SCION

S. L. BHYRAPPA

TRANSLATED FROM KANNADA BY

THE AUTHOR AND SUSHUMA CHANDRASEKHAR

MINERVA PRESS
WASHINGTON LONDON MONTREUX

ISBN 1 85863 464 4

First Published 1995 by
MINERVA PRESS
1 Cromwell Place
London SW7 2JE

Printed in Great Britain by
Antony Rowe Ltd., Chippenham, Wiltshire

SCION

THE SHROTHRI HOUSEHOLD

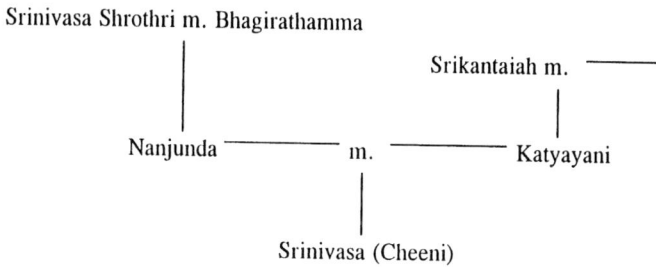

Srinivasa Shrothri m. Bhagirathamma

Srikantaiah m. ——

Nanjunda —————— m. ————— Katyayani

Srinivasa (Cheeni)

Lakshmi	-	a servant maid
Nanjunda Shrothri Senior	-	Srinivasa Shrothri's father
Achamma	-	Srinivasa Shrothri's mother
Kittappa Shrothri	-	Srinivasa Shrothri's uncle

THE RAO HOUSEHOLD

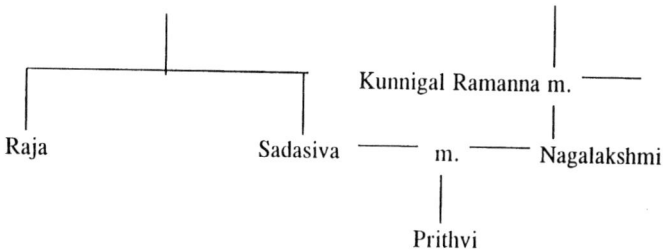

Kunnigal Ramanna m. ——

Raja   Sadasiva —— m. —— Nagalakshmi

Prithvi

THE JAYARATNE HOUSEHOLD

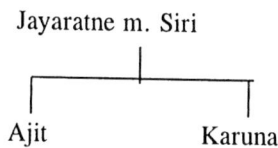

Jayaratne m. Siri

Ajit   Karuna

In 1962, I wrote on an issue that had concerned me for some time. The work was finished in just under a month and was published as *Vamashavriksha*. Now I have had the opportunity to look at what I wrote, when I was in my twenties, in a new and more critical manner. After some months of working with my translator in Scotland, the original text was edited and changed but the essential theme and message remain, I hope, the same.

Previous Publications:

1. Kannada by Sahitya Bhandara, Bangalore. 1st edition: 1965, reprints: 7

2. Hindi by Sabdakar Publications, Delhi. 1st edition: 1971, reprints: 3

3. Telegu by Karnataka Seva Samithi, Guntur, 1st edition: 1971

4. Marathi by Mehta Publishing House, Pune. 1st edition: 1989, reprints: 2

5. Urdu by Mr. Shabbudin (private publication), Shimoga. 1st edition: 1993

6. English by B.R. Publishing Corporation, Delhi. 1st edition: 1992. Translation by K. Raghavendra Rao, published under the name of *The Uprooted*

I

Even after the great flood of 1924, the Shrothri household remained on Sivalaya Road. Indeed, it is not a light matter to forsake the home created by one's ancestors to seek out a newly-built house. For Srinivasa Shrothri, it was inconceivable. During the floods the river Kapila was the goddess who wreaked her vengeance, wrathful and frenzied, her waters turning into an *raga,* the slow music gathering pace, quickening, strengthening, until the melody merged into the beating of a huge drum, until the divinity became inseparable from her dance. In that hilly region thick clouds had gathered and had then poured down, swelling the clear, flat river and bursting her banks. The red water, dirty, heavy with soil, swirled through the small town of Nanjangud. Houses collapsed. As the desperate townspeople looked out, they saw the river carrying off their clothes and pans, their chairs and beds. Tossed around were broken branches, small uprooted trees; they saw bleating goats and sheep, and the bodies of dead deer.

In Shrothri's house, the water poured in until it was knee-deep. While the entire town cursed the river for the devastation it had caused, Shrothri refused to do so. Chanting the Sanskrit hymns devoted to the sacred waters of the seven great Indian rivers, "in the name of Ganga, Yamuna, Godavari, Saraswati, Narmada, Sindhu, Kaveri", he dipped his body in the surging waters at the threshold of his house. His eight year old son Nanjunda, his wife Bhagirathamma and the servant-maid Lakshmi pleaded with him to flee but Shrothri was resolute and uncompromising.

"From time immemorial our mother river has been our saviour. Now she is showing the fearful aspect of her nature. Is this a reason for us to leave? Light the fire upstairs and start cooking."

Although terrified, they obeyed him and went to the upper floor to put the water on to boil. In time, the flood receded and the river lay calm, like the music which slows after the crescendo of the *raga,* governed by a silent, endless, inner rhythm.

After the flood, most of the ten thousand inhabitants moved to ground higher than the level of the river and new neighbourhoods sprung up. The town of Nanjangud lay fifteen miles to the south of Mysore on the way to the Nilagiri Hills, a neat, predominantly middle-class area with straight, dusty roads. It was a pilgrim town which had once been blessed with royal patronage, for the Maharajah of Mysore had been a devotee of the god, Nanjundeswara. Once, a long time ago, the demons and the gods had churned the oceans using the Meru mountain and Aadishesha, the divine serpent, as their rope. The poison that came out was swallowed by Nanjundeswara and to him the temple was dedicated. Due to the presence of the temple, the town was renowned for its Sanskrit learning and its *Vedic* and ancient scholarship. In the evenings *harikatha* was held, when epics were recounted in poetry and dances were performed in devotion to the gods.

II

As the years passed, Srinivasa Shrothri's young son grew into a young man. Nanjunda Shrothri went to university in Mysore, married Katyayani who had been selected and wholeheartedly approved by his parents and became father to a son. When this child was six months old, Nanjunda Shrothri died, a victim of Kapila's fury. It was not that he could not swim, nor was it thought that his arms were too weak to grapple with the violence of the waters. Tall, like his father, with a powerfully formed body, his forehead was wider than a palm and his very demeanour exuded energy. In the morning he had gone to the Manikarnika bank to wash, and though he was cautious, his feet slipped and he fell into the raging water. His arms swung out as he strove to swim ashore. Those who had seen him fall shouted from the bank to encourage him and he too cried back but at that very moment he was caught in a whirlpool and was dragged down into its eddying midst. The servants searched along both banks from Nanjangud to Thiruma Koodalu Narasipura but his corpse could not be found. Four days after the tragedy, the floods receded and Nanjunda Shrothri's death rites were duly performed on the bank of the river. The *puranas* stated that it took the soul eleven days to reach and stand before *Yama,* the lord of death and of righteousness, there to be judged and thus these rites were to prepare and aid the soul on its journey. As there was no body, they put in its place a fistful of clay and burnt it on a small fire. *Mantras* were chanted and incense was thrown on the fire, the air filling with the exquisite scent of sandalwood.

Six months had passed since that event. It is impossible to decide whose sorrow was greater: that of the parents who had lost their son much before his time or that of the loving wife who had lost her husband in her youth. In the span of a month Bhagirathamma turned old. Poor, confused woman, she did not know whether to cry over the loss of a son or weep for the daughter-in-law widowed at such a young age, or to cry her heart out for the grandson who, indifferent to the difficulties of the mature and adult world, played and slept with his smiling face, innocence his form of solace. Katyayani would withdraw into herself and view the entire past of her brief married life in its various phases; her husband whom she adored and who loved her deeply and her parents-in-law, kind, affectionate and temperate. They had celebrated the birth of their son whose childish laughter spread through the house like moonlight. It was a blissful household which would nurture any woman married into it, keeping her cheerful and contented. The family enjoyed great popular esteem in that town and indeed beyond, not only due to Srinivasa Shrothri's agreeable and gentle nature but also to his profound learning in *Vedic* lore and sciences. Katyayani herself reflected on the exercise of unravelling the enigma of existence and angrily found that her mind could not understand it. Frustrated, she blamed this on having stopped her education after passing her school-leaving certificate. Earlier, she had read what literary writers and essayists had said about life and was convinced that none of them would provide a thought, a reason, an explanation for why that tragedy had happened and why it had happened to her.

Katyayani heard someone climbing the steps to reach the upper floor. She bent her head low and began to swing the cradle gently, though the child was already asleep. Shrothri seemed to be thinking intensely and was therefore oblivious to his daughter-in-law's presence. He headed straight to the room which served as his study and library, a spacious area packed with palm-leaf manuscripts, printed volumes, old and new. In one alcove were different kinds of pens and the ink prepared at home by burning *ragi* grain. Near the window and touching the wall was spread a tiger-skin mat on which rested a high pillow and on the mat and in front of the pillow stood a low, foldable stool. For nearly thirty years, sitting in this very room, Srinivasa Shrothri had continued his deep study of the *Vedas, sastras, puranas, Dharmasastras,* and *Ayurveda.* Until the death rites of his son were over, Shrothri had not set foot in this room and had not studied there for two weeks following the obsequies. He had not shed a single tear; at least nobody had ever seen him do so.

"Child."

She raised her head to see her father-in-law towering above her.

"Child, are you reading the *Bhagavadgita* as I asked?"

She did not answer so he repeated the question in the same gentle tone.

"Yes, I did try to read it. But I can make nothing of it. I cannot follow it."

"Well, you must keep studying, taking in as much as you can. In time it will become clear and you will understand."

Katyayani was silent for a while and then said wearily and sullenly, "The wisdom shown in the *Bhagavadgita* is beyond my reach. No *Veda,* no wisdom can wipe out my sorrow, can take it away. There is no use in reading it."

Shrothri smiled ruefully and wisely, explaining, "It is true that we and we alone must carry the burden of our anguish. No book, no person can take our burden away from us, but these books of knowledge and wisdom make us realise the smallness of our own grief when compared to the terrors that strike our world. This awareness may give us the strength to endure our own misfortunes with more courage. Read it carefully."

Shrothri's words were interrupted by the cry of the child. Katyayani moved closer to the cradle, picked up the crying baby and, adjusting her sari, started to breast feed her son. Shrothri, so as not to offend her modest sensibilities, went downstairs. The baby quietened, sucking eagerly and contentedly at his mother's milk. Then he started to smile as he gently scratched his mother's face with his tiny finger nails. Once he gurgled and chuckled so loudly that the sound carried through the house. Amused by such childish defiance, the grandfather shouted back fondly, "Cheeni!" Drawn by the sound, Shrothri went upstairs and seating the child on his shoulder, took him to the cattle-shed in the backyard.

Katyayani hurried to the kitchen to help her mother-in-law who was busy cooking. Noticing her there, Bhagirathamma said consolingly, "Child, it is not good for you to sit alone. You should not brood in solitude."

She added some spices to the steaming pot.

The daughter-in-law listened respectfully.

"You must never be idle. If you feel bored you can always feed the cattle their red beans," Bhagirathamma added helpfully. "It may help ease your sorrow."

Then, after pouring *dhal* into the boiling water and putting the pot for cooking the *saru* on the stove, she made towards the prayer room.

"If anything boils over, call for me. I have to prepare for the evening worship."

And she bustled away.

By the time Shrothri emerged from the prayer room it was eight. He went straight to the back garden to empty the ritual water around the plantain tree, sacred water blessed by invoking Brahma, the god of creation, Vishnu, the god of sustenance, and Siva, the god of destruction. As he was doing so, Katyayani called out to say that Dr. Sadasiva Rao had arrived from Mysore and had been waiting for two hours. Without resuming the chanting of the *Vedic* ritual words but putting away the gourd, Shrothri came out to meet his guest. Sadasiva Rao was a compact individual around thirty five, bespectacled, with most of his hair turning prematurely grey. He was dressed with little care. He sat on one of the lounge chairs, deeply immersed in reading a Sanskrit work and it was only when Shrothri entered the hall that he tore his eyes away from the pages he was scouring.

"You must excuse me. I seem to have kept you waiting."

Sadasiva Rao replied, "You are an elderly man and there is no need for you to excuse yourself on account of a younger person. I have no other pressing work now and I have come with plenty of time to spare."

"How far have you progressed in the writing of your new book?"

"It was recently published in London. In fact, I came out here to give you a personal copy. He rummaged in his miserable brief-case and handed over a book written in English, a beautifully printed volume of some four hundred pages, entitled *The Religious Foundations of Ancient Indian Political Science*. As Shrothri turned the first page, he found written in Kannada, "For revered Srinivasa Shrothri, from Sadasiva Rao, with deepest respect."

"Why so much respect for me?"

"In a way, you guided me in the writing of this book. Most of the information, the refinement of my arguments was collected through intense discussions with you and thus many seemingly impenetrable issues were clarified by your scholarship. I have mentioned this in my foreword."

Shrothri understood very little English. His command over that alien language did not reach beyond the rudimentary and the practical - sufficient for writing postal addresses and bank cheques. Nevertheless, he said politely, "You have written a huge book. I doubt whether I shall be able to read it in its entirety but I am sure that my daughter-in-law would be interested in doing so."

He placed the volume on a shelf and led his guest to the room between the kitchen and the prayer room where they would have dinner. They ate their meal, sitting on the ground, Bhagirathamma serving them as was her duty and her privilege. After a few mouthfuls, Dr. Sadasiva Rao enquired casually, "Will Nanjunda Shrothri be joining us later?"

For just a moment Shrothri was at a loss but, recovering quickly, he said coolly, "Do finish your meal. We can talk about that later."

Sadasiva Rao had been a lecturer of Nanjunda Shrothri, teaching him the history option of his B.A. course and it was through this meeting that Sadasiva Rao was introduced to Shrothri, and eventually was able to benefit from the old man's deep learning and knowledge. Sadasiva Rao was puzzled by this short reply and this bafflement increased as he remembered that it was Katyayani who had opened the door and welcomed him in. He had been a guest at their marriage and he had conversed with her on a few visits to the house. She had talked with him freely, purposefully and with a pleasing directness. But that day, she had been laconic, hardly venturing beyond a few conversational niceties. Her head had been bent down low. As it was considered inauspicious to speak of unhappy matters whilst serving and eating food, Rao carefully left the subject.

It was only after dinner, when the host and the guest had moved into the front hall and the guest was offered betel leaves and nuts, that Sadasiva Rao broached the topic that had so unsettled him.

"Where is Nanjunda Shrothri?" he asked, as nonchalantly as he could.

Shrothri, with inexorable self-control, replied, "My son drowned. In the last rains he fell and drowned."

Rao was aghast. Shrothri, he knew, would never utter such inauspicious words in jest. Yet, he found it impossible to accept what had occurred. Numbed, Rao was silent, staring into the older man's face. In the same placid voice Shrothri continued, "Yes, you must be distressed to hear of the fate of your student, but men must endure everything that befalls them. My daughter-in-law and grandson remain and so instead of grieving, you must bless the child that he shall learn from such brilliant scholars as you."

With that compliment he steered the conversation to other issues.

"What are your plans for the future? A discerning scholar such as yourself should write about the thoughts and values of our ancestors, making their lives accessible to the present generation. Tell me, hasn't it been a year since you last visited Nanjangud?"

Rao had enormous faith in the strength of Shrothri's character and his respect for the old man was limitless. Even so, it was difficult for him to understand how Shrothri could remain so composed in the wake of the catastrophe of losing his only son. As Shrothri had closed the subject, Rao's wishes to return to the issue were blocked and so he turned to his one, all-embracing, all-absorbing topic.

"My book has brought me great success. In fact, several European scholars have written, commenting on and appreciating the work that I have done. During my study of the religious foundations of political science, I became increasingly aware of the fact that not only politics but every aspect of ancient Indian life was underpinned and formed by the prevailing religious system. My ambition is to write a methodical account of the cultural history of this land from the beginning of available historical records to the present day. I confidently believe that this enormous project, covering five volumes, can be completed in twenty-five years. I should request you to help me in my work by extending your blessings and giving the same scholarly support and encouragement that you have shown to my published book."

As they spoke, Katyayani quietly entered the room to prepare their beds. She brought blankets and pillows, arranged them neatly and placed to one side a copper jug filled with water and two copper cups. Without a word, she left. Even as they settled down on their beds, the two carried on their conversation.

Rao continued, "The history of this land has been written and debated by many scholars. Yet, they fall into the category of political rather than purely cultural histories. I propose a different perspective and a new approach. In Indian culture, every aspect of life - art, politics, ideology, the routine and customs of everyday life, all originate from and are supported by an underlying basis of religion. Obviously, the ensuing changes in the cultural configuration of society can be traced to the changes in the dominant religion at a given time, whether Brahmanism, Buddhism or Jainism. I submit that the absence of dramatic changes and sharp variations in society was due to the fact that although different, these three religions originated from a common source. I shall then focus on Islam, its effect on Indian culture and its modern needs. In preparation for this, I have made an extensive study of the classical Indian texts pertaining to ethics, philosophy, art and literature. In the future I hope to read more widely and under your guidance. There is none other who can help me."

Midnight approached and still they were deep in discussion. Rao was clarifying the nature of the proposed work and the principle governing the organisation of the volumes into distinct yet complementary entities. He explained how much he needed time for this project, free, undisturbed and plentiful time. A few assistants would also be of invaluable help as crucial texts would not be available in Mysore and would have to be located in libraries elsewhere in the land. Study trips should be undertaken to allow first-hand observations to be made.

"In short," concluded Rao, "this entails a substantial amount of money. I have sent a petition to Maharaja Krishnaraja Wodeyar along with my published works, asking him for his patronage in this new work. The Private Secretary to His Highness has arranged an audience for me at three o'clock next Monday."

Although it was late, Shrothri listened with interest and by the time they slept, it was two o'clock in the morning.

Shrothri, as was his habit, rose at four o'clock in the morning and went out to the Gundala stream, flowing a few hundred yards from their home. As it was *krishnapaksha* there was no moon in the sky but the planet *Sukra* glimmered. The sky was scattered with numberless stars which provided the human mind with perhaps the only image of the infinite. In the cool, mild hour of the early morning, Shrothri washed himself, and then headed towards the cattle shed. He stroked the cows which stood up expectantly at his approach, checked the quantity of fodder for each one and then tethered them outside. By the time he returned, Bhagirathamma was awake. Carrying a towel and a small pot, Shrothri walked past the front of the temple to the Manikarnika bank. Kapila was flowing in a calm, even, adagio. He bathed himself, washed the cloth he was wearing, filled the pot with river water and as the crows cawed to welcome in the daybreak, he returned home. By this time, Bhagirathamma had finished her bath, washed the floor of the prayer room, decorated it with auspicious, chalk *rangavalli* designs and prepared the ritual items for her husband's morning worship. Such had been their lives for the past thirty years.

When Dr. Rao awoke it was eight o'clock, his usual time. After his bath, he went to the prayer room and paid obeisance to the image of the god. As Rao was served with early tiffin, Shrothri curiously left his guest alone as he ate, returning only by the time Rao had to leave for Mysore. According to custom, Shrothri offered his guest betel leaves and nuts on a platter which also contained gifts - a coconut, fruit and an envelope. Rao realised immediately that the envelope contained money and instinctively stepped back from the proffered gift.

"Whatever you offer me with your blessings I shall not refuse. But I know what is in that envelope and that I cannot touch."

Shrothri replied in a polite but authoritative voice, "You have embarked on a long and prodigious project and you will need money. God has given our family enough to live by and a little more. What better purpose can that little extra serve than to help your laudable work? Please accept it."

"When I mentioned that I needed your support, I meant a different kind of support. Not like this."

"Who am I to support you? You may come to my home whenever you wish and discuss whatever you wish. But you must accept this gift. It is not I who offer it to you for I am not the real giver. What is the value of money if it is not meant for such admirable and valuable work? The ancient moral law, *dharma*, only forbids the acceptance of a gift when he who offers it is a miser in parting with it, when he is offering it at the cost of his household or if the gift is from ill-gotten earnings. If you refuse my gift, you will be guilty of breaking the code of *dharma*, guilty of *adharma*!"

As the train pulled out of Nanjangud, overcome by curiosity, Rao opened the envelope, reached in and his hand pulled out several one hundred rupee notes. He was stupefied. By the time the train pulled into Mysore station, Rao had organised the expenditure of his new wealth - two hundred for a typewriter, a few hundred for buying rare books and the remainder would be used for travelling to places of historical interest.

III

Sadasiva Rao woke at eight but did not stir out of his bedroom as he was busy re-examining the text that he had marked the night before. It was not in his nature to demand anything, to say that he was hungry, but rather to take his breakfast whenever his wife chose to bring it to him. The book he was studying was replete with material and arguments with which he did not agree and so he decided to question them, presenting the correct and definitive position in his proposed volumes. As his mind contemplated existence as it might have been formed and endured over three thousand years of history, he felt a cold palm on his pulsating forehead. Turning round, he saw his wife holding a cup of bathing oil in one hand, massaging his head with the other. Perplexed and not a little irritated, he asked, "Nagu, what are you up to first thing in the morning?"

"Do I have to explain what I am doing? Get up please and wrap a towel round your waist. I shall massage your body with oil."

"Well, I consider that massaging my head is quite enough. Why do you have to start this first thing in the morning? You know I am busy and don't have much time!"

Laughing, Nagalakshmi told him, "Your head is filled with all sorts of books. You can reel off answers to questions such as which ancient king had how large an army and how many elephants! Can't you remember one word of what your wife told you last night? What did I tell you yesterday?"

Rao racked his brain to remember the words. Instead the three hundred pages of the book he had read the night before, reassuringly and inappropriately, flooded his mind. Nagalakshmi said, a mischievous smile on her face, "You will not remember. For people like you, how can a wife be worthy of any attention? Today is your birthday. What I told you was that you should let me massage you and we should eat *payasa* to celebrate. Don't get annoyed that your wife started massaging your head first thing in the morning," she added sweetly.

Rao closed his eyes in horror.

Rubbing the oil vigorously into her husband's back, Nagalakshmi continued, "Have you ever bothered to look at your hair in the mirror? Completely white! You are thirty-four today and already you look so old. Tell me your wife's age," she snapped suddenly.

Rao could not help smiling as he answered, "It cannot be more than thirty-four whatever it might be!"

"You are a very smart person. How can a man who pays no attention to his wife, have any interest in her age? I am two months older than Raja. Raja will be twenty-four years in a fortnight from now. Tell me my age."

"Simple. Two months more than Raja's age."

"Tell me how many years younger I am to you," said Nagalakshmi, secretly enjoying her exasperation.

"Well, let me see. You are younger than me by the number of years Raja is younger than me plus two months."

She tweaked her husband's nose lightly with her oil-smeared finger and said, "Let the oil sink in a little. Keep on rubbing it into your body. I shall not give you anything today unless you pray and bow to the image of God in the prayer room."

Nagalakshmi went into the kitchen. The day before she had cleaned and decorated the house for the occasion, preparing the prayer room for the special ritual worship. All that was now needed was to cook the birthday feast. The rice was steaming, cooked to soft perfection. The curry and the *dhal* were cooked in the traditional South Indian style, with spices, coriander and tamarind. As she was cooking, with the skill of a professional chef and the ingenuity of a housewife, her four year old son Prithvi, who had been away to play in a neighbour's house, rushed to her, complaining, "Mummy, I'm hungry."

Nagalakshmi appeased him by filling his pocket with beaten rice, explaining, "You must wait because today is your father's birthday. If you feel so hungry, eat this."

When she finished her cooking and reached the bathroom, Rao was missing. Immediately she guessed where he had gone, and found him in his study, squatting on a moth-eaten gunnybag, scribbling notes from the book he had read the night before. Moving closer Nagalakshmi urged him, "Get up. You have three hundred and sixty four days to do your reading. On your birthday, at least, you should spend your time happily with your wife and child. Finish your bath, eat and then rest for a while if you want. Tonight we shall all go to see the play *Vasantasena*. It seems the great actress Lakshmi Bai is playing the part of the heroine."

"If you so wish, we shall go to the play. Today let everything be done according to your will. By the way, what is the time?"

Glancing up at the clock on the wall, he exclaimed, "It is eleven already. Hurry up. Get the water ready. I have to meet the Maharaja at three."

"You never mentioned this to me."

"Oh, didn't I? I must have forgotten. Anyway, I noted it in my diary."

"How can making a note in your diary be the same as telling your wife? Oh, what does it matter! Everybody knows that I am so dull and unintelligent. Kunnigal Ramanna's daughter! Do I understand any English to be able to read your diary?"

Nagalakshmi took hold of his arms firmly and frog-marched him to the bathroom. There, she enthusiastically poured bucket after bucket of hot water over him, scrubbing his head, back and body, singing her rural songs loudly all the while. After completing the oil-bath, she worshipped the deity and made him prostrate himself before it, distributing the ritual offering to her husband and son. The three finished their lunch by one-thirty. The used pots and plates were washed and the remaining food tidily packed away. Then she spread betel leaves and nuts on a platter and took it to the study where she found her husband dressed for going out. Even in that great heat, he was clad in a suit, a black tie and also a turban, necessary and customary for paying one's respects to the Maharaja.

"You are going out already! Aren't we at least going to chew the betel leaves and nuts together?" she asked crossly.

"No, Nagu," said Rao impatiently. "It is quarter to two already and my audience with the Maharajah is exactly at three. And if I chew betel leaves now, I shall have to brush my teeth again to avoid presenting myself before him with my teeth and lips stained red."

She moved close to him, held his hands in hers and asked him, "Please look at me."

Rao did so wearily and then she said to him in a voice filled with affection, "You can go now. I am sure the Maharaja will grant your request."

Dr. Sadasiva Rao's father had died when he was ten years old and his brother, Raja, just a new-born baby. It fell to the lot of their maternal uncle, Kunnigal Ramanna, to bring up the two boys. Rao's mother died two years after his father and, due to some careless financial mis-management, there was no property worth mentioning left for the children. And so Rao was placed in a charity home in Mysore to carry on his high school education.

Rao finished his M.A. when he was twenty-four, joining the Maharaja's College as a lecturer in History. From the day he started teaching, he also began to work for his doctorate. Ramanna was eager to see his nephew and his daughter married. Nagalakshmi, who though just fourteen, had nevertheless grown into a tall, well-built girl, well-versed in household chores and possessing an equable temperament. Unfortunately, she was fated to stop her education at the middle school level, believing, like her parents, that such education was of little use to girls. Rao, dedicated and intelligent, ever immersed in the escape of his studies, paid no attention to the problems of his marriage or to would-be brides. He simply obeyed his uncle and married, setting up a modest home in Mysore. His brother stayed with them and continued his studies. Even now Nagalakshmi could relate more easily to Raja whereas she found it difficult to develop any wholly relaxed and easy familiarity with her husband such that he would respond in kind. Their son Prithvi was born six years after the marriage. Kunnigal Ramanna had suffered a stroke four years earlier and had gone to the abode of Yama, his wife following him a year later. The paternal lands were managed by Nagalakshmi's distant cousin and his wife. They had never been very close and now rarely saw each other.

Sadasiva Rao's brother, Raja, was fortunate enough to obtain a teaching position in the very college from which he took his M.A. degree in English and soon after this he won a scholarship for post-graduate studies in England. And now, for the last two years, he had been away in Oxford, two years for Nagalakshmi of inescapable tedium. By nature she was loquacious and her over-studious husband, absorbed in his books, had little time for her. Even when at home, Rao locked himself up in his study until two in the morning, reading, writing some scholarly paper, swamped by thoughts as numerous as the multitude of papers around him. In fact, he did not even find time to write a quick note to his younger brother abroad. All he did was address in English the letters written by Nagalakshmi in Kannada. The time had now come for Raja, after the successful completion of his studies, to return home. His ship was due to dock in Bombay in a few days.

It was a slow, heavy, idle afternoon for Nagalakshmi after her husband had gone to see the Maharaja. Indeed, she did not have much to do in the afternoons. But that day her husband had actually agreed to take the family to see a play. She was excited about it, looking forward to it with a mixture of wifely satisfaction and childish eagerness. She wondered how long her husband's interview with the Maharaja would last. After all, he was a Maharaja and clearly would not be able to spare more than a few minutes.

It was five o'clock and he had not returned. She brought her son back early from the neighbour's home where he had been playing, consoling him with tales of plays and their untold wonders and dressed him for the outing in smart shorts and a neatly pressed shirt. Then she washed her face, combed her thick, black hair and donned a pretty, parrot-green, silk sari for the occasion. Nagalakshmi was saddened that her husband took no interest in his own birthday. It may be acceptable for him to ignore it at whim, but how could she be oblivious to its importance? Her child was getting impatient, asking, "Mummy, father hasn't come back. Does it mean we can't go to the play today? Does it? Does it?"

Quickly she tried to pacify him, saying, "He will be back any time now."

Both waited for Rao. It was six and still he had not returned. She stood near the door in anticipation, her lower lip trembling.

After ten minutes, instead of her husband, a postman came, took her signature and handed her a telegram containing a message of just three words in English. She could just manage to make out that it was signed by Raja. Though she sensed the message to be "Arriving Tuesday evening," she could not be absolutely certain about this. Why did Raja who wrote letters to her in Kannada give the telegram in English? Was it because he wanted to make fun of her ignorance of English? She said to herself, "Let him come. I shall scold him properly."

At last, at eight in the evening, Rao returned home. He saw the telegram and told her, "Raja will be here tomorrow evening."

Nagalakshmi asked, not without a touch of pride, "That means I read the message correctly, doesn't it?"

"Yes, you are a very clever young lady. Well, after Raja comes back, try hard to learn English from him. Then you will be in a position to help me."

Suspecting a catch, she retorted, "Yes, you think I am destined to educate myself and then help you. I hardly think that's likely! I know more than anyone else that it is not in my fate to acquire education. We have missed the theatre..." she was about to complain, but seeing her husband's tired face she stopped and added, "but Raja is coming, so we can all go the day after tomorrow. By the way, what did the Maharaja say?"

"I had sent my new book in advance. It seems he read it and he liked it and appreciated the work I was doing. He was kind enough to extend his support to my five volumes."

In due course, Rao dutifully went to the railway station to meet his brother. The younger brother touched the feet of his elder brother in reverence. As soon as he was home, Nagalakshmi's first comment was, "You have become fairer than before. And thinner."

He answered in good humour, "You see, you were not there to cook for and nurture me. I could not think of marrying an English girl there and enjoying the comforts of domestic life, I was not sure whether you would approve of it. So this is what happened to me!"

"Sit down and be good. I shall get you some fresh lime juice."

And she rushed off, pleased at his simple banter.

Prithvi seemed to have forgotten his uncle. Before his arrival he referred proudly to Raja, mispronouncing "uncle", but now the boy had become, as is sometimes the way with children when they finally meet their much vaunted visitor, shy and aloof. Before his English sojourn, Raja used to look after Prithvi for he had a charming way with children who invariably were drawn to him. After he had played with his nephew, Raja talked to his sister-in-law as she cooked, telling her of the huge impact that her husband's book had made in scholarly circles in England, making her swell with pride and then he would solicitously enquire as to how she spent her time when he was away.

Lowering the fire in the stove, she said, glad once again to have someone who would listen to her woes, "Do you think he can ever change his nature?"

"Well, why don't you ask him?"

But there would be time enough and reason enough to complain of Rao later and Nagalakshmi, who had never left her home state of Karnataka, was eager to hear Raja's news.

"Now, let's talk about you. What did you do there? Didn't you mention in your letters that you were seeing a lot of plays? Tell me about them."

Raja took more interest in drama, stagecraft and theatre in general than in his post-graduate course at Oxford. He had even developed contacts with certain actors in England, managing to learn a great deal about English theatre, from their advanced technology in stagecraft to the most sophisticated methods of production. He began to tell his sister-in-law about these things, realising that she would not make much sense of everything he said and yet, at the same time, knowing it was her habit to listen to any discussion with keen interest. She was an incorrigible conversationalist, as was Raja, and that was how they matched each other. Nagalakshmi kept him posted about the local situation.

"The S.S.S. Drama Company is staging plays here. And do you know? They have been playing *Vasantasena* for the last fortnight and the whole town has gone wild over it. It seems Lakshmi Bai is superb in the leading role. Actually we had planned to see it yesterday but as your telegram came, we decided to see it with you."

Laughing, Raja said, "Nagu, I think you are fibbing. Remember what you said a while back, 'He doesn't talk to me at all'. Now you say that you were planning to see a play!"

"Yesterday was his birthday. I coaxed him into agreeing to go to the theatre. But he went to see the Maharaja and promised to be back in time but he wasn't. Actually he returned at eight in the evening," she said, a little embarrassed.

Rao joined them after seeing off his guest who had arrived to discuss some pressing matter concerning some historical document. He did not quite know what to say and so adopted the opening gambit of saying polite nothings. He remarked, "The English climate must be excellent. You look much better than before."

Raja smiled.

"Have you had a look at my new book?"

"Of course and I have also seen the reviews. When scholars of Indian history at Oxford learnt that I was the author's brother, they were eager to find out more. I learn that you are planning your *magnum opus*. What is it going to be about?"

"How did you get to know about it, all that way in England?"

"Very simple. Nagalakshmi sent me her news bulletin."

"Perhaps it is a somewhat grandiose plan. Srinivasa Shrothri of Nanjangud has blessed the idea and has even given a thousand rupees to tide me over the initial expenses. Yesterday I had an audience with the Maharaja who was gracious enough to offer his support. My research involves so much travelling, and there are no funds for that so far as the university is concerned. Worse still, they are not even prepared to give me a sabbatical or any sort of leave. Perhaps the Maharaja could arrange something."

Raja, familiar with the kind of positive and substantial support extended to scholars and researchers in Western universities, made a wry comment on the Indian reality.

"It is because of the sorry state of our universities that many Indian scholars emigrate to the West. Even your book which has just appeared would be enough to attract the support of an English university for your proposal. Also the source material for writing Indian history is lamentably more easily available in England than here."

Nagalakshmi intervened, "If he goes to England, then it is more than likely he will forget his family and settle down there with some foreigner."

Raja reassured her, "Don't worry. For scholars like him, they fund the travel and maintenance of the wife as well. Don't forget, what could Brother do for his food in a foreign land without you? And you know very well that he will not touch a single meal without your divine *saru*."

"Oh, you talk such nonsense!" said Nagalakshmi, scarcely concealing her delight and taking the ladle, she swirled the *saru* around vigorously.

In the meantime, Rao's mind had wandered to the celebrated British Museum and the renowned universities of Europe.

It took Prithvi just one day to re-establish the former rapport with his uncle and on the way to the play, he clutched Raja's hand. Rao himself was not enthusiastic about the production, but he could find no way of refusing an invitation from a brother who had just returned home from abroad. They walked all the way from Chamarajapuram to Shivarampet. Those were the days when the S.S.S. Company (*sangita, sahitya, samrajya mandali*) had captured the imagination of the people. Everybody, the educated and the illiterate, flocked eagerly to watch their plays. As they approached the theatre, Raja ran into many old acquaintances and friends who would stop and enquire after his welfare. Some senior colleagues of Rao, surprised by the sight of the inveterate scholar visiting the theatre with his family, greeted him, not without a trace of irony. Rao responded courteously, oblivious to their nudges and sly smiles. The theatre itself was a temporary, make-shift structure constructed out of pieces of wood and thin metal sheets. Inside at one end, there was a raised platform, and in front of that a space for the musicians with their violins, harmonium and drums. The lighting technicians also sat there. From the stage there stretched back three classes of seat; carpet (third), bench (second), chair (first), accommodating some two thousand people. Each night the company played to a full house.

Raja's interest in drama had advanced beyond a mere interpretative study and had reached the stage of critical evaluation. Rao watched the play through the spectacles of a scholar. He had read the original Sanskrit play, *Mricchakatika* (*The Little Toy-Cart*) purely from the point of view of historical scholarship and the occasion recalled a historical picture of the original times in which the play was set, its culture and civilisation, daily life, and social conditions. Only Nagalakshmi and Prithvi were fascinated by the prospect of seeing a story unfold on stage - she because it was the first time in her life that she was seeing a play in the company of her husband and Prithvi for the sheer physical and dramatic effect. As a young girl, Nagalakshmi had seen traditional rural performances in her village of plays such as *Sanimahatme* (*The Triumph of the God Sani*) and *Danasura Karna* (*Karna, the Supreme Bestower*). But now her curiosity had been fired by the thrilling and extravagant reports from her friends and neighbours. As soon as the customary invocation to God Rama began, Prithvi craned his neck to make sure that he saw everything that was happening. Nagalakshmi's body tingled with joy.

In the very first scene, the hero Charudatta and the fool, made their appearance. The king's brother-in-law, Shakara, who was chasing the courtesan heroine Vasantasena, described in relentless detail the burning passion within him and then he said, "Vasantasena, you are like Kunti who was caught by Ravana... and I am carrying you off like Anjaneya carried off Viswavasu's sister, Subhadra."

The audience steeped in Hindu mythology saw immediately the absurdity of the comparisons, full of gross errors, and roared with laughter. Nagalakshmi chuckled. Placing her hand in her husband's, she said, "Look, he is supposed to be a king's brother-in-law. And yet he is such a dunce, isn't he?"

Rao was engaged with the historical implications of the situation presented, thinking wearily that at all times the kith and kin of the ruler were accorded high respect, no matter how stupid and unworthy they might be. His wife squeezed his hand and said, "Your mind is elsewhere. You are not watching the play at all."

"No. I am enjoying it. It is very good."

The crass misuse of words on stage, the well-worn jokes and the semantic mess once again prompted the simple-minded audience to fill the theatre with loud laughter. Nagalakshmi joined them enthusiastically but the serious-minded researcher in Rao found the supposed humour old hat and a trifle embarrassing.

Sarvilaka, in the third scene, was breaking into Charudatta's house.

"The wretched bricks will have to be pulled out. They have used bricks of different shapes - lotus shaped, sun-shaped, moon-shaped, pot-shaped, well-shaped. Well, I can meet the challenge. I shall take them out with such skill that posterity will be dumb-struck by my professional artistry in wall-breaking."

This incident did not appeal much to Nagalakshmi for she wondered how a burglar could afford to indulge in such reflections and waste so much time. But Rao found it fascinating, noting mentally yet another item for his study.

"Were they using such a variety of bricks in their architecture? What were the specific benefits for a building in employing each of them? Are these brick-types described in the classical science of architecture? What is the date of the text of *Silpasastra*?"

As for Raja, who had been recently exposed to the British theatre, what struck him was the fact that, although the stagecraft was very simple, it would produce remarkable effects. Prithvi snored gently. Nagalakshmi's interest never wavered for a moment. When she heard Charudatta's death sentence, she wept spontaneously. At the end, Charudatta was declared innocent and he was re-united with

Vasantasena and his wife. However, Nagalakshmi's joy over this was clouded by the thought that Charudatta's wife had to live with a rival spouse, the courtesan. It was four in the morning when the play finally ended. The warm, pleasant night had turned a little chilly and so Nagalakshmi tucked her shawl around her and they walked home.

A week later, Rao received a letter from the university authorities granting him both money and leave for his research. He was also promoted to the post of assistant professor.

Rao immediately sent a letter of gratitude to the Private Secretary to His Highness.

IV

A month had passed since Sadasiva Rao embarked on his research travels. Earlier, he had visited certain important historical places in India and was now re-visiting them in order to gain fresh impressions and insights or meticulously to confirm old ones. The starting point had been Kanyakumari, the southernmost tip of India. The temple there was near the sea-shore and as Rao looked out, he saw the Arabian Sea, the Bay of Bengal and the Indian Ocean meet, their waters stretching out and toppling over the horizon. He continued his scholarly wanderings, visiting the temple at Tanjore, a classic example of South Indian architecture and then Madurai, a spacious temple with a sacred pond whose water common people were not allowed to touch and which was used to wash the stone image of the goddess Minakshi. At Chidambaram he saw the Nataraja temple, the image there was of Lord Siva dancing with one foot on the chest of a demon who represented the evil within mankind. Leaving the Madras Presidency, he went to Hyderabad and from there to examine the Ellora temples executed in the sixth, seventh and eighth centuries. The largest of these was the Kailas temple which was hewn out of the living rock, an outstanding feat of engineering. Every pillar, every step, every image was carved out of that same stone. Inside could be found the most intricate carvings depicting epics of Hindu mythology, showing demons, gods, elephants, chariots, battles. After visiting Devagiri fort which was captured by Tughlak, Rao found his way to Ajanta via Aurangabad.

His modest equipment consisted of a light hold-all, a small trunk for his clothes, a water bottle, a good camera, khaki garb as proof against the interminable, sticky, travel dust, a hat for protection against the sun, a pen, a pencil, paper and a pair of binoculars. He lodged in a room in the Fardapur Guest House from where he made his daily visits to the caves. On the first day, he surveyed the whole area through his powerful binoculars. After that he made the following notes:

"The caves in this horse-shoe shaped valley have been excavated. It is a god-forsaken place where no reasonable human habitation seems possible. Why did the Buddhist monks build their cave temples in the heart of such a forest? One reason is that the rocks of this hill are the right material for the temples. But I might guess at another reason; these temples were ideal places for meditation, undisturbed by other human contact. The existence of these caves was not known to the outside world from the seventh century to the nineteenth century. Indeed, even those inhabiting the surrounding region did not know about them. It is difficult to believe that these wonderful creations of history came to be first known through the courtesy of a few English army officers! It seems more likely that the political conditions and the consequent changes in the religious ideology of the local inhabitants weakened their interest in the caves. As a result, the caves suffered from centuries of neglect. The English researchers and historians write under the illusion that everything significant is their discovery. Were there no human beings before Columbus set foot on America? People before Columbus knew about America."

The day after his arrival in Ajanta, Rao examined the incomplete cave numbered 24. Just then, an elderly couple in their sixties entered and began to stare around them. The man was dark and dapper and carried an umbrella. The woman wore a white sari in a style which prompted Rao to conclude that they were from Ceylon. After a few minutes of looking rather surprised and unimpressed, the man approached Rao and asked, "Excuse me. Could you explain to me why this cave was not completed? Doesn't it look a crude and simple structure produced by utterly unskilled workers?"

Rao answered, pleased at being asked, "Yes, this is an incomplete cave. The Ajanta caves seem to have been excavated and constructed through three stages. First, the unskilled workers hewed the broad cavity in the rock and it is not unlikely that the peasants in the surrounding area contributed their physical labour as an act of religious devotion. In the second stage, skilled professionals carved the pillars and images, in accordance with the instructions of the architects. In the third and last stage, dedicated artists applied their superior skills to fill in the details and give the temple its overall finish. All this took several decades. By the time the first stage was completed in this cave, there may have been political upheaval or the religious ideology of the people might have altered radically, and thus the work was abandoned at that stage. Hence, it was left incomplete."

The old man passed this information on to his wife and listening to their language, Rao was now sure they were Ceylonese. The old man introduced himself, "My name is Jayaratne and this is my wife, Siri.

We are from the town of Kaluthara in Western Ceylon and we have come here with our daughter, Karuna. She did her M.A. in History in London and returned home a year ago," he added with a touch of pride.

And so, as they were engaged in conversation, they walked together towards Cave 12. A woman, around twenty-six, clad in the Ceylonese style of clothing, was busy taking notes. She had a proportionately shaped round face, charming, dignified and tinged with scholarly gravity. Her diamond ear-rings shone against her dark complexion. After mutual courtesies, Karuna combed her memory for some polite starting point and having found one enquired, "If you are indeed Dr. Sadasiva Rao then you must be the author of the work, *The Religious Foundations of Ancient Indian Political Science.* I haven't got hold of it yet but I have read the reviews. I am happy to meet the author of such a work."

Rao beamed.

Karuna asked, "It is my impression that you have seen all of this earlier. Why are you doing such an exhaustive study of the caves? Are you planning any new work?

"Yes. I am planning to do a five volume study."

The Jayaratnes smiled at him expectantly but although Rao was in the company of such educated people and would normally have enjoyed discussing his work with them, suddenly, here in the caves, the mammoth nature of his task overwhelmed him. He was spared an uncomfortable silence by the arrival of the guest house servant who appeared, balancing on his head a basket containing their lunch. The food had been prepared in the Maharashtrian style, consisting *of dhal,* millet *roti*, rice cooked in a little oil with mild spices and sugar. Eating together promoted greater understanding and friendship between them. Jayaratne and his son managed a business enterprise but they also owned rubber and pepper plantations. Being devout Buddhists, they had come to India as pilgrims but their daughter had other interests. At this point Karuna intervened, "An idea formed in my mind of studying Ceylonese culture in the background and context of Buddhism. Although I have covered various historical places in Ceylon and have collected considerable information, I feel that I shall not be in a position to complete the study without some guidance. In the meantime, I thought it would be a good idea to gather as much material as I could."

Karuna spoke English fluently and with a trace of an English accent.

Jayaratne added, "Ajanta has both Mahayana and Hinayana caves, and I am not saying this from sectarian narrowness but the Hinayana temples do not have the images of the Buddha, and hence, no matter how artistic their structure, they look like a house without its householder. In the Mahayana temples, you are in the presence of the Buddha image in the pose of the *dharmachakra,* the very embodiment of peace. This gives us a sense of security, a feeling of being blessed with grace!"

Rao replied, "Hinayana represents the first phase in the history of Buddhism. It was the time when Buddha's original message had not lost its lustre. If everything is blankness, then it would make no sense to worship the image of the preceptor. Ordinary human beings are not fully satisfied with abstract thought, they need a concrete image to focus on and that is why Buddhism moved into an image-worshipping phase. Some historians see in this the impact of Hindu image worship and indeed this may be partly true, but Mahayana also arose for other reasons."

Karuna's mother, Siri, stretched herself on the stone slab, and her husband sat against the wall. Karuna asked Rao, "Have you finished all your notes?"

"No. Why?"

"I just wanted to see your method of taking notes," she said shyly.

"I have yet to do a proper study of Cave 1. Could you spare me some time? It would help me if you could clear up some doubts."

Rao readily agreed, pleased at having a scholarly companion even for just one afternoon.

Outside the sun was scorching. Rao went out, protected by his hat. Karuna followed him with the end of her sari covering her head against the sun. They asked the servant to focus the electric light on the different parts of the cave so that they could study them. As they stared around, Karuna said, "Now we need not take notes separately. You dictate and I shall take down. And tonight I shall make another copy for you."

For a considerable length of time they examined the images and the paintings. After that, Rao dictated his observations which Karuna scribbled down with extraordinary speed.

"The large image in the sanctum is in the *dharmachakra* pose, the posture in which Buddha preaches to his disciples, stressing each point by placing the little finger of the left hand over the index finger of the right hand. The mood on its face varies with the changing nature of the light falling on it. If we focus light near the *dharmachakra* where Buddha sits, the face shows a gentle smile. If the same light is directed from the right, the face wears an expression of profound gravity."

Karuna noted down diligently as Rao described the painting, scenes in which a prince was listening to the discourse of a hermit, where he was bathing, where he was conversing with his spouse, and the scene depicting the Padmapani Bodhisatva. Together they elicited further details about the paintings which reflected the culture of the people who painted them - their eating habits, clothing, ornaments, physiognomy. After the stipulated time the light staff left and Rao had to use his hand torch. But soon it became too dark to do any constructive analysis, yet they attempted, finally leaving to find Jayaratne.

Rao was drained. He tried to lean against the side of the bullock cart, the only means of transport, and to relax but he could not since the cart was overcrowded. Karuna too was tired. Yet, looking at Rao's haggard face, she moved closer to her father in order to leave more leg-space for the exhausted scholar. The cart lumbered along, tossing its passengers, the monotony broken and then added to by Jayaratne's descriptions of what he had viewed in the caves.

The Jayaratnes were to leave the next day but their daughter wanted to stay for two more days, the notes dictated by Dr. Rao being considered very useful. They were able to pool their resources of energy and knowledge to compile copious notes on the caves and also notes reconstructing that culture. Rao would lecture his observations which Karuna would take down, filling three notebooks in closely written, neat shorthand. The following day the Ceylonese family planned to go to Jalgaon, the nearest railway station, and leave for Delhi from there. Rao's plan was to return to Aurangabad and then, from there, return home via Pune, before continuing his quest, this time in the North.

They had all settled into the Fardapur Guest House so much so that they felt disinclined to leave. As the rooms of Rao and the Jayaratne family faced each other, it became all too easy for Jayaratne and Rao to meet casually and then spend the entire evening in protracted discussion. The old man was never tired of eliciting information about Buddhism from Rao the historian, for Rao's perspective differed from that of other historians who merely gave an account of historical events interspersed with biased comments; it threw light on the history of the inner doctrines of Buddhism. As Rao was to leave by the first bus the next morning, Jayaratne left him relatively early that night, but Rao found that he could not sleep. He was still under the spell of Ajanta, mesmerised by its breathtaking beauty. For the last four days, he had been living in the ancient times depicted in the caves but the next day, he would find himself jerked into the modern world as one of its denizens.

The evening wore on and merged into night but he did not notice. In that uninhabited location, moonlight enveloped everything, investing it with a dreamlike, ethereal quality. The Buddhist mendicants and artists had melted the heart of the stone and created new life in such an atmosphere of calm seclusion. Instead of just watching the moonlight outside, he went out to experience its beauty directly. He had almost forgotten the strain of having studied the caves the whole day and his unburdened mind expanded and merged into the night, the soft, dark sky becoming the perfect background for the flow of India's history that he was planning to reconstruct. Like the lucid moonlight, the culture of that country presented itself through its long tradition of centuries. He strove hard to identify the focal point of his writing and now he saw it quite clearly. When did this hoary tradition really originate? Was it like the *Vedas,* a divine creation without any human agency? Or did it begin in about 2,000 B.C. as the historians had surmised? Or 3,000 B.C.? What was its focal point at the start? Was it possible to measure man's cultural history from the perspective of physical anthropology? Rao was totally immersed in a multitude of reflections.

Suddenly he heard a voice from behind.

"You are not yet asleep and you have to leave so early in the morning!"

Karuna came closer, about to ask him whether she was disturbing him but then did not.

"I came to tell you something. Our notes cover three whole books and it would be impossible to make copies of them all. If I handed them over to you, it might be difficult for you to decipher my handwriting and most of it is written in shorthand. Perhaps I could wait until I returned home to Kaluthara and then I would have more time to transcribe the notes in a neat and orderly way?"

At a loss for words, for his notes were so important to him, Rao said reluctantly, "You are aware how much I need this material. Please, don't forget to send it."

"Absolutely not."

They both fell silent, a companionable silence. Rao's mind was still steeped in deep thoughts of Ajanta. Karuna spoke, at exactly the right moment, "I should like to ask you a question. In writing the history of any country, historians divide it into periods such as ancient history, the pre-historic period, early history etc. But the history of no country discloses such sharp demarcations. Don't you think such divisions are somewhat arbitrary?"

Rao responded enthusiastically, "As a matter of fact, I have given some attention to this question. First, let me say that as applied to history, the notion of a period or epoch has no precise meaning, no quantitative boundaries of such a precise nature. The material civilisation of any people reflects its deeply held values. Sometimes such values may have been held continuously for hundreds, even thousands, of years. In this period we can recognise the elaboration and development in its literature, religion, art and material culture. But essentially, there is really no change in their nature and structure for they are all products of a common value system. A new epoch may be said to begin only when there is a real change in the fundamental values of a society. It is then that history takes a new course, a new configuration."

"But how do historians identify such epochal changes?"

"It requires profound, inner vision. Nobody can be a real historian merely by noting the material morphological changes. He should have insight into a people's inner vitality and a society's internal patterns, the clash of values. But we must concede that not only history but other modes - art, literature, philosophy - also capture this reality in their own distinctive styles. Looked at this way, the distance between history and literature is not great. History is really an account of the inner transformations of an entire people, told from a holistic perspective. Literature also captures these changes and transformations in the inner life of a people, but through the depiction of the lives of actual or imaginary individuals. Both history and literature become great works when they reflect fully contemporary life. In India, the awareness of the profound interdependence between the two led our tradition to designate the *Mahabharata* as an historical work."

Karuna sat quietly for a few minutes, trying to digest Rao's words. Then she responded spiritedly, "You are saying that history must identify and describe the epochs representing a certain transvaluation, giving an account of the causes and consequences in such changes and values. But while discussing epochal changes in values, one cannot avoid value judgements. But should one do so? From this angle, is history a story of progress and development or a tragic tale of regression and decline?"

Rao replied, "If we maintain that history is a unilinear progress, we shall be condemning the culture of our ancestors as necessarily inferior to ours. Yet, if we regard history as being a process of regression, we shall be condemning ourselves as being caught up in a process of decline! In the traditional Indian perspective, human history is divided into the *Krita, Treta, Dwapara and Kali* ages in succession, the last one being the age we now live in. This historical scheme certainly presupposes that history is regression. But the age of *Kali* is not the last. This age may be over and then history will be caught in the cycle of repetition of the four ages. After *Kali*, we will have the age of *Krita* repeated."

"Then do you suggest that this cycle is endless?"

"Just as it is impossible to pinpoint the origin of human history, it is futile and foolish to pronounce its end. In this eternal cyclic process, certain values may gain strength sometimes and may sometimes weaken. From such a perspective, human history is just a play of divine will."

Karuna asked him slowly, "For the last four days we have been in Ajanta. In this peaceful place which lets you forget all disputes and debates, and on this calm night, you are saying all this. I feel that I can accept it. Will you do me a favour? I shall be ever grateful to you for it."

Shyly and respectfully she continued, "It has been a year since I returned home from London. My native town has no facilities for advanced research work. I am hoping to join Colombo University next year as a lecturer or a research fellow. Please let me have your views on certain issues and questions of history. I shall write to you regularly."

"Certainly. I shall explain things to you to the best of my understanding. When I am not in a mood to write, you must forgive me."

V

The monsoons came, bringing with them the west wind and the ever-increasing humidity. Kapila overflowed as usual and so the Nanjangud municipality had put up a warning notice in Kannada on the Manikarnika bank, "Danger. Do not swim." Of course that did not prevent people from doing so.

When the monsoons came again, Cheeni was a year and a half old and, even at that young age, had a strong physique and well-defined features; the wide forehead, the tilted smile recalling, startlingly and unmistakably, those of his father. As they had done with Nanjunda twenty-seven years ago, Shrothri and Bhagirathamma devoted their time to the young child. Bhagirathamma would click her fingers before him and pleased by the curious sound he would gurgle. Shrothri would carry him on his shoulder and the child would attempt to speak, mispronouncing his words and pulling at his grandfather's knotted brahmin pigtail. Katyayani could not help but laugh at her son's antics and thus the gaping, inconsolable emptiness created by the death of his father would be filled by these little domesticities.

Bhagirathamma would never tire of telling her daughter-in-law how much Cheeni resembled his father, every act and every characteristic.

"Sometimes he would wake up at night and play in his crib with such a mischievous look and I would have to stay awake too and take care of him. If my attention wavered for even a moment, he would cry so loudly that he would wake his father asleep upstairs."

Katyayani knew the reason why her father-in-law had chosen to sleep away from his wife so early on in life.

The older woman continued, "We do so much for them and then God snatches them away."

Her eyes filled with tears.

"Mother, we are made of straw. He died a year and a half ago and still we mourn. But Father is strong. When he knew, he ran to the river and searched for his son and when he could not find him, he accepted this and returned. He turned to me and said, 'My child, it is at such a time that we should gather our courage to face the truth. God brings this upon us in order to test us.' In my grief, I thought his words so dry and meaningless but with what calmness and gravity he spoke! Do you think that if we had such strength, we too could endure?"

"Perhaps, but one must cry. If we could grieve before him and he before us, how wonderful it would be."

Katyayani considered her parents-in-law. The old couple had never imposed their authority on their son and his wife. Blessed with only one son, they looked upon Katyayani as their own daughter. Shrothri joked frequently with the young couple and if any new drama company visited the town, he would himself urge them to see the performances, even though this was considered very forward. Gradually, as he became increasingly involved in the ritual of worship, Shrothri initiated his son into the role of a householder. The last time that he had visited his lands in the nearby villages to supervise the work was three years ago. By the time of his death Nanjunda Shrothri was almost in command, looking after the household management as well as their landed property. The son's death had now forced the old father to come out of his retirement and resume an active life. Once again it fell to his lot to go to the villages to collect the yield during the harvest and pay the revenue dues.

Katyayani's heart filled with gratitude at the kindness and affection her parents-in-law had always shown her and at the trust they had placed in her. At night, her child by her side, she would suddenly be pierced by the memories of her past - her time with her kind husband, her bodily bliss with him, and his passion for her. Sometimes, if he had not returned from the village, she would wait, watching expectantly at the door. Unable to sleep, she would toss from side to side, and then her mother-in-law would murmur gently, "Are you asleep, child?"

"Yes, mother."

When Cheeni was two, it became impossible for anyone to control him. Inquisitive by nature, he would look with glee at the open front door and chuckling, would run through it. Once he ran all the way to the temple where he explored until his curiosity was satisfied and then, unable to find his way home, he sat down on the steps and wailed. The temple priest recognising him, brought him home to a distraught mother and grandmother. The child was restrained until the month of *Phalguna* when Cheeni chanced upon some new playmates, sons of the local shepherds. As the bed of the Gundala stream was sandy, together they started to build tiny nests. Most of the water had dried up but there was a little left, ankle-deep and pooled in a corner. The young child had drunk some of this stagnant water and by three in the afternoon his body was burning, his face stiff.

The doctor of native herbal medicine, Pandit Venkatachala, was sent for. The doctor felt the boy's pulse, diagnosed a fever that would last for twenty-one days and made up some herbal pills. The Pandit's diagnosis proved correct. The fever did not subside and the boy did not recover full consciousness. His breathing was hard, laboured, the only indication of his continued existence and yet each breath seemed to confirm the impossibility of the boy's survival. The face was livid and lifeless. The legs had gone cold, the forehead showed drops of sweat. Shrothri applied ash to the legs and hands and eucalyptus oil to the emaciated chest. Gently he stroked the child's clammy hair as if to re-assure him and patted the small arms.

For these twenty days mother and grandmother never left the tense agony of that room in which the little boy lay. Lakshmi, their servant maid, continued with her duties. Lakshmi's father had been a household servant during Shrothri's father's time and the daughter too, after her own widowhood, later came to fill this role. It was she who was able to detect the subtle shifts of mood in Srinivasa Shrothri's mind and it was in his wisdom and his courage that she placed herself unreservedly. Earlier she had cared for Nanjunda and now she cared for Cheeni. Now she had to witness the possibility of the Shrothri family tree drying up with no scion, without ever sprouting. Yet it was the knowledge that she would sacrifice her life in the service of this family and her utmost faith in Shrothri's determination that sustained her. Subconsciously she had developed a hardened attitude of neutrality.

On the evening of the twentieth, Cheeni's breathing became very difficult. Shrothri sat cross-legged on the floor and laid the child on his lap. He was a tall, strong and generously built person with the strength to walk more than fifteen miles a day. Against his power, the little body seemed even weaker. As if unaware of the child, he took the small gourd containing water from the Kapila and sprinkled it in a circle around himself, reciting sacred Sanskrit *mantras*. He prayed to the deities, holding the brahman knot of sacred thread with his right hand and closing his eyes, saying the Gayatri *mantra* in his mind.

Shrothri lived his life according to the *sanatana dharma,* fully believing that a man married in order to follow the *dharma* of the householder, and that one became a householder to discharge one's worldly duties and obligations. One begot children later only so that the family tree might continue and not wither. A person dying without issue was the last of the family, and he died leaving behind a branch that was irreversibly stunted. Life was received from one's parents and the offspring incurred a debt that had to be discharged. If one had no progeny, the debt could never be discharged.

Shrothri had enormous pride in his family which he believed to be of untraceable antiquity. For, just as it was impossible to measure the age of the original *rishis* by years, so also it was impossible to identify precisely the early years of an ancient family tree. Its history went back to the misty times when human consciousness had not yet emerged. An individual's status and honour depended firmly upon his family. During his morning and evening oblations Shrothri would feel uplifted when he uttered the name of his *gotra* and *pravara,* his *Kasyapa* ancestry, his genealogy dating from the *Rigvedic* branch. As a member of such an ancient and illustrious family, he was very conscious of his responsibilities and he performed all the rites in such a way as to maintain the honour of his family tree unsullied.

The grandson was the hope and the growth, the scion of this lineage and this tree. Shrothri, who had retired from active life after his son came of age, had now resumed it after his death, enthused by the desire to see his grandson ensconced as a householder. In his scheme of living there was no place for greed, desire and lower passions. When Shrothri's parents passed away, he inherited much wealth and property which he used for religious and charitable causes. He gave to the needy and offered gifts to scholars and musicians in recognition of their excellence. In the lean years of drought, he had stood by those who cultivated his lands. His life was spent acting in the name of God and its aim was to leave for his grandson the honour and the affluence of the family tree.

Though he had cultivated tremendous self-control and trained himself to be neutral and detached in life, the possibility of the death of his only grandson unbalanced his mental equilibrium and pierced his shield of spiritual detachment. His mind refused to take in the recitation of the Gayatri prayer as before but his inner being prayed silently and unerringly to Mother Gayatri that she alone could save the child. Yet, as he did so, Shrothri was ashamed, for he knew that pure devotion could not arise when a prayer was contaminated by a selfish desire. The recitation went on inside him, relentless, unstoppable, the prayer for grandson, his line, pounding in the twisted agony of the night, between the death of one day and the birth of another.

At six the following morning, the Pandit checked the pulse and examined the limbs, pronouncing that the worst was indeed over. On the twenty-first day, as predicted by the Pandit, the boy fully regained consciousness, uttering faintly, "Grandpa..."

Turning to the weeping Katyayani, Shrothri said gently, "Child, as we welcome happiness, so we should bear sorrow. Nothing is achieved by allowing our emotions to dominate us."

VI

After his return from Oxford, Raja Rao infused new life into the extra-curricular, artistic activities of the university. Before going abroad, he had been the President of the University Dramatic Society, and was known for staging polished, student plays. His newly acquired experience of theatrical production abroad raised his status in the eyes of his colleagues and the reputation of the plays he produced increased accordingly. The Principal of Mysore University was keen on promoting extra-curricular activities to the utmost and had placed at the disposal of the Dramatic Society a room and modest financial resources. Raja Rao organised a production for raising funds for the society, and the income accrued from it was used to buy costumes and props. From the very start, Raja had never been the studious type but he was certainly intelligent, and this native sharpness, together with his pleasant and equable nature had seen him through Oxford. He read widely but had no interest in scholarship. He wrote plays for the stage but did not bother to publish them.

Dr. Sadasiva Rao had just finished his study tour of North India and was ready to begin his *magnum opus*. A well-furnished room was set apart for him in the university library so that he could carry on his studies undisturbed and he had even acquired his very own typewriter. Raja was a far better typist, but he was of little help to his brother since he did not share the same scholarly concerns. Since his promotion to the position of assistant professor, Rao was drawing a higher salary and this combined with Raja's contribution meant that the family resources were considerably augmented. With Raja's return, Rao was also freed from domestic banalities. Before, when Prithvi was ill, he would go to the dispensary, and once every six months he would dutifully accompany his wife to the market as an inescapable imposition.

Rao lectured for six or seven hours a week, and sometimes he would not be in the mood for it. Then he would dismiss the class and would head straight for his niche in the library. There, he would plunge into his myriad scholarly activities - reading certain chapters in certain books, taking notes about the life conditions of certain people available in certain encyclopaedias, taking copious notes from the latest research articles in the field of ancient Indian history, searching for old manuscripts in relevant libraries and archives, conducting heated correspondence with Indian and foreign scholars on topics of intense historical and philosophical interest, the scope of his research as vast, complex and disorganised as India herself. By the time he returned home from the library, it would be half past seven in the evening. Oblivious of everybody and everything, he would sit all alone, brooding in an easy chair. On rare occasions, he would force himself into a relaxed mood but mostly he dined in silence, eating a little with indifference, eager to hurry off to his study where he would read until the small hours. As he even went to the library on Sundays, a separate key was placed at his disposal.

Two months after Rao's return from Ajanta, he received a registered packet from Ceylon. Opening it, he found a letter and a typescript running to about sixty pages, a copy of the observations they had made together in the caves. Rao read it carefully from end to end, noting its good, readable English and the systematic organisation of the material. Karuna had edited the material meticulously with the skill of an expert and there was not a single typing error.

The letter read:

"After my return here, I visited the library of Colombo University. The four volumes of notes and sketches of Ajanta by Dr. Ghulam Yazdani were merely descriptive and factual, lacking the kind of historical interpretation and evaluation you were able to provide in your comments. The scholarly world would welcome a small monograph based on a final editing of this material. Should you permit me, I shall prepare the final edited press copy and send it for your approval.

"I fully accept and endorse your historiographical views. I now feel that I should write my own research volume on Ceylonese culture viewed in the light of Buddhism, from the theoretical and methodological perspective you have suggested. Your plan to write the cultural history of India is magnificent and truly awe-inspiring. I pray to Buddha that He should bless you with success in this laudable work.

"My parents remember you and have asked me to send you their regards."

Rao was full of admiration for the foreign lady who, after a brief acquaintance of three days, could show such high regard for his gifts as a historian. He re-read the typescript she had sent and agreed with her assessment that it could be an independent monograph. Yet he did not feel too enthusiastic about the idea and just filed the material away. He wrote and posted a letter, thanking Karuna for the typescript.

Rao had collected all the source material for the first volume of his *magnum opus* and was planning to start the writing after three months or so. After corresponding with the English publishers of his first book, he had entered into an agreement with them for the publication of all the projected five volumes. The publisher had agreed to pay him substantial royalties. The first volume was to open with the key chapter entitled *The Origin and Sources of Indian Culture,* containing a discussion of his perspective and framework and the general nature of the contents of all the five volumes. He had already got a blueprint of the chapter and was about to embark on its creative formation. In the meantime, Karuna had written again.

"I have just finished reading your volume, *The Religious Foundations of Ancient Indian Political Science* and was most impressed by this great work of scholarship. If you agree, I should like to write my book, *Ceylonese Culture in the Background of Buddhism,* under your formal guidance, presenting it as a Ph.D. thesis and then publishing it. My parents and elder brother have blessed the idea. Please, accept me as your student."

VII

In spite of a congenial home, parents-in-law who showered affection on her, a loveable child and material comforts, Katyayani felt dejected and listless. She thrived on the company of her child, playing the usual games with him - hide-and-seek, catch-me! It fell to her to carry out the day's first household chores of sweeping the floor, washing the front yard with water and decorating it with symmetrical *rangavalli* designs.

By this time Shrothri and his wife would have finished their bath, the father-in-law moving into the prayer room and the mother-in-law into the kitchen. Lakshmi took over other more strenuous tasks. Katyayani's duties came to an end after she bathed and dressed her child and hung the washed clothes out to dry. The rest of the time she found hard to spend. Once in a while, her mother-in-law would invite her to a game of dice but this was more a test of patience and filial endurance rather than an afternoon of enjoyment.

Shortly after her husband's death, Katyayani had gone to her natal home in Srirangapatna, a town of seven to eight thousand inhabitants, some twenty-three miles to the south of Nanjangud. It was a pilgrim centre for the god Ranganatha, another form of Vishnu, the preserver, as rural as Nanjangud but without its tradition of scholarly wisdom. However, it did offer some historical interest in being the former capital of Tipu Sultan, the Muslim ruler who had fought the British at the end of the eighteenth century. At home there were her father and her step-mother, an embarrassing mere eight years older than Katyayani. Her rigidly ritual-minded father had hinted that his daughter should, after her husband's death, present a widow's appearance, with her head shaved and the traditional red sari wrapped round her. Thereafter she was to have performed the traditional role of the widow, eating but one meal a day and immersing herself in work and worship. But Shrothri had ignored it. After a few days there, she returned to her in-laws in Nanjangud with relief.

In the beloved house in Nanjangud, she would become nostalgic. She had seen a few girls travelling to Mysore by train to go to university. There some hoped to find the young man that they would marry, or, if not, a degree certainly raised one's suitability in the arranged marriage stakes. Perhaps she could do a B.A. too. Her husband did not take his B.A. examination at the first opportunity and at the second attempt he failed in some subjects. His text books were still there on the shelf upstairs. In some of books, by the side of his name, she could see hers, written by him in pencil and rubbed away by her.

The idea of going back to university grew stronger, undistracted by the occurrence of anything of even minor interest. Though she was not sure that her father-in-law would approve of the idea, she thought it her duty to ask him. When she broached the matter he questioned, "Child, where is the need for you to travel by train every day without eating at your proper times? Why don't you stay at home and live in comfort? Maybe when Cheeni grows up, you can think of continuing your study."

She explained, "He would most certainly have finished his B.A. if he had lived. If I were to do it on his behalf, it would give me some peace."

And then she would be silent, hoping that her father-in-law would not guess at the second reason that she was so bored.

Shrothri was by nature inclined to examine every issue with seriousness. He had observed the sense of emptiness characterising his daughter-in-law's life recently and it occurred to him that if she were involved in some study, she might be diverted away from her preoccupation with her personal tragedy. Yet, he told her, "Remember what I had suggested to you earlier; read the *Bhagavadgita,* read the *Upanishads.* I shall instruct you in their content and meaning every day after my worship. If one lacks the means of livelihood, that is another matter. In that respect, God has not denied us anything. If you ask me, the *Bhagavadgita and Upanishads* are a better remedy for persons like you than a university education."

Though his advice did not appear to contain a single harsh word, his emphasis on the words "for persons like you" pierced her and brought tears to her eyes. Though Shrothri was unable to guess the cause of her tears, he told her consolingly, "Well if you are determined to study, I shall not say no. Why should you cry for it?"

Wiping her tears, she replied, "I did try to read the *Bhagavadgita.* Somehow I was not drawn to it. What can I do? I read some of his books on the shelf upstairs and I seem to like them."

Shrothri said, "Yes, what you are saying is true, child. There is a time for everything."

"After all this, what university can there be? What does she know of the ways of the world? She asks, and you simply say, yes! Wouldn't it be best to stay at home and look after her child?"

Shrothri tried to placate his wife, "After all, she is very young. How can she idle away her time staying at home? Let her go to university for a year or two."

"Don't we, too, feel sorry that this should have happened to her at so young an age? If she had taken the conventional widowhood, at least she could have assisted us in the ritual chores. But now she must spend her time somehow by doing her present work - sweeping the floor, washing the front yard and decorating it. Perhaps she could also help in preparing the wicks and other items for worship or she may observe vows," Bhagirathamma added helpfully.

Lakshmi intervened, "Even if Katyayani goes to university now, isn't it just to complete her husband's unfinished work? She will be studying on behalf of, and in the name of her husband, and not for herself! Let her study. What do you lose?"

Bhagirathamma reconciled herself to the situation but only because it meant that the daughter-in-law was going to bring to the family the B.A. degree that the son had not. Her silence, however, meant only half consent. Realising this, Shrothri said, "Who can be happy at the practice of shaving off a widow's hair when she is so young? It is acceptable if a widow volunteers for it, asking herself why she needs all this outward attraction when the person for whom it was meant is no more. But that must come from within, and not be imposed from outside."

Vasanti, daughter of Dr. Sripad, one of the town's few medically qualified doctors, who lived in the nearby street of shops, learning that Shrothri's daughter-in-law was to attend her university, took the initiative and called on the elder Shrothris, suggesting that she and Katyayani should travel from Nanjangud to Mysore together. They readily agreed, reassured by the arrangement. When Katyayani was about to leave, Cheeni started to cry loudly, demanding that he too should be taken to university. She tried to pacify him by promising to return home soon, to read him the most exciting stories, to play his favourite games, ever conscious of her mother-in-law's telling disapproval bearing down upon her.

Burdened with a vague uneasiness, Katyayani reached the railway station with her friend. It was just ten minutes' walk from home. As she entered the ladies' compartment, she could not control her tears and they spilled out. Vasanti tried to console her but suddenly felt uncomfortable doing so, as she was still a young girl whereas Katyayani was a woman and a mother. As the train moved slowly, Katyayani felt as if it were taking her to some unknown destination and it never once entered her mind that this same train would bring her back home in the evening. The local train moved at a slow pace. The rains had already started and Kapila's waters were brimming over onto the surrounding land. As the train crossed the Dalavai bridge across the Kapila, she had a full view of both banks of the eastward-flowing river. Half a mile away stood the temple of Nanjundeswara and to the left of it was the Manikarnika bank with steps leading into the river. It was at this point that the marital symbol of the vermilion mark had been washed from her forehead. Yes, it was this month but that year the rains had been more torrential. The train left the scene behind and it was only after crossing Kambali Matha that it gathered greater speed. By that time Vasanti had managed to engage her in conversation. They had a slight prior acquaintance which was expected, in the year ahead, to materialise into friendship.

Even before the train touched the intermediate station of Kadakol, Chamundi hill was visible on the right. Katyayani had developed an inexplicable fascination for this hill that stood in that flat landscape so defiantly high. Twice before, and with her husband, she had gone to the top of the hill surveying from a height the surrounding scene - the villages, towns, ponds and that mighty river. And, even though the summit had vanished behind the clouds of the rainy month, the solidity and strength were unmistakable. Katyayani watched the scene through the window of the compartment and as she did so, the hill gave the illusion of changing its position as the train moved. Soon the hill, which had appeared on the right, seemed to stand in the way of the train, and just as it appeared that the train would crash into it, the train swerved and arrived at Chamarajapuram station.

Katyayani opened the door pointed out to her by the attendant and quietly entered the room. Rao, seated in a chair before the table, was talking intensely and animatedly to a woman sitting at the other end of the table who was listening to him with the utmost of concentration and scribbling at intervals. She was around twenty-six or twenty-seven, had a dark complexion and wore a white sari. Now and then Rao glanced at the papers on the table. The room was packed with books, producing a feeling of stuffiness which was accentuated rather than relieved by the fan slowly revolving above. Katyayani stood for about ten minutes without either of them noticing her. She almost decided to go away but she thought it would be improper and so she stood there for five more minutes, trying her best to look purposeful. The woman taking down his words happened to lift her head and, catching sight of Katyayani, motioned Rao towards her presence. It took him two minutes to place her. Removing his glasses, he stared at her with a rudeness that would have been inexcusable in anybody other than an intellectual. Shy and embarrassed, she stood silent, her head bent low. After yet another minute, Rao recognised her, and rising a little from his seat, welcomed her effusively, "Please, come, come. Is it the twenty-fourth already? If you don't make some noise or other to call my attention, well, you will stand there and I will sit here forever! Please, come closer."

The woman in the white sari moved a chair so that Katyayani could sit down. Rao instructed the attendant, "Go to the university and bring Raja Rao."

Then he asked Katyayani, "At what time do you leave home every day?"

"Quarter to nine."

"Quarter to nine! Then you can only get home by six or seven in the evening. My house is here in Chamarajapuram. During the hour and half lunch break, you can go to my house and eat your meal there."

"Thank you, but there are other girls travelling from Nanjangud. I bring my lunch in a tiffin-carrier."

"You can bring it. But you can hand it over to me here and then go straight to my house and take your meal there."

After saying this he laughed loudly and added, "Don't feel shy. My home is your home."

Karuna did not catch the joke implied in Rao's laughing. He and Katyayani were conversing in Kannada and she could understand only the occasional English or Sanskrit word used. Rao's laughter was broken by the arrival of his brother. Suddenly the elder brother realised that he had failed to perform the courtesies of introduction but was rather too quick off the mark, completing them before Raja had even closed the door.

Rao continued, "... of course we have a strong family connection. You remember Nanjunda Shrothri, don't you? This is his widow," he added somewhat tactlessly.

Raja suggested taking Katyayani home with him and she, although nervous, readily acquiesced, glad to escape from that cluttered room and Rao, well-meaning though he was.

Talking to Raja proved to be a rather uneasy experience, even though he was extremely friendly, asking about her options, what literature she enjoyed reading and suggesting a few English novels. To all these she gave short, non-committal replies, annoyed with herself for being so reserved. Katyayani, however, was drawn to Nagalakshmi, to her motherly hospitality and simple warmth. Nagalakshmi in turn felt great compassion for her, insisting with such affection, "You must come here every afternoon for your lunch. You can also come whenever you have any free time. After all, this is your home too."

The tension which had marked her departure from home in the morning, had now been eased by such kindness and solicitude. Returning to university she attended a Sanskrit lecture which she found challenging but not overly difficult and then returned to the ladies' common room. There were seven or eight girls there chattering in a mixture of English and Kannada but Vasanti was not among them. Conscious once again of her alien surroundings, Katyayani wanted to go home as soon as possible. Twice or thrice she went up to the door to see if Vasanti would come back. She was sure that her friend would return by five. So she sank into a cane chair to wait. Her mind filled with memories of her husband.

"How did he spend his time at university? How anxious was he to go home again? As anxious as I am now?"

VIII

During the time that she was free from classes, Katyayani would rush to the Rao household, to Nagalakshmi who would feed her hospitably with her delicious home-made sweets and to Raja. Raja, used to the adoring adulation of teenage students, found much to admire in Katyayani's pleasant manner and mature, dignified presence. Together they would talk avidly for he would speak of his plays, their meaning and stagecraft and his time in England. Although initially nervous, she responded earnestly by telling him of her interest in literature. Her favourite author was the Bengali writer, Sharat. Katyayani was captivated by the strength and originality of his female characters, the fortitude of Parvati in *Devadas,* the independence of the Anglo-Indian Kamala in *Seshaprasna* and the noble nature of Rajalakshmi in *Srikant.* Once, Raja had induced her to stay behind to watch *Hamlet* which he had directed and in which he was also to play a leading role. Although girls from Nanjangud did stay behind for the performances, Katyayani had never done so, always ensuring an early return home. She knew that Shrothri appreciated this as an indication of her responsible attitude and of late he had been increasingly tutoring her in the household finances and the management of their lands. Reluctant to say yes and reluctant to say no, Katyayani had vacillated until finally she promised to be there. Any guilt that she may have felt was soon brushed aside in the thrill of watching Raja in the play. Afterwards, when he asked for her opinion, she responded eagerly.

"You must come again," he insisted. "We need people like you to come and encourage us!"

Katyayani blushed, inwardly elated that he considered her to be a discerning spectator. Nagalakshmi, who had accompanied her, was distinctly unimpressed.

"Not a single song, not a single dance! And in a language totally unknown. What is there in an English play?"

Every iota of her rural simple-mindedness stood up in her defence. Katyayani and Raja smiled, liking her immensely.

The first year of university went by and Katyayani passed her class examinations with merit. Throughout her parents-in-law had been extremely supportive. Shrothri would always take an interest in her studies and was of invaluable help in her Sanskrit papers. Bhagirathamma, overcoming her initial dislike of the university education, had become very solicitous. When Katyayani tried to help her in the kitchen, Bhagirathamma would shoo her away telling her to attend to her studies. If her daughter-in-law protested that she had already prepared for the next day, the mother-in-law would tell her affectionately either to rest or to spend her time playing with Cheeni. Travelling by train every day had become very tedious and so Katyayani looked forward to the summer vacation as a relief from this chore. But when the holidays actually arrived, she began to feel bored and missed university. The novelty of being able to spend a leisurely morning at home without rushing to catch the train soon wore off and as she was contemplating the loneliness of the vacation Vasanti arrived, her face shining with triumphant exuberance.

"Did you get a First?" asked Katyayani.

"Of course not! Anyway, even if they offered me a First I wouldn't take it!" She laughed and swirled round.

Her petulant enthusiasm then melted as she carefully smoothed her new, shining, blue sari and said shyly, "You must be our guest at a feast."

Katyayani was delighted.

"Congratulations. And may I enquire after the bridegroom?"

Details told many tens of times before to relatives, friends and guests were repeated once again with the same excitement as accompanied their first telling for how many times did a woman marry but once? The marriage was a love marriage and not an arranged marriage (in the sense that Vasanti's parents had not selected the bridegroom) but as the young man concerned was of the same caste and distantly related there was little difference and thus did not cause a stir. They had met at university, spending their free time together walking by the Kukkarahalli lake. Katyayani was unaware of this, partly because she had spent most of her time at Raja's house but mostly she guessed because the other girls found it difficult to relate to her as she was older, the mother of a child and a widow. She could sense their attitude, a mixture of curiosity and pity. After Vasanti left, Katyayani felt happy for her friend and within her mind, she prayed to God to grant the future husband a long life. And it was only then that the envy came. Her friend's future was going to be one of marital happiness. She had one more year of university before returning to her old routine. If she were to be confined to the home, there was little real point in a university education. It was an educative experience, instructive in showing her what she could not have. What heaven would her late husband gain if she got her B.A.? A degree was scarcely of use in the management of household work.

Katyayani's mind turned to Nagalakshmi. The memory of her simple, innocent nature and her trustful behaviour touched her heart with feelings of deep friendship. In the whole year, Katyayani had not seen Rao even once and she could guess at the loneliness of his wife. But Nagalakshmi had one formidable consolation - she was not a widow. At least she had the satisfaction that even if away from her, her husband was alive, studying in his library a furlong away. She decked herself daily with flowers. She decorated her forehead with the vermilion mark of marriage. She would wear coloured bangles and coloured saris, not for her the gaping bleakness of widowhood.

Vasanti now busied herself with her new life and so, during the vacations, Katyayani tended the plants and trees in the backyard. It was a spacious yard with a cattleshed at the far end. The garden was a randomly arranged collection of plantain and coconut trees and countless flowers of every hue, deep and velvety, which would be plucked and offered in worship to the image in the prayer room. No matter how many flowers were taken, the bushes would be replenished overnight. The mango tree over which a jasmine creeper had spread, had dried up within becoming ancient and dead. When Katyayani reported the matter to her father-in-law, he called a servant who skilfully axed the tree but saved the jasmine plant. The jasmine creeper was then trained around a bamboo pole. Nearby Shrothri planted another mango tree which Katyayani faithfully watered and, within a fortnight, it put out fresh leaves. Shrothri shifted the jasmine creeper from the bamboo pole and arranged it around the new mango plant. As she watched, the jasmine flourished, entwining itself, curving and clinging.

Holidays were working days for persons like Rao but for Raja they were days of boredom. They signalled the end of theatrical activities and he had completed his duties as an examiner. To keep himself occupied, he did physical exercises in the morning and even went to the university gymnasium for a few days to work out but on the third day he abandoned the idea. Then he thought of taking up classical music as it would help him in his dramatic activities. In fact, he arranged a music teacher at the rate of fifteen rupees a month and bought a violin for a further hundred rupees. For a fortnight and much to the initial amusement and increasing exasperation of Nagalakshmi, he put in a daily stint of two to three hours, labouring over the rudiments, *sa, ri, ga, ma, pa, dha, ni, sa.* The results were none too encouraging and his fingers never seemed to apply the right pressure. The next ploy for overcoming his boredom was a daily bicycle ride on Hunsur Road but this proved to be an equally depressing experience, the fields on either side of the road all dry, greenless and burnt out.

That year the rains came early in the first half of the month of *Chaitra.* The summer heat which had been rising all the time came down sharply and suddenly. Her heat dwindling, mother earth appeared healthier, lively and brisk. Encouraged, nay exhilarated, Raja resumed his cycle rides along Hunsur Road, and what a miraculous transformation! The peasants were ploughing the fresh fields whose small mud boundaries were now green with the young shoots. The trees lining the road swayed gently in the west wind of the monsoon season, filled with squirrels and birds proclaiming and epitomising the bustle and vibrancy of life. At some points on the road, the branches came so low that farmers on their bullock carts would reach out and grasp them with shouts of laughter. Yet, in the distance, Raja could see the low branches being cut to allow the buses to pass along the road. That night, the idea for a new play started to germinate in his mind. Its theme was how man, destroying the beauty of nature, builds his path in history and how the original nature of man and his primal joy were suppressed by the violence of civilisation. But he had no clear idea in his mind as to who could portray the theme effectively and he also had no clear plot in his mind. The picture of man killing nature dominated his thoughts, keeping him awake into the small hours of the morning. Even his elder brother, who had still not broken his habit of studying late into the night, had put out his lamp to go to bed when Raja was worrying his head with the unwritten play.

In the early morning Raja had a gentle, fluid dream. The play had crystallised into some shape, with one character fully visualised and that was a beautiful, young woman - about twenty years of age, a breathtaking presence, her body shining with the lustre of health, her skin tender. She had long fingers, the kind that one found only in paintings. Her hair was loose, long, blue-black. She wore no ornaments on her body and her soft limbs radiated womanly vitality. The gentle, oval face bore no trace of shyness. This astoundingly beautiful woman sat on a slab under a tree, letting her legs down, wholly naked. The streaming moonlight had solidified into her body. By her side was a heap of flowers which she was weaving into a garland. Silently, she was weeping.

At that point, the dream dissolved and Raja woke up. Two days later, the identity of the dream girl came to him.

The summer vacation was over and the university re-opened. Raja sat in a chair in the front-yard to correct and revise the new play he had written in English, glancing surreptitiously at Katyayani who was sitting back in a cane chair, eyes closed, smiling, humming softly, recovering, she said, from a difficult Sanskrit lecture. He leant over and said forcefully, "I know that you can act, that once you acted in *Savitri and Satyavan*. You must, simply must, play the part of the heroine in this play!"

Katyayani became solemn and silent.

"There is a lot of difference between that time when I acted and now. What will people say?"

She considered the constraints on a widow, not only the accepted rule against re-marriage but also the restrictions on participation in aspects of daily life. But objections of social inappropriateness, of the poignancy of the leading role, of the standard of her English, of the time it would take were all counter-attacked as Raja's persuasive powers overcame her inhibitions. Once before she had enjoyed the thrill of acting on stage and was excited by the prospect of wearing make-up again. The fear remained that her parents-in-law would hear of it but this year Vasanti was no longer travelling with her, as she was living in her husband's home in Mysore, and so there was no-one to carry the news home. Every day, Katyayani would visit the Rao household to practice her part.

"It is only when the words are woven into light and shade on the stage that the full meaning of the play becomes manifest," Raja would exclaim and she would agree, staring at his face to understand more carefully the essence of what he was saying.

Once Katyayani asked him how he got the idea of writing such a play. Startled and afraid that she would read his mind and see the very dream that he had had, Raja gabbled insanely about bicycle rides on Hunsur road. Perplexed by his manner and a little disappointed, she nevertheless congratulated him on his perception and resourcefulness.

The play, *Mula Tattva (The Primordial)*, was something of a novelty for the city of Mysore in the late thirties, for it employed new techniques. In contrast to the veritable army of actors that was usually expected and employed, it had just four characters and some of the words were spoken from behind a thin, white screen, others in dim twilight. It was to be performed on a single night and this, coupled with Raja's reputation as a writer/director and rumours of an avant-garde production, had drawn the crowds in vast numbers. As the play was staged in the open air, in a quadrangle at the university, there was little problem with accommodating the numbers. The seats went quickly and the audience spilled out into the archways. The play opened on the first of August and as it was the inaugural performance of the year, the Vice-Chancellor presided over it.

As the curtain rises *Prakriti* (Nature), the heroine is seen wandering silently amidst lush green trees and plants. A voice, sounding as though it comes from the depths of time, speaks, explaining. The woman gathers flowers and then weaves them into a huge garland, gazing at her own creation with pride. Enter *Purusha* (Mankind). Attracted, *Prakriti* approaches him playfully and amorously. She is on the point of garlanding him in marriage and he stretches his hand to reach hers. Just then the silence is shattered by thunder and lightning and the stage becomes dark.

Devaraja's court, the court of the one who rules the world with the royal staff of power. Beside the king sits the *dharmaguru*, Brihaspatyacharya who stamps the former's authority with a religious and moral sanction. Bound in powerful chains, *Prakriti* stands to one side. Brihaspatyacharya presents the indictment, "You have been accused of violating *dharma.*"

Prakriti asks, "What breach of *dharma* have I committed?"

"Earlier you were with another man. That man attained wisdom and fled from you, finding release from your bondage. You, now a widow, now want to garland the neck of another man. This is a violation of *dharma,*" proclaims *Dharmaguru*.

"O, *Dharmaguru,* is it not a violation of *dharma* to force *Prakriti,* who is eternally new and eternally alive to submit to the bondage of artificial *dharma?* My basic and original nature is vitality, life-giving power. The forests that fill the mind with joy, the beauteous sights that thrill the eyes, my expanse which feeds all moving and static creatures - these cannot be consigned to widowhood by any *dharma.* Can you answer but one question of mine?"

"Ask me."

"Doesn't *Purusha's* salvation lie in his relationship with *Prakriti?* If you degrade me with the taint of widowhood, how can the endless crowd of *Purushas* attain salvation? Isn't your *dharma* which comes in the way of their attaining salvation, artificial?"

Stunned into silence, *Dharmaguru* listens. Then *Prakriti* continues, *"Dharma,* morality, royal edicts, social rules, popular censure, which restrain my fundamental nature, are different faces of untruth. *Prakriti* is eternally young and any *dharma* that attempts to destroy her beauty will itself be self-destroyed!"

Again there is thunder and lightning and the stage is left dark. Dim lights slowly appear, giving that world a strange but not menacing quality. Lying lamed on the ground, *Dharmaguru* and *Devaraja* are seen repenting their error. Slowly the light grows brighter. Jubilant, holding the garland in her hand, *Prakriti* comes on the stage, proclaiming her eternal youth. *Purusha* hovers around her but *Prakriti* does not rush to garland him. Perplexed, he moves towards her but each time he is repelled. Finally, understanding, *Purusha* says, *"Prakriti,* you are not a widow. You enjoy eternal wifehood, eternal womanhood."

It is then that she garlands him. She casts a look of compassion at *Devaraja* and *Dharmaguru,* lying on the ground lame and her look of grace restores the natural power to their limbs. They rise and prostrate themselves before her. The lights gradually dim as the curtain falls.

Wild applause.

When Katyayani returned backstage, Raja gripped both her hands and said, "Sublime! You gave my imagination the most perfect articulation!" She smiled modestly, forgetting to pull her hands back from his grasp. Soon after the curtain came down for the last time, hurriedly a table and three chairs were placed on the stage. The Vice-Chancellor, the Principal and Raja took their seats. After the audience quietened, the Vice-Chancellor addressed them, "I used to be a Professor of Biology. Mr. Raja Rao has written an excellent play. I compliment him on your behalf. The lady who played the key role, Miss, Miss..." he looked at Raja for information, "Miss Katyayani gave a wonderful performance. As a student of biology, this is how I understand the message, that nature is perpetually young and new. The cells in our body keep on dying. But simultaneously, new cells are created. Thus the world is saturated with life. This is what we should understand from the play."

Having said whatever occurred to him as relevant to the occasion, he sat down.

It was half past eight when the audience dispersed. Raja accompanied Katyayani to Chamarajapuram station. Katyayani was silent. She was already regretting her acting in the play. As long as she was on stage, she acted the part, forgetting herself. But five minutes after the play had ended, she felt embarrassed. As they neared the station, she said, "There will be people travelling to Nanjangud on the platform. They may misunderstand."

Raja left her without a word.

IX

Karuna's arrival in Mysore enabled Rao to step up the pace of his writing. The content and structure of every chapter were exhaustively discussed before putting pen to paper and she would listen to him attentively, asking him for clarification whenever necessary. When she raised issues, Rao would say, "It is such a good thing you asked me that question. The point certainly needs to be elaborated," and he would make a note at the appropriate place.

She actively assisted him in such matters as locating source material, bibliographical references as well as more specific details. Rao frequently dictated to her, reading from his notes, and she would take down the notes in shorthand and then later type them out in her hostel, performing not only the mechanical service of typing but also improving the style and language. The new typewriter that Rao had bought for himself was soon installed in her room in the ladies' residence.

As she was a research scholar and because Rao had sponsored her, Karuna was given a special room in the residence where she settled in easily, taking somewhat longer to become accustomed to the food. After finishing a late breakfast, she hurried off to the library where she immersed herself in the research work of reading and taking notes. By the time Karuna returned home it was usually seven in the evening and it was only then that she could begin work on her own thesis. Fortunately, even before her arrival in Mysore, most of the data had been collected, the only remaining problem being to find the proper perspective and framework. Within two months of intense discussion with her mentor, Rao, her argument was crystallised and refined. Although the thesis was relegated to a second consideration, Karuna considered herself fortunate in being given the opportunity to serve her *guru* in the writing of his great volume and so worked for him with extraordinary devotion and zeal.

Nagalakshmi, at home, was seething. Raja tactfully remained a passive audience as she continued a vociferous, self-justifying monologue.

"Well, I have been married to him for many years now. In the first few days, he called me Nagu but soon after that he forgot his

Nagu. During the three years of his Ph.D. he ignored me and then he spent the next five writing his book. Now another demon had possessed him, the idea of writing a big book. Five whole volumes of it! It will take him away from us for the next twenty-five years. By that time I will be fifty. God knows under what terrible star this man was born. The local astrologer of our town, Tippa Jois, compared our horoscopes and declared that we were born for each other," she added plaintively.

"Does that mean that you don't want Brother to write great books and achieve honour and recognition? Doesn't it make you happy to see him renowned as a great scholar?"

"How can I not feel proud and happy at his achievements? Am I saying that he shouldn't read and write? But is it right to ignore Prithvi and me?" she snapped back.

"But such is the business of scholarship. Brother's is not a special case for some scholars live like that even in England. We have very few people of Brother's scholarly stature here in India and what he has undertaken requires concentration and an unwavering devotion."

"Well, you have said that there are people like him in England. What do their wives do?

"Their wives do not face this situation because..." Raja sighed, his mind returning to Oxford, to the wives of distinguished professors who possessed the educational experience and intellectual capacity sufficient to enable them to participate in their husband's scholarly life. As a result the couple had plenty to share and discuss, the husband depending on the wife and the wife having no reason to feel marginalised. People chose their life partners on the scale of intellectual and personal compatibility. Raja did not venture to consider whether theirs or the Indian approach to marriage was better.

"Why did you stop?"

"Well, wives in those countries suffer as you do."

Resigning herself to her fate, Nagalakshmi made towards the kitchen. Suddenly she swung round and said eagerly, "Why don't you get married? You are twenty-five and then at least I shall have a companion at home."

Rao returned home at eight to find Prithvi in a particularly intractable and obdurate mood. He was crying inconsolably, pulling at his father's sleeve, demanding that he should be taken for a bicycle ride. Not only was Rao exhausted after his strenuous work in the library but he also did not know how to handle the child, knew not the words to console him. The only words he could find were, "Don't cry unreasonably. Don't pester me. Go to your mother."

As soon as these words came out of her husband's mouth, Nagalakshmi, as if waiting for a cue, rushed out of the kitchen snapping,

"Go to your mother, go to your mother! Well, when have you done anything for your child? If Prithvi is asking with such insistence, what do you lose if you take him out for a while? If you want, I shall come too and all three of us can go out."

Rao did not have the mental reserves to get angry with his wife. What he knew of human nature was that an angry person would become angrier if provoked and so he kept quiet. Nagalakshmi adopted the strategy of using a tone which suggested simultaneously that she was speaking to herself and yet also addressing him.

"Am I his only parent? He cares nothing for his wife. And he has no concern for his own child. You and those evil books. You don't want your wife, you don't want your child. No, you can go on like this. Maybe my death will make you wiser! Let me close my eyes for ever, you will learn your lesson, and you will say, how nice if Nagu were alive!"

This was too much.

"Why do you indulge in such dark thoughts? Come here, close to me."

Hearing his father's loud voice, the child grew silent.

"No, I don't need your kindness - invited after whimpering and begging."

Pouting sulkily, she moved away from him and the boy followed his mother instinctively. Rao held his head in his hands. Whichever way he turned, whatever he did, it was wrong.

After five minutes Nagalakshmi herself softened, came back and sat in the chair.

"You have a habit of taking everything to the extreme. Why shouldn't you let me give you an oil massage every Sunday?" she asked sweetly.

Rao felt rather uncomfortable but he placed his hand gently on her back saying, "I promise to come home earlier in future."

This was enough to pacify Nagalakshmi. That night they slept with Prithvi between them and Rao spoke to his wife with an uncommon intimacy and affection. Their conversation ranged from the jasmine creeper in the garden to the servant maid in the neighbouring house. By way of additional interest she also mentioned the new Hyderabad pulses bought by Raja. By eleven she was asleep and Rao took the opportunity to go to his study to read just a few pages.

His nocturnal reading did not prevent Rao from being back in his special room at university at ten o'clock the next morning, dictating to Karuna.

"Your argumentation and presentation are not coming through," she said directly.

Resting his back against the chair, he said, "Today you may attend to your thesis. I cannot work."

Karuna went to pick from the shelves the volumes she needed and Rao shifted from the office chair to the easy chair. His mind had been disturbed and his concentration disrupted by yesterday evening's conversation with Nagalakshmi. Her words rang in his ears.

"Why did she behave like that yesterday, when she had never before done so? Why did she speak so bitterly and harshly?"

He could easily find the explanation for it. He had often decided to spare more time for amusing conversation with her, but he was helpless in the face of the great work he was writing. For him, living and writing that work had become virtually identical. Bodily functions like sleeping and eating had now become acts which the body performed without any connection with his mind, mechanically. Even to think of sparing half an hour for his family seemed as agonising as changing the essence of his life.

"You need to rest for a few days. You are working too fast and too hard. The human brain is not a machine. Please, go home."

Karuna's words of solicitude were pleasing and soothing.

Tired of not being able to work, he said, "Come, let's go out somewhere and relax."

She paused for a moment and answered, "But this is India!"

"Who are we to care? There must be a train to Brindavan at twelve."

They hired a tonga on Viceroy Road and reached the railway station, entering the third class compartment, as the train had no other class. Karuna had never been to Brindavan. In the early twenties a dam was constructed by the great Indian engineer, Vishveshwaraiah and was named after the very Maharaja Krishnaraja Wodeyar who had extended his support to the five volumes. The dam held back the river Kaveri and the water was diverted for agricultural purposes. Some ten years later, the idea arose of using the space created and the plentiful water to make a park for the inhabitants of Mysore. The park was duly designed, the gardens planted and they also built numerous man-made fountains of different sizes which threw their refreshing white jets up during the day and which were illuminated by different coloured lights at night. And they named this garden Brindavan, the place where Lord Krishna as a young boy played his flute and laughed with cowherdesses.

By the time the train wended its way slowly beyond Belagola to reach Kannambadi, the station for Brindavan, it was quarter to one. As soon as they entered the gardens, the first thing they did was to go to the restaurant and there they ordered *idli* and *dosa* and *kesareebath*. They wandered round for a while and then settled in the shade of a few large trees, beyond the orchard. Rao's mind had now left the world of scholarship, that congested, airless room which was his. Here, he sat under the swaying coolness of a tree. Nearby water was jumping, producing the measured sound of stringed musical instruments. High up in the cobalt sky, a few birds floated on the hot air currents. Rao came out of his silence and asked Karuna, "Within a year you will finish your thesis and you will certainly earn your doctorate. After that you will return home. What do you plan to do there?"

"I don't know."

"Continue your research work. It is the nature of research work to be endless. One perspective in one area of study will take us to another area or towards another perspective in that same area. One thing leads inevitably to another, endlessly. It is ceaseless, limitless. It will stop only with the sheer exhaustion of the researcher's energy and desire."

Then remembering something, Rao added, "Or if you want, you can return home and marry. Perhaps you will be lucky and find a husband with similar interests so that you can continue your research together."

Karuna sighed slowly, hoping not to be heard by Rao. But Rao did hear it. He lifted his face to gaze at hers and changed the topic, "When did you first become interested in historical research and study? Was there anybody in your family who served as a model or inspiration?"

Karuna opened up and began to speak more freely, "In our family, I was the only one to pursue an academic life. My ancestors were agriculturists, cultivating land in a village, named Pelpola but our family's main pursuit became commerce and business. My elder brother, Ajit, and I both studied at the local university and then he went into business and I, to Colombo to do my M.A. course. Professor D'Silva was extremely encouraging and from there I won a government scholarship to London. My time there was stimulating and educative, observing the way historians studied and their approach to the subject. It is from you that I have truly learnt the methods of research investigation. But for the chance of our meeting, I might never have embarked on this writing. Whenever I see your unswerving dedication to research, my mind rises to heights beyond my imagination."

Rao was thrilled at Karuna's flattering reference. Nobody had, before this, paid him such fulsome praise. True, he had received letters of appreciation from foreign scholars and complimentary reviews in scholarly journals. But no-one had so openly expressed a desire to be his disciple and Rao found himself filled with a strange and unfamiliar joy, merging with an unidentifiable anguish.

"Karuna, the life of a researcher and scholar is like the life of a ghost, cut off from all living things, ever absorbed in a half-real world of studies and books, in the eeriness of a library, silent after everyone has gone. Very few can pursue it for they are distracted by the path of common life. Do you have it in you to deny yourself a woman's natural inclination towards married life and pursue scholarship?"

Bewildered and embarrassed by the question, Karuna answered, "Yes, the question of my marriage arose once. Ajit had a partner in the export business and being a university friend he became a regular visitor to our house. I was just twenty and still an undergraduate. He, by now, had started his business and thus being settled, he expressed his desire to marry me and that too in my presence! My parents thought I was silent out of shyness. Ajit was very keen on the alliance. In the meantime I told my family of my deep desire to go to Colombo to do my M.A. At first, they were all very reluctant as they wanted to see me married but when they realised how much a part of me my studies were, they agreed. Ajit's friend believed I would marry him after my M.A. and waited for me but in Colombo I began to see my way more clearly. No, my scholarly life and his business career were totally incompatible, a miserable mismatch. When I told him in no uncertain terms that he should not expect to marry me, he pleaded that he would never come in my way, that he could not live without me. I considered this carefully but felt that it wouldn't work. He might not directly block my studies, but we had no common ground of work and aspiration. Our goals were so sharply divergent. He was as blind to scholarship as I was to commerce. Our marriage would have been a marriage of two blind persons."

Suddenly, Karuna realised that her voice had unconsciously risen in pitch and she fell silent. It pained her to displease her brother and often her mind swung from decision to decision. Perhaps it was folly to reject a handsome and highly eligible young man who begged for her love. Perhaps her scholarly pursuits would not clash with his hopes if he loved her so much. Perhaps she could find some way of combining her household work and the demands of her research. Such questions tended to weaken her resolution to reject him but she held firm. Then a polite invitation arrived, informing her family of his engagement and cordially inviting them to the marriage. The tears came and yet she calmed herself and attended the ceremony in her brother's disapproving company. These doubts and confusions in her mind, Karuna chose not to express to Rao.

For the next half hour or so, neither spoke. Rao was inwardly examining that merciful decision. He saw that by the time Karuna reached marriageable age, she had recognised her life's goal. But his story was different, for he had never faced the question of the compatibility between his scholarly pursuits and the demands of a householder's life. Though he had been educationally and intellectually advanced, he had been otherwise immature at the time of his marriage. As he silently brooded over his past, he saw the Tataya charity school where he had spent his orphaned childhood, his progression to university where he had studied and studied, brilliant enough and shy enough to spend his entire time in the library, possessing neither the courage nor the background to develop the slightest relationship with one or two suitable girls in his class. And Nagalakshmi, who upon being told of their marriage had shyly hidden herself from him, but wherever she had been, she left behind the fragrance of the jasmine blossoms that she wore in her hair and wherever she was, her coloured bangles would jingle softly.

Marriage was something one had to accept as another stage of life. Rao looked up and broke the silence.

"It is not just my personal problem. Our Indian society is now in a transitional stage. Certainly, in the past, the marriages arranged by parents served an important function. In a society with a limited number of fixed castes and occupations, it was easy for any woman to fit into the occupational work of her husband and help him in it. The time for determining occupation by caste or by country is over and now individuals choose their professions and occupations according to their personal likes and dislikes. But the time has not yet come for him to choose his life according to personal predilections. In this transitional time, tragic marriages are unavoidable."

After a pause he continued, "In the old days, the purpose of marriage was to enable one to perform the duties of a householder, to continue the family tree. Now the first purpose survives, though in a weakened form. The second is losing its force. I have a son. I don't know whether he will continue the family name or not. But this volume I am writing is my offspring, should remain immortal, and to this end I am pouring into it my energy, my intellect and my desire. In this task, the wife I have wedded is absolutely useless. And it is you who are contributing to my work."

X

The relationship between Karuna and Rao began as that of co-researchers and developed into a close friendship. Each matched the other perfectly, their lives centred on the same goal. Karuna's level of scholarship was far higher than that of an ordinary student and thus Rao looked upon her more as a colleague and later as a friend. When uncommonly not in the mood for working, they would discuss other matters, though even such talk related in some way to their research, either directly or indirectly. Sometimes they would leave the library and walk along the Dhanvantary Road (the road of the divine physician) so called because of the numerous pharmacy stores that could be found there. They tended to avoid places that were too public such as parks and restaurants for people would stare and comment, especially as Karuna was, due to her darker complexion and different way of tying her sari, so obviously Ceylonese. It was for this reason that they sometimes visited Chamundi Hill.

The writing of the first volume was completed and had been revised thoroughly. Originally expected to take five years, the work had been completed within four. After Karuna's arrival the project acquired greater momentum. Even though Karuna had completed her thesis and had submitted it to the university, she did not want to return home without completing her guru's work and so she sat tight for six weeks, labouring day and night to produce a typescript of Rao's first volume. Finally, tired and elated, she neatly packed one copy of the manuscript and mailed it, with Rao's letter, to the English publisher.

The night preceding Karuna's departure for her homeland was, for Rao, a sleepless one. For the past two years she had been a vital part of his work, functioning as a constructive critic of his writings, bringing to his notice any defects or inadequacies. No paid secretary could have rendered him the kind of meticulous service she had, could fill the dual capacities of scholar-colleague and intimate companion. Rao worried about the future for he did not believe that he could manage the other volumes without her. He rose from his bed. Perhaps he had gone there to the ladies' residence just for a walk, perhaps just to be near her.

At half past four in the early morning, he went towards the Kukkarahalli lake and sat there. Slowly he walked back to the residence, waiting by the gates until she emerged to catch her morning train.

As he stood there, the crows began to caw and light slowly flowed into space. Karuna came out, astonished. He helped her into her jutka. As the jutka was to leave, she turned to him and said, "I am sure your great work will be completed without me. But without you, I shall not be in a position to make best use of what little ability I may possess."

After Karuna had left, Rao busied himself with the preparation of the second volume for it needed to be done and thought that by immersing himself in his work he could block her out as he could block out the rest of the world. As usual he went to the library promptly at nine in the morning and laboured there till eight in the evening. Every moment spent there seemed to emphasise her absence; he could not show his former earnestness and zest for he now had to attend to the problems of hunting references, taking notes and engaging in self-criticism. One of his students on the M.A. course, Honnaiah, had now become a lecturer in the university. Rao tried to enlist his support and assistance for the work but Honnaiah had just got married and could see little beyond the comforts of home and the attentions of his wife. There was none to match Karuna in respect of scholarship, mastery over English, knowledge of the Sanskrit and Prakrit languages, ability to write in shorthand and typing, and above all, commitment and enthusiasm. Yet, he struggled with the project and made some progress. Karuna wrote to him that proofs of the volume were coming fast from the London publisher and that they were waiting for the foreword. There, Rao acknowledged his gratitude to the Maharaja for his encouragement and the crucial help rendered to him in the writing of the volume by Karuna.

Within a month, the volume was out and it was the first volume of a work that embodied Dr. Rao's blood, flesh, intellect and will-power. A huge black volume entitled, *The Cultural History of India, Volume I - Sadasiva Rao,* embossed in shining gold. On the day he received the copies, Dr. Rao was transported, he entered a state of sublime ecstasy. He promised himself that he would not die before completing all the projected volumes. That very day he despatched a copy to Karuna and wrote to the Private Secretary to the Maharaja, asking for a personal audience to present a copy of the volume. The Private Secretary wrote back to say that the Maharaja was indisposed but that Rao could certainly call on him at a later date. Four days later Rao read of the Maharaja's death in the newspapers.

There had lurked in Rao's subconscious the notion that some aggressive and indescribable force lay behind his project, sustaining him, holding him steadfast and resilient. But now with the death of the Maharaja, that force was no longer there. If he ever came across any difficulty, suffered any hardship, there was no-one to help him. When the university organised a meeting of remembrance for the Maharaja, Rao volunteered to speak and it was there that many of the students and lecturers saw their foremost scholar for the first time in months. And as he spoke, Rao's eyes filled with tears of gratitude. Afterwards he left them again to return to his work. The publication of the volume enhanced the reputation of Rao as a scholar and accordingly his colleagues began to consider it a great privilege to meet and discuss some subject or other. It became a point of courtesy with them to enquire politely of Rao whenever they ran into him, "And how far have you progressed with your second volume?"

As the hours, days, and weeks passed the need for Karuna became stronger. He was aware that no scholar could devote adequate attention to the tasks of conceptualisation and interpretation if he were also called upon to do other lesser tasks of source collection and compilation. Even though six months had elapsed, Rao had been unable to organise satisfactorily even the preliminary part of the second volume. Most of his time and energy were wasted in locating sources and taking notes and moreover, there was no-one competent enough and close enough to discuss his ideas critically.

In the meantime, Karuna's Ph.D. results were announced and she not only got her doctorate but the examiners recommended strongly that her thesis be published. In his letter to her, after informing her of the result and congratulating her, Rao had written:

"In your previous letter you had asked me about the progress of my work. Well, it is dragging on. I am weary, tired. My eyes are failing me. I pray to God that I should be granted proper eyesight until I complete my volumes. My life, my work continues in fits. My time and energy are spent in doing secondary chores. The first volume was to be finished in five years. It was over in four. Certain international journals have written very favourable reviews. I don't know why, but somehow I no longer feel confident. Please let me know what you are doing."

Within a week Karuna's reply came, and it read:

"I am overjoyed to get my doctorate but it is you who have blessed it. Yes, I have seen the reviews of the first volume. I feel ecstatic. But in your foreword you over-praise my little service in its formation. My sole intention in doing what little I did was for personal satisfaction. Every sentence in it shines with your luminous scholarship and understanding. And who but I can know it best?"

As she took leave of her *guru* in Mysore, Karuna had been enthusiastic to see her parents and brother and yet, against this anticipated pleasure, the pain of being away from her teacher was overwhelming. The first two days after her return were spent wholly in exchanging news with her family, her studies and the growth of their business. Ajit and his wife now had two children. But she soon tired of the town of her birth. Since her research work had been formally completed, her parents urged her to think of marriage.

Soon after her return home, Karuna started getting proofs of the first volume and spent some two months in looking through them, but she would have been happier if Rao were there in person to appreciate her work. Fifteen days later she lost her mother. The ensuring sorrow was intense and insufferable. Then she realised the best way to forget the tragedy was to immerse herself in research work. She began to borrow books on history available at the local university and devoured them but once she started reading, her mind was inevitably pulled towards Mysore. There would be no peace unless she could rid herself of that all-engulfing passivity. Another letter arrived from Rao.

"This letter is born out of the anguish that I have been suffering since you left. I am sure you will not judge its propriety or otherwise with the eyes of common people. Our relationship has not remained at the level of preceptor and disciple. We are two souls engaged in a momentous task, two devotees worshipping at the feet of a common deity, ready to dedicate our lives to her. If one performs the recitation of *mantra,* the other performs *tantra,* the act of worshipping. Thus it is only when we both join hands that the worship is complete.

"Why should you suppress the call of your soul and torment yourself there? And why should I suffer here helplessly? Come to Mysore. Let us marry. From our marriage may issue forth our ambitions' off-spring, the volumes remaining."

As she read the last line, Karuna began to sweat gently. They had intimate exchanges of thoughts and feeling frequently during her stay in Mysore, conversations as intimate as between any married couple. He had embraced her spontaneously in the green bower on the bank of the Kukkarahalli lake and she had rested her head on his lap. On all these occasions, she had never raised within herself the issue of propriety because she had not yet looked at the situation from the outside world. In all those intimate minutes, he remained a lonely figure, now in greater need of her presence and services than ever before. She knew his feelings towards his wife. But Karuna had never looked at the matter from an ethical point of view and even now she was not really concerned with the moral aspect of the situation; it was not in her nature to cast things in such terms. To her it was simply a social problem of the love of a woman for a husband, her devotion and commitment to him in the face of his indifference and withdrawal. Nevertheless she did ask herself, seriously and properly, whether it was fair and correct to take a husband away and then marry him. Against this she weighed the fact that the two had not, since the early days of their marriage, had a genuine relationship of mutual attachment and understanding.

Karuna was a modern woman with a London education and everything in her mind disapproved of bigamy strongly. Her argument was that it was as impossible for one husband to live with two wives as for one wife to live with two husbands. To her, the issue was whether she or Rao's present wife should remain as the only wife. Since Rao was not really a proper husband to his wife and had no inclination so to be, she concluded by convincing herself that the marital bond between the two was so weak that she was doing nothing so untoward.

A foreigner and one belonging to another faith with a wife still living would be the last person her family would agree to her marrying. Karuna was not prepared to add another burden to their sorrow at the loss of mother and wife and so left, saying she was going to take up a research scholarship in Mysore.

As she left, her father blessed her, "Daughter, may your mind attain peace and equanimity."

Her brother, who had accompanied her to the railway station to see her off, wished her happiness in all that she did, saying that she should never feel shy before him and if she ever wanted to marry he would seek out a good bridegroom for her. Karuna wept at their familial love and affection and because she believed she would never return again and they did not.

XI

After her participation in the play, Katyayani's name became famous, if not a little notorious, in the university circle, both among the students and the lecturers. The women in the ladies' common room, initially aloof, clamoured to make her acquaintance. Despite or perhaps because of her involvement in the controversial play, they were a little in awe of her and Katyayani, regretting ever having been persuaded to do something for which she had not sought her in-laws blessing, did not find it a comfortable topic. She remained grave and unforthcoming. Even though *Mula Tattva,* had been staged in August, Katyayani could not forget the words. When she tried to study, the pages refused to make sense as, in her mind, each scene separated itself layer by layer. The amorous courtship, the condemnation, the refuting of that condemnation, the acceptance, forgiveness and the harmony. From downstairs she could hear the ritual chanting by her father-in-law emanating from the prayer room, loud, systematic and the play in her mind would be lost in the rhythm and the clarity of it.

The chanting would draw her from her studies and she would go outside into the peaceful backyard. The tender limbs of the jasmine plant were around the mango plant, sometimes arching themselves, sometimes moulding themselves gently against the other stem. Katyayani reached out to feel its pulse. The leaves and buds were in pure joy, declaring the primal principle of all living. Words flowed back, "... a vast expanse that can feed the living and the inert. There is no *dharma* that can stain them with widowhood." So far she had only understood the message as a style of social commentary but now, standing in front of the laughing jasmine creeper, she experienced its significance in the very depth of her being. Some incomprehensible and unbearable force entered her body and made it vibrate. Unable to endure the impact of the life force, she slumped to the ground.

Raja had grown up with Nagalakshmi, seeing her first as a childhood friend and then regarding her as a sister-in-law. He was ever-sensitive to her needs, ever respectful of her opinion. After he finished his M.A., and became employed, there was no lack of parents offering their daughters to him in marriage. Nagalakshmi had been insistent but Raja had always pleaded some excuse - he had to study, he was trying for a scholarship to England, he was going to England, he was adjusting to life back in India. Rao was not prepared to force his brother against his expressed desire not to get married, secretly appreciating his brother's reluctance, having known nothing but utter solitude as a married man himself. Some of the more forward girls involved in his plays would themselves coyly broach the subject but Raja took particular pleasure in wittily evading the subject or feigning absolute innocence.

Katyayani. Had she been a simple, unmarried woman, he would not have hesitated to propose but she was not a free person and that discouraged him from making any move in the matter. But he noticed that despite the social and religious constraints of her widowhood, she was showing more than ordinary interest in him. Hopeful and emboldened, he decided to force a decisive situation.

"Come to our house tomorrow," he said, with unnecessary nonchalance for she has never ceased to come to his house.

Recollecting something, she replied, "Isn't tomorrow a holiday?"

Raising his eyes heavenwards and cursing under his breath he insisted, "Come anyway. I want to talk to you about something very important."

"Is something wrong? Is somebody ill?" asked Katyayani with her usual concern.

"No, of course not." He was slightly irritated by her concern as it was totally unnecessary.

"On second thoughts, I shall be waiting for you in the Drama Society office. We can talk there uninterrupted."

The following day he sat waiting nervously in the office of the Society. His mind was full of anxiety and expectation, planning with the skill of a seasoned dramatist, several opening gambits. Unable to find a satisfactory opening, he decided, as he had decided all his life, to leave it to inspiration. And it was just then that Katyayani appeared, as always carrying her books and her tiffin-carrier. He stood up to welcome her, saying, "Please, come in."

But she stood outside the door, somewhat hesitant, unsure of the turn that this special meeting would take. When he invited her in a second time, she came inside and sat in the chair, silent but also full of apprehensive anticipation. After a few unsuccessful attempts to begin the conversation, he said at last helplessly, "At what time does your train usually reach here?"

"Just before ten."

There was a pause. Raja struggled hard to find another opening. Again, equally confused, he said, "You look thinner now than before."

Raising her head, she looked into his face with a mixture of confusion tinged with annoyance. He began to laugh, thereby affirming her suspicions that he had taken leave of his senses. Recovering his gravity, he put a straight question.

"Do you know why I asked you to come here now?"

"No."

"Then you would be lying... we are now not simply a teacher and a student. Though neither of us has said this openly, I am sure you know this."

She was silent. He continued, "I had decided never to marry. But now that decision has collapsed."

These words gave her the same feeling she had experienced when her father had told her he had selected a bridegroom for her, except that now the feeling was more intense and more dangerous. At the same time, what had earlier been unclear now became clear. The past closed in, her child, her parents-in-law and her deceased husband. The complexity and the intractability of her plight enclosed her in its grasp and this was also the moment when she realised the contradictory forces pulling her apart.

"Don't you understand?"

"Of course. I know that you have a child. In England I saw widows with children by their first husbands re-marrying. The children go with the mother. Your child from your first marriage will become my child. I promise not to neglect him."

He had answered the question implied by one of the contrary forces pulling at her, though she had not asked the question. Yet this did not take full account of her predicament.

"My parents-in-law are my responsibility. Their family honour and status are my responsibility."

"All contradictions and conflicts in human life are traceable to the questions of status and position. After all, wasn't this the basic theme of my play, *Mula Tattva?*"

Katyayani sat silent and presuming this to be a silence of consent, Raja caught hold of her hand and went on, "None has a right to violate the basic principle of one's inner nature. I shall be content if you can understand this much."

She did not take her hand away from his. As she sat there outwardly silent and unruffled, a storm was raging inside her and its speed made it impossible for her to comprehend its nature.

Katyayani stared up at him.

"I need you."

With that simplicity and directness there became unleashed the most glorious, the most precarious peace. As she travelled back to Nanjangud by the evening train, nature seemed to be dancing, mad with joy, now no more just a beautiful sight, self-sufficient, but it had become enriched by a new meaning and achievement. The unfulfilled greenness was now approaching the stage of fruition.

When she returned home in the evening, took her meal, and went to bed, her mind began to move suddenly in the opposite direction. This year she was sleeping alone upstairs as Cheeni slept with his grandmother in the bedroom with Lakshmi. Remembering the purpose with which she had undertaken her further education as she bowed respectfully to her parents-in-law, the original purpose of trying to complete her deceased husband's unfulfilled goal of taking the degree, she felt low and ashamed. Remembering that her parents-in-law, especially her father-in-law who had agreed with that purpose and had allowed her to continue her education, never grudging her expenses for university fees, books, travelling, the shame increased pervading her body attacking the newly entered life force. More recently Shrothri had even shifted the financial management of the household onto her shoulders. Her child, now four years old, was due to start school the following year. When a clear picture of the situation rose before her, she saw the immorality and the pain it would bring to this household to leave with the selfish desire to contract a second marriage.

The whole night she was agitated and decided to stop seeing Raja Rao from the next day and also not to see Nagalakshmi. Around midnight she went to the bathroom where she washed her feet and hands. After that she went to the prayer room, bowed to the deity and then started to climb the stairs. Shrothri, who was reading in the hall, said affectionately, "Child, haven't you gone to bed yet? You must not worry yourself about your exams."

After seeing Shrothri so absorbed in his reading, she decided, "After I finish my exam, I shall study the *Bhagavadgita* and the *Upanishads* under his guidance."

One whole week went by without Katyayani seeing Raja. She did not attend his lectures. Afraid that he might send for her, she did not even visit the ladies' common room. A powerful impulse to rush towards him and talk to him came over her and she managed to suppress it with difficulty. Now she was no longer thinking about the nature that surrounded her, or about herself transformed into a drained out representation of that nature, in that state beyond inertia. Notions of *dharma,* social norms, conventional morality had clung to her inside, were spreading through her body and they matched in force the impulses opposed to them. She tried to understand whether her beliefs were her own or whether they were merely the result of her unthinking practice but she found it beyond her capacity to grasp such issues and arrive at a true and correct position. The very clash in her mind between the opposed forces destroyed the mental equanimity necessary for resolving the issue.

One whole night she kept awake. The constant and inconclusive debate in her mind over the issue of *dharma* and *karma,* her own inner values, her own true needs, had left her brain drained and empty. She stood near the window and looked out on a scene bathed in the mildness of moonlight. Her father-in-law had already risen and she heard him walking towards the Gundala stream behind their backyard. Shrothri returned and then, gathering up his clothes, he went to the bathing ghat on the river. At the end of that sleepless night Katyayani felt that she had reached a firm decision. She bathed and wore the ritually pure white widow's sari. Taking a small, bamboo basket, she plucked the jasmine flowers in the yard garden and patiently wove a garland. Once she had finished, Katyayani wrapped it in a banana leaf, packed it into her handkerchief and hurried to the station to catch the train.

At university, instead of evading Raja, she sent a peon to ask him to meet her. Raja arrived, pushing his bicycle and they both took the Hunsur road. As they were passing under the cool shade of the trees lining the road behind the Kukkarahalli lake, he asked, "Why have you avoided me all these days?"

"Don't ask me now."

Verdant fields spread all around them and tall trees stood amidst the fields. Even after journeying for half an hour, they still found people cluttering the road. At last Raja said, "Sit on the bicycle with me. We can go faster. Somewhere away we may be alone, undisturbed."

Hesitantly, she obeyed, afraid that people might see them. Raja took hold of the handle with the support of her shoulders and as he pedalled, bending his body, she felt herself pressed to his chest. One or two stray passers-by looked on with mild curiosity. After they had travelled for a few miles, they reached a village. A little beyond it they came upon a banyan grove. And they went a mile further to reach a spot undisturbed by humans, stopping as they came across a sparkling rivulet. Then pushing the bicycle, they went into a thicket of wild grass.

Katyayani squatted on the grass. Sitting by her side, Raja asked, "Now tell me. Why have you been avoiding me all these days?"

She gave a deep sigh and said, "My mind was torn. I wasn't sure, I didn't know what I was doing."

Holding her hand, he asked, "Are you still under the spell of that confusion?"

"No. I have decided to be with you. When you hold my hand like this, there is not a trace of it."

His eyes alighted on the handkerchief bundle she held. Its contents were easily identifiable through the scent that emanated. She opened the bundle and held the jasmine garland in her hand. Her sitting posture, the sari she wore and the garland hanging from her hand, struck his eyes with an incredible force. He stared at her with intensity. Katyayani was a very beautiful woman for her flesh shone with the glow of health. Her complexion was sheer. A grave yet a gentle face. Her tender flesh appeared to sprinkle the vitality of womanhood. Wonderstruck and reduced to silence, he just stared at all that loveliness.

Raja continued to stare at her. Katyayani garlanded him and closed her eyes. He held her shoulders gently, pulling her towards his chest and embracing her tightly. The trees around burst with a green vitality and the water flowing in the little stream appeared to symbolise a tremendous life force. In that uncertain and overpowering state of mind and body, *Prakriti* danced with primal energy. Watching her magical face with half-closed eyes, he whispered, "*Prakriti!*"

She asked, "Is *Prakriti* a widow?"

They ceased speaking and immersed themselves in the profound silence. The noon sun was slowly sinking westward. And there they knew that there are hundreds of ways in which a woman is cheated of her opportunity to experience life. And all these obstacles, all these ways are solely artificial. A woman cannot successfully counter them with the primal force of her womanhood. Released from the bonds of time and place, the two were now free creatures, back to their original condition. In that kingdom of greeness, there was none to question them and no rule to ridicule them.

That night Katyayani slept soundly. The stage of her mind had now been converted from a battlefield to a beautiful setting for a dance of peace. From that day onwards, she met Raja regularly. One day she got up early, told her parents-in-law that she had to attend a special lecture and left for Mysore by the seven o'clock train, essentially a goods train to which had been attached two carriages for passengers. There was no special compartment for ladies and so she travelled with local farmers. She did not find the congestion of people in the compartment irksome in the least and she did not even mind the pungent smoke of the beedies. Looking beyond the window, one peasant was saying, "Look, this year the *ragi* crop is first class."

Katyayani did not get off at Chamarajapura station, as she used to. Instead she proceeded right up to the main station where there was a shuttle train leaving for Arasikere at eight thirty. Raja was waiting there with tickets for two, carrying bedding and a leather bag, obvious indications of a long journey. He was, even in that sweltering heat, clad in a suit and tie. They took the shuttle and got off at Kannambadi, the station for the famous Brindavan gardens. In the train, she had transferred her books to his bag. Engaging a coolie to carry their luggage, they checked in, paying in advance, at the big hotel in Brindavan, as a couple from Madras. They proceeded to a well furnished room, following the hotel bellboy who carried their baggage.

By the time they finished their breakfast, it was quarter to ten. Outside, the sun was raging fiercely. Yet, at the same time, in one corner of the sky, dense clouds were concentrating. Due to the tense humidity, Raja and Katyayani were both sweating, the tiny rivulets bathing their bodies. As they looked out of the window they could see that heat in the distance rising from the ground. The fan whirring above their heads gave no relief. The vast expanse of dry and parched earth was thirsty and waiting for the rains. The green that had once enlivened the face of the earth was wilting but it was not in the nature of the earth to beg for rain. Soon the sky became overcast with thick, dark clouds. Gradually the density of the clouds increased to such an extent that if they were to burst into a downpour, it would have washed away the green beauty on earth's face and left her disfigured. Yet the clouds refused to fall as rain and continued to hover high in the sky in dignified aloofness. The earth was looking up to the sky in expectation. The new clouds, though unable to carry their own weight, were also too inexperienced to fall as rain. Perhaps, overcome by surprise, defeated by the intricacy of their situation and unable to comprehend the novelty of their plight, the clouds were reduced to impotence and inaction.

In the heat that was scorching and searing the whole world, she became restless, laboured. The rain was badly needed for otherwise this heat would not cease. She saw the clouds drifting indecisively. Once the density of the clouds increased and lightning flashed. In their own light, the clouds could see and understand the beauty of earth and its thirst.

It appeared as if they would crash to earth. Propelled by the force of the water, the uncertainty was washed away, and decisiveness turned into an active force, as the clouds clasped the earth to their bosom. A heavy downpour pounded the earth, a straight and pure, blissful rain, without the bravado of thunder and lightning, undiluted by any squall that could weaken the ecstatic power of the clouds.

By the time they could lunch, the rain had taken away the heat in the atmosphere and a bracing coolness had spread everywhere. The breezes coming from afar carried the scent of soaked earth and the air was so invigorating that they preferred to enjoy it in silence. The verdant face of the earth took on a new sheen. As they finished their lunch, the clouds were once again gathering on a massive scale. Now there was no more the earlier, unbearable heat. It began to rain somewhat sedately, not the mad pounding of the morning and the peaceful earth welcomed the gently falling rain. The sky had cleared and it shone through light clouds.

Raja and Katyayani left Brindavan late in the afternoon. Cooled by the recent shower of rain, the earth smiled. The sun began to reappear and the clouds had vanished. It was five in the evening when they reached Mysore. Katyayani got into the Nanjangud train which was standing ready there.

XII

Rao was busy with his studies or rather not, in his special room in the library. The multitudinous books had piled up higher, waves of them surging through the little room, engulfing the desk, the chairs, the shelves. Tirelessly, he was shifting all those that he needed to his room. Unable to arrange them systematically, he was left to deal with a chaotic heap and it required great effort to select the books he wanted. He was reclining in his easy chair, his mind a yawning gap, conscious only that the zeal for his work had died. Watching the slow-turning fan above creating a creaking spiral and holding his spectacles in his left hand, he stretched out, stretching out every muscle in his sore body. He did not even hear the door being pushed open. Only when a person came very close towards him did he realise that someone was there and he raised his eyes to see who it could be. She was wearing her customary white sari, a matching white blouse.

"Yes. I am here."

Rao found no words to say to her. His heart groaned and overflowed under the pressure. All he could do was to extend his hand to catch hold of hers.

"Where is your luggage?"

She stared at him, surprised.

"Come, let's arrange a room for you in the ladies' residence."

"No, I don't want to stay in the residence."

After a pause, unable to say anything, he managed a, "Come. Let's have some lunch."

They went to the Hindu Hotel. Though he had already had his lunch at home, Rao ate with her to keep her company, some rice and silence, followed by strong coffee.

Rao asked, "What do you think we should do?"

"It is not for me to say. All I want to do is work with you and attain my own fulfilment."

"First, we must marry."

"What if we don't get married?"

"I thought of it. We are not marrying for the purpose for which common people marry. How long can we go on like this? After all, we are to live our entire lives together. And how long can you stay in the residence? If I keep you in a separate house, how can I visit you there without any social stigma? How would it be possible for you to spend the whole day working here? What would people say? And we can't rule out the university authorities accusing us of immoral behaviour. Once we bind ourselves within a marital framework, there will be no questions."

"Wouldn't people question how you can marry when you already have a wife?"

"Yes. But that will pass. Bigamy is not a crime, it is merely outdated. It will not expose us to the accusation of immoral behaviour. Marriage would enable us to work smoothly and effectively."

Karuna wanted to ask him whether he had informed his family at home about this decision, but she did not, thinking it was his problem and it was for him to solve. They booked a single room for her in the first floor of the Hindu Hotel and shifted her luggage to it. Rao paid in advance, explaining, "Miss Karuna Jayaratne is to spend a month here, alone, to conduct her research."

By the time they returned to the library, it was five in the evening. Seeing the books heaped in the room, Karuna set about arranging and cataloguing them. Rao opened his mouth to tell her to rest for a while after the long journey but seeing the vigorous meticulousness with which she carried out her work, he closed it again, happy that she was there.

Though Rao decided to inform his family about his new decision on that very day, it took him a fortnight longer to do so. With regard to how he should begin to explain the situation, how to put things into the correct words and phrases and how to face the consequent reactions, Rao's mind was wavering between the impossible and the insurmountable. He was, of course, fully aware that the news would shatter Nagalakshmi and he was conscious of the fact that his decision would inflict a cruel punishment on his innocent and hapless wife. Yet, he allowed himself to derive moral courage from the thought that if he now backed out of his momentous decision, he would never complete his life's ambitious mission of writing all the volumes. Though he considered Nagalakshmi not specifically guilty, their marriage had become incompatible. But he was not prepared to release himself from that relationship; it was true that he needed Karuna, but it was no less true that he wanted Nagalakshmi.

Somewhat early for him, he put out the light in his study at eleven and went to his bedroom and closed it. On the huge bed, Nagalakshmi was sleeping, Prithvi close to her. His mattress was empty by her side. He had come determined to tell her about his new decision but she was already asleep. He sat by her side and shook her shoulders, calling, "Nagu."

The bedroom bulb cast a dim light. Awake, her eyes half-open, she asked him, "What time is it now?"

"Eleven."

"Really?" She closed her eyes again, embraced her husband, and said, "I am so lucky", without a trace of sarcasm, a trace of rancour.

"Why have you come to bed so early?"

For a moment or two, Rao did not know what to say. He merely whispered, "Nagu!"

Grasping her husband's emaciated body with her arms, she asked in a tender voice, "Did you get tired of reading? In all these years when did you ever come to bed this early and address me affectionately. I can understand everything. After all, aren't I your wife? Go to sleep."

Staring at his eyes now naked without the glasses, kissing them, she asked, "If I tell you something, will you heed my words?"

"What is it?"

"Your body is too hot, appears to be feverish. All that reading has dulled your eyes. If you go on like this and lose your sight, what shall we do? Hereafter every Sunday you must get up earlier than usual. Before you go to the library I shall bathe you. Every day, after your dinner in the night, you must rest for a while sitting in the chair. I shall rub your feet with oils as you sit there."

Rao remained silent. He closed his eyes and resting his face against her shoulder, he tried to sleep. Whispering, "Go to sleep", she patted his back as if he were a child.

Rao's mind was bursting, he had lost control over it. His determination had melted, his courage crumbling in the face of his wife's innocent love. After some time, he heaved a deep sigh. Nagu took his face between her hands, looked deep into it and asked him gently,

"Why? Aren't you sleepy?"

Coaxing him, she continued, "What is tormenting you? Can't you tell me?"

He did not answer. She continued, "If you don't want to tell me, don't. After all, when you lost your parents early in life, who was there to look after you? You rushed off to Mysore to study. There should never be children without mothers! Am I not there for you? Why should you worry? Is it right that you should become dispirited like this?"

She wiped away his tears with the edge of her sari.

That night Rao did not sleep. Nagalakshmi covered him with a blanket and went to sleep at about two, clasping him with her left arm as if he were a baby scared of the night. Though awake, he did not stir for he did not want to disturb her. Rao tried in vain to find an answer to the tormenting question, "What is her fault?"

The only mild consolation was to tell himself,

"Well, I am not deserting her. I am merely accepting another woman to realise my life's greatest ambition. That is all."

The following morning he got up at five. It was Raja's practice to take his bath and go out walking. The two brothers went on a morning walk along Bogadi Road.

"I need to talk to you."

Raja was too shrewd an observer not to have noticed that in the last few days something had seriously been worrying his brother. Unable to decide how and where to begin his account, Rao walked in silence. To help his brother tide over the difficulty, Raja commented, "I learn that Miss Karuna Jayaratne has arrived."

"How do you know?"

"I heard them talk about it in the library. It seems she is staying at the Hindu Hotel."

Though Raja's stock of information astonished him, Rao took the opportunity to speak his mind. First, he described in detail the difficulties to be encountered and the hurdles to be crossed in completing his volumes, the references, the bibliographies, the journals, the momentous and massive nature of the task. Then he explained how his eyesight was getting weaker, concluding, "Without her, the volumes just cannot be completed. And without the volumes I cannot live. It is not socially proper for her to continue her association with me as now and that is why I have decided to enter into a civil marriage with her."

Raja was silent. Knowing that in certain sections of society bigamy had been practised, he had been anticipating vaguely that some such thing might occur, but it pained him to see his own brother consider it.

"Well, as a matter of fact, it was to suggest that you should speak to Nagu and explain the matter to her that I have brought you all this way. I can assure you that marrying Karuna will not mean deserting Nagu."

"The crucial question is, will she agree to it? Even if you say, 'I shall not leave you. You too can stay,' is there any wife who can agree to her husband marrying a second wife? Our maternal uncle brought us up, two orphans. He gave Nagu, his only daughter, to you in marriage. Now he is dead. How do you hold poor Nagu responsible for your difficulties? When you married her, wasn't your willingness more important than hers? It was you who agreed to marry her."

For a minute or two Rao thought over his brother's words. Then he said, "This is not a question that cannot be resolved through mere discussion and debate. I know that you have a deep affection for Nagu."

He paused.

"I too have deep affection for her," he said unable to think of any other way of putting it. "But if this work is not finished, I shall die an unfulfilled soul. Instead of Karuna, can you give me that kind of assistance?"

Raja thought about this but he had neither the temperament nor the inclination to consider or contribute to the aims of others.

Rao continued, "I shall not live away from the house and I shall not desert Nagu. I know that you alone can handle the situation and persuade Nagu to accept it. Please try to look at the matter from my point of view. I doubt that anyone else will."

Raja tried to see things from his brother's perspective. But he had a very deep and special relationship with his sister-in-law. Yet he also had profound respect for his brother's intellectual efforts and took pride in them. He recognised that his brother had gone in too far to retrace his steps. To argue would be futile. Raja came to the conclusion the best way he could serve everybody was to talk to his sister-in-law and try to persuade her.

After she learnt of her fate, Nagalakshmi did not eat for three days; nor did she sleep. Aware that she could play no part in her husband's life as an historian and writer, she had resigned herself to this. Uncomplainingly, she had tolerated her husband's neglect in pursuit of his scholarly preoccupations. But she could not unravel the mystery of her husband's decision to marry someone else just for that reason. Knowing that his sister-in-law was agitated, Raja took three days of his annual leave and stayed at home. On the fourth day after the blow, Nagu had still refused to let a morsel of food pass her lips.

"Nagu, if you behave like this, how can I eat? Shall I starve too?" asked Raja in mock horror and half earnestness.

"It is my *karma* to go without food. You may eat."

"No. I can't eat without you. Please get up."

He tried to force her to eat but could not. Yet, even as she steadfastly refused, she was filled with great affection for her brother-in-law.

"Raja, Mother is no more. Father is no more. And he has begun behaving this way. Why should you waste your affection over me and worry about me like this?"

"You don't understand the nature of his work. His writing has possessed him. Without her, he can't complete it. If he doesn't complete it, he is sure to go mad. Now, can we let that happen?"

Raja phrased this in somewhat melodramatic terms, trying to appeal both to his sister-in-law's tender nature and her rural superstitions.

"Why should he go mad after what is needless and desert me?"

"He never has had, and he does not now have, any intention of deserting you. Even if he marries her, she will stay here. And I am the one who provides this house with the necessities and you are the one who will handle all the matters concerning the household. Let her come and stay. In any case, what else can we do under the circumstances?"

"When he married me he was educated enough to know that I was uneducated. Anyway, if he needs an educated person to help him, aren't you there, his own brother, his own flesh and blood?"

Raja sighed impatiently.

"It is precisely because I cannot be of any use in the matter that things have reached this stage. Nagu, please be reasonable. If you are obstinate, you can only make matters worse. My advice is, it is best to agree to his marrying her. There is no possibility of her harassing you for she can see nothing beyond those five gleaming volumes."

He paused and then said more gently, "You are the mother of his son. I am here to support you. Your position in the household will not change."

Nagalakshmi began to review the situation in the light of Raja's advice; she was, she realised, a far more attractive woman than Karuna with her dark, rural-looking complexion - her body was still fresh and youthful and her face had not lost its original beauty - if anything, the years had made it blossom and curve. She concluded, "How could he reject a beautiful woman like me for that ordinary woman? Surely he must be out of his mind!"

Just then they heard someone entering the house. Katyayani came in, saying to Raja in a low voice, "You haven't been at university for three days!"

Nagalakshmi had not failed to notice the intimacy with which Katyayani spoke to Raja. Turning to Nagalakshmi, she said with concern,

"I haven't seen you for five or six days. What is the matter? You look so worried."

Katyayani took the flowers she had packed in her handkerchief and offered them to her.

Rudely pushing aside the garland, Nagalakshmi said, tears in her eyes, "Why do I need flowers now?"

Katyayani did not know whether to pretend to be ignorant of the situation or to come clean so that she could comfort her friend.

"I heard some rumours," she said apologetically.

"What rumours?"

"It is impossible to believe. Yesterday your brother entered into a civil marriage with his research student, Karuna Jayaratne. I'm afraid the ladies' common room is buzzing with the news."

The new status of being married made little change in Karuna's working schedule. Sensing the strain and delicacy of the situation she did not directly ask Rao about how they should organise their new life. As usual she turned up at nine in the morning to the library and worked there until seven in the evening. At the end of the day she left, taking her shorthand notes which she would type out in full in the hotel. Rao had yet to start the actual writing of his second volume.

When her husband came home to eat, Nagalakshmi served him but she had ceased to talk to him. Prithvi had never had an easy and intimate relationship with his father. Unlike before, Rao now did not sleep in the same room as Nagalakshmi and his child.

The situation was untenable. Karuna, who had earlier promised herself that she would not interfere, decided to do something to end this ugly stalemate.

"Nagalakshmi and I cannot live in the same house. You, whose culture is different from mine, might agree to this arrangement but I belong to a different tradition. I simply could not countenance a situation in which a husband could live with two wives under a common roof. Physical togetherness will not bring about peace. Let me live in a separate house. I shall cook my own food but you can continue to eat with her and spend your nights there. I have no jealousy. After all, we became united for a different and special purpose."

Rao stared into her face. Her eyes were shining with determination and the strongest will-power.

Within a week they found a suitable house to rent in the Saraswatipuram neighbourhood. Fortunately for Karuna, they were able to hire a trustworthy maid. Karuna never openly suggested that Rao should live with her and he continued to live with his first wife, though the two had completely ceased to speak to each other. In fact, Nagalakshmi had shifted her bed to the kitchen and Prithvi, unable to sleep with his father and without his mother, followed her there. Two months passed in this fashion.

One afternoon Rao loaded all his books into a jutka and shifted his home library to Karuna's house but she stressed to him that she was not forcing him to live with her, that he was free to return. Nagalakshmi was silent and outwardly indifferent. Appearing to be totally oblivious to what was going on, she took refuge in the kitchen.

The following day Raja came to the library in search of his brother. He had never visited the study in the library like this before, of his own accord. Karuna left them.

"She is overwhelmed with sorrow."

"I can understand that."

After thinking for a while, Rao said, "I draw twice your salary and I will be getting royalties from my book. Every month, come to me on my salary day. I shall give you some money for running the household."

Raja replied, sadly, "Should I take money from you to feed Nagu? If our mother were alive, would she have taken money from the elder son to live in the younger son's house?"

For a week Karuna cooked Rao's food. It was unbearable. For this reason and because he did not want her to exhaust herself with menial chores, he engaged a cook.

XIII

The *Navaratri* holidays were over, the December vacation had come and gone. Raja and Katyayani would meet every day at university, spending their time in the office of the Drama Society. Although Katyayani continued to visit Nagalakshmi in her household, the latter had ceased to speak to anybody and had turned the kitchen into her fortress. After cooking and serving the meals thrice daily to Raja and Prithvi, she would retire to a corner in the kitchen, where she stretched on a mat, without a word and absolutely motionless. If Raja tried to initiate some conversation, Nagalakshmi would either ignore him or respond curtly. As for Prithvi, he was never at home with his father and therefore found nothing missing in the family life. Now five years old, some excitement and diversion was offered by going to school in the company of the boys in the neighbouring house. His uncle, as before, took him on his bicycle when he rode to the market.

One day Raja asked Nagalakshmi, casually, "Nagu, shall I get married this year?"

Surprised that he was raising the topic, she carried on cooking. "She has a child at home. How can she live without him?"

"How did you know about our secret?" exclaimed Raja, with bewilderment and a particular stupidity that has infuriated women from time immemorial.

"You see, we women have our own special ways of detecting such things," said Nagalakshmi sarcastically. "Anybody who had seen you together for even a few moments would have guessed that you would end up entangled in marriage. Or at least they would unless they had known that she was a widow."

"Tell me, do you approve?"

"Why bother about whether I approve or disapprove? Well, if you set your face against customs and canons and *dharma and karma,* wouldn't it bring evil consequences?"

Raja had, on many earlier occasions made abundantly clear to her, his views on *dharma and karma,* about artificiality, constraints, about a freedom and a social code that operated in a green and pleasant land, far away. And he spoke, albeit tentatively, of the need for true compatibility and commitment. Such words inevitably prompted

Nagalakshmi to recall the fate of her own life but she was not bitter for she had started to regard life with a detachment that merged into indifference. Therefore when Katyayani came to the household to touch the feet of Nagalakshmi in reverence, Nagalakshmi blessed her. It was agreed that this uncomfortable state of illicit meetings could not go on and that the marriage should take place as soon as possible after the March examinations.

Katyayani too was very eager to have the marriage solemnised. For the past three months she had been full of nothing but the idea of marriage, of how to obtain the consent of the elders at home and move into the household of the life-partner she had freely chosen. But she had no doubt whatsoever that her next step would shatter the family's status, prestige and their beliefs passed through generations. Recalling that five years ago she had formally entered the Shrothri household after kicking with her left foot a rice-filled measure, a ritual gesture that symbolised the flooding of wealth into the household, she felt that it was an act by which her name had been absorbed into the Shrothri family tree irrevocably. It was still her household which she was trying to leave, she its hope and seed. From the day Katyayani had opened out her mind and heart to Raja, these ideas were tormenting her, gouging out her insides, leaving a void where more doubts could accumulate and fearlessness could disappear. The unfulfilled marital life had thrown a blanket over these thoughts, invading her mind and body. When the moment arrived for telling her secret to her parents-in-law, she lost her fortitude and her resolution. Raja asked her every day ritually, "Did you break the news to them?"

One day, raising his voice in anger, he asked her, "Why, for God's sake, drag me this far when you lacked the courage?"

Sometimes she thought of running away to Mysore with her child and then writing a letter about her decision but no sooner had the thought occurred than she dismissed it as beneath contempt. The first week of March went by. The university had stopped regular classes as the preparatory holidays began, fifteen days prior to the start of the examinations. For these fifteen days she could not visit Mysore. Before the start of the holidays, Raja threatened her, "If you don't tell them at home, I shall have to write to them about our decision."

In Nanjangud, the atmosphere was close. When Cheeni moved towards her, crying, "Mother, why are you so late?" Katyayani drew him to her bosom, embracing him tightly and then she carried him to Lakshmi's room where she sang to him and patted him to sleep.

Sitting upstairs, alone, she plunged into profound reflection. Gathering together all her will power, she made up her mind to talk to her father-in-law. Shrothri was still sitting in the hall after dinner but she could not find the conviction, the strength to speak to that indomitable old man. As she tried to reach the bottom of the staircase, her legs had become so weak that she was afraid they would give way so she sat down, still. Downstairs, everybody went to sleep and it was only then, when Katyayani was sure that nobody would hear her, should her legs gave way again and should she fall, that she slowly went upstairs. At her desk, suddenly, the inertia that she had been suffering caved in and she began to write furiously, criticising at length the artificial norms that destroyed woman's original humanity, the original and existing need for fulfilment. It was three in the morning when she had finished the sixteen pages of closely written Kannada. She concluded:

"I beg you not to hold to social prejudice and blind norms and to look at the whole matter from the perspective of humanity and compassion. Do as you would do if your own daughter had appealed to your kindness. I am anxious to begin my new life with your consent and your grace. Unable to say all this in person and without inhibition, I have set it all down in this letter. When I return home this evening, I beg you to bless me."

The thickness of the letter did not allow it to be fastened by a paper clip and so she punched through a hole and fastened the pages with some thread. Afterwards Katyayani experienced a peculiarly calm sleep. She got up next day at half past seven and hurriedly went through her daily routine. As she handled the envelope containing the letter she had written the previous night, her hands trembled. Shrothri entered the hall after finishing his morning worship. With unusual determination she went to him and touched his feet, seeking his blessing. Somewhat taken aback, Shrothri asked, "What is this, child, isn't your examination a fortnight away?"

Katyayani handed over the envelope to him and walked away briskly. Nonplussed, he stared at the way she had gone. Then he remembered the envelope in his hand. Opening it slowly, he fumbled at the pages.

When she returned home in the evening, Katyayani was apprehensive and restless, her mind playing out the horrors of betrayals. A formless fear began to invade her. As she entered the house, she saw Shrothri sitting in the front hall, engaged in conversation with a visiting tenant and so she went past upstairs. She did not have the courage to look at her mother-in-law's face. Even under the most trying conditions, her father-in-law would not lose his temper but her mother-in-law was different, flaring up unreasonably and uncontrollably. Sometimes, even Shrothri would have to face the brunt of her wrath. Slowly, she heard her father-in-law call her for dinner. The atmosphere was as still as usual and yet curiously so. Cheeni, more interested in playing with his food than eating it, was scattering rice around, smiling as his grandmother gently chided him. Normality became chilling, inducing a forced passivity and in the midst of that passivity, there twisted a fretful agitation. Restlessly she fidgeted.

"Father, will you go upstairs with me for a while please?"

"Of course. Go and I shall be with you soon."

Shrothri called her to his study and when she entered the room, he was seated near the window on the tiger skin. Then she moved a little closer and sat.

After five minutes of tense silence, she spoke, "Did you read my letter?"

"Yes, I did."

"I beg you to give your consent."

After a minute's silence, Shrothri spoke in his calm, even tone.

"You must try and understand, for there is no question of my approving or disapproving. You are free to do as you please."

There was no rancour in his voice and he had spoken placidly and gently. The words penetrated her.

"How can you say this? You are the head of this household and I cannot act without your permission."

"Do you still accept me as the head of this household? My real authority over you will last only as long as you regard yourself in your soul as a member of this household. When you decide in your mind to tread a different path, from that day my authority will cease."

Katyayani had equipped her mind with all sorts of weapons, tens of arguments to establish the propriety of her decision. Now they had all melted into thin air and her head was like an empty, broken pot. She replied, "In our social order, if a woman suffers a catastrophe, there is no way she can overcome it and return to normality. A widower can re-marry ten times, but a woman can never re-marry. This world has refused to understand a woman's inner nature with any sympathy. Moreover..."

Interrupting her mid-way, he said, "Please let us not enter into a debate or discussion over the social order or the behaviour of the world. We shall make it purely your question. I have not come in the way of your decisions and I shall never do so. You have every right to act as you think right. Yet all our decisions and choices should conform to our *dharma,* responsibilities and obligations."

"Isn't it natural *dharma* for a person to live the effective life of a householder at the proper age?"

"Natural *dharma* is not the only *dharma.* The ultimate and supreme goal of life is not the enjoyment of life as a householder. Its goal is the perpetuation of the family tree, the continuation of its life, its scion. After the family tree grows, if by chance the family life is terminated, it is not *dharma* to return to it. It is only when one is able to transcend one's immediate self-interest and material pleasures that one can discern clearly what is *dharma* and what is not. You referred to men marrying again ten times after each time losing a wife but I have already said that we should not, cannot be concerned with general human problems. A few years ago I had to face a similar issue of re-marriage. But I took the path of *dharma* - no, rather I was guided in my path by *dharma,* saved from *adharma. Dharma* will offer the power of its hand of protection unstintingly to those who surrender themselves to it unreservedly. Your husband might have told you about the matter. If not, you can go downstairs and ask mother or Lakshmi."

Shrothri rose to leave and at the door of the room he stopped and said, "I repeat that you have full freedom to choose your way in this matter. True *dharma,* I believe, is not present in external rules and customs that are imposed on the individual against his or her will."

He climbed down the steps slowly and reached the hall, where he usually slept. When Katyayani realised that that day she had not prepared the beds for her parents-in-law and Cheeni, she felt ashamed. She got up and went to her room, unrolled the bed and slumped on it, huddling on it like a bird that had collapsed to the ground after flying tens and tens of miles. There she recollected her father-in-law and the stringent test of *dharma* that he had had to face.

XIV

At a young age Srinivasa Shrothri was sent to study at the *pathasala* in Mysore, a boys' school of traditional learning where the medium of instruction was Sanskrit. The emphasis was very much on conservatism and traditionalism; a traditional style of dress, a traditional style of thinking and a traditional richness of learning. The boys were well educated in ancient philosophy and literature, gaining a beautiful love for and astounding mastery over their texts. But Srinivasa lost his mother at the age of fifteen and being the only son, he was called back from Mysore and only the two of them remained in the house, the father and the son. They had a small hut then in the backyard of the house, the hut of their loyal servant, Macha, and his daughter, Lakshmi. Macha had not re-married after his wife had died in childbirth. For the first three years he left the baby with relations in the village of Kyathanahalli but later he brought the child back, thereafter father and daughter living together under the benevolent roof of the master, serving him and eating there.

After losing his wife, Nanjunda Shrothri Senior cooked the food as there was no woman in the household. His son, Srinivasa, helped him and during the remainder of the time, he carried on his scholarly interests with the local brahmin tutor, Yankappa Sastry. Under his guidance, Srinivasa was taught the Sanskrit subjects of *Nyaya* and *Vaisesika*. He had memorised *Amarukosha* and in Mysore he had studied the Sanskrit epics the *Ramayana* and the *Mahabharata*. The father did not come in the way of the son's thirst for knowledge but neither did he assist its progress as he was not prepared to spend money, even though the family was then as wealthy as now. In the room between the kitchen and the prayer room, Nanjunda Senior had dug a hole and hidden in it silver coins, heavy silver and gold ornaments. Every night he spread his bedroll across the spot, sleeping there to guard the treasure. Yankappa Sastry, who was aware of the father's stinginess and the son's genuine passion for learning, taught the boy without asking for any fee. Unfortunately the poor teacher could not afford to buy books for his student and to that extent, the boy's education suffered.

Soon Nanjunda Senior tired of the drudgery of daily cooking, his smoke-filled eyes and soiled dhoti. In order to escape this ritual, he

decided to get Srinivasa married. A good alliance could have proved
to be difficult as it was common knowledge that Srinivasa's father had
a reputation of being a mean-minded miser. Even so, with an eye on
the family wealth, prospective fathers-in-law scrambled to seek a
suitable arrangement. Moreover, Srinivasa was a very attractive boy,
tall, slim but well-built, smiling, fair in complexion, and most unlike
his father, dark, dwarfish and permanently sour-faced. Many local
parents from Nanjangud tried to bring off the match but with little
success. Nanjunda Senior was averse to taking a local bride for he
wished to avoid the constant interference of interminable in-laws.
Eventually Srinivasa's marriage was fixed with a girl from distant
Hassan, the additional consideration being that the horoscopes of the
boy and girl matched tolerably well. Indeed, in his eagerness to
escape from the cooking, Nanjunda Senior would have put up with
minor differences. Fourteen-year-old Bhagirathamma was a little dark
in complexion, but otherwise she was an attractive girl with regular
features. Unfortunately she was too short for the groom, causing
much consternation and comment amongst the rural community that
had gathered for the wedding. The bride's father celebrated the
marriage in style for eight days, afterwards offering as traditional gifts
to the bride-groom, a silver rupee coin, a copper vessel, a metal
spoon, a pair of dhoties, some cloth, a pair of chappals and an
umbrella.

But Nanjunda Shrothri Senior was not destined to enjoy the food
cooked by his daughter-in-law. Six months later, he died of cholera.
People, wise after the event, commented that her horoscope stipulated
her marriage into a father-in-law-less household. Before his death,
the father had disclosed to the son the place where he had stashed
away the gold and silver. Once the death rites were over, Srinivasa
Shrothri dug the secret hiding place and found six thousand pure silver
rupee coins as well as so much gold and silver that he could not lift
the bag up by himself. Most of this extraordinary wealth was
acquired when parties who had pawned their valuables with his father
had failed to redeem them. After Srinivasa Shrothri took charge, the
whole household underwent a radical change. Srinivasa offered
Yankappa Sastry one thousand rupees, repaying many years of tuition.
On the advice of his teacher, he bought several books and set up a tidy
library in the room upstairs.

Macha, the household servant, remained. Macha was a tall, well-built and presentable person who had earlier worked in the tea gardens in the Nilagiri hills. There he had fallen in love with a beautiful young woman and had eloped with her. The young couple arrived in Nanjangud where they were taken in by Nanjunda Senior, not out of compassion, but solely because the older man had calculated that Macha, with his powerful figure, would be an excellent guard to protect his wealth and property. Macha was very loyal. His daughter Lakshmi had inherited a fair complexion, her father's height and build and her mother's lovely, ever-smiling face. Since they had grown up together from childhood, Lakshmi addressed Srinivasa Shrothri familiarly as Seenappa. She had also picked up the upper caste Kannada of the Shrothris since she had been brought up in their household. Srinivasa, when he first set eyes on his bride at the time of his marriage, was forced to say to himself, "How nice it would have been if Lakshmi were to be my bride!"

No sooner had the thought sprouted than he plucked it out as evil.

Though he possessed a daughter who was extremely beautiful, Macha did not own the money needed to marry her off. Quite a few people came to him, taking the initiative in asking for his daughter's hand but most were unacceptable. After he took over the management of the household, Srinivasa Shrothri told Macha to search out a suitable match for Lakshmi, assuring him that he would contribute towards the marriage expenses. Shrothri had offered this help as a gesture of gratitude to Macha whose sweat he knew had gone into the making of the prosperity of their household. After a considerably lengthy and protracted search, Macha found an eligible groom in the Kodiyala village of the Mandya district. Lakshmi's marriage was celebrated with great pomp.

A year after this event, Bhagirathamma became of age and came to live in her husband's home. Once again the household became alive with the presence and movement of a woman. Even after his wife's arrival, Srinivasa did not abandon his scholarly concerns, continuing to travel to Mysore to purchase new books and eagerly seeking new knowledge from Sanskrit pundits in the vicinity. So it was that when the new Shrothri household was flourishing, a plague struck Nanjangud town. Among the multitudes carried away by the dreadful scourge, Macha was one, dying before Lakshmi could arrive in time from Kodiyala. Shrothri consoled the grief-stricken Lakshmi, and, when she was about to return, offered her one hundred rupees, saying, "Perform the final death rites of Macha in your place. Remember, you are a daughter of this household."

Lakshmi was dumb-struck by Seenappa's affection and generosity. After touching his feet, she left with her husband.

In the meanwhile, Shrothri's scholarly activities went on with undiminished steadfastness and determination. The early days of marriage, fresh and green days, were full of joy. Though three years had passed in this happy state, Bhagirathamma did not conceive. By this time, Shrothri had acquired considerable command over the *Dharmasastra, Vedas, Upanishads* and *darsanas*. Every day he recited lines from the *Ramayana*. The texts he studied with devotion began to affect him and his life profoundly. He wrestled with essential questions: the goal of the householder's life, the householder's duties and obligations. He was concerned that even three years after the marriage, they had no children, an overwhelming worry because he believed firmly that the goal of marriage was procreation in order to continue the family tree.

One evening Lakshmi arrived unexpectedly. As soon as she came, she grasped Seenappa's feet and began to sob loudly. Then she told him the truth. Her father had been cheated. Her husband was a gambler. He always wore a gold ring and gold chain and this had misled Macha to take him to be a well-to-do, respectable person. Macha had given him money. It was true that he had some land inherited from his father, but he had raised loans by mortgaging it. Some twenty days back, he had won all the money from the other players but by the time the game had ended it was two after midnight and the losers, unable to bear the huge loss, had killed her husband and then fled. Three days ago, the police had caught the killers. Thus destitute, Lakshmi had returned to the home of her birth. Seenappa welcomed her back into the household, saying, "Everything that happens to humans follows the law of *karma*. Lakshmi, don't worry. Don't you have a right to a fistful of rice in this household?"

A little later, Lakshmi had to go to Mysore to give evidence in the criminal case against her husband's killers. Seenappa accompanied her to Mysore three times concerning this matter and supported her as her husband's killers were sentenced to be hanged.

Two more years passed without Bhagirathamma showing signs of becoming pregnant. Once again plunged into deep worry, Shrothri compared his suffering to that experienced in the *Ramayanya* and the *Mahabharata* by rulers who were childless. But he never spoke a harsh word to his wife or displayed before her his agony or despondency but Bhagirathamma sensed it. She loved her husband deeply and had total faith in him, respecting his gentle nature. Together they made vows to hundreds of gods and goddesses. Shrothri vowed that he would make gold feet for Lord Nanjundeswara, the deity of the town's great temple, if they were granted a child. Within a year of this, Bhagirathamma conceived. Though her father had come to take her for the delivery as was customary, Shrothri persuaded them that it should take place in Nanjangud. Three months prior to the date due for the delivery, Bhagirathamma's mother came to Nanjangud. The expectant mother was normal and healthy as the due date approached but, even three days after the pains started, there was no delivery and so on the advice of the local pundit, Bhagirathamma was taken to the government hospital in Mysore where a baby boy was born. Silently Shrothri meditated on the Sanskrit verse:

"He who is unmoved by sorrow and unexcited by joy,
He who gives up love, fear and anger, he has equanimity."

A month later mother and child were discharged from hospital. The doctor spoke to Shrothri in private, telling him that the baby had grown too big for the womb and that if Bhagirathamma were to conceive again her death would be certain. All physical relations would have to cease. The doctor felt saddened to say this as he looked at Shrothri, his powerful build, his youth and the health radiating from his face.

The baby boy was named Nanjunda after his grandfather and, after celebrating the various festivities that accompanied the birth of a new child, Bhagirathamma's mother returned to Hassan. Thereafter the mother and baby slept in the bedroom downstairs and Shrothri slept in his study. During the day, Shrothri was frequently assailed by the temptation to sleep with his wife, especially as while Lakshmi took the cattle out, there was no-one in the house. His wife was alone, and he was at an age when the demands of the body could be irresistible.

The doctor's words were frequently in his ears, ringing like the bell in the prayer room. He would stare at his wife as she fed the baby, the little body filling out and the broad face bright with a smile as he sprawled on his mother's lap, sucking milk from her full breast. Even when Bhagirathamma lovingly invited him to sit down, Shrothri would not stay there but hurried out immediately. Even plunging into scholarly activity did not produce the desired mental equanimity. Most torturing of all, he was assailed by temptations even when he was worshipping in the prayer room, as his mind slickered like a torch burning in a heated wind of sexual desire. He would rise abruptly from the ritual, disgusted at himself.

All this was beyond the comprehension of Bhagirathamma's simple mind. However, she felt helpless, equally haunted. Though she was convinced that her husband would not touch her against her will, even she could not miss the distortions in his behaviour. Unable to offer him bodily satisfaction and service, she compensated for it by serving him otherwise with greater devotion and diligence. Thus passed a few months. In order to suppress his physical urges, Shrothri thought of punishing his body. He stopped drinking milk, gave up ghee, and threw himself with fury into the work of gardening in the backyard. Due to the combined effect of a diminished diet and enhanced bodily exertion, he began to sleep as soon as he lay down and slept soundly. But his body began to get weaker, emaciated. The healthy glow that once shone on his face had now vanished altogether.

Bhagirathamma loved her husband deeply and was proud of his handsome physique; she could not bear to watch his body waste away. She arrived at a decision. She had an unmarried younger sister, fourteen years old, staying with her parents in Hassan who could be brought into the household as a second wife and as she was a sister there would be less chance of any enmity, rivalry or jealousy developing. Every weakening in Shrothri's body strengthened her decision and finally she wrote to her parents in Hassan explaining the situation, everything that she had been too ashamed to say before, everything from the doctor's advice to her husband's deterioration in health. Within a week her father arrived in Nanjangud and put the proposal to Shrothri.

"Marry Kaveri. The sisters will live in harmony."

Shrothri was nonplussed, not to say shocked.

"Did you come here just to say this?"

"Yes. Bhagu wrote to us making the suggestion. How emaciated you have become! I can understand your predicament."

Shrothri was speechless. The father-in-law misunderstood the silence to be consent. He was a man with a colourful background and was reputed to be keeping three concubine families in Hassan. With a presumptuous finality he rose and said, "The horoscopes, too, are favourable. You see, I have come prepared."

That night Shrothri slept in his study as usual. The various texts he had studied began to surface in his memory. The *Ramayana* which he recited daily now rose vividly before him. In the morning after they had finished their morning rite and a light breakfast, Shrothri himself took the old man out. Crossing the Dalwai bridge, they sat by the bank of the river.

"Marriage has only two purposes - to enable one to discharge the duties and obligations of a householder and to perpetuate the family tree. I have a son already to achieve the second goal, and to achieve the first she, my wife, is still alive. I am convinced that it is a violation of *dharma* to marry again. My decision, my final answer is no."

The father-in-law was amazed at the way his son-in-law thought and behaved. Not that they were ideals to which he was a stranger, for he too was versed in Sanskrit and had read considerably in the traditional *sastras,* painstakingly memorising them as a child and conveniently forgetting in the midst of the comforts of life and its material benefits. He tried one last argument, "In spite of what you say, there is also the *dharma* of one's age and that too needs to be respected. Take good care of your health. Life is there only if the body is there. If you decline physically like this, what will happen to Bhagu?"

The son-in-law was tempted but did not yield to his father-in-law's excuses couched in terms of concerned arguments. The father-in-law stayed two more days and during this time his sharp, lustful eyes did not fail to notice Lakshmi. Unable to resist the temptation to interfere, he offered his daughter one piece of parting advice, and placing the gift of one gold sovereign in his grandson's hand, he then enjoyed the privilege of being paid obeisance by his daughter and son-in-law, collected the gift of a dhoti from them and departed.

Though temporarily controlled, the tension continued to smoulder inside Shrothri, the struggle between consciously accepted ideals and the compulsions of natural urges. His learning and scholarship had taught him all these years that human beings cannot achieve freedom until they escape the compulsions of their natural desires. Now he was experiencing the relentlessness of theoretical knowledge directly in his own life, straining himself beyond his resources to wage the struggle against his creature needs. He made it a point to immerse himself in physical exertion most of the day and devote the rest of the time to his studies. Occasionally, whenever he felt as though his mind had found its balance, he was happy that he had at last conquered his passions. But soon a few hours later he would return to the state of tumult and tension. In his mind he would begin to see pictures of the beautiful women he had either seen or heard about in real life. He felt as if he conversed with them and sometimes he felt as if a stark naked woman approached him, took his hand, placing it on her body. His conscious mind tried to control such disturbing images, churned out by his heated head, but unfulfilled desires and youthful urges swept away such efforts with a torrential fury. After a while, when the flood of natural urges became once again placid, repentance would return.

Bhagirathamma disliked her father's parting advice but afraid that her husband's health would suffer, she started to consider it. The advice was practical, and crudely so. Bhagirathamma thought about Lakshmi's plight. She was parentless, and she had enjoyed a married life for the very brief spell of just four years. And wouldn't she welcome resuming a sort of marital life? Moreover, nobody would notice anything if Lakshmi were involved, since nobody would suspect anything. Thus Bhagirathamma's imagination began to throw out all sorts of plans. After all, it was nothing new for men to take what were called kept women, concubines. Indeed, in certain circles it was established tradition and even considered a symbol of economic and social status. She recalled that her father, uncle, grandfather, had all indulged in the practice of keeping unofficial extra wives.

Bhagirathamma and Lakshmi used to sleep in the same room. During the night whenever the child woke up crying, Lakshmi would soothe him and rock him to sleep again. One night Bhagirathamma told Lakshmi.

"He is becoming thinner and thinner every day. Wouldn't you want to save his life?"

"How can you ask such a question? Do you think I will continue to live after Seenappa's death?"

"No-one outside will know about it, this secret between us. You must live with him as his woman. It is my fate to live like this even though married to him!"

She could not control her sobbing, as she continued, "One afternoon you were not at home. The baby was asleep. When I looked at his face, I saw his dilemma and his tragedy, and said, 'The doctor could be wrong. He is not infallible. Just for one day, nothing would happen.' But he was adamant. He replied, 'Why should the doctor tell a lie? What reason can he have to be jealous of us? Even one day may prove fatal. Aren't I human enough to think about your life?'"

Lakshmi was astonished at the words of her mistress. She had watched Seenappa from childhood and, respecting his virtuous qualities and his generous nature, she had developed a reverential attitude towards him. Whenever she saw her husband go out to gamble, she would remember him and say to herself, "If only Seenappa were my husband!"

When she had arrived in the Shrothri household after her husband's death, her mind had gone blank, her only comfort Seenappa's solicitude and Bhagirathamma's kindness. In living with them she could smell the aroma of family life. Though her husband was a drunkard and gambler, he had been her husband and she felt it difficult to endure even the loss of such a man. When she went out to graze the cattle, there were plenty of young men who gave her meaningful looks. But only in the case of Seenappa did she entertain an attitude of respect and fascination.

Lakshmi did not agree to Bhagirathamma's proposition. But over the next fortnight Bhagirathamma persisted in working on her mind with such ideas that in the end, Lakshmi yielded. For the next two or three days, Lakshmi was too embarrassed to look straight at Seenappa's face. Till then, she had always addressed him as in the familiar singular, 'ninu' and that pleased him. Now for the last two days she addressed him with the formal, 'nivu'. It did surprise him, but he let it pass. One night, Bhagirathamma asked her husband, holding his hand, "There is something I want to say. But first promise me that you will accept my suggestion."

Then she made him sit closer to her and explained the proposal. Shocked, Shrothri shouted in anger, "What do you think Lakshmi is?"

"She has agreed. She likes it."

Dumb-struck, Shrothri went on staring at his wife's face. She resumed, "I cannot serve you in this matter. And what I am suggesting is nothing unknown to our society. Though my father has my mother, he does not hesitate to keep other women. The most important thing is that you must recover your normal strength and health. Don't they say that worrying is the death of a man?"

Unable to say anything, he went on listening to her as if in a trance.

"Tonight Lakshmi will be sleeping upstairs. Go to her."

Shrothri said nothing. Immediately his mind was ensnared by the lure of the flesh. During his inner battles, he had never thought of Lakshmi in such a light. He had friendship for her and compassion towards her for she had been born in that household, brought up there. She had agreed to the proposal and it was his own wife who had brought the matter to this point. He did not even have to say "Yes." All he had to do was to go upstairs. Once he was there, the sort of pleasure men die for, though it was not his by right, was waiting for him.

A cool breeze was blowing. Lakshmi slept next to the study where Shrothri himself slept. Unable to calm himself, Shrothri sat up on the bed, his mind in a tumultuous state. That day the full force of his primal nature and its impulses had invaded him with a frenzy and were thundering inside his head. In his imagination, he began to see Lakshmi in a new light or perhaps in an old light that he had blacked out as a young man. Lakshmi belonged to the Nilagiri breed, representing her mother's beauty, but she had got her full-fleshed body from Macha who was a hefty, virile male. Just twenty three, her body burst with curves, full and shapely. He remembered that when she walked outside, she always modestly covered her head with the border of her sari. But he, he could enter her body, experience that softness and that closeness and enjoy her without any interruption from the outside world, in utter secrecy and darkness. His body began to vibrate with an overpowering desire. The mind was caught in a mad flood of passion and his breathing grew reckless.

It had been four years since her husband's death and Lakshmi lay on the bed with hope and anticipation. Seenappa would soon be there. How should she behave with him? He had been, from their early childhood days, a very calm and controlled person. He had looked after the welfare of their family. Now he was utterly dejected and frustrated without the pleasures of his wife's body. If she started this new relationship with him, it would continue until death. Her mind had dreamed and desired so much in her thinking, that she had already begun to imagine their relationship to be as natural as that between a husband and a wife. Startled, she heard the sound of some quick movement in the next room. He must have risen from the bed. She heard steps. Her heart beat faster as she imagined him coming to her, her body shook as she anticipated him penetrating into the depths of her being. Getting up she moved forward, her head bent down, her heart full of expectation.

Shrothri got up from the bed and stood in the room, paused, and then took hesitant steps towards Lakshmi's room. In spite of the chilly breeze blowing in from outside, he started sweating profusely. In five minutes, his dhoti was soaked with sweat. Drops of sweat formed like beads in a row on his back and chest. Wiping his face and body with a towel, he moved near the window. It was pitch dark outside, but against the backdrop of the sky, stars twinkled with dazzling light, shining like this since time immemorial, shining before human consciousness. Leaving the room from another door, he reached the awning. *Arundhati* was there, bright and clear. He turned north and saw *Dhruva*, casting a soft and peaceful light. Standing there he was overcome and his mind struggled hopelessly to measure the history of the stars by the years but realising that it was sheer madness to do so, so he gave up. Something deep inside him told him these were timeless lamps, representing a pure and ancient wisdom. Shrothri remained there for half an hour before returning to the room slowly and there he began to roll on his bed.

Ten minutes later the mental turbulence broke out again. Lakshmi's body began to fill his vision again. His imagination disrobed her. For those ten minutes his consciousness lost control of his mind. He sweated again. Rising slowly, he began to take slow steps towards Lakshmi's room.

Tense with expectation, Lakshmi felt the blood rush through her. Seenappa was walking to and fro in his room. She was aware of his moving to the awning, his standing there, his return to the room to lie down again on his bed and his getting up to walk briskly from end to end in the room. Was Seenappa too shy to come to her? Should she take the initiative and herself go to him? The tremendous vitality within had to be awakened before it could be calmed.

Bhagirathamma, lying downstairs with her child, could hardly sleep. It was already an hour and a half since her husband had gone upstairs and she assumed that their bodies must have merged. It was beyond her reach even to visualise the scene in her imagination. Tears filled her eyes and she began to sob but to prevent the sound of her sobbing from reaching upstairs, she stuffed the edge of her sari into her mouth. She too had the bodily urge like her husband, but what could she do against the doctor's advice? That advice had not killed her natural carnal needs. Her body might not be as strong and vigorous as her husband's but her desires were no less. Yet, it was a night she had brought on herself, with her full consent. The slow crumbling of her husband's great physique was forced back into her mind. His refusal to take a second wife had intensified her love for him. She also remembered her father's kept women and her mother's image passed through her mind. Without waking her child, she gently passed her right hand over him and kissed his head.

Shrothri wiped away the sweat from his face and body. Screening the lamp from the wind through his upper cloth, he scratched a match and lit the lantern. Lakshmi who was sitting on her bed could see the lantern lit in his study. She thought it was now time for him to call her. Blood rushed into her face and made the natural redness of her complexion glow.

Shrothri tried to call Lakshmi but his tongue was dead, inert and useless. He decided to go into her room and he took a few steps but overcome by shame he found it impossible to look at himself. Hiding himself to counter the shame that was engulfing him, he blew out the light in the lantern, taking refuge in the ensuing darkness. Lakshmi, noticing this, was again convinced that Seenappa was too shy to come to her. She could hear steps in the next room and got up, thinking of moving into his dark room and sitting at his feet. As she slowly moved towards the door of his study, her breathing became hard. Some unidentifiable fear swallowed her. Losing all strength and unable to move further, she slumped down near the door.

Just then Lakshmi heard the sound of the wind outside rushing. The doors of the window of the room rattled twice. In the hot darkness he moved towards Lakshmi. Some fear he could not understand, plucked his inner strings and forced him to squat on the floor without moving further. His legs had no strength. Lakshmi was still there, sitting near the door. Shrothri recovered his composure gradually, got up and went to the awning through the other door.

He sat there for one hour, concentrating his eyes on the sky and the effort of concentration, the peacefulness and the majesty of the sight restored his calm. He turned his eyes just once towards the room in which Lakshmi was sleeping, noting that she was no longer sitting near the door. Moving noiselessly, he went to the door of her room and closed it. Then he returned to his room, shut the window, lit the lantern and taking out a Sanskrit book, sat on the tiger skin and began to read from it. It was the *Sankhya Karika*. Shrothri read the last part concerning the relationship between the *purusha and prakriti*.

"Just as the courtesan or the dancer retires from the stage after displaying her art to the audience, so also *prakriti* retires after making *purusha* see his real essence."

What is the purpose of experiencing nature? What is her final goal? He read another verse.

"*Prakriti* is gentle and tender, full of shyness. If *purusha* regards her as other than himself, she will no longer show herself to him."

Shrothri understood these lines to mean that *prakriti* would exercise her sovereignty over us only so long as we have not gained true knowledge. When am I going to attain that knowledge? Shrothri was well aware that it was not the kind of knowledge that could be gained through mere intelligence. He debated within himself whether the liberation from the alluring net of *prakriti* signified the presence of such knowledge or whether the existence of such true knowledge was the pre-condition for the melting away of the bonds of her external attractions.

Lakshmi came down and went to the bathroom. As she went upstairs again, Bhagirathamma heard her feet negotiating the stairs and she understood Lakshmi's visit to the bathroom in the way that only a woman would. Feeling utterly helpless, she alternately sobbed and tried to sleep.

Exhausted by the waiting, Lakshmi slumped at last on the bed. She knew Seenappa's nature for she had grown up with him since childhood and she guessed rightly that he would be wrestling with the problems of *dharma* and *karma*. Lakshmi herself saw nothing immoral in the relationship that was to have been forged between them. It was a simple, practical issue. The parties concerned - herself, Seenappa and Seenappa's wife - agreed and the doctor had advised the couple to stay apart. By now her mental composure was returning slowly. The flood of passion no longer shook her to her roots and her body had stopped trembling. Lakshmi closed her eyes and went to sleep, but even then glimmers of hope ruffled her placidity.

Shrothri read until two-thirty in the morning. Now his mind was no longer agitated and his body was under control. Still, he could not sleep. He closed the book in hand, let the lantern burn, and climbing down the stairs, walked towards the river. Kapila was flowing placidly and so Shrothri seated himself on a rock, dangling his legs in the cool water. Soon the sky was bright with moonlight, the tenth night of *suklapaksha*. Soaking the dhoti he was wearing, Shrothri bathed his head under the water, then squeezed the water out of the wet clothes, wore them again, and returned home. His wife was asleep. Shrothri went inside the prayer room, closed the door, smeared his forehead with the ritual ash and started the morning rite, reciting the great *mantra* one thousand and eight times. Then he prepared the sandal paste and fetched the flowers from the backyard garden. Bhagirathamma was still asleep. Shrothri's worshipping ritual ended at nine in the morning with his prostrating before the deity, chanting inwardly, *"Dharma protects him who protects dharma."*

By the time Shrothri emerged from the prayer room, his wet dhoti had dried. Bhagirathamma had finished her bath and had started working in the kitchen. As soon as she heard the door of the prayer room open, the wife came out of the kitchen and touched the feet of her husband. Then she touched her eyes with the palms with which she had touched his feet first. Shrothri was still uplifted by the worship. He did not say a word and his mind was filled with a strange, inexplicable joy and peace.

When they sat down to eat in the afternoon, he said, "One must eat good and rich food and yet control one's mind, and that's what I have decided to do. I am confident that I shall succeed. From today serve me ghee and give me plenty of milk to drink."

Shrothri could not help smiling inwardly. Although he said nothing further, he resumed eating normal, nutritious food from that day and he again started the yoga exercises which he had done while studying in Mysore. His interest in the studies never slackened, as his library grew larger from year to year.

After the memorable night, Lakshmi slept in the same room as Bhargirathamma and the child. Gradually she began to lose interest in her food. The inner peace she had managed to acquire after returning to Nanjangud from her husband's home had now vanished. Whatever she did, wherever he was, whether sitting or standing, day or night, Seenappa's image stayed fixed before her mind's eye. She visualised scenes of intense intimacy and sexual passion. While bathing, she was obsessed with her body's beauty. Lakshmi stopped talking to her Seenappa, hurt at his rejection of her; she cursed him inwardly with anger, more frustrated still because she knew she still desired him. While she never stopped seeing him in her mind, she fled from him in life, avoiding him consistently.

In the matter of one month, Lakshmi lost weight, becoming as emaciated as a person struck by a plague. The bones in her face began to jut out. Her gait lost its earlier balance and elegance and now she shuffled feebly. She found life utterly empty, totally bereft of meaning and purpose and her mind, trying to control itself, turned blank and vacuous. Her eyes lost their lustre and looked cavernous. Shrothri had no idea of what was taking place. How could he when she hardly showed herself before him? It was beyond Bhagirathamma's comprehension to sense the tremendous battle that was raging inside Lakshmi.

Lakshmi was feverish and the fever persisted through the night. But even this Shrothri did not notice until his wife told him. Perplexed and worried, he went to her, felt her pulse and examined her face. And the realisation struck him. His face, too, looked just like this about a month and a half back, a face which had stared meaninglessly back at him from the mirror when he applied the sacred ash marks on his forehead as he prepared to worship. During her days of sickness, Shrothri never left Lakshmi's bed-side.

During the nights he kept a vigil by sleeping on a mattress laid near her bed. Meticulously, he followed the instructions of the

Pandit. During this time, he could not perform his rites at the auspiciously correct time and he compensated for this by reciting the sacred ritual in his mind. It was also at this time that Bhagirathamma had her period and so she suffered the status of ritual impurity. Naturally it fell to her husband to do the cooking, the cleaning and it was he who would change Lakshmi's sari regularly to keep her dress fresh and clean. Sometimes in her unconscious state, Lakshmi would say in a feeble voice, "Seenappa, if you abandon me, who will take care of me?"

Two weeks later, the fever came down. After regaining her consciousness, Lakshmi watched Seenappa staying with her and the care that he had taken of her embarrassed and touched her. Soon Lakshmi had recovered enough to sit up in bed. Then Shrothri sat near her, took hold of her right hand, and said, "Lakshmi, it takes no effort for a human being to fall, but it needs every effort to rise. Everyone of us must suffer the fruits of his or her *karma*. *Dharma* has ordained that, though my wife is alive, I have to live the life of a celibate. The same *dharma* ordains that, as a widow, you will have to live like this. If we choose such pleasures, we can do so only at the cost of losing our *dharma*. No matter how arduous, no matter how tortuous, we cannot succumb. Anyone violating the command *of dharma* will jeopardise the other-worldly status of the seven preceding generations."

Lakshmi was silent.

Shrothri continued, "Let me assure you that under no circumstances will I abandon you. Holding your hand, I give you my solemn word. I shall perform the worship of the deity and then give you the ritual water. Take it with genuine devotion and you will attain peace."

Within a few days Lakshmi was able to walk about and she began to address Seenappa in the familiar singular. Shrothri later informed her that he had formally and legally placed in her name two acres of crop yielding fields in Hejjige. She should never be dependent, she should never feel dependent, Shrothri told her.

Lakshmi's eyes filled with tears and she asked, "Why? I am happy just to eat in this household and serve you."

Shrothri looked at her and saw her beautiful, pure devotion and was overcome.

XV

Though it was midnight, Katyayani recollected vividly her late husband's narration of a crucial chapter in the history of the Shrothri household. Bhagirathamma herself had once broached the subject with her daughter-in-law and Katyayani had been touched by her narration and by the trust that was being placed in her. And it was then that she realised how much that household was built on love, faith and openness. Katyayani's powerful imagination succeeded in building up a full-blooded picture of the past. Even now, some twenty-five years later, Lakshmi and Shrothri were still close. Lakshmi never ate before Seenappa did and as soon as she got up, she bathed and never touched a drop of water before taking the blessed ritual water offered by Seenappa. In time Lakshmi had come to occupy a distinctive position of her own in the Shrothri household. Of course, Katyayani enjoyed a much higher status in the family, and this they all knew and accepted. Recently Shrothri had given her a role in the financial management of the household. Her father-in-law had consulted her before offering Dr. Rao the financial assistance of a thousand rupees for his publications. Together, they had placed the envelope containing the money on the silver tray as Bhagirathamma sprinkled the blessed water over it. As she recalled this, Katyayani was filled with the affection and trust that she had experienced then and so relaxed and so loved, she fell asleep.

The next day Katyayani planned to go to Mysore to tell Raja what had happened. After all, her father-in-law had clearly said, "You are completely free to decide," but suddenly it did not seem that simple.

It meant it was for her to decide one way or the other and then tell Raja about it but her mind swayed from one alternative to the other, from obligation to need, from one love to another love. Katyayani gulped her food, hurriedly packed her books and, carrying the tiffin-carrier prepared by her mother-in-law, she walked to the station by instinct rather than purpose. Her mind tossed between indecision and uncertainty. Five months had passed since she had told Raja about her decision and since then she had behaved as if Raja were her husband in all but name, the experience of being close to him pulling her towards him with tremendous force. That decision taken five months ago was weakened by her encounter with Shrothri but not completely erased.

Even before the train touched Kadakol station, Katyayani could see Chamundi hill through the window of her compartment. It was summer and the month of *Chaitra* was approaching, burning out all the greenery on the body of the hill, making it appear barren and bald with ugly rocks jutting out painfully. The morning sun had climbed the back of the hill from the east, throwing out huge shadows. Katyayani remembered her father-in-law, his body magnificently structured like the awesome, imposing hill. Even though Shrothri was past sixty, his height, his physique, his firm steps, his sitting posture as he worshipped the deity - all these suggested that mountainous power and beauty.

When Nanjunda died, each person gave way, but Shrothri, in spite of losing his only son, endured the shock, controlled his sorrow and stood like the hill, calm and majestic.

The train pulled into Chamarajapuram station but there was no sign of Raja on the platform. The hill was still visible and though it was ten o'clock and the summer heat of the day was rising, despite the decision that was still to be taken, Katyayani was possessed by an overwhelming and insistent desire to climb the hill. She went straight, crossing the Krishnamurthipuram colony, a middle-class area of neat, clean houses, functional rather than fashionable. Each house contrived to be unique and indeed each was slightly different but not so much as to disturb the impression of uniformity. Each one was pleasant, painted in browns, whites and light greens and each garden held tall, swaying coconut trees and pungent jasmine creepers. Katyayani left this area behind and went beyond Chamundipara, following the road dividing the betel-leaf and coconut gardens. The road was full of dust which blew up into her face and swirled round her body.

As she had climbed the hill before, Katyayani knew about the steps leading to the top. Ignoring the scorching sun raging fiercely down on her uncovered head, she walked on, crossing the Nilagiri road. When she reached the bottom of the steps, a wave of intense heat struck her and turning to her left, she saw a huge fire. Five or six people stood by, watching the flames rise high. One of them held a long bamboo pole in his hand and it was then she realised that they were burning a human corpse. Another threw incense on the raging pyre to mask the smell of burning flesh. Normally the sight should have frightened and repulsed her, but today she found it fascinating. Suddenly she heard a cracking sound come from the centre of the flames and the person with the bamboo pole leapt into action pushing and prodding the blackened and burnt corpse back into the centre. A priest stood there, his head covered with a thin piece of cloth, chanting the ritual formulas with insufferable monotony. A little later, the ceremony ended and the party left to join the living.

The pyre was still burning. Katyayani went near it and stood there watching. The corpse had been charred beyond any human identity, the flesh mixing with the ash from the burnt wood and in those ashes somewhere lay decisions, harmony, sorrow, peace, agony, all indiscernible and indistinguishable. As she turned, she saw yet another corpse being carried by pall-bearers on a bamboo bed. One person walked ahead of the corpse, holding an earthen pot containing smouldering firewood. Behind the corpse walked two persons, their heads bent low. Near them was the priest wearing a red shawl, holding the ritual items in his hand. The group came closer and rested the bamboo bed with the corpse before the pyre. The priest motioned her away, saying brusquely, "Woman, what business can you have here? Go away."

Katyayani moved away slowly and reached the bottom of the steps at the foot of the hill and there, she began to climb the winding staircase stretching out before her. After she had gone a little distance, she felt tired, her breathing became harder and her body sweated. Onwards she forced herself but by the time she had covered half the distance, she was exhausted and she felt giddy. Slowly she lowered herself down and sat, silent and motionless. Below she could see the city of Mysore spreading out in an arc. The magnificent palaces and huge towers which flaunted their glory now appeared dwarfed and humbled from the height that she was commanding. In the west the university sprawled out near the Kukkurahalli lake where Raja was waiting. Ten miles away lay Nanjangud.

Until now, the wind had not been strong enough even to ruffle the leaves but now a cool breeze began to blow. She felt relieved and her mind teetered on the threshold of a decision. Soon the cool breeze grew into a cold wind. The wind gathered momentum, became tempestuous and within a few minutes, the scene was transformed, a whirlwind scattering dust everywhere, circling round the spot she

stood on, bits of leaves, torn fragments of brooms, pieces of cast-
away cloth and pieces of paper swirled inside the tower of the wind.
The whole atmosphere grew dense with red dust, blocking out the city
below. The whirling waves of the wind began to rush towards her,
like the waves of a turbulent river flowing amidst huge boulders.
Katyayani was terrified that the wind would lift her up in his mighty
arms and throw her down into the valley. Instinctively, she gripped a
rock near her, her eyes closed against the coarse dust.

Then, as quickly as it had disappeared, peace stealthily returned,
the tempestuous wind subduing itself into a mild breeze. But when
she opened her eyes, she was puzzled to see clouds collect in the sky.
One massive cloud stood directly over her head, shading her from the
sun. Katyayani got up and started to climb but the cloud had reduced
the heat only to increase the sultriness. Her body began to sweat
profusely, her undergarments sticking to her skin. And she saw
before her mind's eye the flames of the funeral pyre she had seen
earlier. Her mind was beyond thought and begged to be left as it was
exhausted and crumpled.

Drops of rain began to fall. She lifted her head and saw the thick
clouds above, grim and murky. The drops increased as they grew into
a downpour. Katyayani did not run to shelter under any tree but
walked on in the rain. When the rain grew heavier and stronger, she
sat down to be drenched. The rain had washed away the tempest, the
red dust and the cluttered atmosphere. A universal calm prevailed.
The city appeared fresh, illuminated by a new light. Even the tiny
university in the distance wore a new look. The clouds dispersed and
the sun shone on her head, like a blazing ball but the appearance was
deceptive as the sun no longer radiated heat with the same intensity
and sharpness. It was an odd rain, appearing suddenly from nowhere
and vanishing abruptly.

Drying her wet sari against the warmth of the wind, Katyayani
resumed her climb. Now she did not find it so difficult to negotiate
the steps, finding a strange kind of pleasure in climbing. Once again
she remembered her father-in-law and Lakshmi, their happiness and
peace coming from such hard climbing. Reaching the top, Katyayani
went to the temple, offered her worship to the deity and it was only
then that she came out to rest under the shade of a tree. Being at such
a height where the air was fresh, away from the tumultuous world
below, she felt exhilarated, the calm of a river placidly flowing on a

sandy bed, unobstructed by rocks. In that state of composure, she at last arrived at a decision.

Katyayani felt hungry so she opened her tiffin-carrier and began to eat the rice, *saru* and curds neatly packed into it. Then she washed and cleaned the carrier in the water gurgling out of a pipe near the temple and began to climb down the steps. Her sari had dried by this time and only the cardboard cover of her notebook was still wet. The cremation ground at the bottom was deserted and eerily quiet, the fires burning the bodies having been put out by the rain. The rain had washed away the dust in the city also. Though her legs were aching, Katyayani managed to reach the college at four in the afternoon, determined to tell Raja Rao of her decision. The doors of the Drama Society were locked. She stood there, watching, fascinated by the hill in the distance. Something caught the corner of her eye and she looked below. Raja was standing there with his bicycle, sulky and peevish.

Katyayani turned her eyes from him, and stared at Chamundi Hill. After a pause of a few minutes, she said, "No, you come up."

Raja was drained. From early in the morning he had been waiting for her, tortured by whether she would come or not, furious with her for putting him through that misery. In that state, he found her words deliberately calculated to slight him. Angrily he got on his bicycle, which sped down the slope. Katyayani stared at the hill.

After returning home in the evening, Katyayani changed her sari and then touched the feet of her father-in-law reverentially.

"Please, forgive me."

"Everyone has such evil moments when unworthy thoughts occur," said Shrothri in a calm and even tone.

As he was climbing down the staircase, she called him again and asked with some hesitation, "Did you tell mother?"

"No. The letter lies in a drawer in my study. Take it and tear it up."

In the meantime, in Mysore, Raja had worked up a vociferous anger against Katyayani for having made him wait until four in the afternoon and for having treated him in such an unrepentant and offhand manner. Perhaps her parents-in-law had not approved of the idea, perhaps the notion of free consent had been foolishness on his part, perhaps he had been wrong to believe that she would have the courage to leave the household. Unless she did so, there was no chance whatsoever of them marrying. Why had she displayed such indifference, even contempt?

Subdued and prepared to forgive her, Raja went to the university the next day to wait for Katyayani. She did not come and the next three days proved equally disappointing and frustrating. He found solace in the fact that she would have to appear for her examinations in ten days time and that he could see her then. Thus Raja was forced to spend his time at home with Nagalakshmi who spoke non-committally and only when she was spoken to. Whenever he tried to engage her in conversation, she replied in monosyllables, never showing any interest beyond cooking and serving the meals.

One day, while serving the food, she astonished Raja by opening the conversation.

"A priest was visiting our neighbour's house and he said that it will do me a lot of good in the next life if I were to write the name of God Sri Rama. I have decided to write that sacred name at least ten million times before I die. Will you buy me a pen and some notebooks?"

Glad that she had spoken and pleased to be able to do something for her, Raja went out that very evening and bought her ink, notebooks and a beautiful fountain pen but as she said she could not write with a fountain pen, he later exchanged it for a cheaper steel one that had to be dipped in ink. First she poured the ink powder into a bottle and mixed the ink, and then placed the inkpot, the steel pen and the note-book on the shelf before the deity. After sprinkling vermilion and turmeric powder on the objects, she bowed to them and then she took the notebook out and touched her eyes with it reverentially.

"Tell me how many times 'Sri Rama' can be written in one line and how many books need to be filled to have written out Sri Rama's name ten million times?"

Raja carried out the calculations and answered, "One line will accommodate ten units and this works out to forty thousand times for a book, two hundred and fifty note-books to complete ten million."

"As I go on writing, will you supply me the note-books I need? And the ink powder?"

"Certainly. But what will you gain by writing the name over and over again?"

"I am not merely writing a name. It is my devotion to the Lord."

Even Raja's romantic nature could not quite accept this and his scepticism surfaced, making him laugh inwardly at her notion of devotion. Every line, in every page, contained the Lord's sacred name repeated ten times and at the end of every page, there featured a more elaborate invocation. Nagalakshmi's writing experience had been confined to her education at the middle school level but she used to write letters to Raja when he was abroad, as her husband was too busy with his studies to do so. More recently she had had no practice in writing at all and that was why her fingers ached in the beginning and the pace remained slow. Undeterred, she was determined, no matter how slowly, to accomplish the goal before she died. So with determination and hope and devotion, she carried on, her empty mind now filling with a sense of purpose.

Raja was looking forward to acting as an invigilator in the examinations with an uncommon desire. The official timetable had already been organised and the duties allotted so he had no say over which exams he supervised. He did not see Katyayani for six consecutive days. On the seventh day she was there, terrified to see him. While doing the rounds as a supervisor, Raja came near her and whispered, "Meet me after the examination."

"Yes," she answered helplessly.

She met him after the examination and they walked together. As they reached a tree in the west part of the college grounds, she said, "You must forget me."

Her voice was heavy with pain.

"Please don't ask me for a reason. You have wasted your love on an unworthy creature. Marry some other girl and be happy. I feel... I am... too old for you."

Her eyes were filled with tears and she fled from the spot. Raja looked after her as she ran but, overwhelmed by her words, he did nothing. The next day he requested the chief supervisor to assign him some other room. Katyayani, who had injected new life and new meaning into his aimless existence, had suddenly withdrawn from it, abruptly terminating their relationship without giving him a chance to question her. How could he forget her, she who had conquered his mind, intelligence and feelings? It was now surely impossible for him in this birth to marry her. And he started to cry.

Why did she encourage him with such intimacy to end with such a foolish and cruel declaration? Why did she say she was too old? She was the most beautiful woman he had ever met. Raja recalled the days they had spent together - her shyness, sensuousness and passion. When she spoke, she spoke sometimes playfully, sometimes thoughtfully, with eagerness and determination, every tone and lilt of her clear voice echoing back to him her very uniqueness.

On the last day of the examination, Katyayani yearned to meet Raja but she dismissed this thought. But perhaps she should visit him at home and express her gratitude to him as a teacher. Suppressing this, she caught the train for Nanjangud. Reaching home, she told her mother-in-law, "From today the bother of running to Mysore will end!"

Bhagirathamma remembered her son and said consolingly, "Yes my dear. If you pass the examination his name will be vindicated."

Katyayani now spent most of her time with her son. Cheeni was already five and he would be starting school in the coming summer. He had become wonderfully and unbearably talkative. Whatever the object of his attention he would bombard the elders with countless, unanswerable questions.

"What is this? Where did it come from? Why is it here and not there?"

During the day he had taken to going out with Lakshmi as she took the cattle to the fields and at night time, he would insist on sleeping by her side with a child's stubbornness.

During this period of *Chaitra* and *Vaishakha,* Cheeni would have to have his head tonsured and would have to undergo yet another ceremonial initiation. This ceremony involved a ritual *puja* with *mantras*, incense and sandalwood. A silver coin would be placed in the child's right hand. Taking a dish covered with grain, an elder of the family would guide the boy's finger in writing the word *OM* across the rice, *OM* the first letter in any Sanskrit writing, *OM* the sacred word that symbolised the order of creation, sustenance and dissolution. As this ceremony symbolised the commencement of learning, it was a cause for celebration and so relatives and neighbours would be invited to a meal of *chitranna* and *payasa.* Bhagirathamma had decided to prepare the meal and perform the ceremony on a grand scale.

The first few days after the examinations proved tedious and stifling for Katyayani but she thought this would wear off as she became accustomed to the routine of being at home. Although she tried to help with the household chores, Lakshmi and Bhagirathamma had built up a routine during the two years that Katyayani was studying and could manage without her help. So she began to discover new tasks for herself such as reading the *Bhagavadgita* in the afternoons. All her efforts to overcome the tedium proved futile. In contrast to her physical passivity, her mind was in a state of increasing turbulence.

Katyayani felt it impossible to sleep in the night, for memories of Raja haunted her and kept her awake and agitated.

"What is he doing now? Does he think about me? Is he angry with me?"

Quickly she dismissed from her mind the unpleasant question of his marrying another woman.

When her heart secretly wove a web of intense imagination, her mind tried consciously to escape that self-created web. In doing this, she sought the help of the *Bhagavadgita,* whose every stanza she read meticulously and whose meaning she strained to understand. While her intelligence grasped the meaning, her heart did not understand it. Her emotions broke through the barriers set up by the words of the *Bhagavadgita* and overflowed and, against its dictates, her mind would be filled with longing and passion. Every day became as dull as the other and life turned out to be a listless affair. Food became unappetising and unnecessary. Her body which used to burn bright with hope, now wilted like a tender creeper caught in a fire. Yet whilst her body progressively weakened, her hopes ran higher. In the struggle between norms and natural impulses, the latter dominated, filling her life with a hopeless darkness. Raja's face came before her everywhere and all the time, sitting, standing or sleeping. Her memory was alive with her long walks with him, their sitting together, their trip to Brinadvan, and the words of endearment between them. But the memory of these experiences which had earlier cooled her like the touch of white marble, now burnt her more fiercely than the funeral fires.

At two past midnight, a decision emerged tearing through her whole being. But how could she go without telling Shrothri? If she ran away without telling him, wouldn't it be betraying the great trust he had placed in her? But then she recollected that he had himself said clearly, "You are free to do what you want."

But was it the sign of freedom to run away without telling him? Before the flood of her feelings, notions of propriety and impropriety could hardly stand. That night she decided on the direction of her new life. The situation was clear: either she had to flow in that direction or she had to die a slow death. She was not prepared to die.

The next day she told her mother-in-law, "I had forgotten to tell you. Today one of our teachers is getting married. I have been invited for the wedding feast. I have to visit Mysore."

Bhagirathamma was pleased and urged her to go, glad of the opportunity for her daughter-in-law to go out and enjoy herself. As Katyayani came out wearing a clean sari, Cheeni asked, "Mother, where are you going?"

But how could she take him with her until she herself had joined her new husband? She kissed both his cheeks.

"Mother, I want to go with you."

"You can come later."

Then she hurried from there. At the turn of the street, she looked back at the house but the sight was misty. The journey was tortuous and with every jerk of the train, she thought her insides would come spilling out. When she went to Raja's house and knocked, Prithvi came out.

"Where is your uncle?"

Prithvi pointed to the room. As she opened the door and entered the room, she was aghast. Raja had lost so much weight that his bones stuck out of an emaciated body. His face was covered with unkempt hair. He looked at her with suspicion. Bolting the door from the inside, she went to him and laid her head against his chest.

"Please believe me now. I shall not leave."

Raja found it difficult to believe her immediately.

"Look at me. I have come as I am, carrying nothing. Let us marry the way you want. Or, if you don't want any of this, I shall just live with you as your woman."

Katyayani embraced him tightly. Then Raja believed her. He grasped her with force and his palpitating heart found at last its normal rhythm, leading to a curious serenity.

XVI

In Nanjangud, when Katyayani did not return by the usual train at six in the evening, it was assumed she would catch the nine o'clock from Mysore, arriving at ten. Since it was the summer vacation and she would therefore be travelling alone, Shrothri went to the station to meet her. The train came, stopped and then continued its journey to Chamarajanagara. After the departure of the train, Shrothri sat on one of the benches on the platform for a while, disquietened. Over the past few weeks, he had discreetly observed that her mind had been restless, but he had thought it improper to ask her about it directly, telling himself; she is the mother of a five year old son, she has started to shoulder the household responsibilities, she will be finishing her B.A. this year, she is aware of her obligations, her *karma* and *dharma*, and it is not wise to probe her about such a delicate and personal matter. Once it occurred to him that she might have left Nanjangud to be in Mysore, but he dismissed the idea as he did not want to harbour such ugly suspicions without some foundation in facts. After returning home, he said casually, "She didn't come by the nine o'clock either. After all, it is a marriage and her friends may have insisted on her staying for longer. She will be back tomorrow."

Cheeni could not sleep, asking, "Why hasn't mother come?"

Only after his grandmother had assured him, "She will come tomorrow" did he close his eyes.

The night passed, the next morning came, as did the train from Mysore, but the daughter-in-law did not. Forgetting any outside concerns, Shrothri concentrated on his worship ritual. About nine he came out of the *puja* and offered the consecrated water to Bhagirathamma, Lakshmi and Cheeni. Bhagirathamma handed over an envelope which had arrived by the morning mail and inside, somewhere between his stomach and his soul, something turned and he realised what it meant. He moved to the hall, pausing for a moment, trying to recover his balance and poise. Then he opened the envelope. It recapitulated the earlier events - her mental turmoil when she had asked for permission to re-marry, how she failed to be firm then in her decision and the consequent agony that was too great to overcome. It concluded:

"With the inspiration of your lofty character, I tried hard to control myself. I failed, and failed you. Every individual person has his or her own distinctiveness, strength and limitations. Before coming to Mysore this time, I wanted to stand before you and tell you of my final decision but my courage and strength were not equal to the task. In a few days, we shall marry. I do not have the foolhardiness to invite you. Yet, I pray to you and beg you to bless me to attain some peace and meaning in my new life. I lost my mother when I was very young and even though my father was alive, I never experienced true affection. It is only through you and Mother that I realised the deep love of a parent. Let the new life of your daughter be happy with your blessings."

Shrothri sat down, dazed. Though it was beyond his imagination to visualise in detail or comprehend her turmoil, which may have made it easier for him to understand, he had no anger against her. All he could see in her was the picture of an unfortunate woman who had failed to save herself from the onslaught of brute nature. Shrothri was full of compassion for her, recalling what happened and what was said on the day she crossed their threshold as a daughter-in-law, the kicking of the rice-pot, the delight as the rice flooded into the house. Not once had she ever said anything to hurt him or his wife, never defied them, serving them like a daughter born of their own flesh. When her husband was alive she was a loving and attentive wife, possessing the ideal qualities to live in his household, gentleness, compassion, obedience. Yet, in the end, this was what she had done.

Shrothri remembered his family tradition and stature, the deep history steeped in strict orthodoxy and antiquity. Preserved at home was their genealogical record, a description of the family tree, containing the details of twelve preceding generations of Shrothris. The roots of this tree went beyond this record, belonged to a time beyond his knowledge, plunging endlessly into the past. No matter how deep one dug, the roots would be visible, alive and active. The genealogical history referred to persons who had died prematurely, to those with more than one wife living and widows. But there was no record of any ancestor doing what Katyayani was now contemplating. Every woman from another household who had joined this family tree in the past had remained a member of the Shrothri genealogy until death. Shrothri had believed that it was as impossible for a woman from one family to join another family as it was for a tributary to flow into one great river and then try flow into another great river, purporting to retain its original identity. What Katyayani had now done left a stain on the family records which was impossible to wipe out. But, he asked himself, would her act not also stain and destroy the purity of the tree of the other family? Did those persons, who even now were preparing to receive her into their family history, have any knowledge of, or concern for, their family tree? One question answered the other.

It was twelve and he was still absorbed in such thoughts. Bhagirathamma called him for lunch but he could not eat. Unable to put off the moment any longer, Shrothri called Bhagirathamma and Lakshmi to the hall and turned to read out the letter.

Stunned, Bhagirathamma asked, "Does it mean that she had talked to you about this earlier?"

"Yes."

"Why didn't you tell us about it then?"

"Because she had asked me not to. She said that she had realised her mistake."

"Now she has done this, without telling us! Who is the fellow who is prepared to marry her?"

"It is Sadasiva Rao's brother, Raja Rao."

Bhagirathamma's anger reached boiling point and frothed over as she shouted, "Did the brother of a man who enjoyed our hospitality and our support do this to us?"

"How can you blame him for what his brother did?"

"Didn't the elder brother have the courage to decide and advise the younger brother not to do it?"

"Perhaps the elder brother is not aware of it... anyway, he is living with a second wife."

Bhagirathamma gaped at him.

"Oh, Great God! What a family!"

With this added piece of scandal, Bhagirathamma got into her stride, pouring unrestrained abuse on her daughter-in-law and her lover, adding Sadasiva Rao as well to her list for good measure. Shrothri tried to persuade her not to use such abusive language but himself became the subject of the onslaught.

"Keep quiet. You have grown old but without any wisdom or understanding of the world. When I argued with you not to send that wretch to university, it was you who played the musical instruments so that she could dance to her tune and not content with that you got up and danced with her! She went to university to uphold her husband's honour but she brought our family name down to dust. I told you we should have got her head shaved soon after her husband's death, got her to wear the widow's red sari and turned her into a proper widow! But no, you had to understand! It was you who puffed her up, making her take the place of our dead son, spoiling her. Well, now she has taught you a good lesson and you deserve it. Now at least do what I say and save the reputation of the family."

"Tell me what you want done now, but more calmly, please."

"Keep your patience to yourself, you old fool!" Bhagirathamma continued her blistering attack. "But just do as I say. She has written that her wretched marriage will take place soon. Let us go there. We shall give a good dressing down to the fellow who wants to marry her, deliver a few blows to her head and drag her back home with a rope!"

Shrothri paused for a while, digesting his wife's words of advice.

"Our going to Mysore will be utterly useless," said Shrothri patiently and quietly.

"She is not a child. She knows what she is doing. Moreover, she has come to this decision after a considerable struggle within her own mind. Anything done in such matters with force will not endure. People act according to their individual nature and there is little we can do to prevent it."

"Again, your *vedanta*, your philosophy. All right, you are the very incarnation of righteousness. We shall leave you out of it. Lakshmi and I will go and drag the worm back!"

Lakshmi, who had been silent all this time, thinking matters over in her mind spoke now, "Seenappa is right. There is no use bringing her back with force. It is best to leave her to her *karma*."

Bhagirathamma was peeved.

"She is another one to teach me his *vedanta*!" and she stormed out of the room.

In the hall of the Sri Prakasha Boarding and Lodging House, Raja and Katyayani exchanged garlands in the presence of some twenty to thirty persons. The priest, who had charged the couple an extortionate fifty rupees for an hour's ceremony, supervised the tying of the *mangalya* by the groom around the neck of the bride. The assembled company, all close friends of Raja, blessed the couple by sprinkling the auspicious turmeric rice over them and then offered their wedding gifts. As it happened to be the summer vacation and because of the shortness of notice, very few could really be present. Although it was extremely different from the usual Indian weddings that lasted for three days, that were arranged in special marriage halls by the family elders and were attended by some five hundred people, the guests at this small gathering eagerly agreed that they found nothing amiss and it really was a charming affair. Though she had no enthusiasm for going out of the house, Nagalakshmi had come to the hotel but there were no senior couples either to give away or receive the bride ceremonially. Rao was unaware of the whole business as he was away in the North with Karuna studying some rare volumes in the library of Calcutta University.

As soon as the ritual of marriage was over, they retired to the room reserved for them. After bolting the door, Katyayani touched Nagalakshmi's feet in respect, and said, "Elder sister, I don't know whether you approve of what we have done. You are the present mistress of the household. The priest performed the ritual of giving the bride away, it is you who should now accept."

Nagalakshmi replied indifferently, "Once you become Raja's wife, you are part of the family. Hereafter, it shall be your task to manage the whole household."

In the hall outside they had spread the mat for the guests to sit on, and laid out plantain leaves to be used as plates. The guests and the new couple sat together to enjoy the sumptuous meal prepared by the hotel, a variety of hot and sweet items, of delicacies, finished with soothing, cooling curds. Afterwards, the Sanskrit lecturer recited Sanskrit slokas, beginning with *shantakaram, bhujagashayanam*. Another guest, a student in the M.A. Kannada final class, who had an excellent voice, sang the Karnataka poet Bendre's well-known verse on poetic formation:

"Creation came riding on the wings of a honey bee..."

The others applauded him at the end by slapping their thighs with their hands. The guests blessed the couple again and departed. After clearing the hotel bill, Raja, Katyayani, Nagalakshmi and Prithvi returned home in a hired jutka.

The few days following the wedding were days in which the couple lived absolutely unaware of the outside world, so totally immersed were they in each other. As usual, Nagalakshmi took charge of the kitchen and Prithvi was seldom at home, away playing with the neighbouring children. Raja and Katyayani spent most of their time in their room. They had no interest in, or time for, going out, visiting places, going to the cinema or watching plays. They told each other about the pangs of separation, recounted to each other the ecstatic experience of *advaita*, non-duality which they experienced in merging into each other. Raja spoke gently to capture that incredible bliss - the endless, the deathless, absolute truth of the eternal! In the fusion of *prakriti* and *purusha*, night became day and day became night, as time lost its rhythm and steps.

Katyayani had arrived at Mysore only with the clothes she was wearing but now Raja had bought countless, beautiful saris, their colours shimmering and reflecting. Laughing, she would whirl them round in her room and then once she was out of breath, she would slowly wrap and fold the sari around herself. Flowers adorned her hair and the vermilion mark was once again placed on her forehead. Staring at herself in the mirror, she felt her overflowing womanhood, her existence and reality were there.

After a few days Katyayani went to the kitchen to help Nagalakshmi in her domestic chores. Nagalakshmi did not discourage her from doing them, but was indifferent to whether her new sister offered any help or not. All Nagalakshmi now lived for was her household work and after that, she would turn to her great project of writing out the name of Lord Sri Rama. Even when Katyayani tried to engage her in conversation, she showed little enthusiasm. When she realised that her sister-in-law had stabilised herself at this level of existence, Katyayani refrained from drawing her into any conversation.

Prithvi had known Katyayani earlier, even before she came to live in their house. While playing in the street, his playmates had made fun of him, saying, "Your uncle has married a widow!"

He also understood what these words meant. Raja had taught him to address her as aunt and accordingly he did so. His uncle continued to carry him on his shoulder with the same affection as before and still took him on bicycle rides. Katyayani frequently hugged him and passed her palm affectionately across his hair but Prithvi felt shy in the company of his new aunt. Worried of the consequences if he were to run away from her, he would react by using words of formality. Katyayani corrected him, "No, you should not address me that way. Use the same terms of familiarity you use in addressing your uncle."

Thus encouraged, he would try. Once in a while she helped him with his homework.

Whenever she saw Prithvi, she was reminded of Cheeni. But Cheeni was a child born of her own flesh. She recalled that when she left Nanjangud, Cheeni had said, "Mother, I want to go with you."

And she had replied, "You can come later."

Now the vivid memory of the child began to torment her. Yet, how could she take him away? If she took Cheeni from her parents-in-law, they would have nothing of meaning in their lives. Their tree would stop.

From the depths of her being, she would hear a feeble voice questioning the correctness of her conduct in deserting the old couple but her conscious mind would immediately silence it. Raja had no qualms about bringing Cheeni to live with them and when Katyayani told him that she could not find the courage to take the child away, he suggested writing a letter to prepare them for the shock. This she did, hesitantly at first, but then jerked forward by the strength of her emotions, she began to write; no thinking, just feeling. She informed them of her marriage and expressed a wish to see them and seek their blessing. She concluded:

"Three days from today, that is, on the twentieth of this month, I shall take the afternoon train. I beg you to let me take my child with me."

The drizzle of *Jyestha* had already started and in the Malenad region, in the hilly terrain, the rains had been heavy, swelling the rivers. It had been a month since Katyayani had left for Mysore. All the way to Nanjangud, the drizzle continued to fall and the sun seemed to have lost his place in the sky. The rain poured on the train as it halted at the two intermediate stations and as they crossed the bridge, she saw Kapila surging with water and foam. Her eyes surveyed the familiar landmarks - the bathing ghats in a row, the temples on the bank, the mango groves to the left of the river.

As she alighted from the train, her heart thundered, afraid that someone might notice her on the way. Of course, by now her marriage must have become familiar news in that small town.

When Katyayani reached the beloved house, the door was half-open. She entered the hall and beyond was the inner room. The kitchen, the prayer room and the dining hall lay to one side. Lacking the boldness to go further into the house, she perched nervously on the edge of a chair. From inside she could hear the sonorous rendering of a *mantra*. Turning back to the door to see if anyone was coming out, her eyes glanced at the floor and then stared at it. It had been specially cleaned but, unusually, was bereft of the auspicious *rangavalli* designs. It spread out there, bleak and accusingly, the very nothingness of it proclaiming the horrible thing that she had done - she had arrived on her husband's death anniversary. No, but that could not be right! But since she had been living in Mysore she had used the colonial English calendar whereas Shrothri used and the death ceremonies were governed by the different, complex Hindu calendar.

"Should this be the day I so thoughtlessly chose? I should return another day."

She rose to reach the front door but before she could leave without anybody seeing that she had come, Lakshmi came in and urged her to sit down with her natural concern.

"No, Lakshmi, today is the death anniversary."

"Yes, Nanjunda's death anniversary. Didn't you remember?" Lakshmi asked kindly.

Katyayani was about to tell of her mistake over the calendars but felt ashamed, too feeble to be able to vindicate herself. Drained and unable to do anything else, she returned to the front hall and sat in the chair. Lakshmi sat there for a while with her but they could not find the words to say to each other. Katyayani bent her head low. Inside the rites went on with ritual chanting and ritual action, a gripping monotone. As Cheeni, who had not undergone the thread ceremony, was not qualified to perform the rites, his place was taken, as usual, by Kuppayya. The officiating priest was the local man, Subbayya Sastry. Shrothri was explaining the ceremony to the child in a low tone for, one day, it would be his duty to perform it. Katyayani followed the progression of the ceremony by the various sounds, the different Sanskrit *mantras*, the sound of softly spoken Kannada, the clank of metal ladles signalling the start of the customary meal for the invited brahmins.

"What is the difference between the rites relating to the ancestors and the rites relating to the gods?"

Katyayani was surprised to identify the voice of the questioner as that of her own father, Srikanthaiah. His interest in her had not gone beyond taking her home for a few days after his son-in-law's death but after that he had never come again to Nanjangud, nor did he write a single line to her. Though Srikanthaiah had shown considerable affection to his daughter earlier, this had dwindled as she had become replaced and supplanted by her father's second wife. Perhaps Shrothri invited him today to settle the issue of her child.

Shrothri replied, "During the rites relating to the gods, the sacred thread hangs from the left shoulder and the person performing it should sit facing east or north. While offering the ritual water, he must utter, "*swaaha*" and "*vashat*". But in rites relating to ancestors, the sacred thread should hang from the right shoulder and the performer should sit facing the south. He must utter "*swadha*" when offering ritual water. Also in the former, the *dharbha* grass should be snipped, while in the latter the grass should be brought uprooted, with the roots intact..."

His words seemed to be flitting from topic to topic. Srikanthaiah was a lawyer and it was natural that he asked a question concerning the law. "What is the implication of the status of being a son? Does that status apply only to a son or does it also apply to the future sons and grandsons of that first son?"

Shrothri explained, "The *Dayabhaga* legal treatise has an answer to this question. It holds that the term, son, covers three generations, beginning with the biological son and including that son's immediate issue and the grandson. This is because these three are duty-bound to perform the death anniversary of the ancestors; the ritual offering of food by them will satisfy the ancestors."

From the subject of the death anniversary, their discussion shifted to the ancient and traditional system of property inheritance. Shrothri continued, "The son is obliged to pay back the father's debts, even if he does not inherit any of the father's property. And the debt should be repaid with interest. But the grandson is obliged to pay back only the capital, not the interest. If he has no ritual and legal status of a son to the grandfather, why should the grandson repay even the capital?"

Katyayani wondered whether they knew that she was sitting there, whether the words were meant for her ears. Cheeni came skipping out into the hall, relieved to be released from the long ritual, a small boy of just five years wearing nothing more than a loincloth. When he saw his mother sitting there he was confused by her new appearance, the colourful sari, the flowers and the vermilion mark on her forehead. She saw his confusion and sat there embarrassed that her own child had only ever seen her as a widow and never as a true wife.

"Mother, where were you all these days?" His voice was loud enough to reach those inside.

Although she motioned with her hands to call him closer, he refused, standing shyly and obstinately by the door.

"Cheeni, come to me, come to mummy" she called softly.

Remembering the ceremony, the brahmins and what they had all told him, the child replied defiantly, "Today is my father's anniversary. I am in a state of ritual purity. You can't touch me."

And then upset by having behaved correctly, he fled.

Katyayani was shocked and hurt. But after five minutes, the young child returned, made straight for his mother and rested his head on her lap.

"Where have you been?"

Katyayani stroked his childish curls.

Lifting his head, he pleaded, "From now on, please don't go away, leaving me."

She held his head between her hands and bent down to clasp it to her bosom. Then he added, "I shall come back after finishing the rites. They will give us blessed food. I shall give some to you, too," he added defiantly.

Eluding her grasp, he ran to the door.

"Why are you sitting there, Mother? Come inside."

The brahmin guests had finished their meal and once again the rites had started with the chanting of *mantras*, continuing for another half an hour when they abruptly came to an end. After taking the gifts and claiming his officiating fee, Subbayya Sastry left, staring rudely at Katyayani as he crossed the hallway. The other brahmin who left a little later also threw her a meaningful look. Kuppayya went towards the river, carrying in his left hand the *pinda* in a container, and in his right hand a copper pot. He glared at her as he went past. She sat benumbed, staring vacuously at the wall. In the earlier days, he would not even have dared to look at her, always humbly lowering his head in her presence. On his way back from the river, ten minutes later, Kuppayya stared at her again, this time even more insolently, revelling in his power.

After another fifteen minutes, Shrothri himself came out and said, "The leaves have been laid. Come and eat, child."

It comforted her to hear him speak to her in the same manner and in the same gentle tone. He stood there, waiting for her. Although Katyayani did not want to eat, she knew that she could not refuse him when he so kindly offered and especially not today. Shrothri, Srikanthaiah and Cheeni sat in one row facing her. None had the inclination to speak. Bhagirathamma was suffocating silence. The fare was traditional but rich and elaborate, sweet porridge, fried savoury dishes, sliced mango and banana - all crowding the plantain leaves. Srikanthaiah helped himself liberally and Cheeni who had not eaten anything before the ceremony was slurping his food. Katyayani ate a little rice and nobody urged her to eat anymore. By the time they finished the meal with curds and rice, Cheeni was dozing off.

After washing her hands, Katyayani returned to the hall and sat in that same chair. For the next half hour she was left all alone and each minute that went past bore down upon her, crushing her. Finally Shrothri came there and sat on the edge of the divan near her. Five minutes passed.

"Your letter came."

Plucking up her courage, Katyayani said, "I explained everything in that letter."

Bhagirathamma came out of the kitchen.

"You would write it, wouldn't you? You have done great honour to the parents and to the household which received you. And now you are here to take away that innocent child, to brainwash him into your wicked ways that violate our customs. You will turn him into something worse than an untouchable. You want to destroy this house."

The words tumbled out of her mouth in one breath. Katyayani's father, Srikanthaiah, followed Bhagirathamma into the hall and sat on the divan in another corner. He was a tall and bloated figure, orthodox in his pragmatism and when it came to himself, pragmatic in his orthodoxy.

Bhagirathamma continued her onslaught, "It was not enough for you to have done all this damage to our honour and custom. You have now come to take the boy away and present him to your new husband, saying 'Cheeni, this is the father who begot you!' Is that why you are here? Have you any sense of shame? Your own father is here. Let him judge your behaviour. Tell your father whether we abused you, persecuted you, starved you!"

Srikanthaiah coughed. He had travelled some distance and was ready to have his say. The silence in the air had become frozen. He coughed again but his daughter remained silent. Once more he coughed, loudly and uselessly. Then he started to speak in English. Even though Bhagirathamma did not understand a word of what he said, she nevertheless recognised and was impressed by Srikanthaiah's experienced courtroom style of speaking. Shrothri, even though he did not catch the details, managed to grasp the general drift and sense of the words. After referring to the *Dharmasastras* for quarter of an hour, her lawyer father finally made a point of law, "Even in English law, the guardianship of the children is vested with the biological father and his family. Even when a mother is widowed and re-marries, the children continue to carry the surname of the original father's family."

Then he came to the theme of how she had brought disgrace on her father's unsullied lineage. He concluded with straight abusive language, "You are a wretch, a filthy disgrace to the family. Better if such an unworthy daughter were not born..."

He would have continued but for Shrothri's intervention. Shrothri had caught the tone of his in-law's arguments and he said, "Now what has happened has happened. It serves no purpose to blame each other. Let no foul words come from our mouths. Please go inside. I shall sort everything out."

Bhagirathamma felt great strength and substance in the in-law's English presentation and it gave her an inexplicable sense of confidence in her own position. She refused to follow her husband's suggestion and said, "What do you know? You are a blind follower of *dharma*. He is a lawyer and he will handle the problem. Leave it to him and keep out of it."

She stood there. By then Katyayani was unable to control the anguish that was building up within her. Her father had never visited the Shrothri's household, had never enquired whether his daughter was alive or dead and now he was here treating her little differently from the way he would treat criminals. The pent-up grief and pain burst out and she began to sob loudly and without restraint.

Shrothri told his wife once again firmly, "Go inside."

Defiant and weeping, Bhagirathamma replied, "No, I shall not leave. He is not just your grandson. It was I who bore his father. How can you understand my pain? The boy is my branch, my flesh. It is I who am bringing him up."

Srikanthaiah tried to pacify Bhagirathamma, "You are an elder and if you cry, it will be inauspicious."

Shrothri now spoke in an authoritative and final voice, "Leave the final decision to me."

He gently but firmly pushed them out of the room. Bhagirathamma was still crying. Shrothri bolted the door of the hall from the inside and he and Katyayani were now in the front hall alone.

Katyayani had not stopped crying. Pulling a chair near her and sitting down, Shrothri said, "In such matters, crying is of little use. Calm yourself. Now there is no-one here to hurl angry words at you. Please tell me whatever you have to say."

Katyayani raised her head and looked into his face. Shrothri's face was as calm and as unruffled as ever. It took her some time to control her tears. Wiping them away with the hem of her sari, she said, "You know how hard it is for a mother to be separated from her child, born of her flesh. What more need I say?"

Shrothri nodded. She continued, "I do realise that his absence... will make you... unhappy. Yet how can I live without Cheeni? Please send him with me."

"Child, this is not merely a question of sentiments or emotions, the heart or the mind. The question needs to be seen from a much wider perspective. No doubt a mother has attachment to her child. But don't we also have our attachment? Our claims? You lost a husband, but you have found another husband. Can we get a new son in the place of our dead son?"

Katyayani had no answer.

"The dead son belongs to us. How can his son belong only to you? Children do not belong exclusively to either a father or a mother for they are the wealth of the family and the lineage. They are our scion. If anyone of us tries to stake our individual claims over them, they will elude us all. Only those prepared to be part of the family and lineage can exercise collective rights over the collective nature of the family and the lineage. Once you choose to tear away from the circle, what right can you have over the centre-point of that circle?"

"I am not talking the language of rights or authority. I am a mother without her child."

"No shoot can talk of motherhood once it leaves the family tree. The sense of motherhood, fatherhood, brotherhood, all these have meaning only in the context of the lineage, the family tree. The goal of marriage is merely to promote the interest of that lineage tree. If this is so, where then can the claim of motherhood arise?"

His arguments roused Katyayani and she replied spiritedly, "Your outlooks on life and mine are totally different. You consider the individual as an instrument of family or lineage goals, whereas I attach the highest value to individuality."

Shrothri was silent, reluctant to continue the futile debate. He simply added, "When we encounter such a fundamental difference and disagreement, there is no point in prolonging this debate. At least do you concede that children are as much the grandchildren of grandparents as they are the children of their parents?"

Katyayani remembered when Cheeni was a six-month old baby, she and her husband were in a playful mood. Her husband was saying, "This child is mine."

She would counter him, "No, he belongs to me."

Just then Shrothri came there. Nanjunda laughingly appealed to his father for justice. Shrothri had replied, smilingly, "Children belong neither to the father nor the mother. They are simply the grandchildren of their grandfather!"

She recalled then that she and her husband had then accepted this verdict, even in the midst of their amusement, as something irresistible and unchallengeable.

"Suppose you took Cheeni away. Can you assure me that you will bring him up in such a way as to uphold the traditions and values of the Shrothri lineage? Should not the child be made aware of the semen from which he has sprung? Will he be in a position to perform the death anniversary to his ancestors and discharge his debt to them, as he did today? Don't you agree that in the environment of your new household these values appear to be absurd and irrational?"

"I do not believe in those values and practices."

"You may not believe in them. When that child grows up later, the laws of the government will confer on him the right to enjoy the entire Shrothri property. What justice is there in his enjoying the property of the family whose beliefs, faith, culture and moral responsibilities he has chosen to reject? As soon as we receive our body from our parents, we also inherit their physical characteristics, their values, their traditions. We cannot simply say that we can keep the physical heritage, our body, and reject the other heritage as not our own; it is a perverted perspective."

Katyayani was silent. She was unable to pursue any kind of argument.

"It is in order to promote the growth of another family tree that one lineage offers its own soil in which the seeds from another family strike their roots and grow. The soil so donated will realise its objective only when it can receive the seeds of the family and sprout new life. Once you become a mother, you are a mother for ever. How can you resume the status of a wife by becoming once again a virgin maiden? It is against the rhythm and rule of nature for experience which moves forward from stage to stage to regress to an earlier stage. In the process of progressive development, it is sin to revert to an earlier already transcended stage."

Wrinkles of pain showed on Katyayani's face. Shrothri saw them and softened his tone.

"Please believe me that I didn't say all this to cause you pain. Unknowingly my tongue has said so many things. According to the law of the government, you can take the boy with you. But the law does not reflect *dharma*. I shall not allow the honour and status of the Shrothri lineage to be dragged into the courts. I shall make one last suggestion."

Now his voice was firm but not rough, as he spoke, "The final decision shall be yours. I have no authority to hand over the child to you. One branch of a tree has no authority to cut off another branch and give it away as a gift. I shall not beg you to leave the child here for my sake or for the sake of that woman weeping there. I do not have the low desire to want the child to support us in old age. The child is sleeping upstairs. Go up. But before that, think over what I have said. If your conscience tells you to take him away, then do so. If my wife or your father tries to intervene, I shall take care that they do not hinder you."

After speaking these words, he rose and left the room. Bhagirathamma, who was eagerly waiting near the door, asked him anxiously, "What did you do?"

Shrothri took hold of her arm, led her into the kitchen and bolted the door from within.

The abrupt and unexpected turn of events, the twist in his words, the burden was too much for Katyayani to bear. Before arriving there she had decided unequivocally to battle with Shrothri, but he did not give her scope for her arguments, for a self-justifying debate. She had come determined to let him hear the voice of humanity, the voice of an anguished mother but he recast the situation in his own way, making his own position very clear, gently, firmly, placing the agony of the decision upon her. He could have shown anger against her. No, instead of that, he led his weeping wife inside and bolted the door from within, knowing, enabling her to take the child away, unimpeded.

Katyayani tried to visualise the situation through the eyes of the old woman crying behind the bolted door, tried to see torment from another angle. She had a new husband in place of a dead one but they had no new son to be their son. For Shrothri, his beliefs and values came from a time and tradition which began before consciousness, and everything - affection, love, emotions - gained significance only in the context of familial relationships. He attached no value to motherhood torn from the context of lineage and future generations. Yet what pride was there in his final words!

"I shall not allow the honour and status of Shrothri lineage to be dragged into the court."

His authority, his trust enveloped her.

"If your conscience tells you to take him away, then do so. If my wife or your father tries to intervene, I shall take care that they do not hinder you."

Her heart turned tense with irreconcilable elements, unresolvable issues. Thoughts and ideas began to dispel the mists of her motherly love, starting to invade her, rushing to the core of her being, naked and exposed. The forces ranged against her maternal instincts were powerful yet they could not vanquish the primal feelings rising from the depths of her being. Paralysed by love and horror, she did not have the strength to get up. Her mind refused to think, to bear the burden of the decision and so her heart became unbearably heavy. It took every ounce of her energy to stand up. Before her was the door of the room, wide open. Beyond were the steps climbing up to the upper hall where Cheeni was lying asleep. Her legs managed to drag themselves towards the staircase. Downstairs, there was an absolute silence. The house wore the look of a deserted, ruined building, the silence eerie. Katyayani started to climb the staircase, slowly, the only sound that of the swish of her sari as it caught the steps. Up there in the hall, where she had studied for her degree, on the tiger-skin rug, Cheeni was asleep. Lakshmi had covered him with his grandfather's blue shawl but the shawl had slipped down half-way, exposing the child's stomach and the side of his chest. Cheeni was breathing rhythmically, evenly, undisturbed. Katyayani sat near her son and looked deeply into his face, a face that reminded her so much of her first husband, the same, straight, prominent nose, the wide forehead - the face, the build of the body, even the sleeping posture was his. The physique of his grandfather, reflected in his father, was gently moulded into that tiny body. Whose child is he? She could not make herself believe that there was no connection, no line that led irrevocably to the Shrothri household. Rich soil that had belonged to this lineage had received a Shrothri seed, and it had now grown into a tree. Unerringly and naturally, the tree displayed the distinctive qualities of that seed.

Perhaps the blood and flesh and the milk from her breasts secreted by her inherent nature, her hopes, ambitions, love, for the child had no value. Did she need to build up so laboriously a case for authority over this child? Had the reality and self-evident truth of her maternity become so weak as to need the support of arguments and justifications? Perhaps she had fallen so low as to have lost her motherly claims. Something was probing, then driving and twisting. She felt a strange, gurgling pain in the pit of her stomach. From within forced forward a stream of hot tears, and she began to sob loudly. Disturbed by the crying, the sleeping child lost the rhythm of his breathing and rolled to the other side. Now the shawl had fallen to one side, fully uncovering the body. She controlled herself and suppressed the tears, silent as she watched the boy's body, saw it with eyes of desperate longing and expected fulfilment. The sight filled her eyes and heart. Again she remembered her first husband, Nanjunda Shrothri and her chest appeared to burst with unendurable agony. She bent her head slowly to kiss the boy's sleeping head, hiding her face. Gently she bent to kiss the small feet. Once again the flood of tears was rushing from within. But, before it could turn into an audible cry, she stuffed her mouth with the end of her sari and hurried downstairs. It was as silent as before. The door of the kitchen was closed as before. Before the suppressed sobs could escape, she crossed the threshold of the household and went out into the damp air.

A mild drizzle fell. As the sky was completely blacked out with tense, dark clouds, it was impossible to guess the time. Night was falling prematurely. The road was muddy, made worse by the cattle. Katyayani walked as hurriedly as the squelching mud would permit her. As she was turning towards the station road, she met Lakshmi. Katyayani reached out and took hold of her hand.

"Please, come with me for a while."

Lakshmi moved the umbrella so that it covered Katyayani's head as well as her own. Inside the station they sat on a bench. Lakshmi could imagine how Seenappa would have handled the situation and the words he would have spoken.

"When did my father arrive?"

"Yesterday evening."

"Who invited him?"

"Bhagamma."

"Not father-in-law?"

"No, but even then she wrote to him, asking him to come."

Katyayani sighed slowly. Turning to face her, Lakshmi asked, "Why did you do all this?"

"How can I explain this to you of all people? You should understand yourself."

They sat there in silence.

"It is the fruit of our *karma* and we are made to act according to it," said Lakshmi wearily.

Lakshmi's foreboding concern unsettled Katyayani. She wanted silence, the sticky, cheerless silence of the station.

"It is dark. You had better go home."

Lakshmi placed her hand on Katyayani's back and said, "Thinking will only bring unhappiness. Turn your mind and heart into stone."

Darkness covered everything and the train had not yet arrived. Katyayani remembered that she still had to buy her ticket. At the ticket office the man paused, with unconcealed annoyance, from reading his Kannada newspaper to tell her abruptly that there would be no trains until the next day as a goods train had derailed near Kadakol station. He had been chewing betel leaves and his teeth and lips dripped red. It was quarter past seven on the railway clock. Though she knew several houses where she could seek shelter for the night, she had no mind to do so. Katyayani decided to spend the night in the station but was worried that if she stayed there any longer she would be recognised. No, the best thing to do would be to go away somewhere and then return to the station late at night when it would be deserted.

Walking through and beyond the Pindargeri neighbourhood, her body moved forward mechanically and unconsciously like a puppet possessed by a strange spirit. It was the area where the servants lived. It was filthy, rubbish piling up all around, a dark putrefaction, stray dogs barking, howling and fighting. She could hear the sound of water; a drain had burst and then blocked. The stench of the sewer was rancid and overwhelming. The smell of cooking floated out, mingling in her mouth with the taste of choked vomit. Inside the tiny, crowded huts, paraffin lamps burnt and she could make out long shadows against the walls and grasping voices belonging to those shadows, reverberating in her mind. She walked onwards, away from the harshness to somewhere where it was quiet. The river bank appeared before her and the Gaurighat where she sank down on one of the steps. The river was flowing in its routine fashion, sedate and sustained. In the chilly darkness, there was an island of light cast by a lonely, electric street lamp but it was a hazy light in which things were blurred, hovering and looming. The drizzle continued to fall, wetting her sari. She covered her head with the wet sari and tried to think.

The afternoon repeated itself in her mind. Then, in the numbing voidness of herself, a day, five years ago started to form, the same *Jyestha* and the very day. Yes, she recalled, I too wanted to end my life, unable to endure a life without him. Perhaps her father-in-law recognised this for he would sit close to her, saying consolingly, "You have to live, at least for the sake of this child."

Now that child was asked to live without her and she without that child. Her eyes turned on the river. It called her to become a part of it. Already she could feel the water gurgling and rushing in her ears. The death-wish was invading her, her body, mind and soul. But there was deep inside her a silent force that held her tight. When her life had lost all meaning, she was perplexed by that power that pulled her back. Filled with this thought, twice she went close to the water, squatting on the lowest steps at the very edge. In that lonely peopleless place, the rain-fed river flowed, making a sound like that of milk boiling over. Down below, it would be peaceful, the fluidity of an escape. From the murkiness, she would look up and see the moon and the electric light, distorted against the surface of the water. Deeper and deeper, she could merge into the waters, floating endlessly, suspended there for all time.

Suddenly she felt something focusing on her. She shied away but it directed its gaze onto her. In the darkness, she could just make out the form of its liquid murkiness. Calmly, she stood up, without fear, staring at the figure. It hesitated, as if unsure, and then it moved slowly down the steps, faltering a little but never ceasing to stare at her. The fluid figure moved closer to her, reached out for her hand. He was cold, unbelievably cold and wet. Weak, faint, she rested her head against his body. He sat down beside her, holding her close. Her sari was now dripping. The dizziness increased, and she felt as if she would finally lose all consciousness. Then she clung, embracing him, sobbing loudly.

"Why have you come for me? I am a sinner."

"Come, let us go," whispered the voice in her ear.

"Yes, yes," she murmured, "Take me back with you."

The body pulled her up, held her with an unusual firmness and she prepared to enter the waters with him.

But the body stopped and then shook her violently. It shouted at her in horror and astonishment. The strength and ferocity of the voice brought her out of her dizziness.

"What are you doing? How could I have lived if you had ended your life? I knew the train had derailed and I came to look for you."

She realised then that it was not he but Raja. Shocked, she cried loudly and agonisingly like a wounded animal that nobody would pity. The rain fell harshly and steadily. The force of the water calmed her and she began to realise. Turning to him, she pressed her body close to his as if she wanted to become part of it, "You came in the rain in search of me, so exhausted!"

XVII

After eight years of married life with Karuna, Dr. Rao was able to bring out the second volume of his projected *magnum opus* and submit the typescript of the third volume to his London publishers. Rao had by now established a formidable reputation in the world of scholarship, leading to an invitation to preside over the annual conference of the All India Historical Association. A few American and British universities had extended visiting fellowships. Impressed by this recognition, Mysore University made him a fully fledged professor which brought the benefit of being able to live in the spacious quarters of the senior teaching staff.

The daily routine underwent no change. As usual, Rao went to the library at nine in the morning to leave it at eight in the evening. Karuna would either work in the library with him or if there was any typing to be done, she would spend a few hours in the study at home. In the evening they ate their dinner prepared by the cook, Raghappa and would then go for a walk. Yet, even while walking, their subject of discussion was their research work or matters relating to it. Rao would use this time to try out fresh ideas that might have occurred to him during the day, and Karuna would respond critically. After further protracted deliberations, Rao would arrive at a final position. Sometimes, so absorbed, their walks would last longer as they lost track of time. On returning home, he would put down in writing the ideas and thoughts crystallised during the discussions.

Though the typescript of the third volume had been submitted three years ago, the material had not yet been sent to press, languishing in the basement of a publishing house. The Second World War was raging and paper scarcity had become a global phenomenon. In any case, the printing presses were heavily involved in the war effort.

The London publishers had written to Rao informing him that although commercial printing had temporarily ceased in London, his volumes would most certainly be published in the future, even if by the offices in New York, Toronto and Sydney. As London was being heavily bombed, Rao was advised to keep several copies of the volume in India. The war affected Asia too. Java, Borneo and Sumatra, places of historical interest which were to be visited in connection with the research were declared high risk zones. Even travelling within India had become difficult. As all the European countries were involved in the war, Rao's letters to scholars there seldom reached their addresses and even if they did, responses were rarely forthcoming. A professor in Paris had sent a curt reply, "Mankind must survive this war. Then we shall consider its history."

Four years after her marriage, Karuna lost her father. Unhappy that his daughter had married a foreigner in Mysore whose wife was still living, Jayaratne nevertheless had to acknowledge his own helplessness after the event. Some consolation was derived from the fact his daughter and Rao had a common goal and that their marriage was a marriage of minds. After she learnt of her father's death, Karuna went back to Ceylon to be with her brother but since then she had neither the time nor the inclination to visit her homeland.

These days Karuna had picked up enough broken Kannada and explanatory hand gestures to communicate adequately with the cook. Raghappa was a Madhva brahmin, a cook more by wishful thinking than by profession. From childhood he had been singularly lacking in both common sense and imagination. Orphaned early in life, he had earned his living by doing odd jobs in middle-class houses. When he first joined Rao's household, Karuna had taught him what little cooking she knew. Raghappa simply continued the same simple fare he had picked up from her with monotonous regularity - a light *saru*, vegetable curry, always tasting the same. Though they could easily have got a better cook, they kept him on. He was past fifty and they knew the poor fellow would not find another job. Also he was a thoroughly honest servant who made all the purchases for the family and gave scrupulously correct accounts. Even if they were out for a month, they could rely upon him to take care of the house.

The subject matter of the fourth volume was to be an account of cultural life and its conflicts in India from the tenth century to the end of Muslim rule. Their research involved visits to the beautiful, white, marble palaces of Rajasthan built by the Rajput kings. The architecture was both Mughal and Hindu in origin and the palaces themselves were wonderfully spacious and airy, perfect in that scorching heat. Jutting out were large balconies from which could be experienced the exquisiteness of the moonlit night. Then they went to Pune, the capital of the Peshwas, the rulers of Maharashtra in the seventeenth and eighteenth centuries and examined their administrative records. Yet, wherever they went, they realised how much more they could do and so Rao did not have the confidence to start the actual writing of the text. Indeed, he still had to collect more information on the fabulous trading and cultural history of Vijayanagar before he could begin.

Towards the end of February of that year, Rao's health began to deteriorate. For the last twelve years he had laboured to produce this work, ceasing not even for a single day. While his enthusiasm for work was boundless, his body found it increasingly difficult, if not impossible, to cope with that ardour. Now, when they went out for a walk after dinner, he would feel short of breath after a mere five minutes. Sometimes when he was in his easy chair, holding a bulky volume to read, his hand would give way, and the volume would slip down from it. Or when he was discussing some reference with Karuna, he would feel suddenly too weak to speak. The Honours and M.A. classes demanded at least six hours of lecturing every week. At Karuna's insistence, he went to see a doctor who recommended a total break.

Although initially reluctant, Rao accepted Karuna's suggestion that they recuperate in a hill resort and even feebly began to look forward to the idea. Accordingly, they hired a taxi and went to Nandi Hills. There they booked into the Cubbon Guest House, which had been named in honour of an English government representative to keep him in good humour. It was an ordinary, clean, guest house, neither cheap nor luxurious.

The fresh air and the greenery on the hills were tranquil and restful. The station was small, perched on the top of Nandi hill, consisting of a few buildings and neat, symmetrical gardens maintained by the government horticultural department. Those who came there were of a certain social and economic position; a quiet and reflective clientele. It was the very essence of organised upper-middle class relaxation. Now Rao and Karuna went to bed early and rose at five in the morning to enjoy a calm, dawn walk. Sometimes they walked down to Nandi village beyond the Veerabhadraswamy temple. When they felt a little tired, they rested in a ruined shelter on the way. In the evening they walked about a mile along the tarmac road. The afternoons were spent under the shade of a tree or taking a nap. Karuna found it difficult to sleep in the afternoons and so she would wander out by herself. Until now her mind had been so completely absorbed in books, notes and shorthand that this was the first time that in their life devoted to their work that she began to reflect on it. She sat down on the grass, surveying the vast expanse of the land below. Although the Nandi hilltop was lush and placid, the land below was deadening, the dull sameness devoid of any beauty. The small manmade lakes below sparkled in the sun like silver foil and near them were clustered small villages with dirty, white walls and roofs covered with burnt, red tiles. There was a point in the distance where the air was so clear and pure that it appeared as if the tips of the hills were purple and blue, merging into the horizon. Despite this row of small hills, the impression was one of monotony, of oppressing silence, the pain of nothing.

As she sat like this, she remembered her parents. Her mother had been eager to see her married and settled and looked forward to playing with her grandchildren. Now she and father were dead and she had none but Rao who could lay claim to her love and whom she could regard as her own. Even Ajit had stopped writing, but this had not disturbed her as she had been too busy to notice. Ceylon, home, was no longer and she had found a new life elsewhere, an intellectual life, devoted to research. Although Rao joked with her and talked to her with intimacy, though their relationship had gradually formed into a physical one as well as an intellectual one, she knew that he would never descend from the heights of scholarship. She had grown so accustomed to this life that she did not even wish for any other and yet she felt the need for a relationship rooted in personal affection, perhaps even love.

In the past she had dreamed of being the mother of a living child, the fruit of her married life. Often she had yearned to hold her own child, to play with him but the overriding demands of her work had offered little scope for such dreaming and wishing. The idea was pushed out of her mind as an impossibility, no, an impracticality. Thus had passed ten years of her life.

Two months of leisure, of total relief from work, provided ample opportunity for reviving her maternal instincts and her motherly aspirations. Every day when she returned her child would be waiting for her! She imagined the child crying on seeing her! She imagined him feeding against her breasts and clasping him whilst, contentedly, he fell asleep. Her imagination worked to surround her with such pictures and illusions of motherhood. Of course, she would continue her work and she would appoint a nanny when she herself was busy pounding away on the typewriter. Maybe she would snatch a quick look at her baby's smiling face before going back to her work. Maybe she would go home before Raghappa brought the afternoon tea, would kiss and cuddle her child. When they went out for a walk after dinner, her child would be in her arms. If they sat down to talk anywhere, she could put the little one to sleep on her lap. He should be like Rao, imbibing his peaceful nature and ending up, also like him, a great scholar, turning out to be a distinguished historian.

Karuna felt her age close in on her for she was already thirty-seven. Had she married at the usual early age she would by now have been the mother of a twenty year old girl, perhaps even a grandmother.

"It is not too late. I should try to become a mother even now."

But she knew that the older the woman, the greater the problems of conception and delivery, the endangering of the mother's life. This thought hung in her mind and she visualised the eventuality of her dying in childbirth, lying down screaming with pain beyond her endurance. A nurse nearby was trying to console her, put courage into her. For two days she would so suffer, teetering between agony and death and then she held her fist tightly, as if clutching her very life and closing her eyes, she delivered her baby. She was lying unconscious, her breath shortening. Her heartbeat and pulse-rate were slowing down. The heartbeat tapered off to an eternal stillness and silence. She would die. My child? Karuna began to pray in her imagination.

"Oh, God. It doesn't matter if I die. Please save my child, keep him alive. Let him survive as a proof of my motherhood."

Who would take care of her child after if she should go? Nobody. But between life and motherhood, she had chosen the latter. A life without motherhood is more pitiable than death. She decided to tell her husband about her agony, but ashamed, did not for she feared that he, all that she had, would despise her weakness.

As they lay later together in bed, the cool hill breeze caressing them, Karuna asked her husband, "After death which legacy that a man could leave behind would give him the greatest satisfaction?"

Putting to use his historical knowledge, he answered, "Each individual human being is moved by an aspiration distinctive to himself or herself. Some are empire-building. Some devote their energies to constructing mighty temples. But very rarely does one find a person who wants to discover a new truth and spread it before he dies. But of course, the majority of mankind looks to the self, the family and children."

"Then do you regard the persons in the last category with contempt?"

"Of course not. I consider none as deserving contempt."

She didn't answer him, but held his hand as she lay, asking tentatively after a brief pause,

"Tell me. What is the progeny of our married life? What is it that we shall be leaving behind after death?"

"There is no doubt that anyone interested in human history will not ignore our volumes. No future Indian historian can take even one step forward without considering our work as a crucial starting point. Even now our work has gained universal recognition by scholars. What more or better legacy can we leave behind to the world and its cultural wealth?"

Karuna was silent. She was aware of the praise showered by the world on the volumes they had brought out so far and the universal respect commanded by them in the world of scholarship.

In her mind, there was no doubt whatsoever that their joint work would keep alive their name after their death for decades. She now felt proud that no children they could produce could hope to equal their scholarly account of man's cultural history. Rao had settled down to sleep, closing his eyes. No, she would ask him tomorrow. Lovingly, she stared into his face in the dim light; he was a kind man.

The next morning, they got up later than usual, full of an unusual spiritedness and now speaking to each other in a tone of intimacy they had never before employed. They held hands as they walked down the hill and the gentle warmth of the sun fell on their backs. A distance away were two small towns and as they had not ventured that far before, Karuna suggested visiting them. They reached the foot of the hill. The first place they touched was Sultanpet and after walking down its only street they went on to Nandigrama, where they visited the small, nondescript Bhoganandeeshwara temple. By half past ten they had finished their small tour and started their ascent of the hill.

The sun was scorching them from the left, a wild fireball revelling in its merciless intensity. After climbing up some hundred feet, Rao was tired and had to rest before continuing up the steep hill. But by the time they could negotiate half way, Rao again felt the strain. Dizzy, the sweat pouring in streams down his back, he clung to her. Lowering himself onto the step, he let his body go limp. Scared, Karuna placed his head on her lap and began to wipe away the sweat from his face and neck. She unfastened the buttons of the shirt and protected him from the glaring sun by screening his face with her sari. Rao was not unconscious but his heart-beat appeared to be faster and his breathing had yet to become normal. After five minutes he opened his eyes and saw her fear saying,

"Don't be frightened. I felt a little pain in the pit of my stomach. That's all."

The sun was growing sharper. Karuna carefully helped him stand up and walked him to the shade of a nearby tree where she made him sit. There was not a drop of water anywhere for him to drink. Down she went to the village and there in her broken Kannada engaged two strong palanquin bearers, agreeing to their demand for ten rupees. It was half past twelve by the time they reached their room. After a cooling bath and lunch, Rao rested but could not sleep as well as before. He tossed on the bed in pain and his head hurt because of being exposed to that beating sun. As the afternoon faded into evening, he began to run a temperature. When she felt his body and forehead, her concern grew into alarm but Rao re-assured her, "Don't be alarmed. The hill was too much for me. After all, I am forty seven."

In the afternoon mail, there was a letter for them. The markings on the cover indicated that it was a letter from London, addressed to Mysore and redirected from there. It was from the publisher who was pleased to inform them that commercial printing had now resumed and that the proofs of the third volume would be arriving shortly. Of course, they hoped that the fourth volume was progressing equally successfully.

It was happy news indeed and Rao seemed to be infused with a new vitality. In the afternoon he slept to regain his strength and Karuna went out to the gardens to sit on a bench in the shade of a tree. The engulfing space had been swallowed by the silence that surrounded her. In the distance she saw the same lakes, towns, hills that she had seen every day. In the afternoon heat, the sky stood above her head in a sultry silence and the atmosphere was one of introspection. Seriously and calmly, she started to think of her future. In three weeks, the proofs would start arriving from London and attending to this would consume all her time. After that, she had to prepare the index to the volume. Of course she would have to assist in the writing of the fourth volume. The collection of the material would have to finish within the next year and thereafter the long, laborious process of the writing, organising, re-phrasing and crystallising. An additional complication was that they now saw that the scope and size of the volumes would go beyond that which they had originally planned. They needed at least another eight years. The effect of the work was enormous and she knew that she had become physically less capable due to age and worry. Yet she was fortunate to have a tough constitution that had helped her to endure the work but that could not be said of her husband's physical capabilities.

"Will his body withstand the strain of this work?"

Suppose she were to become pregnant. Certainly she would not be able to work as much as now, and after the delivery she would need complete rest. The child would make his own demands. The voice of the imagination that had evoked the utter simplicity of a child's smile, the horror of dying in childbirth now told the mind, "He will die without finishing his work."

She could not believe that such a feeble voice could be so harsh. The honesty in it was impossible to ignore. Her face became worn out with worry and sorrow. Wrinkles appeared on her forehead, joining her eyebrows.

Yet, with pride, Karuna recalled her will-power, her capacity for unequivocal action. It was with such a will that she had sacrificed her native homeland, her parents, and her roots, to unite with him. Now it was this very same will-power and determination that showed her the way forward. The goal of their marriage should not go unrealised. She would see that he lived to finish his great work. Yet, when she remembered his emaciated body, she lost her courage and hope. His body had thinned out, there was no definition of muscles and it looked as light in weight as that of a child. His eyesight was failing.

"No, I shall be content with this. I shall give all my love, all my devotion, all my strength to the completion of his great project."

But even as she reached such a determination, her eyes were clouded with tears for her unrealisable motherhood. Her hands grasped her sides and then she brought them together pressing against her belly, as if she were stifling a child gestating there in her womb. Her body fell forward and she hid her face between her knees and sobbed loudly. For the last two days she had been dreaming and imagining her new life as a mother, and her body had acquired a new glow, a new vitality, because of that new desire and new hope. An undercurrent of a life-force that had been running parallel to her intellectual life had overtaken her, gaining an illusory strength, taking deep root in her being. Now she was required to nullify it, under her imagination, and revert to the old path, the old rhythm of life.

XVIII

The eight years of Katyayani's new life had brought about significant changes. Her husband's faith and love were enduring and there had developed no conflict or hostility with her new elder sister, Nagalakshmi. Yet, once one enters a new life, the old self cannot follow. After her final return from Nanjangud, Raja had advised her to study, to do her Honours and then a Masters degree. This Katyayani welcomed for she had discovered that the mind needs more than love. However, she found it embarrassing to study in the same university with her new identity, meeting the same students and teachers whom she had known before her new life had begun. At last she and her husband came to a decision: Raja must teach her at home for the M.A. degree of Benares University as a private candidate. Being an industrious receptive student, she did not find the task particularly difficult. After two years of such study, she took her M.A. degree.

When Katyayani went to Benares with Raja to take her final examination, she was carrying their child. As she had to concentrate on her work, a maid-servant was engaged to do the household work and Nagalakshmi continued to manage the kitchen. It was only when they were returning from Benares, after she had thankfully written the last paper, that Katyayani began to show concern for her future child. Raja was naturally enthusiastic. He had always had an instinctive understanding of children. Now Prithvi was a schoolboy and Raja missed childish laughter and games, the cry of a child begging to be taken for a bicycle ride. The feeling stronger, the pleasure deeper he told himself as it would be his own child. After their return from Benares, he kissed his wife's swelling belly, hoping to kiss the child growing inside, and would gaze expectantly at his wife's face. Understanding, she would embrace him as if he were her child. Every evening, she and Raja walked about two miles, a necessary activity as he was feeding her incessantly.

Even as the second child was growing within her, she would think back. Surely he must be studying in the Kannada primary school and his grandfather would be teaching him at home. Shrothri would be introducing him to the orthodox brahmin Sanskrit lore, learning by heart the sacred *slokas* and the countless stanzas in praise of God.

Then her mind would turn to the child inside. Would it be a boy or a girl? She had given birth to a boy already, and wished for a girl now. But she would be suddenly jolted from her dream-world, when she realised that her first son was no longer hers. The new family tree to which she was now grafted would also need a boy. Katyayani passed into the sixth month of her pregnancy. She was ordinarily a well-shaped, attractive woman and her new condition enhanced her, made her seem more beautiful, more fulfilled with the ripeness of motherhood. Absorbed in her new beauty, she would let her eyes roam over her body. Watching her do so, Raja recalled a time when they had taken Hunsur Road together, to the trees and plants around bursting with life.

Katyayani was in excellent health. Raja was away at college, which had just re-opened after the summer vacation. As usual the first rains of *Jyeshtha* had started. At this time, unknown to herself, her mind tended to plunge into turmoil. Indistinct pictures of what happened two years ago flashed in her memory - the full, flowing Kapila river, her desire to put an end to her life on its bank and Raja's arrival to take her away from there. The memory of Cheeni would also come before her. Suddenly she felt an acute pain in her stomach. In half an hour the pain became intolerable and fear built up inside her. The pain resembled what she had felt seven years ago. She told Nagalakshmi who phoned Raja and they went to the hospital. Nagalakshmi could not watch that agony. Katyayani's legs were splayed and she clutched at herself. Contractions and convulsions shook her body. Nagalakshmi placed her left hand on her shoulder while gently massaging her back and waist. This excruciating, hellish pain had been endured when Cheeni was born. The blood began to flow out and it took one hour to bring about a full abortion. Her body lay in a semi-conscious state, a strained face, wan and bloodless, her hair knotted and sticking to her temples. Her fingers were hanging limply, defeated. Her arms spread out and then drooped, hollow and gnarled.

After four days she recovered enough to talk feebly, but the doctor said that it would take another fortnight for her to be able to sit up. Therefore, Nagalakshmi would go home in the morning, cook the food, have her meal and return to the hospital with food for Katyayani. There she would spend the rest of the day and the night. A week after he lost his child, Raja went to the library to inform his brother. With some anger, Rao asked Raja why he took so long to do so and immediately he and Karuna hired a jutka and went to the hospital to see the patient. Karuna stayed for an hour, talking to Katyayani with her pleasing simplicity and affection. She understood and therefore did not attempt to console.

Afterwards Rao came to visit Raja at university. He pushed a cheque into his brother's hands. It was for a thousand rupees.

"Take good care of her. She is very weak and you should not want for anything."

Some time afterwards, Katyayani became pregnant again. She suffered her second miscarriage.

A year later, Raja was promoted to the position of assistant professor and was transferred to Bangalore. Although happy at the recognition, he was unhappy to leave behind the Drama Society he had built up so assiduously. Katyayani was enthusiastic, glad to go to a new place. Nagalakshmi accepted the shift passively and indifferently. As far as she was concerned, there was no difference between the two places, for her lot in life remained the same - working and cooking in the house and when not busy with it, writing out the name of Sri Rama. For the last two years the act of writing Rama's name had given her mind peace, and her anger against her husband had been diminished to such an extent that she was prepared to talk to him, should he ever visit. At home, Raja continued to treat her with the same respect and care. Katyayani showered affection on Prithvi and they took a special interest in his education. Yet, Nagalakshmi had started saying to herself, "When all is said and done, this cannot be my real household. My home is where my husband is. Even if he lives with her. I can do the cooking that I am doing here for him there."

When the whole household prepared to move to Bangalore and the day of departure approached, Nagalakshmi hoped that, at least now, her husband would come and see her. But he did not. Therefore, once settled in Bangalore, her work of writing the name of Rama resumed with the same zeal. In the last four years she had written the sacred name two million times, filling fifty notebooks. In the last page of every note-book she wrote, as a concluding piece, the Sanskrit verse which ran:

Bestower of every prosperity, the wind rising over every
mountain,
Incarnation of limitless compassion, I salute, Anjaneya!
Destroyer of all impediments, source of all wealth,
Lord Rama, Lokabhi Rama, I salute thee ever again!

The notebook would then be offered for worship by smearing it
with vermilion and turmeric powder, and placing it on a shelf near the
image of the deity in the prayer room.

"How many names would fifty notebooks cover?"

"Two million."

"How many more years are required to reach ten million names?"

"In four years, you have finished two million. If you keep up this
pace, you will finish in sixteen years."

"No matter what the cost or effort, I must finish ten million before
I die. Lord Sri Ramachandra, please grant me another sixteen years!"

Katyayani asked her, "What do you gain by simply scribbling the
name like this?"

"Sri Rama will grant me a better life at least in my next birth."

Katyayani recalled the story of Sri Rama. No doubt he was a
brave, heroic figure, capable of great self-sacrifice, but in the end,
fearing public censure, he deserted his wife.

His wife, Sita, was the very incarnation of purity, born of Mother
Earth herself. Katyayani did not approve of the latter part of the
story. She told Nagalakshmi, "Whatever you may say, I don't think
Rama was right to send a devoted wife like Sita to the forest in exile,
fearing public condemnation."

"Tut, tut. You shouldn't talk like that. Who are we to judge Sri
Ramachandra and find fault with his act? After all, he is God. Isn't
he all-knowing?"

The whole of Nagalakshmi's mind came to be filled with the
memory of her husband and she was as Sita, deserted and exiled by
her husband. Unlike Rama, however, her husband lived with another
woman and the fact that Rama had not done what her husband had,
increased her devotion to the God.

After Raja started teaching in Central College, a vacancy arose for
the position of a lecturer in English. This he suggested Katyayani fill.
At first, she was afraid of the job but was re-assured by the fact that

her husband was working in the same college and that too as an assistant professor. Raja wrote to his elder brother, suggesting that he should use his substantial influence with the university authorities. Katyayani was successful in her application and in her life she tried to forget the unwanted past. Soon their lives developed a new rhythm and a new routine. Raja started a Drama Society in Bangalore and, as in Mysore, it flourished, earning him immense popularity. As Katyayani was now working, Nagalakshmi had to shoulder most of the household work. Noting this and knowing that with a second salary the household income had increased, Katyayani suggested employing a cook. Her sister-in-law was not impressed.

"Before you came into this household as a bride, didn't I do all the work? It is no burden for me."

Four years had passed since Katyayani began working in Central College and teaching was no longer something to feel nervous about but merely happened. Very soon she became bored of her life, as she felt increasingly isolated, intensely lonely. Occasionally she remembered Cheeni and felt a powerful urge to see him. She was consumed with curiosity about him - would he still remember her? Did he ever feel like seeing his mother? Did he, once in a way, ask his grandfather about her? She thought he must be grown-up by now, tall like his father. Of course, the thread ceremony would have been performed when he was eight and by now he would be trained in the *Vedic* lore. She regretted that she had not made use of the opportunity to learn Sanskrit literature - the *Vedas* and the *Upanishads*, from her father-in-law. Her son would increasingly be called to her mind, she would build him up in her imagination and thus she escaped loneliness in the company of her imaginary yet real child.

In the meantime, the signs of pregnancy began to appear. Raja was delighted and this time swore to take no chances. A doctor examined Katyayani, recommending various tonics and pills and then as precautionary methods, a monthly testing of urine and blood and a weekly check-up were organised and paid for in advance. By the end of the sixth month, Katyayani's body began to glow, and her features acquired the shine and swell of a mango, filled with red, ripe fruit. Her body burst with the vitality that came from carrying within itself another growing life. She gazed at herself in the mirror. Along with the sheer joy produced by it, there was present a vague fear, shapeless and yet real. She felt unable to confront fully and directly the beauty of her still developing and ripening body.

This time they were not worried about what might be the gender of the coming child: they were more anxious that the mother and the baby should be back to the house after a safe and normal delivery. Each thought it but did not tell the other, each prayed silently. But Nagalakshmi warned them, "The eyes of people are not always benign and they may be casting evil. So when you go out, wear old saris in order to keep their eyes away from you. Evil eyes will fall on you if you dress attractively."

Suspicious and frightened, Katyayani followed this advice, and Raja too, accepted its wisdom.

She had just completed the sixth month of her pregnancy. One day Raja was busy lecturing his class when a peon handed him a note from Katyayani saying that she was in great pain. Dismissing his class, he hurried to the common room and rushed her to Vanivilas hospital. Even before they reached the hospital, that cruel pain had started and blood had started to flow and stain her sari. As they took her away, Raja knew what would happen.

After some two hours, the ward boys brought Katyayani on a stretcher and laid her on the bed. The nurse announced that until next morning nobody would be allowed the see the patient or talk to her. It took one day for Katyayani to regain full consciousness and when she had, another half-an-hour to comprehend what had happened to her in the past day. Then, in spite of her feeble body, she began to cry loudly. Nagalakshmi, who stood there dumb, began to hold Katyayani's head between her hands. A doctor motioned Raja to come out.

"There is no danger to life I hope."

"This time her life could be saved because you were able to rush her to hospital in time. If she were to become pregnant again, the same danger will persist. And next time, if this is repeated, the chances of her survival will be minimal."

Raja became pale. The doctor continued, "For the next twelve months she should totally abstain from sexual activity. It is not advisable for her to become pregnant again. I would advise you to undergo a vasectomy. How many children do you have now?"

"None, we are childless."

The doctor said sadly, "Well, you must make your own decision. We can't tell you what you should do or should not do. I have offered advice to the best of my ability and the decision must be yours."

Katyayani stayed in bed for a month after her return, subsisting on a daily regime of medicine, tonics and fruit juice. A doctor would visit to check on her progress. Once glowing, her face now resembled a mango after it had been squeezed of all juice. Once attractive, her fingers now looked like long sticks, so thin that her rings became loose. Her eyes had lost their lustre and dejection now slunk on her face. Even the hair on her head had shrunk to a handful. Except for the hours in college, Raja sat by her bed, abjuring his favourite theatrical activities. When he was away, Nagalakshmi would take his place. These days, Nagalakshmi performed the Sri Rama puja every Saturday and read the full story of Rama in Kannada. Sometimes she read out this story to Katyayani at her request, squatting on a low wood platform. Katyayani listened to it avidly, temporarily immersed in her own devotion to Rama.

Sometimes she would sink into her own thoughts, trying to make sense of her predicament, why that awful, unbearable thing had happened to her thrice. Her husband had taken every precaution possible, in addition to the expensive check-ups by a specialist doctor, and yet it had happened, when before, when she had given birth to Cheeni, it had not. Bhagirathamma used to give her some traditional herbal medicine she had learnt from her mother and that too only from the seventh month. Yet that delivery was a pain that was productive and creative.

Two days later Raja had passed on to her the advice given by the doctor, that her future pregnancies would be fraught with similar risk and danger, that her life would certainly be at stake. When she attempted to use the explanations she was accustomed to, her mind ran towards such ideas and accusations as sin and spiritual merit.

She had not married Raja to help him to perpetuate his lineage, at least not as an explicit purpose. Raja, too, had no such idea. Theirs was a union of mutual love which was limited to the idea that they could not live without each other. Perhaps that had set the limit to their marriage and its strength. They had joined each other as a response to the call of life - like *prakriti* and *purusha*. Yet wasn't it also natural that they should have aspired for the next goal, the goal of parenthood? He was obsessed with the desire to become a father. She was equally yearning for motherhood. But she did not subscribe to the idea of mothering a lineage. Rather she thought in the simple terms of being a mother of a new child and that meant the exclusion of the notions of motherhood, fatherhood and the lineage. Shrothri had told her that it was against the rhythm and rule of nature for experience which moves forward from stage to stage to regress to an earlier stage. In the process of progressive development, it is sin to revert to an earlier, already transcended stage. As a virgin and as a wife, she had had her first experience and bliss, and later attained motherhood. But then, later, she loved another person like a virgin maiden desiring his love and became his wife. Did it mean she could not become a wife or a mother to a new lineage?

"Are we joined in a marriage which is genuine or is this just an illusion of sin?"

She asked Nagalakshmi, "Sister, can you explain to me what sin is?"

"How should I know? You are an educated person. You should tell me."

"I don't know. Tell me what you think."

Without any deep or concerned reflection but basing herself on her simple faith and devotion, she answered, "It is sin to cause suffering to others, and it is sin to cast eyes of desire on what does not belong to us."

"Then does it mean that there are no other sins in the world besides these two?"

"How should I know such things?"

Katyayani considered this.

"Whom have I caused sorrow and pain till now?"

Sharply would be recalled the faces of old Shrothri and his old wife. Could it be that the old couple were now suffering acutely the loss of a daughter-in-law? Maybe it was her duty to serve the old parents-in-law. Another aspect of Nagalakshmi's answer would stab her sharply. She had said, "It is sin to cast eyes of desire on what does not belong to us."

After some two months Katyayani was able to rise from her sick bed and move about, did not have to sleep in the afternoon and took evening walks covering about a furlong. Prithvi was taking his high school examinations and she helped him with that, her health gradually returning. After another month she had to go back to work at college. Though her body did not glow with health as before, it started to look much better, the skin regaining its earlier tautness and shine.

When they were alone, Raja asked her, "Recently you have become stronger, don't you think?"

Understanding the undercurrent of affection beneath the words, she clasped him, entwining his neck with her hands, "Were you bored all these days?"

"No, no. Nothing like that."

"I understand. You need not lie to me."

Staring into his eyes, she continued, "It was marrying a person like me that brought you to this plight."

They remained silent for a time. She broke the silence herself, "Did the doctor advise you to do it?"

"To do what?"

"A vasectomy."

"Yes."

"Suppose I get operated instead of you?"

"There is no difference between the two."

His voice was weak with sadness.

The following day she went with her husband to the hospital. When he heard her suggestion, the doctor did not agree as Katyayani was still frail. It would take much time for her body to recover enough strength to undergo a sterilisation operation. The response from Raja was silence. What saddened him was not just the fact that it was dangerous to resume physical contact with her without an operation. No, it was rather the frustrating thought that even after all that they had suffered, they were doomed to a life of childlessness. Ten years ago, if anyone had mentioned the misery and misfortune of a couple without children, he would dismiss it with a laugh, considering it an obsession. Of course, he was immensely fond of children. He had always enjoyed playing with Prithvi. He used to think, "Why should one have to enjoy the company only of one's own children? Children of other people should do equally well for the purpose."

He asked himself now, "Why should I now feel dejected that my wife will never bear my children?"

Katyayani was tormented. Suppose, frustrated with her, he thought of another marriage? Such doubts often assailed her. How could one maintain with firmness one's status as a wife without the supplementary status of being a mother? One day the fear of her plight if he remarried became so over-powering that she burst into open sobbing.

Now Raja slept with Prithvi in the hall outside. Raja moved closer to the boy and held him tightly with his right hand and they both slept peacefully. He said to himself, "I am now thirty nine and middle age is fast approaching. How much longer should one attach oneself to a householder's life? If there was no chance of producing children, what is the point of maintaining a physical relationship with the help of such artificial aids as an operation? No, no operation is necessary. I shall embark on the life of a celibate. I shall not sleep with her, but spend the nights out here with Prithvi."

But two days later, he wavered, finding it difficult to keep to his earlier decision. He lost faith in his own natural qualities. Realising that it was impossible for him to abstain, he came to an ultimate decision with difficulty and a sense of failure, shamefully recognising his need. After the visit to the hospital, no rationalisation of the loss of an essential power and capacity could succeed in consoling him.

XIX

Shrothri, over the last eight years, was gradually withdrawing from the active life of a householder. The process had, in fact, started much earlier with Nanjunda's marriage, so that in time his son could take over the reins of management. The untimely and unexpected death of Nanjunda pulled him back into family life. Two years later he started to transfer his responsibilities to his daughter-in-law, but the hope that she would take over similarly collapsed. Now past seventy, Shrothri realised that it was only after his grandson grew up, married and assumed responsibility, that he could expect to retire. Therefore he detached his mind from the world and developed an attitude of indifference and uninvolvement. He even considered the idea of embracing a state of total disengagement from worldly affairs, accepting *sanyasa*. After so many years of involvement in family life, he now began to develop an intense desire to give up all attachments and emotional entanglements, spending his days in divine meditation. As a *sanyasi* he would wear an orange-coloured cloth, the only colour permitted, would live by begging, sleeping where he could, abjuring richness and comfort. In recent days, he had begun to read with keen interest detailed, ethical and religious works on *sanyasa*, *Sanyasopanishad, Vaikhanasa Sutra, Dharmasindhu* and *Jivanmukti Viveka* - all dealing with the rationale, purpose, modality and morals of living a life of renunciation.

Of course he knew it was a violation of *dharma* in his present position to desert his responsibilities and embrace *sanyasa*. *Dharma* required that *sanyasa* should not be undertaken until one had placed the family's dependants in a secure situation, taken their permission, and, if the spouse were alive, her consent. Now the grandson who was to carry on the name of the lineage was so young and it would take many more years before he could marry and begin to shoulder the responsibilities of the household. Bhagirathamma was sixty and he was sure that she would not permit him to enter into this fourth and last stage. He was aware that like all desires, the desire for *sanyasa* could also turn into an evil if carried to the point of a feverish pitch, undermining one's mental equanimity. *Sanyasa* was a form of formlessness, a state of neutrality and positionlessness. If one's mind became distorted and unhinged in its pursuit, that itself would constitute a severe hindrance for its attainment.

In the year the daughter-in-law left, his grandson started at the government primary school, and that was also the year in which the boy's tonsure ceremony was performed. Bhagirathamma was planning to celebrate the ceremony on a grand scale but finally it was a solely ritualistic affair without any suggestion of festivity. When the boy was eight, his thread-wearing ceremony was performed and this time Bhagirathamma was more enthusiastic and though Shrothri had no interest in social elaboration, he did not prevent her from inviting their friends and offering a sumptuous meal. For him the ceremony was simply to initiate the boy into the recitation of the Gayatri *mantra*, the thrice daily ritual of worshipping the Gods, the *sandhyavandana*, and imbibing the *Vedic* lore. On an auspicious day at the auspicious time, Shrothri sat the boy on his lap, covered his head, and whispered the Gayatri *mantra* in his ears. As the rite required, the novice had to go round with a begging bowl. Bhargirathamma was the first person to put alms in the boy's bowl. Smearing his forehead with sandal paste, wearing a cloth smeared with vermilion powder and yellow turmeric, Cheeni recited the Sanskrit formula of his lineage:

"Born of *Kashyapagotra*, and of the Naidrava lineage, professing Ashwalayana *sutra*, belonging to the Rig branch, grandson of Srinivasa Shrothri, son of Nanjunda Shrothri, I, Sri Srinivasa Shrothri, offer my obeisance..."

As the boy recited this before begging from the women, Shrothri became acutely conscious of his ancestry and felt proud of it. When his own name was recited as part of the illustrious lineage, he felt a surge of affection and pride.

The next day, Shrothri personally instructed and supervised his grandson's *sandhyavandana* ritual and the ritual of worshipping the god of fire. Since the boy had grown up in a Sanskrit, orthodox atmosphere, his tongue was fluent in chanting the sacred words. Every evening the boy recited and memorised the *Vedic* text and Shrothri would explain its meaning and significance.

Recently Bhagirathamma's health had begun to deteriorate. She no longer possessed her former physical strength and her daughter-in-law's desertion had sapped her mental reserves. Nowadays she slept in the inner courtyard. Next to her slept Cheeni and next to him Lakshmi. A little away from their heads slept Shrothri.

Bhagirathamma often remembered the daughter-in-law, and thought that she should have been with them to give them support in old age by shouldering all the responsibility. She should have taught Cheeni English, looked after the family affairs but no, she had to abandon this and flee. The old woman got angry, worked up inside herself, wondering whether God would grant Katyayani peace after death. At night she would express these pent-up thoughts to Lakshmi, sleeping next to her. But Shrothri would intervene.

"What has happened has happened. How often should I tell you not to rake up these old issues? Why should we worry about the punishments God awards others after death? If you go on repeating such things, would it not poison the boy's mind against his mother? There is no sense in worrying about these futile matters."

After that Bhagirathamma would become silent, and although she saw sense in her husband's words, once in a while her feelings burst out and she had to express them openly to Lakshmi. Lakshmi understood the old woman's anguish but neither supported nor condemned her words, tactically the perfect listener.

In time, Cheeni completed his middle school studies. He was an able and enthusiastic student whom his teachers had predicted would pass the examinations with a first class rank. Though growing up, Cheeni continued to sleep cuddled against his grandmother. Time was spent in school, studying Sanskrit with his grandfather or with his doting grandmother. It was she who fed him all sorts of news about the town and satisfied his boy's curiosity. He would ask her, "Why is it Grandmother, that Auntie Vasanti from Dr. Sripada's house brings biscuits for me whenever she visits us?"

Grandmother would answer, "Well, she has always been very fond of us."

Then he would ask, "Grandmother, is it true that in Chakrapani's house they hide their silver coins, burying them under the prayer room?"

Or, "Is it true that near the Parasurama temple there are seven cauldrons of gold coins guarded by a seven-hooded serpent?"

Or, "Last time, when we went to Hejjige, at Papayya's house they gave me a ball of butter and half a block of *jaggery*. Do they eat so much butter in their house every day, Grandmother?"

There was no end to the boy's curiosity as he rained his questions on her. Cheeni knew of his father's death because annually he performed the death anniversary. But he also knew that his grandfather performed his mother's death anniversary. Of course, he remembered that before his tonsure there had been a woman whom he called mother. But one day, during a quarrel with a playmate in school, the other boy taunted him, "Your mother ran off with some man and left you behind."

After returning home, he asked his grandmother, "Granny, Nani from the Agrabara said that my mother ran away with someone. Is it true?"

She replied sharply, "Because some fellow says something, you should not believe it and talk like this."

Cheeni was shocked and frightened by the anger in his grandmother's voice and from that day never asked anybody about it.

Around the time that Cheeni was in high school, his grandmother fell ill. Although she had had attacks of ill health before, this time she was bedridden. Shrothri administered Kashaya, a traditional herb potion, but it produced no result. On the third day, it was decided that the Pandit should be called in but he was out of town and would not return for another month. Bhagirathamma's temperature rose alarmingly. Her whole body was in pain. Soon Bhagirathamma's system refused to take even milk, and she began to vomit whatever was given to her. Frightened, Shrothri decided as a last resort to call the government doctor. Shocked, his wife protested, "I have never to this day let anyone belonging to another caste touch me. I shall never drink water from the hands of non-caste persons."

She was adamant and refused to allow her husband to leave the house the whole day.

But that night she lost her consciousness and Shrothri was at a loss as to what to do. Lakshmi had to rush to fetch the government doctor who came, examined her and gave her an injection, commenting that he had been called somewhat late. After the prescribed medicine had been brought from the small Nanjangud dispensary, they tried to administer it to her through a plastic teat. The old woman's lips were sealed together and after some time Shrothri did not try to push the medicine inside because, even in her unconscious state, she was refusing to take that which was given by a doctor of another caste. Three more days passed without treatment. Lakshmi and the young grandson were exhausted, their faces slumped and wan. But Shrothri was already ahead of time as he inwardly prepared himself for yet another stage in his life. Gently he recalled fifty years of his life with Bhagirathamma - how she had arrived as a bride, how they agonised over the lack of children, the birth of a son, his grim determination to lead a life of celibacy, the old woman's careful and devoted rearing of the grandson after the daughter-in-law had left. Bhagirathamma was a good woman who never wished ill of anybody, who tried to help others as much as she could. But she was by no means a person who had conquered anger and other baser instincts. Shrothri had made ample allowance for this. Until she became bedridden, she had served her husband with exemplary devotion.

"In this householder life, what more should one expect from a wife?"

Around midnight she began to mumble incoherently about Cheeni. Cheeni was terrified by the eerie scene of these disjointed, disordered words pouring out of his grandmother's mouth in her unconscious state and in the dead of the night. Lakshmi looked into Shrothri's face and he stared back dumbly for he sensed that the patient had realised the inevitability of her fate. Her breathing lost its rhythm and from this, Shrothri estimated the time of her death. He went to the prayer room and brought out the vessel in which the sacred water of the Ganga had been preserved. Slowly he poured the water into his wife's mouth. Ganga flowed into the dying body and then half an hour later that body itself stopped. As Shrothri took his fingers away from under Bhagirathamma's nostrils, Lakshmi began to sob loudly. For forty five years the old lady had fed Lakshmi, had shared in every happiness and misery and once a long, long time ago had even desired her husband to experience that pleasure that she, his wife, could not give him. Later, when Shrothri had gifted away two acres for Lakshmi, the old lady had given her unqualified approval. Shrothri turned to Lakshmi saying, "Men are destined to die one day or other. You have forgotten it."

But even as he said this, he felt a lump in his throat. He continued in a sorrow laden voice, "None can escape anguish. We must learn to bear it."

In the slow, gentle dawn people gathered from the neighbouring houses. Someone went off to fetch the wood. Someone looked to the arrangement for a cart. Soon the ritual fire was blazing. The news spread throughout the small town. Women and children poured in to get a last glimpse of Shrothri's wife. The dead body was lifted and taken to the cremation ground. When he had to pour grains of rice into his grandmother's mouth, Cheeni felt dizzy and clasped at her body. Starting from the seventh day, Bhagirathamma's death ceremony was performed strictly in accordance with the ritual requirements.

Shrothri's household underwent a dramatic change. Although the old man rose at the same time, he cut down the time he spent worshipping and meditating in the prayer room. There was the child's milk to boil and the food to prepare. Although Lakshmi continued her servant duties, another person was engaged to ease her burden. As usual, Cheeni had his evening sessions in learning the *Vedic* lore and though the grandfather urged the boy to go out to play on Sundays, the boy would not, remaining at home to help the old man in his tasks. The young boy's face now showed unnatural gravity and sometimes emptiness. This prompted Lakshmi to suggest to Seenappa that in four or five years time they should think of Cheeni's marriage.

"These days, is it possible to marry one so early?"

Lakshmi would respond, "Why not? How old were you at your marriage? Times might change but our boy will obey our wish."

XX

Katyayani tried to control her mind and she studiously avoided being alone. Every evening she went out with Raja for a walk and as in the early days of their marriage, they often went to the cinema. Under Nagalakshmi's benevolent guidance, she would take a greater interest in her household chores and would cook delicacies and sweets of every kind. Every Saturday she would be a willing participant in the elaborate Sri Rama worship. Yet, no matter how she tried, she could not forget either her three unborn children, nor Cheeni. Often she wondered in which class he would now be studying and whether he remembered his mother. If he had ever asked his grandmother about his mother, there would be nothing surprising if he were told, "Your mother is a bad woman. She ran off with some man and left you behind."

Would he recognise her if she passed before him? He had last seen her when he was a five year old child. He was sure of receiving the endless love of his grandparents.

All her love became relentlessly focused on Prithvi. Whenever she went shopping with Raja, she would come back with something for the boy, a bat and ball or new clothes. She saw to it that the child dressed properly before going to school and took an interest in his studies, helping him with the lessons that he found difficult and even those that he found easy. Prithvi adored his aunt and yet he sometimes felt inhibited, his feelings towards her a mixture of fear and devotion. When she scrubbed his back after an oil massage he found it embarrassing. Instinctively, he would shrink from her and she would have to hold him with a firmness verging on force.

After his operation, Raja too began to centre all his affection and attention on Prithvi. The sixteen-year-old boy was entrusted with the management of the house, including the finances, and in fact had access to the steel wardrobe in which the cash and valuables were kept. Every day Raja would eat his meals with the boy, addressing him, not as Prithvi, but as "Child". Katyayani understood her husband's feelings, and felt no sense of jealousy, only a deep sorrow that they could not realise their natural desire.

In spite of her normal working life, her daily walks, Katyayani never regained her former physical form and elan. Her reddish-white complexion was now a pallid milk-white. Gone were the fresh glow of the body and the physical vibrance. To please Raja she took the tonics that were prescribed by the doctor but left to herself they would have stagnated on the shelf.

The summer holidays came, the heat intensified and the sameness of life continued. That evening the college peon came at five and gave Raja a telegram which he informed him had actually arrived the day before but since it was addressed merely to Raja and not Raja Rao, some confusion had arisen. The message was clear, and it read, "Your brother and his wife are seriously ill. Come immediately - Raghappa."

As Raja stared at the telegram, dazed, Katyayani ran to hire a taxi to take them there as soon as possible.

Nagalakshmi was adamant, stoutly refusing to go to Mysore.

Raja tried to persuade her.

"The telegram is dated yesterday. God knows what might have happened by now. Nagu, you shouldn't talk like this, not now, not when things have come this far. After his death, will you be able to see him again? Will you find him there to be served by you?"

Wiping her tears, she silently nodded her consent. It had been ten years since her husband had moved away from her with a second, educated wife. She recalled his efforts to talk to her even after the second marriage, her repulsing of him and finally his total breach with her. Rao used to despatch the volumes of his work to Raja as they came off the press. The three fat volumes were kept in a row in a prominent place in the hall, three huge books, hard bound with her husband's name embossed in gold on the front cover. Raja used to show them off to visiting friends, saying with unconcealed pride, "These are my elder brother's works!"

Inwardly Nagalakshmi too felt proud. Raja tried to explain to her how the new wife was helping her husband in his scholarly endeavours. Initially she had not attached any significance to such explanations, resorting to the ritual of writing out the name of Rama. In time her thinking had become calmer, changing to such an extent that she was even prepared to live with him and his new wife if only he openly asked her to do so. But her husband never came to invite her. She said to herself, "Had I been there, I would have looked after them well."

She trembled and her heart beat faster. She offered a prayer to her Rama silently. "Sri Rama, spouse of Janaki, protect them and see that no ill befalls them."

Prithvi remembered his father as a man with white hair and spectacles with a red frame. He also knew that his father had married another woman besides his mother in order to write a book and that the woman was his student. He wondered why his father had deserted his mother and in seeking the answer he would compare his teachers in school with his father. Of course, his father would be better as he was a great scholar, Uncle Raja had declared that so many times. But why did such a great person marry a second time? Yet his uncle had enormous respect for his father, and hence he must be a good man.

As the car pulled into the professors' quarters at quarter past eight, they were greeted by a distraught Raghappa. As she crossed the threshold, Nagalakshmi experienced a peculiar sensation, the feeling of being a stranger in her rightful place. Inside the bungalow she found unfamiliar furniture, and all the doors of all the rooms were open. Everywhere there were books piled up and manuscripts scattered. In one corner, a typewriter rested on a table. On another table were kept his volumes. The walls were white and blank with not a picture hanging from them to break their monotony. There was no sign of the floor ever having been decorated with *rangavalli* designs. No door was decorated with the auspicious buntings of mango leaves.

By the time they reached the hospital, the doctors had finished the night rounds and only the nurses were left to look after the patients in the special ward. They obtained the doctor's express permission and entered the special ward which provided each patient the luxury of a single room. Rao was lying on a bed, sleeping on a white bedsheet, covered with a red blanket. There was a small stand next to the bed on which were placed medicines and a glass of water. From it hung the board containing the patient's medical notes. Beneath the bed in a corner was a bed pan. Near the door stood a chair for the nurse. Rao's face was smothered with a dying forest of hair and the eyes looked strange and weak without his glasses. His eyebrows were sickly and bleached. Though he was unconscious his breathing was normal. Leaving Nagalakshmi and Prithvi with Rao, Raja and Katyayani went to visit Karuna.

Nagalakshmi was aghast at her husband's condition. After Raja left, she could not control her sobbing, and started to cry loudly. A nurse approached her, requesting her not to disturb the patient and then asked her, "Who is he to you, madam?"

"He is my husband."

"Isn't the lady in the female ward his wife?"

When Raja and Katyayani went to her room, Karuna had just recovered consciousness, but even so she was unable to recognise them. The doctor explained that there had been an influenza epidemic in the town and indeed it was still raging. The Professor and his wife, their resistance low, had fallen prey to this. The family doctor saw them and apparently they were recovering, the doctor warning them however to take every precaution as full rest was essential in the post-recovery stage. Ignoring the advice, they had resumed their project. Three days later the fever returned in the night. When the doctor returned in the morning, they were both semi-conscious.

"Now there is no real danger. Once your brother wakes, you need have no fear."

A day after he regained his consciousness, Rao was able to recognise people, though not to talk to them. As he turned his eyes to the floor, Rao found Nagalakshmi squatting there, on a low wooden platform. Nagalakshmi felt his eyes flicker open, trying to focus on something. There was no-one else in the room. Nagalakshmi turned round to check, but no, the nurse had gone into another room and could be heard gasping out her gossip. So she concluded, he must be looking at her. Rao wanted to speak but he was too feeble to do so. Nagalakshmi was a mixture of anger and shyness, each one pulling in different directions and she felt helpless caught between contradictions. For nearly half an hour, she just sat there, her head bent low. But after that some inner force transcending the conflicting feelings gave her the strength to lift her head. But by then the patient had closed his eyes and gone to sleep.

Disappointed, Nagalakshmi got up and stood close to him, placing her hands lightly on his shoulders, and bending low, gazed into his face. He was not fully asleep. At one point, the rhythm of his breathing changed and he appeared to be waking up from his slumber. Quickly, she pulled her hands back and returned to her original spot where she squatted as before, her head bent low. For the next two days, she continued to stare at him, narrowing her eyes.

Day merged unnoticed into night and in the early hours of the morning there was nothing but the snores of the night duty nurse asleep on the veranda and the sterile dim light cast by the electric bulb. Unable to sleep, Nagalakshmi rolled on her mat on the floor. Once, when she lifted her head, she found Rao's eyes trained on her with profound intensity. Again, she lowered her head. In a feeble, hardly audible voice, he mumbled, "Na... gu."

It took her by surprise and she was not sure whether she actually heard him utter her name or whether it was an illusion, a hope played out by her own mind but it filled her with joy. Again, the same feeble voice called the same name. Now all the complications contorting her mind, all the contradictions dissolved, melted into an endearing call. She got up and went near him. Rao moved his hand slightly and placed it in hers. The fringes of his eyes were wet with tears. Unable to control herself, she broke into loud weeping. Rao was too weak to pacify her with words. She got hold of herself and covered his face with her sari. Then, holding his hand, she sat by his side on the bed. Neither spoke for he was too weak and she too overcome.

Within four days, Rao had recovered enough to be able to talk. The doctor advised Nagalakshmi to go home as the worst was over but she had turned her nose up at this and ignored it. Now she administered the medicine to Rao at precise intervals, changed his clothes deftly, emptied his bed pan. When no-one was about, she held his hand.

"But why did you desert me like that? Of course, I have had no problems there, in Bangalore. Raja is more fond of me than before, and Katyayani treats me as her elder sister. But would that make up for a life without you? No matter what you do, can I ever get the contentment and peace that I shall get by cooking your food and serving you? Well, you married her but who can look after your health as I can? That Raghappa may be a good and honest man, but he cannot cook. If the food had been tasty, you would have eaten more. Your health would have been better."

And a lump hurt in her throat. Nagalakshmi entreated, "Even now will you accept my suggestion?"

"Tell me."

"I shall live with you. She will stay with us. After so many days and with so little time left, I shall not mind the way you both live. Raja says that she helps you in her own way. Would you agree?"

By the time she finished her proposal, her eyes had welled up with tears for she sensed that she was outlining her new role as a person, reaching a new stage in her life, sacrificing something essential to her dignity.

Rao's heart broke within, his chest constricted and his breathing became heavier. He remembered his own past, starting with life as an orphan in his maternal uncle's house to their boyhood days. When he married her, Nagalakshmi was a slip of a girl, and with what organisation and confidence she ran the new household in Mysore! With a tender, ever-smiling face she would carry out the household chores, and with what economy she managed his meagre salary, so well as to set by some money for his books. And how solicitously she looked after her husband as if he were a child. Over the last ten years he realised the preciousness of what he had lost. Now that same preciousness had returned to him of her own accord, in search of him. He was overwhelmed by gratitude. Holding her hand, he said, "Yes. We shall do as you say. If I have erred, forgive me."

Within a week, Rao and Karuna were discharged from hospital and shifted home. While they had been ill, the copies of the fourth volume had arrived. Relaxing in a chair, Rao took a copy and began to turn its pages one by one but he was looking at the pages neither with full attention nor with any clear, definitive intention. It was more a mechanical gesture of habit, something done in the absence of serious study. He had dedicated the third volume to the memory of the late Maharaja and the fourth was to be dedicated to Srinivasa Shrothri of Nanjangud. Gradually the rough outline of the volume took some organised form within his mind.

The guests from Bangalore - Raja and the others - were still there with them. Nagalakshmi organised the cooking so well that Raghappa and Karuna could only look on in shame and delight. She served the whole family. Karuna and Nagalakshmi exchanged not even a single word. Nagalakshmi never left her kitchen fortress and Karuna never entered it, imprisoned in her study room, checking the notes she had typed out earlier for the fifth volume, now under planning and preparation. Sometimes Rao came there and they discussed the source material and content of the fifth volume. Nagalakshmi had vowed not to speak to her husband unless he came to the kitchen to talk to her but as her cooking built up his strength, he spent his time increasingly on his fourth volumes. Also, he had little time for Prithvi so Raja gave the boy ample money to go sight-seeing. Karuna noted how well dressed the boy was, wearing clothes more expensive than that of his fastidious uncle and how much he resembled his father, the same stance, the same eyes and nose, and was saddened.

Rao and Karuna took their evening walk, slowly, for it was the first time that they had done so for almost two months.

"I want to ask you about something."

"What is it?"

She sounded half enthusiastic, half resistant.

"This time when they go back to Bangalore, let us ask Nagalakshmi to stay back."

Karuna's face was sober and thoughtful. Trying to read her mind from her face, Rao continued, "This time it was she who served me during my illness. She will not show any jealousy towards you even if she were to stay here with us."

Rao grabbed her hand.

"Instead of Raghappa's food, we can enjoy her food. Once we entrust our health to her, we will be free to concentrate on our writing work. Moreover it would probably be a moral lapse on my part to leave her alone like this."

Karuna did not dislike Nagalakshmi, nor was she jealous of her. In fact she had compassion for her, sympathy for a woman who had married before her husband's understanding had matured and who suffered separation from her husband through no fault of her own. Karuna wanted from her husband an altogether different kind of relationship and she had it to her satisfaction. She had no objection to any kind of help Rao wanted to extend to Nagalakshmi but she had set her face against any arrangement in which one husband and two wives lived under a common roof. In her long study of Indian history she had come across cases of bigamy and polygamy and no matter how accommodating the wives turned out to be, they could not overcome normal human nature, filled with jealousy, enmity and insatiable desires. Her own first-hand experience of European family life had shown her that when a husband or wife found it impossible to be together, they resorted to divorce and started their marital life with a more compatible companion. It was not merely a matter of legality but it was part of their culture and social norms.

"Why are you silent? Please say something."

She emerged from her thoughts and replied slowly, "I had never asked you to neglect her. Even now you can live with her in a separate house or both of you can stay in this house and arrange a small house for me elsewhere. You can stay here. The important thing is that the purpose for which we married should not suffer. I can endure living away from you as long as our work progresses."

"Can you live only for work and abjure our natural marital life?"

"Yes, I can."

She said it too quickly, her voice shaking.

He extended his trembling hands to catch hold of her right hand. Tears were collecting in the corner of his eyes.

"Why this stubbornness?"

"No, it is not stubbornness. Inside, I could never accept bigamy. We came together for a specified and limited purpose and I care only for its realisation. It is my good fortune to be part of that purpose. Of course, in these years of life together, we have been more than partners in scholarship. We have grown into each other emotionally. But no, you should set up two homes. Live there and visit me. I shall have no jealousy."

The whole night, Rao thought over the matter, seeing it from different angles. There were just three days left before Raja and his family were to leave for Bangalore. Nagalakshmi was expecting and hoping that Rao would come to her and reiterate his need for her, telling her to stay behind. The future was harsh, a life without Raja, Katyayani and Prithvi, a life in which her husband would spend his life with another woman, absorbed in his work, leaving her alone. However, she consoled herself that even there she could continue her project of writing the name of Sri Rama and she would spend her time in their service. Her husband said nothing. Her pride and modesty balked at the thought of questioning him directly. Finally, she asked Raja when alone, "Did your elder brother say anything?"

"About what?"

"No, nothing really."

She said nothing more, and did not explain, even when Raja asked her about it again. The day before they were to leave, Nagalakshmi could not sleep. However much she tried to suppress them, the tears caught the back of her eye-lids. However, she brushed them away before anybody would notice. After a sleepless night, she got up early and cooked breakfast. Their train was in the morning and the taxi ordered the night before drew up in front of the bungalow. Raja put the luggage in the car and he, Katyayani and Prithvi waited for Nagalakshmi. As Nagalakshmi slowly came out, Rao was standing near the small garden gate. Calmly, she walked forward, bent down and bowed to her husband respectfully. Neither Rao nor Karuna came to the station. Only when the taxi had started, did Rao lose his control and wipe the tears from his eyes. As the speeding vehicle made the bungalow vanish from sight, Nagalakshmi started sobbing loudly. Katyayani, sitting next to her, took hold of her hand and said, "Sister, console yourself. The work for which we came has been done."

"But, he forgot the promise he had made, forgot the words he had spoken!"

XXI

Rao felt ecstatic that, at the age of forty-nine, he was able to bring out the fourth volume of his ambitious historical project. There was but one last volume to write. The material collected for all the volumes was so great that he toyed with the idea of using the unused material for writing three or four smaller volumes. For instance, the material for the fourth volume was so extensive and so original that the publishers had suggested that the material not included could form the basis of another separate work. Although Rao had not been to Nanjangud for the past ten years, he nevertheless dedicated the nine hundred page fourth volume to Srinivasa Shrothri as an act of gratitude and remembrance for the old man's assistance and scholarship. As he had once done, he wished to visit Nanjangud to present a copy. Additionally, there was also some clarification he required from Shrothri regarding the review of the third volume by a German professor who had questioned the veracity of some of its statements.

Initially, Rao was worried about the possibility of facing Shrothri's hostility as his younger brother had loved and married a Shrothri daughter-in-law. Although his own knowledge of the old man's nature and philosophy assured him that Shrothri would not behave that way, he had seen that throughout history men had behaved unpredictably under pressure. He had no idea of the origin and development of the Raja and Katyayani episode. When they married, he and Karuna were in Calcutta and it was only after his return that the two had come to receive his blessing. Like the historian that he was, Rao arrived after the drama had enfolded and all he could do was to acquiesce in its existence. He wondered whether he would have prevented it had he ascertained its progression. Perhaps. Due to his profound respect for Shrothri, he would have explained the effect it would have on the household and then Rao would have left the decision to the persons concerned.

Rao wrote a letter to Shrothri, asking whether it would be possible for he and Karuna to call on him. She too, was eager to see Shrothri. A reply came three days later. With his natural courtesy, Shrothri welcomed the visit, writing:

"I am in the grip of old age. Can there be any greater fortune for me than the company of such distinguished scholars? Please, do come."

The train took them past Chamundi Hill, over the river Kapila and when they reached Nanjangud station, they hired a coolie to carry their books. As they walked to Shrothri's house, Rao explained the historical significance of the town, pointing out various buildings and houses with his right hand, carrying their small suitcase in his left. They arrived at Shrothri's neat, white house but the door was strangely and inhospitably closed. The second time they knocked however, the door was opened by a teenage boy, who led them into the front hall. A few minutes after the boy left, Shrothri came out, joining his palms in welcome. Ten long years on, Shrothri's head was virtually bald, his face covered by a white beard. As always he was wearing a hand woven, white dhoti with an auspicious red border and a blue shawl over his shoulders. His forehead was covered with wrinkles but his teeth were intact. Although he had hurried out to meet them, they saw that he stooped perceptibly as he walked. Shrothri was most solicitous towards his guests, telling Cheeni to put their luggage upstairs, bidding them wash the dust from their hands and feet and offering them fresh milk.

After they sat down in the hall upstairs, Rao took out the four volumes and set them down in front of his host and mentor.

"These are the fruits of your blessing."

Shrothri picked up each volume, relying on his scant English to make out the title, the author's name and the publisher. On the first page of each volume, there was an inscription in Kannada, "To revered Srinivasa Shrothri, with devotion - Sadasiva Rao." But when Shrothri opened the second page of the fourth volume, he was surprised by what he saw. Though he could not make out three or four words, he could read the dedication in thick letters,

"This volume is dedicated to revered Srinivasa Shrothri of Nanjangud, with utmost gratitude."

Shrothri put his finger on the dedication and exclaimed, "This is the one thing you should not have done."

"But why? You had offered substantial financial support in the writing of the volume. With your profound learning you enriched my knowledge but above all, your blessings inspired me and enthused me in this work. Who else but you should be remembered in its dedication?"

Shrothri replied slowly, "Where is the need to dedicate it to anybody? It was God who inspired you to write a work like this and it was the same God who inspired other people to come to your aid. It was my fortune that He prompted me to be one of them. Is it not our *dharma* to offer a flower in your worship of knowledge? Why should we be thanked for doing our duty in accordance with *dharma*?"

Rao did not know what to say. For the next ten minutes Shrothri turned the pages of the huge book. Then, turning to Karuna, he asked, "Can you follow our conversation?"

Karuna stared at him blankly and Rao, having concluded with relief that Shrothri must know about his second marriage, answered on her behalf.

"Not very well. Following the tone and tenor, she can grasp the general sense but she has picked up enough to handle the servants at home."

Then Shrothri said, "Please, rest. I shall leave you now."

It was his time for worship.

Rao gave a summary of the conversation in English to Karuna and after that they spent the remainder of the afternoon and the early evening studying the books and palm-leaf manuscripts in the study.

At eight in the evening, Shrothri called them for dinner. Three leaves were spread in the kitchen and the old man asked his grandson to sit for the meal.

"Are you not eating?" enquired Rao, puzzled.

"No, I shall serve you."

"But, where is the mistress of the house?"

"I shall tell you later."

The strangeness of the situation haunted Rao. Furthermore, he was embarrassed that a seventy year old person should be serving them. The old man appeared to find nothing amiss and conversed lightly and easily with his guests as if nothing had changed at all, as if the mistress herself would appear at any moment, offering the hospitality of the house. The food was simple, steaming and delicious.

An hour after dinner, Shrothri joined his guests in the hall. Before that, Cheeni had placed there a plate containing betel-nuts, leaves and lime paste. Rao asked, "Don't you take betel-nuts and leaves?"

Shrothri replied, "No. I gave up long, long ago. Moreover, I am no longer a full householder."

"Why? What happened?"

"Two years ago. What else could be the reason? Old age. She was sixty. These days, the traditional blessing, 'May you live for a hundred years,' is a mere saying."

He smiled.

Rao was saddened. Had it been anyone else, he would have ventured to offer some consolation but he was unable to offer that to the old man before him, so superior in age, knowledge and wisdom. Now it was he who changed the subject.

"We shall be here for four days. We find it embarrassing when you cook, for it should be our duty to serve you. My wife is of a different religion. If you give us a few pots and some rice and *dhal*, she will cook for me and for herself."

"Do you think I am cooking especially for both of you? We all have to eat. All I do is add a little more rice and a little more *dhal*. And that's all the cooking I do! How can that cause trouble to this old fellow? Please don't feel embarrassed."

They became immersed in a serious, scholarly discussion which continued until midnight. As the small hours of the morning drew closer, Shrothri himself led them upstairs where Lakshmi had made up their beds.

Thus four days were spent in such a manner and during this time Karuna's respect and regard for the old man grew. Impressed with the way he carried the burden of old age, with dignity, with nobility, she tried to compare him to other people she had seen; her father, her professors in Ceylon and in England. Shrothri, however, set himself unconsciously apart. His unusual personality overwhelmed her. To find a parallel to him, she had to go to the ancient Indian texts - the *puranas*, the epics. Her historical mind turned to Bhishma, who had taken a vow of celibacy to allow his father to marry a fishergirl and who had always striven to uphold the tradition and dignity of his Kaurava clan; to Vasishta, one of the seven great sages from whom *dharma* was given its form; to Yudishthira, the eldest of the Pandava brothers who was obedience itself. Again Karuna looked at Shrothri. His daughter-in-law had deserted him by marrying Rao's brother and it was through Rao that the brother had been introduced to her. Yet, the old man did not show a trace of anger or hostility over Rao's action or inaction.

Whilst engrossed in discussion, the Sanskrit *slokas* flowed freely from his mouth and the very manner in which he enunciated the words, stressing some and separating the syllables of others, brought out fully their meaning and implication. As Karuna could not understand the deep and difficult discussions which followed in Kannada, she listened to the man and not to his words. Though past seventy, his face glowed with radiance. Every gesture, every action represented the essence of an ancient culture and its tradition of courtesy and consideration for others. Whenever he had any doubts about any matter, he picked up the original text in his study to clarify it, his study overflowing with printed books and palm-leaf manuscripts of texts on *Dharmasastra, purana, tattvasastra*. Often he carried on the discussion in fluent Sanskrit with incredible ease and grace. Karuna was impressed by his presence, his immense learning and overpowered by his profound humility.

After the discussions came to an end, Shrothri would head towards the kitchen in order to prepare the meal. Rao would give Karuna an English summary of the talk which, compared to the stature, the eloquence of the old man, appeared deficient, almost distasteful. But, Karuna dutifully took down the summaries in shorthand. Shrothri's comments on the German reviewer's criticism, backed up by the original texts, supported Rao's position and provided substantial material to produce a paper out of it, vindicating his stand.

The thought that had once assailed him ten years ago and which had somehow got lost somewhere in the middle of his research, now fully entered his mind. Rao realised that, though Shrothri lost his wife due to the natural process of old age, he would not have been subjected to so much hardship if his daughter-in-law were still living with him. But then Shrothri was so constituted that he would not regard any burden as a burden at all. His essence was resilience and resourcefulness. Rao had observed Cheeni carefully. The young boy was tall and sturdy like his grandfather, had a broad face in which were set eyes that sparkled. Yet, the boy had developed a gravity of manner, unnatural and undesirable for his age. The old man and the boy were relaxed in each other's company but the strange situation in that household had produced in the boy an unusual degree of stand-offishness and seriousness.

Rao thought, "Poor Raja had no idea of the situation in this household. In fact, it was through me that Katyayani visited our home and met him. And this is how it all ended! But I had no idea of the beginning of the affair. I was too absorbed in my own work. My life took a new turn. I wasn't there when they got married."

Rao felt that had he been aware of the situation, he could have offered some advice and as he had not done so, he decided to ask for Shrothri's forgiveness.

The day before they were to return to Mysore, in the evening Rao and Shrothri went for a walk, past the temple and reaching the steps of Manikarnika bank. After the fury of *Jyestha* and *Ashadha*, the river was flowing sedately, a half moon afloat in the waters. The banks that rose up on either side watched the movement of the river warily. On the far bank the paddy crops, moulded into the earth over the centuries, stretched for miles and miles. The crop swayed gently, the darkest of greens, giving a sense of a dreamy infiniteness. To the right lay the Nanjundeswara temple, a vast, silent structure creating a white island in the ever-reflecting moonlight. The gold capped tip of the temple reached out into the heavens. Rao and Shrothri sat close to each other on one of the steps, silently watching the water below.

"What is the matter?"

"It is difficult to express."

"Please try."

"My brother's marriage and how it all originated - I did not know anything about it. Maybe if I had known I would have intervened. Your daughter-in-law belongs in this household. I beg you, on his behalf, to forgive him."

"Why are you saying this? Where is the need for anyone to forgive anyone, and for what great crime?"

"You look at everything from your noble eyes, seeing good everywhere, but now, in the circumstances, your daughter-in-law should have been here with you."

"If things always happened as we wish, how could we call this our world?"

Shrothri spoke in a calm tone. Then he continued, "It would have been good if my wife were alive. Even better if my parents were alive! But everyone stays with us only as long as mutual debts are discharged, not a moment longer. After that, they must go away from us. While some move away from us after death, others move away from us even when alive. These things should be accepted and one should never feel sorrow because of them."

"Did you never feel hatred or contempt for your daughter-in-law?"

"Why should I?"

Then he smiled gently, and continued in the same placid voice, "Once our relations of mutual indebtedness were finished, my son drowned in the river and went away from me. For the same reason, my wife died after an illness. How can I show them contempt or resentment? In my eyes their going away after death and my daughter-in-law going away while alive are identical events. She too left us for the same reason. And how can you blame her?"

"At least for the sake of the child." Rao interrupted.

Shrothri said, "Yes, you are right. When we see things through the eyes of a child, we sorrow. But do you mean to say that she felt no anguish when she left the child of her womb? Yes, she felt immense grief at leaving her child. But, then, the natural force was more powerful than grief, it governed her behaviour. Don't we call nature, *prakriti*, an illusion, *maya*? We live in this world subject to nature and its *dharma*. Is it an easy task to live here and yet escape the power of nature? It is not surprising that she succumbed to it. Why should we condemn her for that?"

Of course, Rao was familiar with this philosophical understanding. But what he now encountered was an old man who tried to live according to such understanding. His respect and admiration for the old man increased.

"Don't you ever think about your daughter-in-law?"

"What is the point of endlessly mulling over what one has lost in life? If one keeps on thinking about the dead wife and son, one's mind becomes feeble. Don't I have enough work on hand as it is? I have to bring up and educate my grandson and I am already seventy-two. Only after taking my grandson to a certain stage shall I think of liberating myself from worldly concerns. Sometimes, memories float. But I do not brood over the past."

Rao, however, began to go over his past life in his mind.

"Shrothri never did anything in life that led to duality and self-contradiction. That is why his sights are always directed towards his future goal. But in my life, the one duality I am guilty of pulls me back perpetually into the past. It drowns me in memories and renders me helpless. How can I overcome it?"

Hoping that Shrothri might suggest a way out of his duality and its contradictions, Rao resumed the discussion, "Are you aware of my second marriage, its purpose?"

"Yes."

"Without her, I could not have accomplished my goal. She was absolutely indispensable to my writing work. But my first wife is an innocent person, guilty of no wrong or crime. In such a situation, do you think I was wrong in the step I took?"

"How can I say that you were wrong?"

"I am aware that it is not in your nature to pass judgement on others and their actions. I do not want an answer from that perspective. In my position, what would you have done?"

"It would be absurd to state what I would have done precisely if I were in your situation. It seems you said one day in your history class, 'A beggar told an emperor that he would not have let blood flow had he been an emperor. The emperor replied that if he had been a beggar, he would have never even remotely thought of war!...'"

Then, pausing for a minute, Shrothri continued, "You feel that your second marriage was strictly for the purpose of finishing your volumes. Writing a volume is a work of intelligence and intellectual activity, an aspect of *prakriti*, of nature, of the physical. Thus a marriage contracted to promote intellectual activity is also a response to a natural impulse. But some enter into another marriage merely to satisfy their bodily urges, others to satisfy another type of urge. Though the intellectual urge is superior to the bodily one, it is not in essence different from the latter. But true understanding transcends intelligence, not merely the body. It needs no external support and it rests on nothing but the genuine call of the soul."

Rao intervened, "What value can a marriage have if it comes in the way of one's life's supreme goal? How can you say that a marriage entered into for the purpose of promoting that goal is the result of a natural impulse?"

"Yes, from one perspective you are correct. In our changing social circumstances, the goal of marriage is changing. It is not for us to say whether this is right or wrong. Once one marries a person, whether knowingly or unknowingly, how can one dismiss that marriage lightly and ignore the claims of the other innocent person?"

Recalling his own marital life, Shrothri continued, "Well, I confess, I too used to think like you. Increasingly, I became fascinated and absorbed in my study of Sanskrit texts, trying to master the systems of *Vedanta, Tarka* and *Mimamsa*. It was my lot to have a wife who was not only absolutely ignorant of Sanskrit but who could not even write competent Kannada. But with what devotion she served her husband! She gave me a son to perpetuate my lineage. She offered flowers, fruit and sandalwood paste for my daily worship. In terms of intellectual capacity, we were so far apart. And yet she was my wife."

Shrothri realised that his words had hurt Rao, so he continued more gently, "Just as it is absurd to state what I would have done in your situation, its converse is also equally absurd. It all depends on one's outlook in life. When one tries to go along a path, one runs into dualities, but if one were to choose to retrace one's path, one might run into a different set of dualities. Your present achievement is not small. You must complete it. I can assure you that I fully understand the compulsions that drove you into a second marriage. But why should you keep your first wife away?"

"My second wife rejects bigamy uncompromisingly, is categorically opposed to the idea of two wives under a single roof."

"This is one face of modernity. It is not all wrong. She agreed to marry you even when you already had a wife and for an ideal. But she could have compromised with bigamy by concentrating on her goal. Whether in the life of an individual or a society, every method has its own specific use but in unusual situations, they should not be given an overriding status. If one is clear about the primary aim of life, one can go on making small compromises consistent with the primary goal."

Rao plunged into thought. He said nothing. They both sat silently for a while and then went home, reaching there about eleven. Karuna was talking to Cheeni in the front hall. As they entered, Cheeni went inside.

The next day, as Rao left, he tried to touch Shrothri's feet to seek his blessing, but Shrothri would not allow it.

"Only God deserves that," he said.

Karuna bent low and joined her palms in obeisance.

Shrothri was sad to see them go for he did not believe he would see them again.

Nevertheless he said with equanimity, "Please visit me now and then. I am an old man. I cannot stir out."

When Rao and Karuna reached Mysore it was quarter past ten. They were surprised to see Raja sitting in a chair in the front yard, putting on his shoes.

"The transfer order asking us to move here came last week," he informed them. "I wrote to you but after we arrived we saw the letter lying there unread. It appears that you went to Nanjangud. Is everybody well there?"

A subtle shade of sorrow clouded his face but Rao did not notice. "Shrothri's wife died two years ago." And he went inside.

Nagalakshmi and Prithvi were in Bangalore, to arrive after Raja had found a house. Nobody had particularly wanted to move to Mysore but they had no choice but to obey the transfer order. That Raja was a brother of Rao was of much help as they applied for Katyayani's transfer to be with her husband. Raja was assigned to the Maharaja's College while Katyayani taught in the nearby first grade college.

After learning about the visit of Rao and Karuna to Nanjangud, Katyayani was anxious to hear about the Shrothri household, to satiate her deep desire to know about her earlier home and about the son born of her womb. After her third miscarriage, her eagerness to see Cheeni had intensified. She tried to imagine him as a grown up boy, wondering if he remembered her and whether he got on well with his grandparents. If she had stayed, she could have helped them in their old age, assuming complete responsibility for the management of the household. Shrothri could have continued his religious worship and study undisturbed.

In the afternoon when everyone was out, Katyayani asked Karuna to tell her of what had happened in the years that had passed since she had left her child in Nanjangud. At first Karuna pleaded ignorance, citing her lack of Kannada as an excuse. But, on feeling the frustration and longing on Katyayani's face, she relented.

"I thought your father-in-law was a very fine man."

She paused and added helplessly, "He made a great impact on me."

"How are the others? Cheeni, my mother-in-law, Lakshmi?"

"Your mother-in-law has been dead for two years."

The pillar sustaining her controlled peace collapsed. She cried, "Who looks after the household work now? Who takes care of the boy?"

"Your father-in-law gets up early every morning, goes to the river to bathe and then finishes his morning worship. The boy will be taking his S.S.L.C. examination this year. He also gets up early and sits down to his study after his morning rites. At ten o'clock, his grandfather serves him with the food he cooked earlier. After the boy returns from school, he instructs him in the *Vedas*. The old man cooks the evening meal."

"How is he? Does he remember his mother? How has he taken his grandmother's death?"

Karuna recounted how she had been impressed with the boy though their conversation had been difficult, for although Cheeni understood English, he did not seem to have any command over the language. In fact, he used Sanskrit. She noted that she was impressed by his excellent grounding in *Vedic* lore, his recitation of the *Mahabharata* and *Ramayana*. Of course, he was the mirror image of his grandfather, his height, broad chest, shoulders, wide face and shining eyes. Then, having said whatever seemed appropriate whilst still avoiding the issue, she stopped.

"Does he remember his mother? Did you ask his grandfather about it?"

She asked this question with all the force of her desire. Karuna could not give any immediate answer. Confused, she appeared to fall into deep thought, hoping that Katyayani would guess, so that she would not have to explain.

"Say what you have to say."

"I asked him myself, 'Where is your mother? Do you remember her?' From the expression on his face I knew that he did not like my asking that question. It is my feeling that he does know about his mother but I am not sure whether he knows that I am related to his mother. Then I changed the topic. He seems to have been very fond of his grandmother. Though his voice and tone were even and flat, I could infer this from the expressions on his face while he spoke. He told me about her illness, the cause of her death, the death rites. And he has deep regard for and devotion to his grandfather."

"Did he strike you as a relaxed boy with a boy's natural playfulness and lightheartedness? Or was he thoughtful and serious?"

"It is my guess that during the time his grandmother was alive, he must have been a natural, young fellow with boyish playfulness. There is another old woman in the household called Lakshmi and he seems to be greatly attached to her. His bed was close to hers. But his face looks too grave and grim for his age."

Then Karuna spoke about Shrothri, "He is the living example of our culture. His knowledge is very deep, and his mental equanimity astounding. It is as if he belongs to our age and yet not. When I look into his face, I see a brightness attained only by those who are *sthithaprajna,* the ideal person of the *Bhagavadgita,* who is in the world and yet out of it. Yes, he is a gentle and mild mannered person, but I had the feeling that somewhere are lodged a strange harshness and indifference. His life is governed by a tremendous will power and an uncompromising sense of duty."

Katyayani's mind was filled with the faces of Shrothri and Cheeni. Her memory loomed before her and her imagination supplied the passage of time. She now knew that the boy had profound affection for his grandmother, so much so that he gave a vivid and detailed account of her last days and death. He did not want to talk about his mother.

"But does he know about me?"

Then she recalled that Karuna herself had felt that he knew about his mother. She wondered whether it meant that the boy had contempt or even hostility towards his mother, his mind poisoned by being told of what she had done. Immediately she abandoned such ideas as she was certain that Shrothri would not descend to such depths but her mother-in-law had had a long memory and a short temper.

"Instead of running away from there, had I just died, he would not have had contempt for me. He would have accorded me the same respect that he gives to his dead father and grandmother, perhaps even more to my memory. Which life can be worse for a woman than one in which her own son has contempt and hatred for her? Why did I not think of this, realise this earlier? If after the marriage I had taken my boy with us, this would not have happened. He would have loved and respected me. He would have shown respect to his step-father. Father-in-law offered me the freedom to choose - to take him away with me or to leave him behind. Why, when I went upstairs, did I not pick him up and take him away? What was the force that prompted me to decide the way I did? I realise now that I should never have left my child."

XXII

A fortnight later Raja managed to find suitable accommodation. A week after that, Nagalakshmi and Prithvi came to Mysore and were duly impressed by the house. It was a spacious, white building situated in the Lakshmipuram neighbourhood, an affluent upper-middle class area of landowners, leading lawyers, doctors and businessmen. The garden was flourishing with bright and pungent flowers and creepers grew around the veranda. Inside it was very comfortable; large rooms, which seemed even larger because of the big windows and the expanse of the light, pink-cream floor. The house was filled with books and cane furniture covered in cushions embroidered by Katyayani.

After their departure, Rao and Karuna missed their company for all four would sit together after dinner, talking light heartedly, infusing some normality of family life into an otherwise extreme existence. Raghappa's insufferable cooking thankfully improved under the guidance of Katyayani. But now with their departure, Rao's household had relapsed into its old tenor and monotony. The same routine of work in the library and preparation of source material continued as before. The material for the fifth volume was being collected briskly but even in the midst of his concentrated work, Rao could not avoid the feeling of duality that had turned his life into two worlds. Whichever one he chose, he would be ceaselessly and restlessly looking over to the other.

Frequently, he would remember Shrothri's words, his assertion that intellectual power was also an aspect of *prakriti*, of the physical, that marriage if caught in the net of intellectuality is an expression of a natural impulse. True, some people marry only in response to physical attraction but though the intellectual one is superior to the physical one, they are not fundamentally different. Then he would re-examine the background and nature of his marriage to Karuna. He knew that, without her help, his work would not have been completed with such speed. There was no one else who could give him such support. There was no one else who could devote themselves to this project with such concentration and single-minded dedication. He remembered one thing: and he experienced it even now. When Karuna referred to their achievement, praising it, Rao's heart swelled with pride and conviction. He was more inspired by her words than by the commendations or excellent reviews of other scholars from all over the world. When she referred to the work as "our work", his heart would thunder inside him, overflowing with joy. Whenever they discussed spiritedly some important issue and she squeezed his hand in admiration during their after-dinner walks, or when she made notes at home after they returned, on the basis of such discussions, he would feel then that she was his real wife. Suppose my helper and collaborator had been a man, would I be having such feelings?

In the same way he often thought about the marital life of Shrothri and his underlying ideals.

"Shrothri immersed himself in the study of Sanskrit texts, studying *vedanta, Tharka, Mimamsa* and *Dharmasastra* with profound intensity. His wife was not even as educated as Nagu. Why did he not feel the need of another woman as I do?"

"But," Rao told himself severely, "that was because he had not embarked on any unique project of writing as I had done. But suppose Shrothri were to be in my position. Though the comparison cannot be identical, I am sure he would have finished the work unaided. He would have hired a typist and would have laboured over the other work all by himself. He would not have trodden the path that I have taken."

Nagalakshmi edged in and out of his mind and now she lived about half a mile away from their bungalow in Mysore. How sincere and devoted to him she was and how she offered to live with them, serving them! Forgetting the injustice done to her, she had offered to cook for him and the rival wife and care for their health. Lacking in formal education, she had nevertheless developed a strong and individual personality. In the family circle she was supreme, brooking no opposition. Though she did not consciously try to establish her authority, it was unquestioningly accepted. The ultimate source of her strength was her maternal solicitude and love for others, her trustworthiness and her service.

There, against the sick atmosphere of the hospital, he had acted towards her in such an affectionate manner and in return her every gesture and word was full of a secret intimacy. But once he was well and home, he became engrossed in his work and he had little time for her. Karuna's presence offered him what he could not otherwise have and he became captivated by it. He remembered Nagu's face when she touched his feet before leaving for Bangalore, proud and yet, wilted. Of the two forces, which should I accept and which one should I reject? Study and writing are the very breath of my life, Nagu's memory has become a fire that can burn my inner soul and this breath of mine fuels and fans that fire. But he knew well that Karuna was indispensable for the completion of his work. But suppose he gave up the volume itself! He recalled Shrothri's words, warning him that if one should try to avoid conflict by retracing one's steps, then a new conflict would surely ensue. Rao was convinced that he would lose his mind if he abandoned his volume or slowed down its production; he had to complete it whilst his stamina remained. Some voice from the depth of his being told him that he was not going to live long. Day by day, his mental agony increased while his physical strength decreased.

In fact, Rao did not suffer from any disease, but his physical strength was declining, leading to a corresponding decline in his ability to carry on his study and research. He found that he could not digest his evening meal and had to substitute in its place, bread and milk. Reading, he would not grasp what his eyes scanned and Nagalakshmi and Karuna would crowd his mind.

Karuna, who had been watching his deteriorating health, took him to the doctor who again recommended rest and a change of air. Rao did not agree and adamantly refused to entertain the idea of slowing down the work of his volume.

"I cannot tell why, for I do not know why, but I know that my days are short."

This fear and this impetus forced him to concentrate his will and energy but the body refused to co-operate with the mind or was it the mind refusing to co-operate with the body? Karuna pleaded and then shouted angrily, "Why don't you follow the doctor's advice? Why are you so stubborn?"

She resorted to fasting without an afternoon meal with him as a form of protest. In the evenings she insisted on taking him out for a walk. During such a walk the mood instead of being more relaxed as it usually was, grew tenser and tenser and although they were in the open air, it seemed as if the world was a small, shallow box, containing but the three of them.

"I can understand. Tell me."

Slowly lifting his head, he gazed into her face. Even in the dim light of the street-lamp, he could see the gravity etched between her eyebrows and straining at her cheekbones.

He answered, "You know it already. And the solution is in your hands, not in mine."

Karuna was silent and helpless, thought blocked.

"During my illness she came and served me. And with such devotion. Not merely a duty, but a tradition, a whole Hindu tradition, a culture built up around the devoted wife. With such selflessness, consoling me, 'What has happened has happened. Give me a chance to serve you.' She was prepared to cook and serve us both. She has transcended the mere consciousness of wifely duties. Enveloping us in her maternal security and warmth she has reached the highest stage of being a mother to us all. This is my torture."

A sudden silence fell between the two. Neither spoke. Rao broke the silence and told her of his discussion with Shrothri, finishing by saying, "If the fundamental and primary goal of life is clear, one can assign to minor goals their proper role and act accordingly."

In the diluted darkness, Karuna led her husband homeward. As usual Rao went to his study and Karuna to the hall where she started to type, mistake after mistake. She took her fingers away from the keyboard and thought about what her husband had said.

The fifth volume was sluggish, lumbering along, existing rather than rejoicing in that existence. Her mind ran to the deteriorating health of her husband and she knew that because of this his worry was increasing, destroying the very energy and vitality needed for its completion. She turned to Nagalakshmi who had worked like a cook uncomplainingly in the household of a husband whom she had wedded according to the *dharmic* rites.

"She had reached the height of being a mother to us all."

Karuna finally accepted that Nagalakshmi had reached a higher stage than herself, a state that for her, with all her scholarly wisdom, was unobtainable. With the consequent sense of liberation, but mingled with a vague sense of pain and loss, she finally said to her husband, "Please, go and bring her. We shall live together."

Rao stared into her face. Her eyes were pools of peace. They had always convinced him of the strength of her belief.

Had Rao refused her suggestion in the hospital itself, Nagalakshmi's sense of rejection would not have been lessened but it would not have been so lasting, nor so bitter. But in the hospital, he had told her with such emotion, such honesty that he wanted her to live with them. There she had wanted to serve him, setting aside the rival wife and her pride. Every day she hoped that he would tell Raja, "Leave Nagu behind." But he did not and so she left for Bangalore.

The first few days after their return from Mysore dragged heavily for Nagalakshmi, the thought that her life had so cruelly turned out to be insignificant, in turn, dulled and tormented her. She lost interest in her food, in her work. Raja and Katyayani, when they heard of what had happened, felt saddened and Raja, feeling utterly helpless, began to pay greater attention to his sister-in-law. Katyayani asked her, "Sister, how far has your project of writing out Sri Rama's name progressed? How many note-books have you filled?"

" I don't know. I haven't counted."

"I notice you have not been working on it recently."

"What is the point of writing out any God's name? It is all a waste." Nagalakshmi spat out her bitterness.

"Sister, we should not blame God for our accumulated fate, the fruit of our past life and deeds. Need I tell you this? As a result of some previous life's *dharma* and *karma,* we suffer in this life. How can you neglect God in this life? Don't you want a better next life? If you worship Sri Rama with sincerity and devotion, the fruit of your devotion will benefit your brother-in-law and others. From now on, spend less time in household work and give more time and energy to your devotion to Sri Rama. After Prithvi returns from college, he will buy ink-powder from the market and I will prepare the ink. How many note-books are left?" she asked briskly before her elder sister could object.

Nagalakshmi realised that it was wrong to have neglected her project of writing Sri Rama's name all these days. Within herself she prayed to Rama to forgive her for the lapse and resumed her writing with fresh determination. After a few days, Nagalakshmi regained her former equanimity and she assured herself,

"Let the whole world desert me. My Sri Rama will never abandon me," and she prayed to him within herself.

"I am forty. What do I have to look forward to? Let Raja, Katyayani and Prithvi prosper. And let them prosper too."

She tried her utmost to forget what had happened in Mysore and as she did so unconsciously a hardened attitude of indifference towards her husband formed and solidified.

None of them had been particularly enthusiastic about the transfer to Mysore but they soon became accustomed to their new lives. Raja and Katyayani settled down to teach and Prithvi enrolled in a nearby college. Nagalakshmi managed to control herself and sat down to continue her project. By now she had written Sri Rama's name four and a half million times, filling well over one hundred and ten notebooks. Each day more and more time was spent on this exercise. The traditional Saturday *pujas* became increasingly more elaborate, with longer *mantras*, repeated many times accompanied by the offering of fruit and flowers.

When there was no-one at home in the afternoon, Nagalakshmi would sit out on the veranda, absorbed in the task of writing Rama's name. The lines filled and Nagalakshmi prided herself on her well-formed hand, the correct angle of holding the pen so that it touched the paper at a perfect slant, just the right amount of pressure on the nib, her fingers relaxed, hand steady. The pen was dipped skilfully into the ink and it moved elegantly across the page. Not once did the ink blotch, nor did it smudge. The characters were carefully written, each the same height and width as the other, perfect uniformity, perfect harmony.

As she wrote, she heard the long squeal of an unoiled door as someone opened the gate. She raised her head to see and saw her husband. Instinctively she gathered up her notebook and pen and hurried inside. Rao entered the front yard, moved to the veranda and sat in a chair. There he stayed silently for some minutes, then he called out, "Nagu, are you there?"

Silence.

"Nagu, I have come to take you back."

Rao repeated the words. Then she cried out from inside, "I am happy by myself. I don't want anyone to take me anywhere!"

"Please don't speak with such anger. I felt miserable after you left for Bangalore. Now Karuna has agreed to everything."

"I don't need to come there with any woman's approval. No, I shall not go anywhere."

"Please Nagu, don't talk like that. I have come myself..."

She interrupted him from inside the house, and said, "No matter who comes to call me, who comes to take me, I shall have the same answer."

Rao remained silent for some twenty minutes but Nagalakshmi did not come out, nor did she say anything. At last, he stood up and said, "I'm leaving. Think about it. I shall explain things to Raja."

"Raja knows. Everybody knows. Nobody will change my mind. Why waste your breath? I can always earn a fistful of rice by working in anybody's house. I have my own self-respect and my own pride."

As she hurled her words at him, Rao stood there and then slowly left. When she finally heard the clank of the metal gate as it closed, she sobbed loudly. Katyayani found her half an hour later, still crying.

Rao went straight to the library and told Karuna of Nagalakshmi's refusal. For the next week his mind was in a tumultuous state. Until then he had assumed that he had the right of a husband over her but now that feeling, if not that right, had been smashed. He knew he had lost something exquisite and beloved, and the lonely, dense feeling he had when he was in the school for orphans, returned. He would do as he had done then, work and study, losing himself in the culture of his land, imbibing the lives of those who had made his country great. Yet never before had he experienced this sense of powerlessness. His achievement followed in a trail behind him and stretched out before him. But he resisted and tried to overcome, remembering inside that he did not have long to live. He told Karuna, "We must work faster, faster."

And Karuna dutifully plunged into her labours with fanatic and relentless zeal.

XXIII

Constantly Katyayani meditated on the force that had divided her life into two, throwing it into a perpetual, dualistic conflict. When she remembered the sacrifice her husband Raja had made for her, she would be thankful that at least she had not eloped with an unworthy person but her life could not be sustained by thankfulness alone. The pitiable and proud state of the Nanjangud household turned in turmoil inside her and tormented by the memory of her son, she felt an irresistible urge to see him, but calmly Shrothri's commanding figure stood before her. And the old man in his stage of life, even after having lost his wife, was devoting himself dutifully to bringing up his grandson. Karuna had been overwhelmed by that sense of duty and the strong determination to follow the dictates that governed life. Katyayani had experienced this strong will earlier, the profound faith in life that had given the capacity for an unbelievable steadfastness. It was this total commitment which manifested itself as a sense of duty. Successfully Shothri had suppressed the myriad currents and conflicts that were trying to fragment his life and developed a single force, driven by a single energy.

Once she even thought she would go to Nanjangud alone, see her Cheeni, and fall at Shrothri's feet, begging him to bless her with peace. Her own fear of herself filled her. Yet she was sure that if she did go, Shrothri would not utter a single harsh word but would bless her by touching her head when she touched his feet in contrition. If she visited Nanjangud now and then, maybe this, instead of tearing her apart, would bring her some peace. But her courage failed her for she could not bear to look into the compassionate mirror of his eyes.

Classes started and hoping that teaching would occupy her mind, she eagerly went to university but inauspiciously, on that very day, a former teacher had died and the university had been closed in remembrance. The students, murmuring, left for their homes. The teachers' room was empty and the rain outside reverberated in the unfamiliar silence. The noise of the rain reached inside and drew her to Nanjangud. The force inside built up until she felt that unless she went, she would surely go mad. Outside she opened her umbrella with a shattering snap and headed towards Chamarajapura station.

Students chatted noisily on the platform and the noise turned and increased inside her ears, hurting.

As the train started moving, she stared out of the window, each scene that went by seemed to have been plucked out of her memory and run by, in order, on a screen before her. When the train passed South Mysore station, Chamundi hill became visible. Below the clouds that had smothered the sky, the hill appeared magnified as if seriousness had solidified in form. If she had followed the decision she had made that day on that hill, then she would not be in the situation she found herself today. The groups of trees on either side of Kapila looked the same as before but the temples and bathing ghats showed their age. At Nanjangud station she stood on the platform as the other passengers and students left. Fear crept into her. Seeing her standing there, dazed and confused, the ticket inspector approached her saying, "Give me your ticket. Where do you want to go?"

She handed over the ticket and came out of the station.

As she walked, she looked suspiciously at the windows and doors on either side to see if anyone was watching her. In that drizzle the street was empty and the shutters were closed. Forward she moved until she stood in front of the house that had once been hers. She remembered that the front door would be closed during the rains. The impression of shoes freshly made on the muddy ground told her that somebody must have just entered the house. By the side of the impression of shoes could also be seen a thin line of water which had dripped from an umbrella. Her entire body began to tremble. Even when she stared out of her eyes, everything was trembling - her whole body, hands, and the umbrella in the hand. In spite of the cooling rain and the cold air, she sweated profusely. All her attempts to understand the fear proved futile. She tried to raise her hand to knock on the door but she could not and so it hung there. Suddenly, she heard a voice from within. If they came to open the door, they would see her. She shuddered, and turning, walked briskly away.

The next day, too, it rained. Exhausted from a sleepless night, Katyayani went to university. As soon as she entered the lecture hall, the students rose without a sound for they were facing the very first lecture of their university terms. Katyayani sat in her chair and started to call out the attendance, a tedious task as there were one hundred and twenty students. After calling out the names of the first fifty, she marked the rest present mechanically. After closing the attendance register, she placed it on the table and started to gaze at the hill. The green foliage had become black under the cloudy sky, grim and foreboding. The students watched her for some five minutes, and then broke into subdued whispers and murmurs and in another few minutes the voices rose to a crescendo.

"Silence."

The students obeyed her instantly and she took out a collection of Keats' poems set for that year and started her lesson.

"Come in," she snapped as someone knocked at the door.

The door opened and the class turned to stare. The feet appeared uncertainly around the door, clean, polished, laced shoes. The new trousers gleamed where the hot iron had been passed over them and the white shirt sat stiffly. He was a tall, well-built, young man, with a broad face, a long nose and striking eyes. His hair was cropped, newly-cut, and combed back with coconut oil and his forehead carried the ritual mark of an orthodox brahmin. A wet umbrella dangled from his hand. He walked unsteadily and unnaturally in his new garb. The boy crept along the wall to reach the empty desk at the back and then sat down. Katyayani was mesmerised. The students started to whisper again. She picked up the text and began to read but she had hardly got past two lines when the late-comer said, "Madame, attendance?"

"Your name, please."

"N. Srinivasa Shrothri."

Katyayani's hand trembled imperceptibly. Her face began to perspire and drops of sweat appeared on her forehead. Finding it difficult to stand, she sat down in the chair. Just managing to get hold of her voice, she resumed her teaching but found herself unable to remember what it was she wanted to say. Her head became a vacuous sphere. Deciding that it was better to stop teaching than to teach in an haphazard and irrelevant manner, she closed the text and told the boys to leave in silence. But before the first student reached the door, she was standing there. That hall had only one door and the boys were leaving one by one. Moving down from the last row of desks, she saw Cheeni approach her, certain that he would talk to her, he knew who she was, he must have known who she was, and she stood there full of anticipation. There was no reason for her confidence but she did not find it necessary to find any reason for it. Almost three quarters of the students had left. Cheeni, too, came at last, talking animatedly to another student. Surely he would speak to her, for he has that same face, the moulded features he had as a child. As he came closer, he stopped talking to his student friend, lowered his head, grabbed his books to his chest and then tried to leave without saying a word to her. She called his name, and he stopped in his tracks.

Srinivasa Shrothri stood, his head lowered.

"Where do you come from?"

"Nanjangud, madame."

"You travel every day?"

"Yes."

"By train?"

"Yes."

Moving close to him, she said, "Come, visit my home today."

He did not reply.

She repeated her suggestion, "Come, child, let us go."

"Madame, it will be late for my train."

"Your train is at half past five, isn't it? It is now just four," she said sweetly, as if coaxing a child.

For a minute he said nothing.

"No, madame. It will be late for me."

Now Katyayani was certain that he knew who she was. Immediately she was angry at his arrogance in so curtly refusing her invitation as a teacher, ashamed of his behaviour as a mother.

The whole day she was in unbearable agony. Her conscience now assured her that he had recognised her as his mother. If he had respected her request and confronted her with the question of why she had done what she had, then at least she would have had an opportunity to explain. Suppressing her shame, she would have told the truth and asked him to forgive her. Had he openly hurled his accusations at her standing before her, she would have endured it. No, he was not merciful. No, he refused her, rejected their relationship as a mark of dishonour, a punishment pre-meditated. By evening her head became hot and an acute pain shot through it.

Katyayani was laid up with fever for one whole week. After recovering, when she returned to work, she was so weak that she began to teach her classes sitting in her chair and in a low voice. Srinivasa Shrothri was attending his classes regularly, sitting in the same place in the last row. No matter how hard she tried to control her desire, she would not resist the temptation to look at him now and then. He fixed his eyes on the pages of the text and listened to her lecture. As usual, he was scribbling the meaning of new words. She decided to tackle him once again and invite him to her house.

On Tuesdays, she lectured his class at ten-thirty in the morning. From the teachers' room, she sent word with the attendant to fetch Srinivasa Shrothri, a student in the D section of the Intermediate Science Junior Class. She asked him to tell the boy that she wanted to see him, and she added that other students should be informed that she was not taking their class that day. After five minutes, the attendant returned, Cheeni following him. As he had his books clasped to his chest, as usual, she noticed a new watch gleaming on his wrist.

"Today, there is no question of being late for the train, child. Come home with me. When I invite you, you should not give discourteous answers."

Without giving him a chance to say anything, she hurried him along. She led and he followed. When they reached Ramaswami Circle, she turned to him and said, "Why are you behind? Walk with me. Don't be shy." She slowed down to fall in step with him.

Today he was wearing chappals, not shoes and on his exposed feet she saw the small weals where the shoe had pinched. Duty-bound he walked.

At home, Nagalakshmi was alone in the kitchen, immersed in writing Rama's name. As Raja and Prithvi were at university, there was no-one else in the house. Students often came by to the house and therefore Nagalakshmi took no notice of the new arrival. Katyayani came out of the kitchen with a plate full of rice and curds, a glass of milk and a glass of water. These she placed on a low table and invited the boy, who was standing uncomfortably in the doorway, to come in. The haunting and yet real face now blushed from shyness and confusion.

"This is for you," she said.

Then she went to the door, closed it and sat in the chair.

"No, madame. I've had my meal."

"This is not a meal. Eat a little. When a *guru* offers something, you should not refuse."

"This is too much for me."

"Take as much as you want. Don't worry, you can leave the rest."

He took the plate, set aside the spoon and began to eat with his fingers.

"You are from Nanjangud?"

"Yes."

"Your father's name?

"Nanjunda Shrothri."

"Both your parents are alive?"

"No."

"Both are dead?"

"Yes."

All the time he spoke and all the time he was silent, his head was bowed. Katyayani sensed that he did not want the food.

"If you want, leave it."

Placing the plate on the floor, he went to the window and though the bars were close together, he manoeuvred his body around, stretched his hand out and pouring water over it, washed it.

"Who looks after you?"

"My grandfather."

"His name?"

"Srinivasa Shrothri."

When she asked him whether it was not difficult for his grandfather to look after him all by himself, he did not reply. After a prolonged pause, she said, "One of our relations knows Nanjangud well. She told me that your father drowned in the floods and that your mother is still alive."

He said nothing, staring blankly at the floor.

"I don't know."

Again there was a long, tense silence.

"Do you remember your mother?"

"No."

"I learn that she is alive. Is she mentioned at home?"

"No."

"Didn't you ever want to meet her?"

Again he fell silent. When she persisted in the question, he said, slowly and deliberately, but in a tremulous voice, "No."

Katyayani felt as if a huge slab had been placed on her chest. All her hope seemed to have been destroyed in one second by this brief answer. Darkness from within seeped over the inside of her eyelids. She felt dizzy and closed her eyes, sinking back into the chair. When she opened her eyes a generation later, she saw him still sitting there, the same height, physique, face, posture. His somewhat thicker lower lip and his hard straight look recalled his grandfather, symbols of hardness and decisiveness.

"Your mother is here. In this city. She is a good friend of mine. She is yearning for you. Shall I ask her to come?"

He fell silent again.

"Child, answer me."

He did not reply but sat there like carefully sculpted stone.

"Say something... I shall ask her to come."

"Please don't, madame."

Once again that inner murkiness came over her. Her eyes were half-closed; she could neither shut them, nor open them.

"It is getting late, madame."

As she opened her eyes, she saw him move away, pass under the doorway, his head bent. Her strength had gone and she had no power to grasp him by the hand, crying, "Stop, don't go."

Her tongue was dry and dead.

He put his feet into his chappals and she heard the sound of them on the ground as he moved away, the sound becoming ever more distant. Through the window she saw him walking away, his head still bowed, as if heavier than the rest of his body.

"Cheeni, you are my child, my son, born of my womb."

Exhausted, she slumped on the floor and rolled on it. Her head on the cold stone, she thought how cruel and contemptuous he was towards her! Hard-hearted enough to sit before his own mother and listen with indifference to her words. Anyone else in his place would have at least once shed tears, even moved closer to her, calling, "Mother."

And then he departed as if nothing had happened, nothing had been at stake. Perhaps he was naturally harsh, perhaps not. Although he was capable of the old man's hardness and grimness of determination, there did not reign on his face the same kind of knowing peace.

Katyayani developed a high fever which subsided three days later. On the fourth day she went to the university in a jutka carriage, but she was too weak to take any class. Two days later she went to take the lecture, determined not to look at him. But her desire to see him overcame her. Defeated, she turned her eyes towards the last row of desks and to the particular seat usually occupied by him. She combed the whole class. She called out his name from the register, and there was no answer. For the next two weeks, there was no sign of him. One day she checked in the university office. The concerned clerk checked with the concerned register and reported, that N. Srinivasa Shrothri had taken his transfer certificate to another college, after remitting a term's fees.

She took this as his final rejection of his mother. She wondered about the college to which he might have taken the transfer. Of course, with a little effort, it would not be difficult to locate him. However, there was little sense in seeking the iron rod that refused to be moulded.

XXIV

Cheeni certainly knew all about his mother. Even when he was at school, some of the children had talked about it amongst themselves, repeating what their parents had mentioned to each other at home. At his house, the matter was never raised as it was obviously a hurtful one. Yet, by and by his grandmother had gleaned some scant information, such as the move to Bangalore and the subsequent job as a lecturer. Later he had discovered the name of her husband. His grandfather had never once referred to the subject and understanding the reluctance, Cheeni never asked him. Lakshmi, in obedience to the old man's wishes, joined the principle of silence. He had developed towards his grandfather an attitude which combined a sense of awe with a sense of devotion. The old man's life - his dutifulness, the enormous respect shown to him by others and the way he cooked and fed the boy like a woman - made a deep impression on the young mind. Lakshmi gave him an oil massage once a week. After the bath, she would go to the boiler and reach down to where they had laid firewood to heat the water, and taking some of the cinders would mark them on the boy's forehead, a mark of respect for Agni, the god of fire.

"Child, touch the feet of God Yagneswara. Then the feet of your grandfather."

"And what about you?"

"It is enough if you do so to Seenappa. It is as bowing down to all the deities."

Thus his mind shaped and mesmerised by the old man and his life, Cheeni did as he was told.

He had arrived on the first day the university was to begin, but when he learnt that there were no classes in remembrance of a former teacher who had passed away, he, along with other students had returned to Nanjangud by the noon train. Chakrapani, son of lawyer Venkata Rao, was in his class and the two had promised to save seats for each other.

"Do you know our English lecturer's name?"

"No. Why?"

"Mrs. Katyayani Rao. Her husband works in the post-graduate college."

It was then that Cheeni realised.

"I went to my aunt's house and my cousin told me all about them. It seems that they had a widow's marriage."

Then Chakrapani stopped as if he had bitten his tongue.

Chakrapani knew exactly who their new lecturer was; but his intention in referring to the matter had not been to hurt Cheeni, but rather indirectly to tell his friend before he heard of it from another source.

The next day, Cheeni had felt too shy and too frightened to go to his English lecture but forced himself. Unfortunately he had arrived rather late and so had compounded the embarrassment. Cheeni had been attracted by the teacher. He would watch her face slying, burying his face in his book and squinting up when her eyes were elsewhere. When she had invited him to her house, he had been confused by the unexpected gesture, given the first excuse that had entered his mind and had run away. Fascinated by the experience of slowly discovering what he had always longed to know, his mind became filled by a consuming curiosity. The next day he had gone to the post-graduate college to see her husband. Just as he sat down in the unfamiliar lecture hall, Raja Rao arrived. The subject of the lecture was Shaw's play, *Saint Joan*. Though Cheeni could not fully understand the lecture, he saw other students enjoying it because of its presentation through the accomplished acting and the fluent English. After he came to know that the new teacher was his mother, though he had to accept the truth, he had previously entertained no strong feelings either way about her husband. Now a subtle undercurrent of contempt for him was developing in his mind. He remembered his father, or rather found that he could not for he had never set eyes on him, had never seen a photograph. Raja Rao's lecture suddenly seemed brash, proud, self-parading. He felt like leaving but disliked the rudeness of walking out half-way through.

Cheeni's mind was caught in a whirl of emotions and thoughts which he could scarcely comprehend. An urge formed to talk to his mother, to ask her why she had gone away with that man and had left him. Grandmother mentioned that his mother had been a student of Raja Rao and her friendship with him grew through theatrical activities because he was excellent at producing plays. But when he thought about the sequel to their plays, he felt disgusted. Yet he was not sure why. Once he considered going to her and confronting her with his questions. But she might question him back, "Who are you to ask me?"

For two or three days he did not want to eat and spent sleepless nights. The notion of turning to his grandfather was dismissed for he could not hurt and sadden the old man. Better to do what his grandfather would do, swallow the pain and carry on with fortitude. During his morning *sandhyavandana* ritual, he added a few more to the Gayatri *mantras* he recited.

His grandfather had told him several times that a person's *dharma* and *karma* involved but that person and it was not for others to concern themselves with it. Cheeni was endowed with the power of an incredible will and so he pushed his mother's behaviour out of his mind. Unexpectedly it nagged him. If she should come to him, declaring herself to be his mother, he did not know whether to respond, saying, "Yes, I am your son."

If he accepted her as his mother and their relationship, his trust in her might increase and he might decide to live with her. He grieved that he should do what his mother had done, repeat the same act of abandonment in its cruelty. But he could not be a son in two places, a misfit of dual parentage. Cheeni had already grasped some teachings of the traditional *sastras* and thus he had a fairly well developed consciousness of identifying in terms of the family, the *dharma* of belonging to the tradition of that lineage. During his daily *sandhyavandana* ritual, he would recite his genealogy and this had intensified his pride, conscious of his grandfather's dictum that everyone should not only preserve the honour of the lineage but should try to raise it to a higher glory. In the *puranas* he had read about how rulers in the past tried to enhance the prestige and power of their lineages - traceable to the sun or the moon. Reflecting on the situation, he told himself that he, as one born to the *Kashyapagotra* and Shrothri line, could not regard himself as the scion of another tree. It was the essence of his upbringing to consider every elder with the respect due to a parent but he considered it the height of impropriety and absurdity to desert his lineage and start a link with a mother, a connection without a basis.

But such ancient beliefs, such steadfast decisions did not solve the problem of how exactly he should behave if his mother were to claim him openly one day as her son.

Certainly he would not repulse her with a rude answer for that would surely hurt her. His grandfather has constantly emphasised the principle that one should never use rude words and cause pain to others. His ultimate decision was not to further the relationship, to break it off at its very stem. As he went with her to her house, walking slowly behind so that she would not see his face as he attempted to steel himself, he felt a sudden weakness within him. In the house he survived but when he came out, he went a little further and then, standing forlorn under a tree by the road, he sobbed.

University was a daily chore and he went dutifully but was frightened by the possibility of her inviting him again, of her crying before him and he before her. He saw from the notice board that she would be on leave for four days but, after those four days respite, she would surely return. Inside he wanted to see her again, to say, "I am your son, I am Cheeni."

But then the desire would be smothered by his grandfather's advice: "Contact with an object, any object, results in attachment to it. Once the attachment develops, it would be impossible to escape from its hold. Therefore we must abjure such contact."

Yes, he thought, he must abjure, stop seeing her altogether, leave the university and then his mind would become controlled.

That night he complained to his grandfather of the poor teaching at this particular college and told him that he wanted to go to another college. At first his grandfather was reluctant, telling him not to be hasty but when Cheeni insisted with a curious and passionate impatience, his grandfather agreed. The term's fees would still have to be paid at the first college but Shrothri advised the boy to disregard this factor. Accordingly, Cheeni enrolled elsewhere.

XXV

Katyayani was increasingly losing all her resilience and all her faith in life, her health deteriorating from day to day. But the fever did not return, there was no headache and she was not bed-ridden. Despite the lack of visible signs of an ascertainable illness, she was losing her resources. Once rounded with healthy flesh, her body had now become skeletal as if in the night it were being eaten away by worms. A doctor advised certain tonics, fruit and eggs. Katyayani, a brahmin and a strict vegetarian, was aghast at the thought of eating eggs but Raja cajoled and forced her. All this failed to improve the situation and she continued to lose her health and strength. After the university, she would retire to the loneliness of her room, and sit there with an empty mind, staring vacuously through the window at the trees lining the road, winding out of her vision, imagining herself as one of those trees, rejected by a branch put out by its own body. Suddenly she would feel the urge to try to go back to Nanjangud again. But when such thoughts sprouted, her ruined body would shiver and she would return to her emptiness and solitude.

Recently Katyayani had started to mutter words incoherently during her sleep. Sometimes, words tumbled clearly out of her mouth. At that time, her husband sleeping next to her, would shake her gently and ask, "Why are you muttering like this in your sleep?"

She slept on. One midnight, Raja suddenly woke up. When he opened his eyes, he found Katyayani missing, her mattress empty. He got up, walked out of the bedroom and noticed the front door, wide-open. About a furlong away, he saw the dim figure of a woman, walking slowly towards the Chamundipuram neighbourhood. Identifying her as Katyayani, he ran towards the figure. Catching up with her, he asked, "Where are you going?"

Her eyes were open, but the face was still asleep, a sleeping purposefulness. She did not recognise the person before her but still she answered, "To Chamundi hill."

"Why do you want to go there?"

"Why? How can one live without climbing heights? In my dream I was climbing down all the time. Now I am awake. I am going to climb up."

"Come back with me. We shall both go there in the morning."

She patted his back as she said, "How sensible you are!"

He brought her back home, holding her hand. Then he closed the front door securely, took her to the bedroom and made her lie down on the bed.

"Are you asleep?"

"No. I am always awake."

Her eyebrows which had been knitted together, relaxed and her sleep deepened.

Raja did not know how to deal with the situation and as his turmoil increased, greater became the demands on his love and affection. She developed an insatiable greed for his attention. If he were to attend to some work and hence not talk to her, she would immediately interpret it as a decline in his love for her. Even if he became mildly annoyed with her for anything, she was terrified that he might desert her. One day, when he was sitting on the bed, she touched his feet and implored, "If you keep me away from you, what will happen to me? Why don't you care about me?"

He tried to console her, "What have I done to you now? You are worrying without cause, needlessly imagining things."

He continued, "I am not unhappy with you. I am doing my best to see that you put on more weight and regain your normal health, and yet you are going down. Can't you, at least for my sake, seek some kind of a peace?"

"Don't you see that it is only to gain that, that I am struggling so hard? How much sorrow I bring to you! You are such a good man." Then she embraced him tightly and started weeping.

His increasing awareness of her helplessness deepened his love for her. He made it a point to spend as much time as he could in her company. Once, he suggested going to Nanjangud.

"No, I can never go back there. I would rather die here than fall unconscious in front of him."

Raja felt utterly helpless.

"Why don't you follow Nagu's example and pray to Sri Rama?"

"I am trying. But Sri Rama cannot grace a person such as I."

XXVI

Rao and Karuna toiled without reprieve over the fifth volume, covering in rich detail the cultural history of India from the time of the British to the present day, focusing on the transformations in the matter and meaning of Indian culture. In order to spare Rao any unnecessary strain, Karuna herself undertook the arduous task of tracking the source data, sifting through and refining it. Rao used to explain and outline the theoretical perspective on the material and the overall framework of the volume. Karuna would then search out other texts that either supported or questioned Rao's viewpoint. Thus they worked in regular tandem, relentless organisation in search of originality. She took good care of his health, and took him out without fail for a walk in the evening. She also saw to it that he did not read too much at night and went to bed early.

It was around eleven. Rao was sitting in his room, making some notes. Karuna was in an easy chair just behind him, reading. All of a sudden, even though he was sitting, Rao felt giddy. The room spun round. He flickered his eyelashes but could not see the pencil in his hand. As he slowly removed the glasses with his left hand, he felt semi-conscious and a vibrating darkness filled his eyes. He felt too weak to move but cried out feebly, "Karuna."

She was just behind, and hearing him, she lifted her head, prepared to respond to his new viewpoint. Suddenly, Rao felt an acute pain in the left side of his chest. It clutched him and pulled tighter. His breathing became hard and his chest congested. He closed his eyes and bit his lips. As he was trying to lift his right hand and place it on his chest, Karuna got up and moved close to him. Then she clasped his head to her chest. For a full minute she saw on his face the contortions of a fatal agony. As the pain subsided, he rested his head against her arms.

Karuna was aghast. It took a few minutes for her to realise that it was a heart attack. Even so, she mustered enough courage to feel his breathing by placing a finger near his nostrils. The breathing was somewhat slow. It was the fate of those who dedicated their lives wholly to art, scholarship and research to face a cruel end. A sort of emptiness enveloped her. In the distance, she saw the vision of an imperfect tragedy. She screamed for Raghappa and sent him to fetch the heart specialist, Dr. Anand.

After the doctor left, she dissolved a pill in water and made Rao drink it. He was now fully conscious and had stretched himself on the bed, his body relaxed. Karuna sat in a chair close to him. Though she was somewhat mollified by the doctor's assurance, there remained the numbness that had frozen her mind, making it heavy and cumbersome. The light was very dim and outside the crickets could be heard, the essence of the dead of the Indian night.

For two whole months, Rao rested and arranged a routine around the strict conditions prescribed by the doctor. Mysore University offered him medical leave during his time of convalescence. Mornings would consist of a slow walk to the Kukkarahalli lake and a slow walk back. An hour or two would be spent teaching the M.A. class and then he would return home. Karuna slaved in the library. After another two months, the doctor made a thorough check-up and warned that the condition of the heart was still very delicate. No more than a daily stint of one hour's teaching would be permitted and the reading, writing and researching would have to be curtailed for an indefinite period.

"If these instructions are not strictly followed, the consequences could be fatal. Anything may happen any time."

Karuna was thoroughly shaken by the doctor's admonition and warning. She imposed a strict regime of discipline on Rao who was not allowed to read or write even a line. She was aware of the size and scope of the fifth volume and busied herself collecting material for it. As she did so, she arrived at a strategy to deal with the new situation; she herself would not only collect the information but would write the first draft of the volume. Karuna would read the information to him, note his comments and suggestions, and write the volume herself, but under Rao's active and continuous supervision. Rao agreed with her plan which had been inspired by her affection and concern for his health.

With the decline in Rao's health, Karuna was forced to consider more acutely the uncertainty of her future. Many years ago, her parents had died and the only symbol of her family at home, Ajit, had ceased to be a part of her life. Until that moment when their routine of so many years had been broken, she had given no thought to what would happen to her if Rao died. Her financial situation was relatively secure but she believed that she would have nothing to live for, no child, no person to claim her. After all, one can only live for oneself for so long. A cruel and meaningless future stared her bleakly in the face. Terrified by it, she was determined to keep her husband alive at all costs.

For the first few days, Rao faithfully followed the doctor's instructions. Thus he managed to control his body but his mind jerked continually. He remembered Shrothri and told himself to emulate that old man's equanimity. If intelligence, the attraction and functioning of the mind are a form of *prakriti,* then if the mind is without occupation, it should lead to the goal of spiritual liberation. He was familiar with the meaning and implications of spiritual liberation in the Indian metaphysical tradition but now he was thinking about it from a purely personal angle as a problem of individual liberation. The liberated soul has no use for the intellect. When he himself is the supreme knowledge, there is no need for intellectual and mental activity.

"But then, can I attain that sort of liberation?"

He would remember the complicated and arduous practices necessary for its attainment and would reflect, "But I tread an altogether different path. At this stage of my life, it is an impossible goal for me. I am old, my hair is falling out. If I continue the road I have taken so far, I may finish the work on hand. Instead, if I try to go after another ideal, deserting the old one before attaining it, I shall gain neither."

Before his heart attack, Rao had made a thorough study of the material Karuna had collected for the volume. He had no doubt regarding her intellectual ability and her command over the source material but was uneasy of her writing it, for he knew that a text was the reflection of its writer's inner power.

"The hand that wrote the first four volumes alone should write the fifth and final volume. No matter how hard Karuna tries, her version of the fifth volume can never reflect the inner force of the person who had authored the earlier four."

That month when he went to the doctor for a check-up, he broached this matter. The doctor, in the meantime, had become acquainted with Rao's profound scholarship and his respect for him had increased accordingly. After listening to Rao's words he said,

"Of course, I can understand your concern. In medical matters, no expert can claim to predict beyond reasonable doubt. Yet, I still maintain that if you refrained totally from work it is likely that you will live ten years longer than otherwise. Did you say that the proposed volume will run to more than six hundred pages?"

"Yes."

"But once you begin the work and your involvement in it intensifies, would you accept a restriction in the number of pages you write each day?"

"No. When I start writing something, then within a week, I lose control over it, and in fact, it will start controlling me. It will proceed with its own pace and rhythm. 'Til it finishes, my mind will not tire. Unfortunately the body does not keep pace with the mind and often it becomes exhausted. But I myself will not be conscious of my body's failure."

With admiration at the commitment and the frankness, the doctor watched Rao, nodded his head in approval, and then asked, "Then what do you want me to do?"

"I cannot live without writing. A physical existence that is intellectually impotent is of no value. The world of scholarship is not interested in one author, Sadasiva Rao, who suffered from a heart disease, lived for such and such number of years, in constant fear of death! They would be interested more in whether the author of the four volumes completed the fifth. When I am not writing it, my life is utterly worthless. I shall fulfil my ambition. It will be enough if I can prepare the first draft in four months. If I die after producing the first draft, my wife can always edit it, revise it and finalise it. But would it be possible for you to keep me alive once I begin the work until I finish it?"

The doctor meditated on these words and as he did so, a weak, gentle smile formed on his lips. He was familiar with the examples of researchers in his own field of medical science who had sacrificed their lives in the cause of knowledge.

"If no-one had sacrificed life in the cause of promoting the growth of knowledge, human civilisation would not have attained the level it has."

If his words as an expert in heart diseases could help in the writing of a great work of learning, he should not hesitate to put them to such a use. Therefore, he held Rao's hand encouragingly and said reassuringly, "Don't worry. I shall use all my knowledge and experience in looking after your health. I can assure you that nothing untoward will befall you as long as I am here."

Rao was elated. He had no words to express his gratitude to the doctor. When Rao told Karuna about his new decision and the doctor's supportive assurance, she was stunned. In no time her eyes filled with tears. Rao asked her in surprise, "Can you cry like other women?"

"Am I not human? You owe a duty to the world of scholarship. But have you no duty to the wife you have married and have you no relationship with her?"

Unable to answer her, Rao lowered his head as if looking to the spot where her words had pierced him. For his sake, for the sake of his ambitious project, she came to him, sacrificing everything, dedicating her life to his cause and slaving for him. In return, he had offered her little. But he knew that she had done what she had done without expecting any reward or return. Perhaps the greatest gift to her would be to live longer.

"I have decided not to write the volume myself. But you should start writing it soon. I shall read what you write and revise it and finalise it."

Karuna squeezed his hand in affection and gratitude. Within a week of this decision, she started to write and was able to write forty pages in the next ten days. As it would be difficult to read her hand-written manuscript, she typed the material and her husband read at the pace of four pages a day. As Rao ran through the pages, he was all admiration for her English style, the richness of the content and her dedication. But he hardly needed fresh evidence of these qualities in her. He was also aware that her writing lacked the inner strength and energy of the preceding volumes. Karuna readily agreed with his critical evaluation.

Rao's life began to move on a more even keel than before. He found it difficult to live a life bereft of work, geared to his life's supreme goal. He had always been a hard-working person and this enforced idleness irked him, perhaps death was preferable, perhaps it was not much different. Within a fortnight his mental condition began to have its effect on his physical health. Karuna was able to see his agony helplessly. One day, he confessed to her, "Karuna, you did not marry this inert, goalless, soulless body. Help me to complete the work for which you married me. Don't look at the situation from the angle of an ordinary woman, worried by the question of what would happen to you after your husband's death. You are not one of them, you are utterly unique."

Karuna became grave and she resisted. The whole night she thought over her situation, examining it from every angle. When Rao returned from his walk, he found that she had washed the pen that had been lying uselessly for the last six months and filled it with ink.

"Until now I have been wandering in the darkness of ignorance. Whenever it is necessary, dictate to me. I can use short-hand. I shall not leave this room. Write."

XXVII

The elaborate study of Sanskrit, the *Vedas* and the *Upanishads* suffered as Cheeni left for university at eight in the morning, returning after six in the evening. During the holidays Sanskrit and *Vedic* studies commenced in the early afternoon. The solicitous grandfather now fed him with more milk and ghee as Cheeni needed more energy to travel between Nanjangud and Mysore. Even when the boy volunteered to help in the kitchen the old man would refuse, urging him to go back to his books, especially now as he was entering his senior year.

Karthika month came and the death anniversary of Shrothri's father was due to be performed. As Shrothri found it, at his age, a physical strain to cook whilst fasting, they engaged a helper, Kuppayya. Kuppayya would arrive the day before and would perform the ritual cleaning of the kitchen, would collect the ritually pure water and prepare the chilli powder and pepper spices. Shrothri performed the death anniversary of his parents and ancestors with the utmost seriousness, ritual correctness and devotion. Equal faith was given to worshipping the deities and the ancestors, for he held the deep conviction that a family could not prosper unless its ancestors were properly and ritually propitiated. The most orthodox and ritually purest brahmins were invited to eat at the ceremony. These brahmins had to satisfy stringent qualifications: they must have performed the *sandhyavandana* regularly, they must be physically in good health and they must be skilled in uttering clearly and correctly the *Vedic mantras* and most importantly, there must have been no moral lapse in their lives. Shrothri gave generously to the brahmins during the death anniversary ceremonies; copper spoons, new pots, dhoties, silver rupee coins, prostrating himself reverentially before them. The old man fasted the night before and did not touch a single drop of water until the ritual was completed.

This time, as before, Kuppayya had come the previous night to prepare the kitchen and Shrothri cooked the day's food in a mud oven. The evening before, Shrothri was searching for a book in his study upstairs for he wanted to clarify some issue relating to the rites. Vaguely, he recalled that the point was discussed in *Gobhila Smriti* but could not remember the exact *slokas*. He did not possess a printed copy of the text but indistinctly remembered writing them in a notebook in his own hand. Upstairs, he rummaged in one of the several old trunks but despite searching diligently, he could not find it. Marginally frustrated, he was about to close the trunk lid when he spotted, quite by accident, an old piece of paper, so old that it almost disintegrated as he picked it up. It was part of an old letter from a time far, far back.

"... are a vile man, you who ruined so many, you who cheated your own brother. For the sake of a family feud and some property! We all know of the tale of Shyamadas. Seven generations of Shrothris will be sent to *naraka*. God will judge you."

It was signed Kittappa of Edatore.

During his youth Shrothri had heard the name of Kittappa, his father's younger brother. It was part of the family lore that the two brothers had quarrelled bitterly and had turned into implacable enemies. Shrothri wondered what could have been the evil deed of his parents which condemned seven generations of Shrothris to *naraka*. As the next day was the day of a death anniversary, his mind naturally focused on his ancestors and he could not even begin to think of them being consigned to *naraka*. But who would tell him the truth? He was already seventy three and the undated letter was very old, ancient beyond reckoning. Lakshmi. After all, she was born in this very household. Women, he knew, had a way of discovering things, a way not open to men. Lakshmi was squatting in the middle hall, preparing the vegetables for the next day's cooking. He asked her in a forthright manner, "Do you know a Shyamadas?"

Lakshmi was dumbfounded.

"Yes, I have heard the name."

She stopped as if she had taken a wrong step and was eager to retrace it. He read out the letter in his hand and asked her, "What is this matter for which my ancestors are to go to *naraka*? Tell me the story of Shyamadas."

"I don't know anything Seenappa. I have heard that he used to visit this town for his story-telling".

Shrothri's curiosity had reached a feverish pitch and his doubts became agonisingly acute. He stretched out his hand and said, "Lakshmi, hold my hand."

Confused, she asked, "Why?"

"Do as I tell you."

Then he took hold of her right hand and asked, "Touching my
hand, will you swear to speak truth? If you tell a lie, you will go to
naraka after death. Do you know anything about that letter?"

Lakshmi lowered her head. When Shrothri repeated his question,
she asked him, "Seenappa, why have you pushed me into this
impossible situation?"

Her voice was full of anguish. But Shrothri was adamant and
relentless.

"What do you gain by hearing that story? Why are you so
stubborn?"

"I am consumed by curiosity. No matter how diabolical the deed,
tell me about it. I can withstand it. On your faith in me, tell me
everything you know. Do not omit a single detail."

"What can be more important for me than to obey your wish?"

Greedy by nature, Nanjunda Shrothri Senior, Srinivasa Shrothri's
father, had taken possession of the ancestral property by the time of
his father's death. At twenty eight, when he assumed control over the
household, his younger brother, Kittappa Shrothri, was twenty four.
The younger brother was the exact opposite of the elder in nature, the
latter disgustingly avaricious, the former generous to a fault. Where
the elder viewed existence from a cold-blooded, business angle, the
younger was deeply emotional, with a devout belief in God and
dharma. Their wives too were perfect matches to their husbands.
Naturally, when the brothers were hostile to each other, how could the
wives behave as sisters? Kittappa's wife bore him a son within a year
of the nuptial ceremony but Nanjunda Shrothri's wife, Achamma,
though twenty four, did not conceive. When the two wives wrangled,
Kittappa's wife would not hesitate to say, "God grants children
according to our *papa* and *punya.*"

Invariably on the occasion of their father's death anniversary, the
two would quarrel. When Kittappa wanted the brahmins to be offered
a gift of silver rupees, Nanjunda would retort, "You can do that when
you earn your own money. As long as I live, I shall give only a
quarter of a rupee coin."

In the natural course of time and tempers, the quarrel went beyond
mere words and the two came to blows. Kittappa, being the stronger,
rained quite a few blows on his elder brother. Achamma joined the
fray, followed by Kittappa's wife, and so they created a pretty tableau

of Indian, village life. For about a month after this fracas, Kittappa could not suppress his anger, but irritatingly Nanjunda Shrothri would smile disarmingly at his brother, even the day after the quarrel, incensing him further. Kittappa retaliated by ridiculing him, calling him a shameful miser.

A year later the feud between the brothers culminated in the legal partitioning of the property. The partition was executed by four *panchas*. The two fathers-in-law insisted on being present and thus the process continued with the maximum of squabbling and the minimum of efficiency. While detailing the assets and liabilities of the family, Nanjunda Shrothri showed a liability of twenty thousand rupees against the landed property and produced a legal document, showing the loan. In fact, he had obtained a blank piece of paper signed in advance by Kittappa who was not particularly knowledgeable in practical matters. Kittappa lost his case and he was eventually left with a paltry two acres property. Managing to sell it, he left the village with his wife and three children and became the official priest of a temple near Edatore. The anger remained.

During the night Nanjunda Shrothri was accustomed to going out to answer the call of nature, and usually he went to the Lakki bank of the Gundala stream behind their house. One night, when he was there, somebody hit him from behind and before he could yell, another stuffed a piece of cloth into his mouth. Together his two assailants stripped him of his dhoti and tied his arms and hands with it, beating the naked body with a birch stick until it was red with weals. One attacker stood before him and spoke in a tone of mocking vengeance, proclaiming wildly that this was the punishment to be meted out to a cheat. Nanjunda recognised the voice as that of Kittappa.

Unaware of these happenings, Achamma was asleep in the house. When she found her husband missing in the morning, she thought that he might have gone to the fields and returned to her household chores. A woman, who had gone to fetch water at seven in the morning, saw Nanjunda Shrothri, almost naked, his hands and legs bound, his mouth stuffed, thrown on the bank of the stream. Blushing at the sight, she rushed to Shrothri's house and informed his wife about it. The neighbours untied him, laughing amongst themselves. Nanjunda could not sustain his accusation in court as there were no witnesses.

Very soon after the partitioning of the property, Nanjunda
Shrothri's income and wealth showed a great upswing. Lands near the
Deverasanahalli village were haggled over and bought and a huge
profit was made out of his money-lending business. Due to his
charging an excessive rate of compound interest, the money owed
swiftly exceeded the value of the goods pawned. Within ten years
Nanjunda had amassed a wealth that was astonishing for that rural
town. The old house was suddenly deemed too small and was
demolished to be replaced by a new one which even had an upstairs!
Achamma's body was garishly and insensitively covered in pawned,
gold ornaments. But as the days passed the couple began to worry.
Who should be the heir to all this wealth? The idea that the money
could be given away to a charity was never considered. What was
worse from Nanjunda's point of view, was that after his death the
whole property would be given to Kittappa and his children. His heart
twisted at the very idea. The thought of how his brother had
humiliated him by thrashing him and leaving him naked fuelled his
wrath. But what could he do? He was thirty-eight and his wife was
thirty-four. One who had never given away even a paisa for a
charitable cause, now vowed to the deity, Manjunatha of
Dharmasthala, that if he were to become the father of a child, he
would weigh it against silver when it became five and then offer that
silver to Him. As a symbol of his vow, he tied a silver quarter rupee
coin in a piece of turmeric-washed cloth in the deity's name. He
began to recite the *Lalitasahasranama* every day and even served the
brahmins *payasa* and betel leaves with nuts. Somebody said that if
you worshipped the snake deity you would beget children. That he
had done on the bank of the river, spending fifteen rupees. Still they
had no children.

It was at this juncture that he became acquainted with Shyamadas,
a man who made his living by travelling from village to village,
reciting sacred tales from the epics and *puranas*. Originally he came
from the town of Kollegal and his own family still lived there. His
recitations attracted large audiences because of the mellifluous,
melodious voice in which he sang and the clear pronunciation of the
Sanskrit *slokas*. Physically he was a well-built man with a broad face
and long nose. Knowing that Shyamadas was well-versed in Sanskrit,
Najunda Shrothri invited him to his house and asked the itinerant
story-teller about what he should do to beget children. On the advice

given, he went to Tirupati, climbing the steps of the seven hills to Tirumala, the temple town of the god Venkateswara. There he prayed and performed rituals but still there came no child. Finally, turning to his ruthless practicality, Nanjunda went to Mysore and was examined by a medical doctor regarding his sexual potency. The doctor informed him that he would not produce children because of a physical deficiency. When he realised that no deity would help him, he thought of adopting a son, but none nearby was prepared to give his son. In the meantime, gossip had it that Kittappa was boasting that, after the death of his childless elder brother, the property would come to him and his children. Nanjunda Shrothri's body began to burn with anger and hatred.

He shrieked, "It does not matter even if all my ancestors languish in *naraka*, I shall see that not even a pie of mine will go to that wretched brother or his offspring."

The anger was fuelled by his three burdens in life - his childlessness, his incapacity and an intense hatred. The evil idea that had occurred to him earlier, and which he had dismissed, was given fresh life by his brother's boastful statement.

At first, Achamma did not agree with him. She was forty and in these years she had displayed innumerable human vices - greed, selfishness, deceitfulness but she had never abandoned her devotion to her husband. The long, unfulfilled desire to become a mother tempted her and yet her husband's plan repulsed her. At the same time she could not tolerate the idea of their property going to the children of her hated rival - her sister-in-law! Slowly the desire to become a mother sprouted again in her. Shyamadas was about her age or perhaps slightly younger, and he used to visit Nanjangud twice a year. Even though his performances took place in the surrounding villages, Shyamadas usually stayed in Nanjunda's house. This time, when Shyamadas came to stay with them, Nanjunda Shrothri absented himself on the plea of visiting his lands. After a month Achamma began to vomit in the mornings and showed signs of pregnancy. Nanjunda Shrothri was worried that Shyamadas might divulge the secret so he invited Shyamadas to his house, gave him a thrashing and shouted at him, "I thought you were a virtuous person. I entertained you as a guest in my house and fed you. What did you do, you ungrateful wretch, in return for my kindness? If you ever show your face anywhere around Nanjangud, I shall make you regret the day you were born."

When Shyamadas went inside, Achamma offered him a bag containing five hundred silver rupee coins and said, "You don't know him. Don't ever return. I am sure that he will have you murdered."

Shyamadas had no regrets. He never again made an appearance in that area.

After nine months, Achamma gave birth to an attractive male baby, full of health, his body filled out, his forehead wide and his face broad. Nanjunda Shrothri named the child after his own father, Srinivasa Shrothri. Some people in the town knew the truth but none had the courage to open his mouth to speak out, for practically everybody was obliged to Shrothri and some time or other, everyone had to borrow money from him by pledging their gold and silver.

The brilliant boy, Srinivasa, was initiated into his brahmin life at the age of eight through a grand thread-wearing ceremony. The young brahmin initiate was told to recite his genealogy by his father, relating his *gotra* and *pravara*.

... and Lakshmi finished narrating what she knew.

"Is this all true?"

"How can I say? Have I seen them with my eyes? When I was young, I heard my father telling all this to somebody whom I didn't know. I only remember overhearing it."

Shrothri fell into an abysmal silence. He remembered Nanjunda Shrothri and the mother who had borne him. He remembered his father as a short, squat person, dark in colour, blunt nosed. His mother too, was no better in appearance; she had a small, round face. Then Shrothri reflected on his own physique and appearance. Though seventy four, he was a tall, sturdy figure. His face was striking, broad and his eyes large, his forehead wide and his nose long and straight. Though he had never been attached much to his body, he had been content with its strength and health, the greatest wealth a person could hope to gain. Now he began to hate his body as something unclean, repulsive.

Shrothri came down and slept on his bed, a storm raging inside his mind. Of course he had always known about his parents' greedy and miserly lives and that his father made his wealth through lending. After his father's death, when he came to head the household, he had not only stopped that business but he had also given away almost three quarters of his father's wealth in the form of gifts and donations to charity. Yet he was never ready to pass moral judgement on anyone, least of all his own parents. But now a deep-rooted belief of his life seemed to have been axed. Shrothri had enormous pride in his family history and its distinctiveness. The humiliation now was to see the crumbling of the Kasyapa lineage, a lineage stretching back to the beginning of time, a lineage to which he thought he belonged.

Even if he had been a child born of another family and had then come to the Shrothri line as an adopted son, he would not have been so tormented. Even if his parents had bought him for three fistfuls of rice from poor parents and brought him up, he would not have worried. Adoption, he knew, was sanctioned by tradition as a legitimate mode of acquiring parenthood by childless parents. Nanjunda Shrothri's action, however, was not motivated by the desire to promote the interest of the lineage or the desire to have a son to perform his death rites. It was from sheer malice, from the desire to prevent his brother from getting his ill-gotten property, an act of revenge and hatred. He asked himself with unbearable pain, "I am a child born as a fruit of that deed, a child called into existence to satisfy my father's basest desires. What is my lineage? Where then is the purity of my genesis?"

Instead of condemning his parents, Shrothri began to condemn himself and his birth.

Lakshmi, who was lying in a bed next to Cheeni's, could not sleep either for she had anticipated the devastating effect on Seenappa of these ugly revelations. All these years, she herself had been wrestling with the question, "How can a person born of such parents and brought up in such a household turn out to be a person of the highest moral righteousness?"

She had not found an answer. Perhaps there was none alive in Nanjangud who knew the truth and, even if they did, they would not have the courage to speak of it, for Seenappa had the reputation of being a *rishi*, a sage. Who could raise his voice against him? As for Lakshmi, she believed that a man's worth depended not on birth or lineage, but his own individual qualities and achievement. She regarded Seenappa as a god. She tried to comfort him, "Who knows the absolute truth? I have always regarded the question of birth as an unimportant one. God rewards people on the basis of their deeds of sin and merit. From the day I first set eyes on you, you have lived an exemplary life of righteousness. Even the most exact weighing by the god of death, *Yama*, should earn you a place in the highest heaven."

Shrothri remained silent. He heard her words but his mind could not respond as it was caught up in its own chaotic oscillation. He thought of himself as the topmost branch of a tree that had grown from the depthless earth up towards the sky. The branch was sawn off and it fell from that great height. The magnificent tree appeared to be standing indifferent to the fate of the falling branch, as if it had nothing to do with it. Shrothri felt he was an orphan, a directionless entity, an illegitimate child born for illegitimate purposes.

Again, he remembered his parents. They had undoubtedly brought him up with love and care. Nanjunda Shrothri was by nature greedy and miserly but otherwise he had been a solicitous parent. His mother had been inordinately fond of him and for her, feeding and dressing him was a source of great joy. These memories lingered with him for many years after their death and every year their death anniversary was an occasion for remembering them with filial love. It was terrible for him now to contemplate that his status as their offspring was thrown into such illegitimacy, a colossal farce.

The story of the epic, *Mahabharata*, came to his mind. It was customary in the days of the epic for a childless person, desirous of a son to perpetuate his lineage, to let another person impregnate his wife. However, the stringent condition was that the stranger involved should do this without sensual or selfish gratification, with the mind of a lofty sage who had attained mastery over the senses. He must donate his semen and seed as a spiritual deed, and the process itself was like a spiritual rite, a *yajna*; they called it *niyoga*. But in this age of *Kali,* that practice had disappeared. The spirit of this age and its customs were very different. Moreover the *niyoga* practice stipulated that the act should never involve such base motives as greed for wealth or sexual gratification.

Shrothri realised that the next day he would have to perform the death anniversary of Nanjunda Shrothri, as his son. He saw the situation as a horrible travesty. Until now he had been performing the death anniversary of a person who was not his biological father, to whose lineage he had not been attached according to *dharma*, who had his wife impregnated out of a sense of hatred and thus been the unsanctioned cause of his birth. It amounted to a travesty of true *dharma*. Shrothri was aware of the custom of performing the death anniversary rite of a person on the basis of affection, and not a blood relationship. For instance, if a friend died childless, surviving friends could perform his death anniversary rites. But this was not such a case at all. He called Lakshmi.

"After knowing the truth, there is no point in performing the anniversary tomorrow. In the morning I shall go to the invited brahmins and tell them not to come for the rites."

Lakshmi replied, "But for so many years it has been done..."

Shrothri interrupted her, "When one does not know the truth, one can continue a tradition or practice. Because of ignorance, it does not become right and legitimate. I am now a different person, a different entity with a different status."

Lakshmi kept silent. Shrothri was immersed in thought. After half an hour, Lakshmi said, "Didn't you say that one shouldn't do anything impulsively, in the heat of the moment? You also used to say that the line of *dharma* is thin and delicate and that it required the deepest reflection to arrive at its precise nature. Don't act hastily. Let tomorrow's ceremony go on as planned. Who is more knowledgeable in these matters than you?"

Shrothri said nothing.

Neither of them slept that night. Shrothri did not get up at his usual time but lay lifelessly on the bed. Kuppayya had arrived before eight, drew water from the well in the backyard and poured it over himself. Thus ritually purified, he sprinkled water on the vegetables to purify them too. Cheeni bathed and wrapped around his waist a piece of wet cloth reaching down to his knees, also in ritual purity, and went into the kitchen to assist Kuppayya. All the items were being cooked in pure ghee and the cooking went on with full force and speed. But Shrothri had not yet bathed. He was in the cattle-shed, stroking the cows. Did the animals possess consciousness? If so, did they have any awareness of their lineage? Thus many unresolvable and unfamiliar issues crowded his mind, floating like directionless, drifting clouds. By twelve noon, Subbayya Sastry arrived. For the first serving of the meal, the brahmins came, wearing ritually pure dhotis, their foreheads smeared with ash, carrying gourds and small ladles, both made of shining copper. One of the brahmins, Master Anantaram saw Shrothri still unready for the rite and was shocked.

The rites started after midday. As the ritual formulas were uttered in Sanskrit, Shrothri, an expert in interpreting them, was unable to make sense of them. He even forgot to which finger he should fix the ritual *dharbha* grass loop. The chief officiating priest had to remind him of the ordinary routine details. Thinking that Shrothri was perhaps unwell, the priest slowed down his chanting of the ritual words. Then Shrothri sprinkled on his head the water with which the feet of the brahmins had been washed. The meal began. Instead of Shrothri, it was Cheeni who started to serve the food. The priest was surprised. Shrothri had lost control over his mind, which was scattering in several directions at the same time. The main priest uttered the crucial instruction, "After the brahmins have eaten, the performer should offer ritual water and *pinda* to the dead ancestors."

Shrothri heard and the brahmins washed their hands.

Then the priest spread the *dharba* grass towards the south and instructed Shrothri to take out the *pinda* out of the dry leaf containers. After Shrothri sat down, holding the rice ball, the priest chanted the formula, "This is for my father, Nanjundadeva of *Kashyapagotra*, of the Vasu form, I offer him this *pinda,* offering it at the feet of Sri Rudrapada in Gaya... now please place this *pinda* on the *dharba* and take the next *pinda*..." and thus went on the recitation in sonorous Sanskrit.

As soon as this formula fell into his ears, Shrothri felt giddy and his eyes were covered with darkness. He tried his best to overcome it but it had grasped him. Totally exhausted, he collapsed there on the bare floor. Master Anantaram who had completed his meal got up, scared and came close to him and took Shrothri's unconscious body and placed it on his lap. After water was profusely sprinkled on his head and he was fanned, it took Shrothri ten minutes to recover consciousness. He tried to get up but could not. Bundling a dhoti into a pillow, the priest placed it beneath Shrothri's head and said to the cook, Kuppayya, "You should come. Wear the ritual *dharbha* loop and carry on the remaining part of the ceremony. It is permitted."

Kuppayya wrapped a piece of cloth around his waist and sat for the rites. Shrothri closed his eyes.

As always, the rites were ended by the offering of gifts of dhotis, copper vessels, copper ladles and silver rupee coins to the brahmins. It was then that Shrothri opened his eyes and was able to talk. But the officiating priest regarded the interruption of the rites and Shrothri's withdrawal from them midway as harbingers of some great catastrophe for the Shrothri household.

A few days passed and Shrothri said to Cheeni, "Cheeni, take two days' leave from university. We have to go on a journey."
"Why Grandfather?"
"I shall tell you on the way."
Leaving Lakshmi at home, the two went to Mysore and from there caught a train for Edatore. After they sat down in the compartment, Shrothri explained to the grandson, that Nanjunda Senior had a brother by the name of Kittappa who was entitled to an equal share in the Shrothri family property.

"I had never seen him but I have heard that he was cheated of his due. It is for us to find Kittappa's children and grandchildren and transfer to them half of our property. That is *dharma*. I am asking you because your signature is necessary on any document which transfers our property to them. My life is uncertain and I may die anytime. You are the heir to the property and therefore I want to consult you."

The grandson replied with the utmost of respect, "As you say, if it is *dharma* to give them half our property I agree with all my soul. Your words always reflect *dharma*."

Shrothri was overjoyed at his grandson's words. They reached Edatore Station at two in the afternoon, hired a horse carriage and went to the house of an acquaintance in the Nagara area. When they started their search for information about Kittappa who was forty years old some seventy five years ago, it transpired that there was none in the place belonging to the Shrothri lineage. In fact, there were no persons there belonging to the families that had migrated from Nanjangud and none of the present priests at the temple had a grandfather with the Shrothri surname. At last they were successful in finding an eighty-five year old person with some recollection.

"Yes, I remember that when I was a young man, a person called Kittappa lived here, a man from the Nanjangud area. He had three sons and he was then about forty or forty-five. A very short tempered man. He became the priest in a temple in a nearby village. Once there was a fight between him and the temple guardians. It seems he beat the persons involved very badly indeed. The fault was another's but he was the relative of a local wealthy and influential family, and he saw to it that Kittappa and his family were ostracised and made to leave the town. Nobody knows where he went with his children."

Realising that his efforts had failed, Shrothri returned to Nanjangud with his grandson, disappointed. Days rolled on and the old man showed less enthusiasm in the boy's *Vedic* studies. Sometimes, while teaching, the old man's mind would wander away elsewhere. At that point, the instruction stopped abruptly. He was seized often by the thought, "This house, landed property, this money, none of it is mine. If I chance upon members of Kittappa Shrothri's family, it is *dharma* to hand all this over to them. But how to find them?"

Shrothri lost his appetite and began to eat very little. When he saw the rice on the leaf, he felt he had no right to it as it did not come from his lands nor was given in legitimate charity. With that thought, he got up from the meal and then washed his hand.

Nanjangud was a regular haunt of itinerant story-tellers, wandering brahmins, and people raising money for marriages and thread-wearing ceremonies. Everyone of them invariably visited Shrothri's house and they left its doors with generous gifts and donations. Whenever such persons came to their house, Shrothri made it a point to ask them, "In your wanderings, did you ever come across members of the Shrothri family? Or hear about them?"

The answer was always in the negative. Then he would request them, "If by chance you do run into them, please write to me about it."

Then he would give them his address and add, "It is not enough if it is just a Shrothri family. In their genealogy, there must be a grandfather or great-grandfather with the name Kittappa Shrothri. He was from Nanjangud. It would be of great help to this old man."

He placed an advertisement in the newspapers:

"If there is anyone belonging to the Shrothri family of Nanjangud, please contact so and so." None replied.

These days Shrothri often remembered Katyayani and her transgression of the rule of widowhood. Having borne the issue of one family tree, she had married into another lineage. In his mind he began to form a comparison between the behaviour of his nominal father, Nanjunda Shrothri, and his mother, with that of Katyayani. Such a comparison convinced the old man that Katyayani had not committed any reprehensible act for she had done nothing to satisfy such base desires as wreaking vengeance or expressing hatred. She had acted simply as a natural consequence of the spirit of the modern age which had engulfed her, her only deficiency her inability to resist the heat of her youthful urges. But when he recalled the deed of his parents, he was filled with repulsion, contempt, anger. Soon such feelings would subside, replaced by a profound repentance. He would pray within himself, "Why should I lose the equanimity I have attained and enjoyed for so long? Why should I make room in my mind for such base emotions as contempt and hatred? If God has willed for me this kind of genesis, who is to blame? What authority do I have to judge and condemn my parents? Oh God, grant me the detachment I have so far enjoyed, not to measure the sins and merits of others."

XXVIII

For five months Rao worked on the final volume with fierce and sustained concentration. Each day he awoke to its presence and it drove him onwards, exhausting his frail body. As he wrote, he came closer and closer to the present day, closer and closer to the reality of his time. The work shone out from behind them, a stupendous catalogue of the culture of a land, which would stop when the authors could go no further, when they realised that they themselves were history in the making.

"Finished!"

Karuna's heart was full and gently she squeezed his hands.

"Your work is over. Buddha has blessed you. Now follow the doctor's instructions."

From that day on, Rao began to derive an indescribable joy from life. Decades of uninterrupted labour and single-mindedness had borne fruit, a symbol of Karuna's devotion and faith, the completed work.

"Every individual must realise the goals of life in his own way. Up to a point, I have realised mine. The material collected for this work has not been used wholly and can yield three or four short volumes and some ten research papers. I have no energy left to do these things. Let Karuna do them by herself. If God grants me some more years, I might help her in finalising these publications."

But Karuna herself had much left to do for she had to check the source material cited, edit the style of writing, consider the presentation and finally type out the material to be sent to the publisher. Rao wanted to dedicate the last volume to Karuna but she did not agree, arguing ingeniously that no father would dedicate a child to the mother who had borne it.

Rao took his daily walk towards Lakshmipuram. Raja and Katyayani were at home. Katyayani brought out a glass of milk. She was thin beyond recognition and it appeared that even the most thorough search would not yield even a drop of blood in her body. Rao looked at her compassionately and turning to Raja said, "I have come to take Nagu with me."

Surprised and slightly apprehensive, Raja went inside and conveyed the message to her but Nagalakshmi was adamant.

"I shall not go to any other house."

Raja explained to her that Rao was badly sick and that he had completed his writing.

"It is likely that worrying about you caused his heart attack. His health remains delicate."

"Why do you think of such bad things?" she said crossly.

"It will take just an hour to finish the cooking. Let him stay and eat with us. I shall serve all of you first and then go with him. But Katyayani's health is so bad. How will you manage?" she added with concern.

Raja assured her, "We will manage somehow. I shall help her. Prithvi is here. If need be, we can ask the cook there, Raghappa, to come here."

Nagalakshmi remembered the name of Sri Rama and she praised Him in her mind, "You will never abandon those who put their trust in you. Sri Rama, Jaya Rama, I surrender myself to you."

The moment Nagalakshmi set her foot in Rao's household, it acquired a new life, a new spirit. That very afternoon she sent Raghappa to buy spices, and fried and prepared her spice powders. In the evening she sent him to the market to buy lemon, raw ginger, betel leaves, a small limebox and a variety of vegetables. That night she cooked the food and served Rao herself and she also served Karuna. When Karuna addressed Nagalakshmi as "sister" in English, Rao told her to use the Kannada "akka".

The next day Nagalakshmi got up at five o'clock, lit the kitchen fire and boiled the early morning milk for the household. Rao went out for a walk, cane in hand.

"Sister, shall I help?" Karuna enquired politely, unsure.

"No. Your work is reading and writing. You do what you can do best."

Karuna's face showed a gentle smile and, uncomfortably, she felt as if she had chanced upon a hitherto ignored treasure. Returning to her manuscript she plunged into her work. Rao returned from his walk at half past eight. Nagalakshmi led him to the bathroom, scrubbed his body and bathed him. When he asked her, "Am I a baby?" she replied, "What else are you? A child unable to look after its health."

She pretended to be angry but beneath the ill-fitting mask, there was great joy and enthusiasm. At ten, she asked both of them to pay

their reverential salutation to Lord Rama before inviting them for lunch. They obeyed her.

After lunch, Karuna collected together the pages of manuscript and hurried to the library. When Nagalakshmi sat down to eat, Rao came into the kitchen and started to serve her, regretting those days that had passed away. He suggested that Raja, Katyayani and Prithvi could come here too and they could all live as one household. She agreed that the bungalow was indeed very big. She offered him betel leaves but he refused as the doctor had forbidden this. He urged her but, no, she did not indulge either.

Nagalakshmi was almost fifty and most of her hair had turned white. Nevertheless she had carefully combed and plaited it. It glistened and the chrysanthemum tucked into it was very becoming. There was a large moon-like vermilion mark on her forehead and a smaller one below it. Her face shone with an innocent beauty, a tender saintliness. As before, her arms were covered with different coloured bangles. Her cheeks, toes and palms were smeared with turmeric, enhancing her quiet beauty. Nothing brash or garish, everything subdued and soft.

"I deserted you all these days. I would have been stronger and healthier if I had lived with you."

Nagalakshmi bowed her head shyly. Seeing the tears, Rao became solicitous. Holding her hand, he asked her to sit closer and consoled her, "Don't cry. I shall never leave you now."

She made him lie down. Rao made her lap his pillow and stretched himself on the bed. Holding his face between her hands, she asked him,

"When you were sick, why didn't you send for me? Of course, when you came then to take me, I was very angry. But am I such a great sinner as not to serve you during your illness?"

"Don't say that. You are the one with spiritual merit and I am the one who is a sinner..."

She interrupted him, "Tcha, you shouldn't say that," and covered his mouth with her palm.

Taking hold of her palm, he said, "No, I am not judging from the point of sin and virtue. I married her for no base purpose. But for her I wouldn't have finished my writing in time. Otherwise it would have taken ten more years to finish. We could have lived together like this right from the start but with her modern outlook she was

unwilling, unable. Without her constant companionship, my work could not have been completed."

Rao's joy was measureless. There was no conflict in his life and he had attained an elusive harmony. He said in a voice all the more powerful for its quietness, "I have written the history of this great country's glorious culture. It is a culture that has given the world, the most elevated and noble philosophy, art and religion! I have tried to describe the inner strength of countless great souls who acted as many Gangas whose water joined the great ocean of this culture! This writing has given me ecstasy and fulfilment. Perhaps, Nagu, our separation all these days, your suffering all these days were necessary for the success of this work. Now all that is over, and we have reached that end, our re-union and the blissful moment for resting my head on your lap. Nagu, are you aware of how happy I am? Bend down and put your head on my chest. Embrace me."

Rao clasped her by the waist. She bent down and gently pulled him to her. Rao murmured, "Nagu..."

He was too full of happiness to say anything more. He felt his breath choking and he began to sweat. His left chest was in mortal agony. He shifted one hand gently and placed it there. Nagalakshmi was petrified. For about half a minute, Rao's face was contorted with terrible pain. Not knowing what to do, she called Raghappa.

By then Rao's face showed less pain, his eyes were closed and his limbs were motionless. As Raghappa ran to fetch a neighbour, Nagalakshmi knew that her husband was dead. The neighbouring professor's wife rushed there and held Nagalakshmi's hand as her crying increased in volume and pitch. When Karuna entered the room, she saw the motionless body, that weeping woman and wanted to scream at her. But she could not and she tottered forward and collapsed on that very lifelessness.

As soon as the news of Dr. Rao's sudden death spread, teachers and students of Mysore University filled his bungalow to pay their respects. The principal declared that classes would not be held that day as a mark of respect. The next day a ceremony of remembrance was arranged and on the table on the dais were piled the published works in a prominent manner. Next to the books was a photo of Dr. Rao, which had been decorated with a huge garland. Speaker after

238

speaker showered spontaneous praise. It was a tribute to a dedication and a single-mindedness beyond comprehension.

According to ancient custom, the death rites were to be performed by Prithvi but his thread ceremony had not taken place and so it fell to Raja to do the duty.

For Nagalakshmi, the darkness and despair of her life appeared to have been dispelled when her husband had taken her in a jutka to their home. The next day, at the same time, her husband had rested his head on her lap and breathed his last. She wept, telling herself that the sins of her past life had now been visited upon her in this birth. Widowhood was a cruel fate. Ritually, even after her husband's death, Nagalakshmi was not fully regarded as a widow until the tenth day. Neighbours and friends came to put the vermilion mark on her forehead, deck her hair with flowers, put bangles on her wrists as this was the last time they could do so. As the tenth day approached, Nagalakshmi's agony increased at the thought of losing her right to these signs of being a wife. Earlier she looked at herself in the mirror just once a day, but now she would peep again and again at her face, the symbols of her wifehood. Often, when the sorrow became too much, she would roll on the floor and howl.

"Raja, when the breath of my life has stopped, what is the sense in preserving this wretched body? Tomorrow let this hair, this sari and all this, let it go. Fetch my widow's red sari."

"Don't talk like a person from age and a custom gone by. Let the rites take place as usual. But don't let them shave your head. And you can wear a white sari."

"I want to take the full vows of a widow."

Katyayani felt a sharp stab. It was difficult for one who had known Nagalakshmi earlier as a beautiful wife to imagine the new Nagalakshmi, wrapped in a red sari. Her own widowhood, pummelled into the past, revived itself and dragged its beaten form before her. Twenty years ago when she had lost her first husband, she too was allowed those ten days of wifehood before entering the night of her widowhood. On the tenth, she had swooned. They wrapped a white sari round her to mark the end of her joyful life. Her mother-in-law, Bhagirathamma, had suggested that she should have her head shaved and that she should be asked to wear the traditional widow's red sari but Shrothri himself had disagreed as he did not want to wound the modern sensibility of the young daughter-in-law. Her life too had changed its texture and tenor from that day.

"What she says is right. Do it."

Raja replied in a choked voice, "But I can't bear the sight of Nagu in a red sari."

"One must endure sorrow. In these matters her mind is more mature than yours. She has vowed to accept her new status in its entirety. You cannot change the reality of her status, you cannot pretend just by rejecting the symbols. In such matters, a woman's instinct and her inner inspiration should prevail over a man's worldly thinking."

Raja was silenced. The next day Nagalakshmi was taken out of the house. While the outward signs of her lost wifehood were taken away from her one by one, she sat tight-lipped, determined not to cry. The bangles snapped, the hair fell, swishing at her feet. After the rites were over, she sat in the backyard, where a potful of cold water was poured over her. The following day, Nagalakshmi sat before a picture of Sri Rama, and declared, "Sri Rama, I have placed all my faith in you. You allowed this to happen to me and yet I shall continue to worship you. Ensure that in my next life I die as a wife and not as a widow. Lord, favour me in my next life by granting him as my husband".

From that day, she began to spend more of her time writing out Sri Rama's name. During all this, Katyayani looked after the household but her sick and deteriorating body found the task beyond its ability. In a few days, she ran a high temperature and then as there was no-one else to do it, it fell to Nagalakshmi to look after her.

Since she had not wished to hurt the Rao household by leaving earlier, Karuna waited until the thirteenth day, until the death rites had been fully performed. After she became Rao's wife she had put the vermilion mark on her forehead and had always worn a white sari. On the tenth day, without any rite, she wiped away the vermilion mark. After the last day of the rites, when the soul of the dead person has entered the heavenly abode of Vaikuntha, the home of Lord Vishnu, the preserver, Karuna told Raja, "Now I shall leave here."

Raja was surprised.

"How can you go back to that bungalow to live alone? The university will take possession of it as per the rules. We shall shift the books and other things to this house. You can use one of our rooms here and finish the remaining work. After all, aren't you my sister-in-law?"

Karuna thanked him but insisted firmly. With Raghappa, she moved back to the bungalow.

The same evening the neighbouring professor and the Vice-Chancellor visited Karuna to offer their formal condolences. They sat in Rao's room and recalled his sterling virtues, telling her of the many letters that Mysore University had received from scholars abroad. Obituaries were to be published in scholarly journals in Europe and America. To help with the redrafting of the fifth volume, the Vice-Chancellor would issue a special order exempting her from paying the rent and Mysore University would donate a few thousand rupees towards the publication.

A few days later she received a letter from the publishers, expressing their profound regret at the death of such a scholar and politely they enquired after the fifth volume. Promptly, Karuna wrote back to say that Rao had completed his work. She would get the press-copy ready in three to four months. One month was spent in the library, locating and checking sources and citations. Then she began to work on the type-script, working without respite. If time was spent relaxing then the old, painful memories would return and deepen her depression. Raghappa was an ideal servant and although worried about his own future, not once did he mention this to her.

After four months, Karuna completed her work. She finished typing out the material, corrected the typescript and arranged the manuscript neatly. The publishers had asked her to write a brief biographical account to be included in the preface. By the time the material was ready to be posted, it was ten in the evening. Laying the manuscript out, she stared at it gently, stroked it, re-arranged the pages carefully, stroked it again, gazing at it. She sat back in the easy-chair, totally, totally relaxed for the first time in so many years. Suddenly and unawares, she started to weep. Over the last months, she had worked and slaved over the volume as if he were still alive. While typing, she felt that she was hearing his voice dictating to her. While writing the preface she thought he was sitting before her, speaking to her, and that she was taking it down in shorthand. Now in the cool night there was nothing but a sense of emptiness and meaninglessness. For nearly an hour she sobbed loudly. At last she got up and went near the window to see the darkness stretch out endlessly towards Ceylon.

Slowly she went to the front door. Raghappa was sleeping in the outer yard.

Carefully, so as not to wake him, she opened the door, locked it behind her and walked out into the street. As it was a spacious area, the distance between street lamps was considerable and so, as she walked, she lurched continually from glaring light into darkness. In time, she came to the raised bank of the Kukkarahalli lake. After climbing up the slope, she reached the green bower to the left and sat down on the stone bench beside it and remembered. Once full of sorrow at the prospect of being separated from him, she had rested her head on his lap and cried. Rao had embraced her, the sweetest moment of her life. Drowned in the memory of that moment, she forgot herself and wept. Now she found it impossible to sit there. She got up abruptly and walked towards the university. After the lake came the grounds, surrounded by a few trees. It was under one of those trees that she and Rao used to sit when they came for a walk after dinner and deliberated the context and direction of their work. After the discussion there would be a brief interlude of silence. When they left there, if the light was too dim, she would lead him, holding his hand. She turned her eyes towards the university. Rao had taught for some thirty years, his dedication and achievement part of the very breeze that blew there. She walked further and saw to her left the library building shining with its own light beneath the dark sky. It was in this building that she and Rao had laboured together to create the volumes. As she stared in the windows, she saw the way they worked, Rao's posture as he dictated the material to her. Unable to experience any longer what she had for so long accepted as her life, she walked back to the bungalow.

"If Nagalakshmi had joined them or if she alone had lived with him, maybe he would not have had any occasion to run into situations of such excitement. Maybe he would have lived for another ten years!"

The whole night she could not sleep. She sat in the room till half past eight and then picked up the parcel to take to the post office. A neighbour, also a professor, was standing in his garden and seeing her called out, "Are you going to the post office? Give me the packet. The servant can do it."

"Thank you, but I shall do it myself."

After she handed over the sealed material and obtained the receipt for it from the post office and was returning home, her mind felt utterly empty, its silence haunting her. A major goal of her life had now been realised. Yes, she had to write short papers on the material collected but unused in connection with Rao's volumes. Somehow, out of the void of her mind, she would have to create. Calmly, she walked to the university and waited for Prithvi. As soon as she sighted him, she called out and invited him to the bungalow. He accompanied her.

Sitting next to him she asked, "Have you read any of your father's books?"

"No."

"Why not?"

"I am a science student."

Sadly she smiled. The son had no interest in the books written by a father who had sacrificed his very life for scholarship and learning. And he was a student of a subject unrelated to that of his father. Then she raised her face to look at Prithvi's face. In essence, it was Nagalakshmi's face, but the eyes and the nose had taken after the father. Karuna moved closer and asked him, "Come, place your head on my lap and lie down."

He lowered his head out of shyness and did not stir.

"Don't feel shy. Come here. I, too, am your mother."

She took hold of his arm and made him lie down with his head on her lap. Holding his face between her hands, she asked him, "Child, your mother suffered by being separated from your father. Will you blame me for it?"

"No."

"Wasn't it because of me that your father did that?"

"But I have learnt that, because of you, he was able to write all this. Uncle and Aunt told me."

Karuna bent down and put her arms around the boy, forgetting her own plight. When she woke up at five in the evening, Prithvi had gone and her mind reverted to a sense of emptiness which scared her. The past was coming back through memories, the time on Nandi Hill. After dinner, when she tried to sleep, sleep refused to grace her. She had been all these years a person deeply engaged in active work, and now suddenly she found herself unoccupied, the foundation of her life collapsing. She tried to console herself, saying that as a historian she ought to know that indeed life was not a perfect realisation of every aspiration.

After dinner in the evening, she went out for her customary stroll. Within half-an-hour she had returned. It was impossible to live in this town. The person for whom she had lived, the purpose for which she had laboured were now gone, both a cold comfort. She was totally, utterly alone, a solitary, deserted figure. Ceylon remained, her brother; he must be about fifty now. He might not recognise her and she had stopped writing or visiting a long time ago. But now she remembered him with a love and affection she had never before felt for him and so she sat down and wrote a copious letter. As she wrote, she found herself caught up in a strange emotionalism and she concluded the letter:

"I was able to accomplish an important goal I had set for myself in life. But now that it is over, I find myself facing the frightening prospect of a life of emptiness and darkness. I can only hope that you will allow me to take refuge in your company. After I hear from you, I shall return to the land of my birth. Maybe I could get a teaching job in a university there."

Calmly she packed and then went to Raja's house and told him that any money, saving one thousand rupees for the faithful and diligent Raghappa, was to be transferred to Nagalakshmi. The royalties from the volumes would be given to Prithvi.

"I shall continue the research work and publication left unfinished by my husband, and thus pass the remaining days of my life."

In spite of Raja's protests, she transferred the balance to Nagalakshmi's name. Karuna moved to the bedroom to take her leave of her other sister. Katyayani's condition was graver than described by Raja. Her body had lost all its freshness and had become pale but she managed to talk.

Standing before Nagalakshmi, Karuna said, "In life we have and we shall continue to suffer. For any wrong I have done, please, forgive me."

Then she took Prithvi's face between her hands and kissed his forehead.

"Though you are a student of science, try to read your father's books."

XXIX

As he could not trace any information about Kittappa Shrothri's family, Srinivasa Shrothri abandoned the idea of finding them and his mind began to move in an altogether different direction. When he told Lakshmi of his intention, she was furious, telling him in no uncertain terms that he must have taken leave of his senses.

"*Dharma* is delicate, Lakshmi. It cannot be grasped by mere popular customs and practice."

That Sunday afternoon, while teaching the *Vedas* to Cheeni in his study upstairs, Shrothri stopped mid-way, waited until his grandson had lifted his head expectantly from the text and said, "Child, you have often asked me what it is that I accept totally. I have discovered an answer. I shall do nothing without your full and free consent."

"Grandfather, can there be anything you say with which I do not agree?"

Shrothri hesitated for a minute before answering and then he explained to the young boy the truth about his birth and parentage. Cheeni was dumbstruck. Before he could recover himself and cry out in anger and amazement, leading him to a downward spiral of inequanimity, Shrothri continued, "At first, I thought of handing over half of the property to Kittappa Shrothri's family and their children, whether in Edatore or elsewhere. But now I have changed my mind for I feel that I do not have any claim over any part of this property. What right have we to enjoy the property of a lineage to which we are not joined through blood? If I am a bird that has occupied the nest that does not belong to it, you, my grandson, have no right. We are not entitled to be called members of the Shrothri lineage, for we are not their scion. To carry on the ritual of *Brahmopadesha*, one must have a definite and legitimate affinity to a *gotra*. As members of the *Kashyapagotra*, we were given *Brahmopadesha* and since then we have been faithfully performing all our duties. But now that we have failed to locate the family of Kittappa Shrothri, the legitimate heir to this property, our duty now is to give away this property, either to charities or deserving causes. That is the only way left for us."

Cheeni paused to consider the matter. He speculated about their situation, financially and socially, if the property were given to charity. But he had an unshakeable belief in his grandfather's understanding of *dharma*, and so he answered, "What you say is right. I shall give up this property that does not belong to me. After all, I am young and if I find a job somewhere, then we shall manage to keep ourselves."

Shrothri was overjoyed.

"These are words worthy of one who has studied the *Vedas*. We must give up the wrongfulness of this property for if we do not, then someone in our family tree will lose it through a violation of *dharma*. What is ruinous is not their loss of the property but that they do so by treading the path of *adharma*. There is no greater loss than the accumulation of sin."

Then he explained to Cheeni the last stage of his life.

"Even by the time your father married, I had planned to live a life of a retirement of sorts and had begun to do so. But his sudden and untimely death prevented me from so doing. Over the last eight years the thought has grown and intensified, the thought of embracing a life of renunciation, of *sanyasa*. The truth of my origin has strengthened that desire. Although there is now no issue of labouring to elevate the status and glory of the family tree, I still attach great importance to it and regard it with deep respect. Consent to my retirement."

Cheeni's eyes were filled with tears.

"Grandfather, I accepted your first plan without a qualm. But what have I done to deserve your second plan? It is natural that you should detest this property. But why should you go far away from your grandson?"

"No, child, it is not you. These days, all these days, I have maintained the life of a householder but in that final stage one should follow a life suited to that stage, withdrawing completely from worldliness and absorbing oneself in meditation on *Parabrahma*, the ultimate reality. As we shed our years, so we should alter our aims and our lives to a way befitting our changing perspectives. Otherwise we sin. The state of *sanyasa* should have been assumed long back. My obligations as a householder are over. All that remains is your consent."

Cheeni found no answer. His mind was discerning enough to understand the subtleties of the *dharma* explained by the old man but his heart was unwilling to accept the argument.

The old man continued, "I realise that my duties to you have not yet been fully carried out. It remains for me to find you a bride from a suitable family and initiate you into the next stage of life, that of the householder. That I shall certainly do. Your degree requires two more years study and for your expenses until then, you may use some money out of the Shrothri family property and deposit it in a bank. You are entitled to it because I am entitled to it. I have laboured for it by looking after it carefully for so many years. Your obligation to me lies in studying for the next two years and following the life of a householder, with your wife, according to *dharma*. You must continue, you must perpetuate. Two acres of land near Hejjige were placed in Lakshmi's name. They shall remain hers. Your duty is to provide for her for as long as she lives. Before her death, it is for her to use the land for some religious or charitable purpose."

The grandson was bewildered. His grandfather concluded, "It is from me that you have learnt the *Vedas*. Examine them. Think it over."

Cheeni studied the books his grandfather was now reading - the *Sanyasopanishad, Vaikhanasa Sutra, Dharmasindhu, Jeevanmukti Viveka*. Some pages caught his immediate attention as they had been set apart by a peacock feather bookmark. Certain sentences were underlined in ink. Cheeni turned to a page in Sankaracharya's interpretation of the *Brihadaranyaka Upanishad*. The passage was in Sanskrit:

"He who wears a soiled cloth and hence is indifferent to appearance, whose head is tonsured, who neither expects nor acquires, who is always pure in body and soul, who deceives none, who lives by begging and who is ever wandering without a true dwelling, it is he who attains *Brahmatva*."

Cheeni understood the ancient and complex Sanskrit *slokas* without any difficulty.

"A person aspiring to the status of a *sanyasi* should perform the *Prajapatiyajna* and gift all his property and worldly goods to the poor and the needy."

"After leaving his wife and children, he must live outside the boundaries of towns and villages. Homeless, he must live where he is, in empty, unpeopled houses, under trees, or where he finds himself at sunset. During the monsoons and only then may he remain in one place."

"The *sanyasi* should beg in seven random houses. The offerer, before he offers cooked rice, should sprinkle water on his palms."

"He may eat but not fill his stomach. He eats only enough to keep himself alive. He should not feel joy on the day he receives food, nor misery on the day he does not. All he possesses is a gourd, a piece of cloth for soaking in water and then squeezing that same water out, a pair of sandals, one wooden seat and a pouch to receive alms."

As Cheeni read further, he felt increasingly dejected.

"The *sanyasi* must sleep on raised earth, shall not despair if sick, must not invite death but shall not love life. So as a servant who waits for the end of his servitude, so must he await his last day."

Shrothri had also marked a passage from the *Anushasanaparva* of the *Mahabharata*, mentioning the four types of *sanyasa* - *Kutichaka*, *Bahudaka*, *Hansa*, and *Parma Hansa*.

"The *Parma Hansa* lives under a tree, in a peopleless house or by a cremation ground. He may be clothed or naked. He is beyond the reach of the conflicts of *dharma* and *adharma*, truth and non-truth, purity and impurity. He sees the spirit and soul even in material possessions such as land and gold. He accepts alms from all, regardless of caste. The rules and injunctions of the *sastras* do not bind him."

As Cheeni read, one by one, the stringent rules of the life his grandfather wished to embrace, his heart filled with increasing sorrow. Until now *sanyasa* had been a concept to be studied but now he could not accept the possibility of his own grandfather enduring the rigours of such a life, no, not at that age.

Later he explained to Lakshmi what this new life would entail, the very harshness of it and begged her to persuade him to abandon the idea.

Lakshmi mused sadly, "If he were to allow me, I would go with him, I would serve him. He will not, for he will go alone. He is equal to a god. He has committed no sin in his life. Isn't he content with the spiritual merit already accumulated?"

But she thought, he is a learned man, and we have no competence to advise him.

Shrothri continued to teach Cheeni the *Dharmasastra*. The old man cited examples from the lives of great-sages and characters from the *puranas* and epics, would pick up Sanskrit texts and urge his grandson to read them. As he listened to that gentle voice, so calm and serious and sincere, Cheeni would be overwhelmed by this man who lived by his ideals and would see *sanyasa* as the furtherment of those ideals, the inevitability of the next stage.

The rumour spread through Nanjangud that Shrothri had decided to give away his property and wealth and become a *sanyasi*. In reply to their excited queries he said, "It is nothing. I am getting older and it is my *dharma* to become a *sanyasi*. My grandson does not want the property so I shall be giving it away."

Almost every day visitors came to the Shrothri household, some to discuss the aspect of *sanyasa*, some to forward their case as being persons deserving of charity. Cheeni was now certain that his grandfather was committed to his decision and he realised that it would be against *dharma* to deflect his grandfather from the laudable goal through love for him.

On an auspicious day in the month of *Chaitra*, Shrothri asked Cheeni to invite Master Anantaram to the house. Master Anantaram had lived in Nanjangud for the past ten years, working in the school there and in nearby villages. He was already fifty and he would retire in another five years. During his life, he had carefully saved his money, had built a house for himself in the Chamaraja neighbourhood and had invested in three acres of land.

He had attained considerable command over Sanskrit and as he often approached Shrothri to clarify difficult points of *dharma*, a close understanding had developed between the two. Having been impressed by the person's virtuous and serene character, Shrothri had always invited him to eat with the brahmins during the death anniversaries.

Master Anantaram arrived at eight that evening and Shrothri led his guest out for a stroll. The Master knew about Shrothri's decision and he too had politely asked the old man not to leave the town but being well versed in the *Dharmasastra*, he did not press the issue.

After a contemplative silence, Shrothri recounted the tale of his family history and the truth about his birth, his attempts to trace the survivors of Kittappa Shrothri's family and his failure to find them.

"I cannot leave here without seeing my grandson initiated into the householder stage. In you, I have placed the fullest confidence. The issue concerns your youngest child, your daughter, Lalita, I believe she is sixteen years old. Please consider giving her to my house as a bride. My grandson is still studying and I have set aside a sum of five thousand rupees for his further education. Sometimes I have doubts about the propriety of taking that money from the Shrothri property but if I do not, I shall be regarding the property of the Shrothri lineage with unacceptable contempt. It would be *adharma* to desert my grandson as he prepares for the future. Let him complete his B.Sc. It would be your responsibility to see that your son-in-law finishes his degree and treads the righteous path. There is nothing that I have hidden."

After thinking over the matter in silence for some time, the Master asked, "You are of *Kashyapagotra*, are you not?"

"As I have already said, we do not belong to the Shrothri lineage. But I received the *Brahmopadesha* in the name of *Kashyapagotra*."

"I accept your offer. I know that the culture and qualities of the grandfather have gone into the making of the grandson."

Lalita was a neat, pretty girl studying tolerably well at the local high school. Excepting that by contemporary standards she was too young, in every other respect, she was considered an excellent match for Cheeni. Shrothri suggested that though the marriage could be performed soon, the nuptials being postponed until after Cheeni completed his B.Sc. By then the girl too, would have finished her high school study. One auspicious day, at an auspicious moment, in the month of *Vaishakha*, Cheeni's marriage was performed simply and correctly in the Nanjundeshwara temple, planting him firmly in the householder stage of life.

Shrothri then surveyed the entire landed property and enquired about the farmers who cultivated the land. If the land were taken away from them, they and their families would starve and thus

Shrothri decided that none was more deserving of this gift than these peasants. The silver and gold in the house was sold and the money donated to the temple. All his beautiful Sanskrit books were given to Cheeni.

The day for Shrothri's *sanyasa* was yet to be decided. He planned to leave his town on an auspicious day and travel to the holy places of Haridwara, at the foot of the Himalayas and Badari, in the midst of the Himalayas. There he would seek a worthy *guru* and ritually terminate his householder status. He chose the fifth day of *Jyeshtha*. Shrothri was calmness incarnate, waiting quietly for the day of his irrevocable departure.

On that day Shrothri ate a feast in the house of his in-laws. He left Master Anantaram's house with the dhoti he was wearing, two clean dhoties, one pot to carry water, all bundled and hanging from a bamboo stick and a cash amount of one hundred rupees to cover the cost of the railway ticket to Haridwara. Shrothri himself was unruffled and he tried to console them. The rain started in the cool of the early evening. When he arrived on the platform, a huge crowd had collected there to send him off, despite the downpour. They gathered round him, bowing reverentially, offering him their obeisance. Master Anantaram, Lalita, Lakshmi and then Cheeni touched his feet reverentially. As the train pulled out of the station, Shrothri stared back, saying softly, "From untruth to truth, from darkness to light, from mortality to immortality. Let there be peace."

When the train reached the Dalwai bridge, the rain thundered down onto the roof of the carriage. Shrothri watched the river Kapila through the window, flowing between dense trees. From the day he could remember, he had always bathed in this river. Whenever he found time a cumbersome occurrence, he went to her steep bank and forgot, mesmerised by her beauty and her unmatchable power. Trying to feel neither grief at her having swallowed his only son, nor gratitude for the food grown from her waters, he thought back to his mother and Nanjunda Shrothri. He began to imagine the figure of Shyamadas. His wife, Bhagirathamma, son Nanjunda, Cheeni, daughter-in-law, all appeared before him. Many years had now passed since he had last seen her and he wondered where she would be now. The desire to see her, once again, before cutting himself off from worldly life suddenly became overwhelming. Perhaps he could

visit Sadasiva Rao in Mysore and find out her address in Bangalore
from him.

He asked directions at the station and managed to arrive at the
house. A neighbouring professor, sitting near the door in a cane
chair, upon hearing Shrothri's enquiry, shook his head dolefully.

"Sadasiva Rao is no more. He passed away eight months ago."

Shrothri was saddened by this. He asked, "Where is his family?
Do you know where his brother lives?"

"The Ceylonese woman returned to her native land but his first
wife is living with his brother in Lakshmipuram."

As Shrothri moved towards Lakshmipuram the size of the houses
and their surrounding gardens increased. He noticed that people, who
had been sitting out their verandas, enjoying the cool air, were now
being driven inside by the beating rain. The rain fell steadily and soon
he was soaked, his dhoti dripping water. He opened his bundle and
took out another dhoti and covered his head, remembering that soon
he would have to reduce the number of possessions he would be
allowed as a *sanyasi*. The air became filled with the smell of
pounding rain. Finally Shrothri stopped before a spacious, white
house and knocked on the door. It was opened by a woman wearing a
red sari.

"Whom do you want?"

"Please tell them that I have come from Nanjangud."

Raja rushed out, bowed and asked, "Did you come alone? Didn't
your grandson come? Where is the taxi?"

Shrothri did not understand.

Raja beckoned him in and led him to a bedroom. On the bed lay a
woman, her body wasted and near death. Shrothri stared at her. She
was fully covered with a thick pile of blankets. She had been reduced
to a skeleton, a horrible emaciation. Her eyes were closed, the face
was bone covered with sagging skin, like the loosened canvas of a
painting. She wore no ornaments. The pause between each breath
was full of an agonising suspense.

"What is her illness?"

"It is one that no doctor can cure. The doctor said that she won't
last the night. She wanted to see you and Cheeni, so I sent a taxi to
fetch you both. I don't know whether the son will come. We are
fortunate that you have done so."

"No. I am certain that he will come."

"Maybe, but when he was at college, he found out she was his mother. She brought him home herself. Perhaps he was angry or hurt or for whatever reason he repulsed all her attempts to be close to him. He even went so far as to arrange a transfer to another college. You probably know all about this."

Shrothri was astonished.

"And the miscarriages, and her son did not want her... lost interest in life, developed this will to die. Well, I don't think the boy will come. You have come. That is enough."

Raja's eyes filled with tears and he bent down and touched Shrothri's feet. The old man placed his hand compassionately on the bowed head before him.

"All is the will of God."

Recovering himself, Raja got up, moved closer to the bed and bent down close to Katyayani's ear, saying firmly, "Your father-in-law, Shrothri, has come."

He repeated this a second time. Her face showed signs of her having understood him and she tried to lift her eyelids. Raja turned her on her side, and arranged her hands so that they touched Shrothri's feet. Perhaps Katyayani was conscious of it.

The sound of car tyres driving through the mud and water broke the moment. The brakes screeched on the slippery ground as the taxi stopped.

"Come child, serve your mother at least now."

Cheeni stood near the bed.

"Hold your mother's hand."

He did as he was told.

Katyayani's breathing was now faster, strained by Raja turning her onto her side. Shrothri gently pushed up her eyelids, examined her eyes and then checked her pulse.

"No, it is not mere tiredness. She is nearing the end. Fetch a doctor."

"The doctor can do nothing now. She doesn't want to live. The last three days, she has been telling him not to come."

Shrothri stared at the dying woman and said, "Bring some Ganga water. Or any clean water."

Nagalakshmi brought some pure water in a silver cup and stood at the threshold of the door.

"Child, serve your mother," said Shrothri.

Shrothri opened Katyayani's lips and Cheeni poured a little water into her mouth. She swallowed. As she did so her breathing grew rapid, quicker and quicker, her chest heaved, pounded and then finally slowed down its rhythm.

Her breathing became peaceful, peaceful became her breath.

Cheeni carefully gave the water to his mother again but now it trickled out of the side of her mouth and onto the pillow.

Raja crumpled, sobbing loudly and without restraint. Prithvi and Nagalakshmi wept, huddled in a corner. At this hour of the night the cremation could not take place and therefore there was little point in informing anybody about the death until daylight. Shrothri folded the hands and legs of the corpse inwards, and placed a knife near it, according to custom. He led Raja out and made him sit on the veranda. Nagalakshmi was still crying in the room, holding Prithvi close to her. Cheeni sat in a corner, buried deep in thought. Though his face was full of grief, he did not cry.

Time passed. The cawing of the crows could be heard. Shrothri stood up and scanned the sky.

"It is four o'clock. The rain has stopped and now you must perform the rites. I must go on my pilgrimage."

"You are leaving now?"

"It saddens me to leave but I must reach Haridwara soon."

Shrothri tied his dhoti in a thin towel, making a small bundle out of it. Then he left. Raja watched the majestic and gaunt figure of the old man moving away from him.

Shrothri had walked a short distance, the air dark and strange as the street lamps were not yet lit. In this darkness, the deep darkness before dawn, Shrothri walked towards the railway station. From behind, he heard the voice calling, "Grandfather."

The grandfather stopped. The boy moved towards him.

"No, I shall not weep before you. I want to ask you something."

"Ask me, child."

"She is my mother. Her life began in some way and ended in another. Should I perform her death rites? Tell me before you go."

Shrothri closed his eyes and thought.

"Child, we have no right to determine the sins and merits of others. To do so in the case of one's parents is the greatest wrong. Our duty is but to do our duty. Perform the death rite of your mother with the purest of devotion. It was she who gave birth to you. And perform it on the bank of the Kapila."

Cheeni stared at his grandfather. The old man turned to take his next step.

"Now you may go. Today's cremation is your birth duty."

GLOSSARY

adharma -	see *dharma*.
advaita -	non-duality.
Amarukosha -	thesaurus.
Arundhati -	star named after the wife of a sage who herself had attained spiritual eminence.
Ashadha -	August.
Ayurveda -	the medical science of life, preventive and curative.
Bhagavadgita -	holy book of the Hindus, revealed by Krishna to Arjuna on Kurukshetra battlefield.
Brahmatva -	attaining the highest reality.
Brahmopadesa -	initiating a person into the pursuit of Brahma, or the ultimate reality.
Chaitra -	March/April.
chitranna -	spiced boiled rice.
darsanas -	different philosophical schools.
Dayabhaga -	treatise on the division of property.
dhal -	lentils.
dharbha -	grass considered auspicious when performing death rites.
dharma -	the principle which in its different forms holds the physical, moral and spiritual universe together. Hindu social organisation and behavioural codes are governed by the application of this principle. *Adharma* is its opposite.
dharmachakra -	wheel of *dharma* which Buddha set in motion and which should continue endlessly.

Dharmasastras -	the study of social, moral and spiritual codes as formulated, interpreted and codified by different sages.
dharmaguru -	a teacher of *dharma*.
Dhruva -	the north star.
dosa -	a type of South Indian pancake.
Dwapara -	There is the theory that time passes in a cycle of four ages. In the first age, *dharma* is wholly present. In the second age, it decreases by a fourth and so on until the last age when there is only a quarter of *dharma* left. The cycle begins again. *Dwapara* is the third age.
gotra -	Each person traces his affiliation to an ancient sage. Until her marriage a woman belongs to her father's lineage and after to her husband's.
harikatha -	story of God and creation, narrated before large audiences by wandering storytellers, interspersed with philosophical and moral discourse. Often the story is in the form of poetry and is accompanied by musical instruments.
idli -	steamed, beaten rice cake.
jaggery -	brown sugar.
Jyestha -	July.
Kali -	the fourth age (See *Dwapara*).
karma -	This literally means action. The effects of all our moral and immoral actions affect us either in this birth or the next.
Karthika -	November/December.
Kashyapa -	an ancient sage from whom a *gotra* originated.
kesareebath -	a semolina pudding.
krishnapaksha -	the fortnight when the moon is waning.

Krita -	the first age (See *Dwapara*).
Mahabharata -	Indian epic.
mandali -	company.
mangalya -	necklace which signifies the fact of marriage.
mantra -	religious stanza or chant.
maya -	illusion.
naraka -	hell.
Navarati -	a festival celebrated over a period of nine days in October to mark the triumph of good over evil.
ninu -	Kannada word meaning 'you' used for elders.
nivu -	Kannada word meaning 'you' used for relatives and close friends.
Nyaya -	school of thought concerned with logic.
panchas -	mediators.
papa -	sin.
paisa -	equivalent to a penny.
Parabrahma -	the ultimate reality.
pathasala -	school of traditional learning in which the medium of instruction is Sanskrit.
payasa -	sweet pudding considered auspicious.
Phalguna -	February/March.
pinda -	ball of boiled rice, ritually offered to ancestors on the day of their death anniversary.
Prajapatiyajna -	form of offering oblations to the creator of the universe.
prakriti -	nature.
pravara -	a stanza which consists of a *gotra* and names of ancestors.

puja -	religious worship.
punya -	merit.
puranas -	literally means narration of the past but concerns mythology.
purusha -	mankind.
raga -	type of Indian music.
ragi -	a kind of grain.
Ramayana -	Indian epic of Lord Rama, a form of Vishnu, the preserver.
rangavalli -	design drawn with white stone or chalk powder.
Rigvedic branch -	classification of a *Veda*.
rishi -	sage.
roti -	Indian bread.
sa, ri, ga, ma, pa, dha, ni, sa -	do, ray, me, fah, so, la, te, do.
sahitya -	literature.
samrajya -	empire.
sanatana dharma -	ancient moral code.
sandhyavandana -	thrice daily prayer.
sangita -	music.
sanyasa -	the last of the four stages of a person's life, student, householder, retirement and wandering mendicant who renounces all relationships.
saru -	thin, soup-like curry eaten with rice.
sloka -	stanza of prayer.
sthithaprajna -	one who has supreme control over his mind.
swaadha -	type of *mantra*.
swaaha -	type of *mantra*.

sastras -	codified moral injunctions strengthened by ancient custom.
suklapaksha -	the fortnight of the month when the moon is waxing.
Sukra -	Venus.
sutra -	aphorism.
Silpasastra -	*sastra* on the science of sculpturing.
tantra -	physical act of worshipping.
Tattvasastra -	science of reality.
Treta -	the second age (See *Dwapara*).
Upanishads -	last portion of the *Vedas*.
Vaishaka -	April\May.
Vaisesika -	school which propounds the theory of atoms.
vashat -	type of *mantra*.
vedanta -	philosophy.
Vedas -	mankind's earliest philosophy in the form of Sanskrit poetry, expressed by Aryan sages. These became the basis the later Hindu religious and philosophical development.
Yama -	god of death and of righteousness, who judges the souls of the dead according to their past action and inaction.